STRAIG   G

Best wishes

About the Author

Born in 1947, Deborah Fowler has been writing fiction since she was seventeen. She has written over 600 short stories for women's magazines and *Straight on Till Morning* is her sixth novel. Together with her husband, Alan, she has also written a number of small business guide books, and several books on various aspects of childhood, the latest being *A Guide To Adoption*.

Deborah lives in Cornwall with her husband and four children, two of whom are adopted.

STRAIGHT ON TILL
MORNING

DEBORAH FOWLER

POCKET
BOOKS

LONDON · SYDNEY · NEW YORK · TOKYO · SINGAPORE · TORONTO

First published in Great Britain by Pocket Books, 1995
An imprint of Simon & Schuster Ltd
A Paramount Communications Company

Copyright © Deborah Fowler, 1995

Simon & Schuster Ltd
West Garden Place
Kendal Street
London W2 2AQ

Simon & Schuster of Australia Pty Ltd
Sydney

A CIP catalogue record for this book is available from the
British Library

ISBN 0-671-85224-8

Typeset in 11/14 Optima by
Hewer Text Composition Services, Edinburgh
Printed and bound in Great Britain by
Harper Collins, Glasgow

For the children of Romania –
please God may the world never forget them.

FOREWORD

This book is a work of fiction, but the subject could not be closer to my heart. Alan, my husband, and I have six children, two of whom are adopted. Michael, now aged six, is from Romania and Edita, now two years old, came from Bosnia. The circumstances of their arrival with us has propelled our family into the very heart of Eastern Europe's struggle to find herself, and the suffering we have witnessed has changed us all irrevocably. We will never be free to walk away from it. It has also bred in us a deep frustration.

We are all part of the same continent yet, largely, we sit back and watch as Eastern Europe tries to cope with the aftermath of raising the iron curtain. How often are Romanian orphans mentioned in the news today? Yet their plight is even more desperate than it was on the day Ceauşescu was shot. The orphanages are overflowing because foreign adoption has been stopped and contraception, although now legal, is not available.

The cost of living continues to spiral upwards – ordinary people cannot afford to support themselves, never mind their children, and much of the aid has dried up as the world's attention becomes focused elsewhere. Michael's orphanage was drastically over-crowded when it housed two hundred and fifty children in 1990. Today, over five hundred children try to survive in the same building.

And what of Bosnia? We watch helplessly as that country destroys herself and, as always, it is the children who suffer most. There is an orphanage not far from Split where six hundred orphaned children are cared for by four monks – in the early days, desperately cutting up their habits to use as nappies. In refugee camps and orphanages all over former Yugoslavia, traumatised children live a life without hope – mal-nourished, starved of attention by hard-pressed helpers, disorientated and haunted by fear.

What can we do – we, the little people who have no real influence, no real power? We can care and maybe, in time, that will force tangible understanding and help from the Governments of Western Europe. 'Love is the same whichever country it is given in,' said Dr Liliana Bacile at Orphanage No 1, Bucharest, in January, 1990. It should be . . . it certainly should be.

Deborah Fowler
Cornwall
1995

The way to Neverland –

*'Second to the right, and
straight on till morning'*

J. M. Barrie *Peter Pan*

CHAPTER ONE

MARCH 1989 – LONDON

He should have slowed down. It would haunt him for the rest of his life, the fact that he did not, the fact that she was old, frail, hovering in the rain on the pavement's edge. There was plenty of time to stop and normally, of course, he would have done so. Charlie Edwards, veteran London taxi driver of nearly thirty years standing, was used to people doing daft things. Yet she had been staring straight at him; she could not have failed to see him. If only he had not been in such a hurry to reach home. If only Old Street had not been so busy. If only, if only . . .

She stepped off the pavement, right in front of his cab. He slammed on the brakes but the wheels locked on the wet, greasy surface. Her body caught the full impact of the bonnet with a sickening thump, which threw her into the air. Desperately he swung the steering wheel to the left but by now the cab was crazily out of control. The back wheels caught her; he felt the terrible jolt as they crushed her tiny body under the full weight of his cab. Then he hit the lamppost and for a while at least, all was merciful oblivion.

'Sal, there's a call for you on line two.'

Salvena Saunders looked up from the computer, her exasperation evident. 'Judy, I told you to hold all calls.'

'But it's the Charing Cross Hospital.'

'So?' said Sal. 'Be a love and give me a break. It's Friday night, it's been a hell of a week and this story has to be finished before I can go home to Toby. You take it.'

'They say it's urgent. It's the Accident and Emergency Department.'

Sal felt the colour drain from her face. Toby, something had happened to Toby. He was dead — an accident on the rugby field, he had been run over on the way home from school. 'Put it through then, Judy.' Her hand trembled as she picked up the telephone. 'Hello?' Her voice sounded hoarse.

'Is that Sal Saunders?'

'Yes, yes,' she said desperately. 'Is anything wrong?'

'This is the Charing Cross Hospital. We have your mother in here.'

The relief that it was not Toby was so profound that for a moment Sal could make no sense of what she was being told. 'My mother, are you sure?'

The voice sounded hesitant. 'I – I presume so. Her name is Barbara Saunders . . . Beehive Cottage, Horton-cum-Studley in Oxfordshire.'

'Yes, that's right,' said Sal, with mounting astonishment.

'We assumed it must be you, as soon as she mentioned her daughter worked for the *Daily Record*.'

'What's . . . wrong with her?' Sal asked.

'I'm afraid your mother has been run down by a taxi cab. She is quite seriously injured. We think it advisable for you to come in straight away.'

'Yes, of course,' said Sal. 'I'll be with you in about ten minutes, traffic willing.' She put down the telephone carefully, thoughtfully. How long was it since she had last seen her mother . . . five, no probably six years, when for Toby's sake she had felt she should make one final attempt at a reconciliation. It had been a complete fiasco – there was too much bitterness between them. Now it could be too late.

Sal felt all the old insecurities come flooding back – the need for her mother's approval, which had proved so unattainable, the guilt at so clearly having failed as a daughter. Their relationship seemed always to have been a disaster. Sal sat slumped in front of her keyboard, momentarily unaware of the bustle of the news desk around her, in her effort to try and analyse her feelings. Even in the midst of what could be a life and death drama, her mother seemed to have the upper hand. Sal was already convinced that somehow this accident was her own fault. She felt nervous, jumpy – a little girl again. If only her father was still alive. He would have reassured her, taken charge of the situation, soothed his wife's anxieties.

Yet maybe . . . maybe now this was a role she could fulfill. Maybe she would be able to break through the barrier of her mother's cool indifference. *At last.*

The shrill sound of the telephone on the adjoining desk snapped Sal out of her reverie. It was only as she stood up and reached for her jacket that she realised how odd it was that her mother was in London at all. Sal could not remember a time when her mother had voluntarily left her rural idyll to go anywhere, other than the very occasional expedition to Oxford.

'Anything wrong?' Judy asked, seeing Sal's stricken expression.

'Family problem, I have to go out,' Sal replied, purposely vague.

'What about the article?'

'Tell David I'll do it later, but in time for the deadline. See you.' She hesitated by the door. 'Have a good weekend.'

'Thanks,' said Judy, 'and you.'

'Has she arrived yet?' Bob Green put his head around the door of Reception. The receptionist frowned. 'Who?' she asked, bewildered.

'Salvena Saunders, Mrs Saunders' daughter – the journalist. You telephoned her, at least I hope the hell you did.' Bob Green had been on duty for fifteen hours and he still had another three to go. It was Friday night and the Accident and Emergency Unit was already hotting up. He'd had enough.

'Of course I did,' snapped the girl. She had only been working in the hospital for a few weeks and still did not appreciate the pressure under which everyone worked.

'Well, wheel her in the moment she arrives. I mean the moment she sets foot through that door.'

'What's wrong with you then, Bob – got the hots for her?' Chris Jennings, a junior registrar, joined them. He was still smiling, but then he had only just come on duty.

'Shove off, Chris.' Bob hesitated. 'Look, can I ask your advice? I have a real problem.'

The bantering atmosphere died instantly. 'What sort of problem?' said Chris.

'It's Sal Saunders' mother. She's in her late seventies and she's been knocked down by a cab.'

'Yes, I heard,' said Chris. 'How bad is she?'

'Well, on the face of it, not too bad. She has a broken leg, a great deal of superficial bruising and grazing, but no apparent head injuries. However, I do need to organise a laparotomy urgently. There are signs of internal bleeding and at her age there's not a moment to be lost.'

'So?' said Chris.

'She simply won't have it. She says she will scream the place down and drag herself out of the hospital unless we wait for her daughter. She says she needs to talk to her and won't agree to any treatment or any tests until she arrives.'

'Well, you have a simple choice then, don't you?' said Chris. 'You either ignore her and press ahead, or sit tight. I think I'd go for the latter. Anything for a quiet life.'

'But if something goes wrong . . .' Bob began.

'If something goes wrong, you've done your best, provided you've made sure she understands the risks. You're never going to stand the pace in this profession if you get all worked up about something so relatively minor.'

'But it's not minor, is it? Sal Saunders is a household name. If her mother goes and dies on me because I've failed to give her the necessary treatment, it could be all over the papers.'

Chris smiled suddenly. 'Problem solved, mate. Here she is now.'

Bob turned and followed the other doctor's gaze. It was strange, but she stood out, even among the teeming mass of humanity that was the Accident and Emergency Department on a Friday evening. It was hard to define why. It was certainly not her height. She was short, probably not a great deal over five feet, and there was no attempt at making an entrance. She was hurrying, head down, her shoulders tense and slightly hunched. It was her hair, Bob decided. He had not realised it was so fair – almost white, thick and shining, hanging to just below her shoulders.

She reached Reception, lifted her head and stared straight at him. He caught his breath. He had seen her on television, of course, and thought her very pretty, but in reality, she was beautiful. Her large brown almond-shaped eyes were set wide apart, her skin was warm, glowing from recent sunshine, and her nose was small, *retroussé* – slightly at odds with the full mouth and strong jawline of a determined woman.

He cleared his throat. 'Miss Saunders?'

'Yes.' The voice was husky, deep and instantly recognisable.

'Would you come this way? My name is Dr Green. I'm treating your mother and I would like a word with you before you see her.'

Her eyes widened. 'Is she very badly injured?'

'This way,' he said, struggling to get a grip on himself. He ushered her into a waiting room. 'Please sit down.'

She ignored him, moving restlessly around the room. 'Dr Green, can you tell me what happened?'

There was clearly no room for prevarication with this woman. 'Your mother has had a nasty altercation with a taxi. She has a broken leg, some bruising and lacerations, but I am concerned that there may be internal injuries. She urgently needs a laparotomy, which is a—'

'I know what a laparotomy is,' Sal interrupted impatiently.

Chastened, Bob continued: 'The point is that she won't have one until she has seen you.'

'Seen me – why?'

'She says she has something to tell you.'

'That's ridiculous!' Sal objected. 'She hasn't seen me in years.'

'Well, whatever,' said Bob, 'I would be most grateful if you could persuade her to postpone the chat until we have checked up on her. If there is any internal bleeding we need to sort it out quickly.'

'Yes, of course,' said Sal. 'You'd better lead me to her.'

She had aged almost beyond recognition. Bob Green withdrew, and for a moment Sal stood in silence by her mother's bed. Her eyes were closed and so it was possible to study her for a moment undetected. She was thinner than Sal remembered and far more lined. Her hair, now completely white, was spread untidily on the pillow. Her complexion was almost grey. She looked old, tired, frail, and so very alone.

Why had their relationship always been such a lost cause? Sal asked herself. God knows, she could have done with a loving mother over the years, particularly as a single parent. And this old woman lying before her should not be alone in the world, no matter what differences there had been between them. Sal felt a rush of compassion – love, even. Maybe it wasn't too late. Maybe they could start again . . . if she lived. *Please God, let her live.* Tentatively, Sal touched her hand. 'Mother, it's me.'

Barbara Saunders' eyes opened. She stared blankly at Sal for a moment, and then there was the ghost of a smile. 'Good, I'm glad they found you. I didn't even know if you would be in the country. That ridiculous job of yours could have taken you any-where.'

Criticism in the first words her mother had spoken to her in years. Sal fought to control her disappoint-ment. 'I got back from Hungary the night before last,' she said lamely. It was no use, nothing had changed. She remembered why she was there. 'Mother, I understand you're being awkward about having a laparotomy. You really do need one urgently. I'll wait here in the hospital until they've run the tests. We can talk then.'

'No, I must talk to you first.'

'Mother, please,' said Sal, 'we haven't seen each other for at least five years. Surely whatever you want to talk to me about can wait.

'Salvena!' Her mother winced and for a moment closed her eyes. When she spoke again, her voice was weaker. 'Why must you question everything? I need to tell you something and it cannot wait. Do you understand me?' There was an urgency and an authority in her mother's voice that brought back many dramas from the past. They had always argued, indeed they agreed about virtually nothing. Sal's lonely childhood had been heavily restricted, fenced all around by her mother's stringent rules, always delivered in the same accusing tone as now.

'Will it take long?' Sal asked, realising as always that she was hopelessly defeated.

'I doubt it, but I'm going nowhere until I have talked to you, so the sooner we start the better.'

There can't be much wrong with her, Sal thought, as she is still so much in control. 'All right,' she said. 'I'm listening.'

For the first time, the old woman's resolve seemed to weaken. She shook her head on the pillow as if to clear her mind. 'Give me your hand,' she said. Sal was astonished. Even when the relationship between them had been less acrimonious, her mother had shied away from physical contact.

Still, she did as she was asked. 'Salvena, this is going to come as a terrible shock to you, but there is something I should have told you years ago.' Again, she hesitated. 'The man who you believed to be your father, my husband Tim, was in fact not your father at all.'

Sal stared at her mother like a madwoman. 'I don't believe you! You mean to say that Daddy— ' She stopped short. Sal had adored her father, idolised him. Although for much of her childhood Tim Saunders had been away pursuing a career in the Army, when he was with his family he had been the centre of Sal's universe. He had died when she was eighteen and Sal sometimes felt she was still getting over the loss.

After a moment Barbara continued. 'I know this is difficult for you, I know how fond you were of Tim, but it is important that you know the truth. I can't go to my grave . . .' she paused, then: 'Your father, your biological father, was my first husband.'

'First husband?' Sal burst out. 'But I don't understand!'

Barbara dropped her daughter's hand with apparent exasperation. 'Listen, please listen.' Her voice was barely above a whisper now. 'Your father was a Yugoslavian, an Army officer, too. I met him in Cairo, before the war. How I ever came to marry him, I don't . . . Still, that doesn't matter now. We married and moved to Belgrade. He was a great deal older than me, eleven years, and I was only eighteen at the time. We had a son, Georges.'

'A son – a *son*, Mother?'

'Yes.' Barbara's eyes suddenly filled with tears and she began rubbing furiously at them. 'Don't interrupt, Salvena, I have to tell you this while I still can. When Georges was eight, I had another child, an unplanned child – you. Shortly after your birth, I discovered the truth about my husband. He was a traitor, a member of the KGB. He was spying on Tito, leading a double life. He had been a respected Army officer, then a member of the Government and yet all the time he was working for the Russians.' Barbara's condition was deteriorating. She moved her head restlessly from side to side, clearly in great pain.

'Mother, I think I ought to fetch the doctor,' Sal said.

'No – just listen, will you, you stupid girl. I know this all sounds improbable, but believe me, it's the truth. Your father threatened to have us all killed – you, me, Georges, but then he relented. He said that you and I could be given a new identity and return to England. He said he could arrange for our "death" to be faked so that we wouldn't be in any danger from the KGB, I suppose. I didn't trust him, but surprisingly he kept his word. We escaped to England without incident, although I have to say, I never felt safe again. I still don't.'

At the mention of her mother's almost paranoid insecurity, the preposterous story suddenly took on a degree of realism. 'And Georges?' Sal asked.

A sob broke from Barbara's lips. She began to cry and then choke. She seized Sal's hand again. 'I don't know,' she said. 'I had to leave Georges behind. I never saw my son, my beloved son again.' There was a gurgling sound in her throat; blood started pumping out of her mouth. Sal screamed and stepped back. A fountain of blood hit her in the chest and began dripping down her jacket. Her mother slumped forward.

'Mother, Mother, I'll get someone!' She rushed to the curtains. 'Nurse, it's my mother. She seems to have— '

Bob Green was standing outside the cubicle. He looked at Sal's jacket and rushed past her. 'Stand back, we must get her to crash.' He pushed Sal aside. 'This nurse will take care of you.' The bed, instantly surrounded by people, disappeared in a moment. The last sight Sal had of her mother was of her untidy white hair on the pillow.

Back in the waiting room a nurse brought her a cup of tea.

'I'm afraid we haven't any clothes to lend you,' she said, looking at the bloodstains, 'but I have brought you a flannel and some water. Do you want me to help you clean your jacket, or will you do it?'

'I'll do it,' said Sal.

'Shall I stay with you?'

Sal looked at the girl. She was very young and obviously upset. 'No, I will be fine. I think I'd rather be alone.'

As soon as the door was closed, Sal slumped into

a chair. What her mother had told her was ludicrous. That perpetually middle-aged, middle-class, *ordinary* little woman could not possibly have ever been married to a foreign spy! She simply did not have it in her — and yet . . . Somewhere deep in Sal's subconscious, bells had started ringing. It was certainly true that her mother had been frightened all her life — maybe, just maybe, with some justification. And why were she and her mother so different — so impossibly, incredibly different? There was literally no common ground between them; there never had been. Sal suddenly thought of her own name, Salvena. It was an Eastern European name. Her mother told her she had been named after a great-grandmother on her father's side. Naturally, Sal had assumed she meant Tim's, but now . . . And what of her own attraction to Eastern Europe? Was it chance that she was the Daily Record's Eastern European Correspondent, or had she been drawn to that part of the world by some genetic force?

Chaotic thoughts chased each other around her head. Could she really have a brother — and if so, where was he? She thought of her many trips to Yugoslavia over the years. Perhaps she had passed him in the street, or even her father. She dismissed the idea. Timothy Saunders had been her father. Dad — not her father at all? The pain almost made her cry out. Yet he had loved her, she was sure of it . . . loved her *and deceived her*. Why had no one told her all this before? Why only now, when it was too late?

There were so many questions she would have asked and now never could – for long before a sombre-faced Bob Green entered the little waiting room, Salvena Saunders knew that her mother was dead.

To get away from the hospital – to get out, to get some fresh air – that was the priority. Sal was halfway across the Reception area when a small dapper man stepped into her path. His hand briefly touched her arm. She recoiled. Normally good with the public, at this moment the intrusion was intolerable. At the expression on her face he stepped back smartly, his eyes widening at the sight of her blood-splattered jacket.

'Miss Saunders, I'm so sorry to detain you. It's about your mother.'

'My mother? What the hell has she got to do with you?' The angry retort was out before she could stop herself.

'I'm sorry,' the man repeated, stammering. 'It's just that I . . . I saw what happened. I'm her banker, you see.'

'Banker?' Sal stared into the thin, pale face level with her own. The man dropped his gaze first.

'I've obviously chosen a bad moment,' he said quietly, 'but I came with her in the ambulance. There was no one else with her, no one who knew her. How is she?'

'She's dead,' said Sal flatly, and the man's hand flew to his mouth in dismay. It was a tiny hand, beautifully manicured. Sal felt oddly repulsed.

'I'm sorry,' she said, 'but I have to get out of here.'

'Of course, of course,' he fussed. 'Would you mind if I walked with you? I'll find you a taxi.'

They did not speak again until they were outside the hospital. Sal walked fast and furiously, as if putting some distance between herself and the building would reduce the impact of what had happened. The little man beside her had almost to run to keep up. At the crossroads she was forced to pause while the London traffice roared past. 'I'm sorry, I'm being very rude. It's just that it's been a hell of a shock.'

'Yes, yes, of course.' Brightening a little, the man held out his hand. 'My name is Adrian Drummond. I work for the Swiss Federal Bank. Your mother is – *was* – one of my customers. She was leaving my office when this unfortunate accident occurred.'

'Are you sure we are talking about the same person?' Sal was bemused. 'Mrs Barbara Saunders?'

'Oh yes,' said Adrian Drummond. 'Mrs Saunders was a very valued customer. She'd been banking with us for many years – well over thirty, I would think.'

'I had no idea,' Sal told him. 'What sort of money are we talking about?'

The shutters came down. 'I'm very sorry, but even in these tragic circumstances, Miss Saunders, I cannot discuss your mother's finances.'

'But I'm her daughter, and she's dead – and apart from any other consideration, I must be her sole beneficiary, I imagine.'

The little man shook his head. 'It's not quite that simple, I'm afraid. You see, Miss Saunders, your mother's banking arrangements are very tightly controlled.'

'I just don't understand,' said Sal, 'but then I don't understand very much at the moment. Look, Mr Drummond, could I come and see you, and talk to you about my mother's affairs?'

'Yes, of course. I don't know how much I'll be able to tell you, but I'll help in whatever way I can. How about on Monday, at eleven o'clock?'

'Good, I'll see you then. Where is your bank?'

'It's the Old Street branch, in the City.'

'I'll find it.' She started to go and then abruptly turned back to him, with the ghost of a smile. 'Thank you for travelling in the ambulance with my mother. You must have been a great comfort to her.' In a second she was gone.

Adrian started to call after her, to suggest he found her a taxi, but the words died on his lips. With her striking looks and well-known face, Sal Saunders could pick up a taxi far quicker than he. He let out a sigh and started walking slowly towards the tube station.

Extraordinary how different the mother and daughter were. He had liked the mild, lightly bantering manner of Barbara Saunders, and she had trusted him completely. In fact, since her husband's death she had come more and more to rely on his advice. He was pleased to be in her confidence. As he crossed the road, a gust of wind tugged at his trouser leg and he shivered, feeling a little faint and suddenly very, very old. He ducked down into the subway, but the coldness persisted. It was the shock, he told himself, unaware that despite the fact that she was some fifteen years older than him, he had been more than a little in love with Barbara Saunders.

Sal walked towards the Editor's office. 'Is he in?' she asked his secretary.

'Yes, but you can't disturb him.' The advice came too late; Sal was already in the lion's den.

'For Christ's sake!' David Thorson looked up from his desk and anger was replaced by concern. 'Sal, what in God's name has happened to you? Is that blood?' He rose to his feet and came around the desk. It was not just her dishevelled appearance, the girl looked completely wiped out.

'David, I'm sorry to barge in like this, but my mother has just died, and your office seemed to be the right place to come.' Carefully David removed her jacket, then folded her into his arms and pressed her head against his shoulder. She stood in his embrace awkwardly, stiffly. He could feel the tension running through her; she was trying desperately to hold herself in check.

'It's always worse to lose someone when the relationship has been strained,' he said gently. 'What was it, a heart attack?'

'No,' Sal mumbled into his shoulder. 'She was knocked down by a cab in Old Street. She had internal injuries, then she haemorrhaged and they couldn't help her in time.'

'How awful,' said David, 'but what on earth was she doing in Old Street?'

'I don't know,' Sal lied. She moved away from him. Already she was more composed.

She's shutting me out, David thought. I wonder why. 'A drink?' he suggested.

'Yes, please.'

He produced a bottle of brandy and two glasses, and poured them both a hefty measure. 'Well,' he said, 'I'm sorry she had to end like that. There was no love lost between her and me, of course, but then she had every reason not to approve of me. With you it should have been different. She should have appreciated you and your achievements, the sort of daughter she had. It is a damn shame she never realised.'

'Perhaps she did,' Sal said. There was a catch in her voice, as if she was close to tears.

'Judging by the state of your jacket, you must have been with her when she died,' David said, and Sal nodded. 'Was she able to talk? Did she say anything to you?'

Sal hesitated for a split second. 'No . . . no, nothing,' she said. The lie came easily and with it, a sense of release. She had slammed the door on what had happened. If she was not even going to tell David what her mother had said, she would tell no one. If she shared that last conversation with no one, then maybe it had never happened.

She downed her brandy in one and stood up. 'I'm sorry, I'm all right now. God, I must look a mess. I'd better go home and change and then I'll come back to finish that article on Raisa Gorbachov.'

'No, you won't,' said David. 'I'll take you home now, and there you will stay. I'll get someone else to finish your article.'

'It's in a heap all over my desk. I just left it when I got the call from the hospital. No one will be able to understand my notes.'

'OK, so we'll use something else. Don't worry about it, it's my problem. What time is Toby back from school?'

'About six normally, on Fridays.'

'Good, so if we hurry there will be time for you to change and pull yourself together before he gets back. Don't forget he's lost a grandmother as well as you losing a mother.'

'Some grandmother!' said Sal. 'I don't think he would have recognised her if they had passed one another in the street.'

'That's as maybe,' said David, 'but when you think about it, your mother is Toby's only other known living relative. Her death is cutting his family by fifty per cent. You should take that into account.'

'What's that supposed to mean?' said Sal, immediately defensive.

David sighed and sat down behind his desk again. 'It's not supposed to mean anything, Sal, but since Toby has never known who his father is, the only certain thing he has in his life is you. So, up to a point, your mother has to have represented a degree of security in his life. Like, if something happened to you, there would be her. I'm not making a heavy point – just asking you to think about what I've said.'

Sal smiled at him. 'You're right, of course, much as it pains me to admit it – but then, much as it pains me to admit it again, you usually are.'

'That's better,' David grinned. 'Now, give me a couple of minutes to reorganise these piles on my desk and we'll go home.'

Sal watched him as he worked. As a young man he must have been impossibly good-looking. Now at fifty-five he was still one of the most attractive men she had ever met. His hair, blond once, was now grey but it suited him and despite it, there was still so much of the boy in him. It was easy to imagine him as he must have been in his schooldays. He sat at his desk now, his hair flopped over his forehead, his tie askew and the sleeves of his shirt rolled up. His enthusiasm for life was unquenchable. Despite his chosen profession of journalism, miraculously David Thorson seemed to have retained a sort of innocence which Sal realised was part of his charm. If you saw the world as David saw it, you saw a place full of interest and opportunity – his glass was always half-full, never half-empty. And she was lucky enough to have this man as her boss. To have his friendship, to have him as her mentor . . . she knew she was blessed indeed. At this moment, he had known exactly how to handle her. Too much sympathy, too many questions would have sent her flying from his office. Instead he had known when to back off, and yet the warmth and comfort of his presence had reassured her. Just for a moment it had seemed as if her world had gone mad, but David had put it back together for her.

But then he always knew how to handle her. He always had . . . except for once – once, when she had hurt him more than anyone else had ever done.

CHAPTER TWO

The call, when it came, was a blessed relief. Sal and Toby had been snapping at each other all morning. The air was heavy with tension.

'Sal,' said David's familiar voice. 'I've managed to escape from the mountain of paperwork. I thought maybe you and Toby would like lunch out, say at Covent Garden, and then we could have a spot of kite-flying in the park – something to take your mind off things.'

'Toby's too old for kite-flying,' Sal said ungraciously.

'No, I'm not,' said Toby from the other side of the room. 'Who is it?'

'David,' Sal replied tersely.

'Kite-flying with David would be great! When can we go, Mum – today?'

'I heard all of that,' said David smugly. 'You're outnumbered. I'll be around in half an hour.'

'I don't want to go out to lunch,' Sal told him. 'I'm not in the mood. There are things to be done.'

'But not on a Saturday,' said David. 'That's one of the reasons you should come out with me. You have to be in some sort of limbo at the moment, and in a state of shock, I should think. How's Toby coping?'

'Fine,' said Sal defensively. 'We're fine, absolutely fine. We're not a charity case.'

'Oh, for heaven's sake, Sal, stop being so prickly,' said David. 'If you don't want to go out to lunch, that's fine, but Toby does and I'm on my way.' The phone went dead.

'Is he coming?' Toby said, his eyes bright with enthusiasm.

Sal resented his obvious eagerness. She let out a sigh. 'Yes, he's coming, but I can't understand why there's all this excitement. You wouldn't think much of flying a kite in the park with me.'

'No, I wouldn't,' said Toby, 'because you're no fun any more. You're either working or moaning at me.' His colour was high and he was suddenly close to tears.

The unexpected outburst surprised them both. Toby turned and ran from the room, slamming the door as he did so. For a second, still stunned, Sal stood rooted to the spot. They never argued, she and Toby, they both hated confrontations. Then, as if from nowhere, David's words of the night before came into her mind. Perhaps, despite his apparent indifference, Toby's grandmother's death had affected him. Certainly the previous evening he had been very quiet after she had broken the news.

'Toby!' She rushed across the room and bounded up the stairs.

His bedroom door was shut. Just for a second she hesitated, and then turned the handle cautiously. The door was not locked. Toby was lying face downwards on his bed. For a moment the back of his head reminded Sal painfully of his father. She dismissed the thought hurriedly and walked over to sit gingerly on the edge of the bed beside her son.

'Toby, look at me.' There was no response. 'Toby, I'm sorry. I haven't been much of a mother recently, I know. It's just that my work—. Well, it's getting more demanding all the time and when an assignment comes up, I just have to take it. If I start turning down work because of my family responsibilities, I'd be out of a job in a week.'

Toby turned over and regarded her solemnly. He was a startling child. He had Sal's white-blond hair, but matched with blue eyes and high cheekbones. At ten years old, it was obvious he was going to make an extremely attractive man.

'Why don't you get another job then?' he said rudely.

'Because I'm not trained to do anything else,' Sal explained, fighting a sense of injustice. 'Toby, come on, be reasonable. You like the house we live in, the fact that we have a garden. You like your private school, the nice clothes you wear, the holidays we have, the way we can afford to take friends to the cinema, then there's your mountain bike . . .'

'I don't really care about any of that,' said Toby passionately. 'I'd rather have you at home.'

'I think you do care about those things, really,' said Sal. She suddenly felt desperately uncertain and well aware she was treading on dangerous ground. Whose standards were they living by, she wondered – his or hers?

'Not if it means you getting killed, or something,' Toby said. 'You always seem to be going to dangerous places where there's wars and things.'

He looked very young, eyes wide and fearful, and Sal suddenly glimpsed an insecurity she had never seen in Toby before. She reached out and took his hand. He did not resist her.

'They sound dangerous,' she agreed, 'but they're not really, at least not for journalists. Yes, of course I cover wars and revolutions – that's my business, but reporters are always very well protected. We have access to the very best information, so we don't need to go anywhere that is too dangerous.'

'Journalists are always being killed,' said Toby firmly. 'I've read about it.'

'Not this one,' said Sal, trying to lighten the mood.

'Now that Granny is dead, what happens to me if you are killed?'

David had been right. 'I won't be.' Sal pulled Toby upwards and into her arms, holding him close to her. 'I'll always take great care, I promise.'

'But what if?' he persisted, his voice muffled against her shoulder.

'Well, I suppose you would live with Louis and Evelyn, if that's what you'd like. Is it what you'd like?'

Toby nodded, and then quite unexpectedly he began to sob. It was some years since Sal had seen her son cry, other than briefly as a result of a cut or a bruise. Like her, she supposed, he kept his feelings to himself and seemed happy to do so. Now he clung to her, weeping as if his heart would break — and hers with it, as the sense of guilt, never far below the surface, threatened to engulf her.

'If you like, we'll draw up a new will putting Louis and Evelyn in charge of your affairs. You can see it, so you'll know it's all properly arranged. How about that?' Her voice sounded falsely hearty.

'I wish Granny hadn't died,' Toby said between sobs.

'But you hardly knew her,' Sal said. 'You hadn't met in years.' She was genuinely confused.

'But I knew she was there,' he said. 'Just in case . . . you know.' He drew away from her, his face ravaged by tears.

Sal smoothed his hair back from his forehead. 'Everything is going to be fine, Toby, I promise. I'm sorry your grandmother's death has upset you so much and I'm sorry you never knew her better — but she and I just didn't get on.'

'Why?' Toby asked. 'I thought people always loved their mothers.'

Sal smiled sadly at him. 'I did love her in a way. It's just that we were so different, we seemed to have nothing in common.' As she spoke, the thoughts she had been trying to keep in check during the last twenty-four hours came crowding in again.

'What sort of different?' her son persisted.

Sal forced herself to concentrate. 'Oh, I don't know. Granny was a very fixed sort of person, with definite ideas you couldn't alter. She was a very anxious person, too. She always wanted everything done just right and she never wanted to stand out in a crowd. She was very conventional and private.' Her words carried a new significance, she realised. Why had Barbara been almost a recluse? It was as if she was hiding from something or had something to hide. If so, then no wonder she had hated her daughter's very public job. It explained so much.

'She certainly doesn't sound much like you, Mum.'

'You mean she didn't have my loud mouth!' Sal smiled at him and was rewarded by a smile back.

'What was her life like?' Toby asked.

'I don't know much about her life,' Sal admitted cautiously. 'But when I have sorted out her affairs, maybe I will.' A thought suddenly struck her. Of course, going through her mother's papers might well reveal the truth, or otherwise, of her claims. Damn David! But for him, she could have gone down to her mother's cottage today . . . Still, there was tomorrow.

'Toby, why don't we go down to Granny's house tomorrow? I have a key and I ought really to do a few things there. I should have thought of it before. We could look out some photographs and you can have a good laugh over the ones of me when I was little. I was a real fright with braces and freckles.'

'I'd like to do that,' said Toby cheerfully.

'Good, now dry those tears,' said Sal. 'I can always

ring David and put him off if you're not in the mood
to go out.'

'Oh no,' said Toby quickly. 'I'd like us to go out with
David. It'll do us both good.'

Sal couldn't help smiling. He had moved from Little
Boy Lost to being the man of the house in a matter of
seconds.

'OK,' she said. 'You're the boss. Go and wash your
face, and then we'd better change. We can't have David
taking us out in our scruff, can we?'

Toby shook his head, and hesitated.

'What is it?' said Sal.

'I'm sorry I shouted at you, Ma.'

'I deserved it,' said Sal.

'No you didn't.'

Sal stood up. 'I'll try and be a better mother, Toby.
I promise.'

'I like you just the way you are,' said Toby.

Sal felt a warmth flow through her, calming her
troubled thoughts. She loved him so much, yet what
was it, this devil which sat on her shoulder and drove
her on in her chosen career? She had not been honest
with her son. There were plenty of jobs she could do
which did not involve her being away from home,
let alone taking her into the heart of so many major
conflicts. Yet it seemed she needed to test herself again
and again . . . as if I need the buzz, she thought. Sal
continued to ponder the folly of her ambitions as she
mechanically slapped on some make-up for David's
benefit. Children change so rapidly – that's what I've
not taken into account, she thought.

From his babyhood, Toby had been blessed by the ministrations of Jenny, the near-perfect nanny-cum-housekeeper, who adored both mother and son and frequently turned her own life upside down to accommodate them. When Toby had been a baby and a small child, Sal knew that she and Jenny had been entirely interchangeable. But he was growing up. He was aware now, presumably not only of the nature of her job, but also of the fact that she had choices — choices she made which deliberately took her away from him. She would have to be more careful in the future. His grandmother's death should not have affected him. The fact that it had done demonstrated his vulnerability and lack of security. She must consult him more and take his feelings into account when planning her life. The child/parent relationship was due for review. They needed to be partners. Perhaps if Toby understood her work more, it would pose less of a threat.

Lunch with David was a big success. They went to Tuttons in Covent Garden and gorged themselves on pasta and garlic bread, David and Sal splitting a bottle of wine.

The tension between mother and son had gone. Toby seemed relaxed and happy and there was no trace of his former anguish. His fears, however, had taken their toll on Sal. She tried to be lighthearted and vivacious, but it was an effort. She caught David watching her a little quizzically from time to time. It was not until Toby was absorbed with his kite that they were alone for a moment.

'What's up?' David asked bluntly. 'I've known you long enough to know when something's really bugging you.'

'My mother died yesterday. That's enough, surely!'

David hesitated and slipped an arm around her shoulder. Sal did not pull away, but she remained rigid and unyielding.

'Loosen up,' he said, shaking her a little. 'There's nothing to be ashamed of in feeling a sense of grief.'

'I don't feel grief exactly,' said Sal. 'I feel regret for the relationship we might have had; guilt, too, for not being the sort of daughter she wanted, but it's hard to miss someone who was really no part of your emotional life. I did try to love her, David, I really did.'

'Of course you did,' he said comfortingly. There was silence between them. 'Toby seems fine,' he added after a pause.

'He wasn't this morning,' Sal admitted. 'You were completely right, David, Mother did represent some sort of security for him. He wanted to know what would happen if I died. It's clearly something that has been worrying him.'

'I'm not surprised,' said David. 'Well, you needn't worry about that. You know I'd always take care of him.'

'No,' said Sal, a little too hastily. 'No, it would be impossible for you to cope with no wife and the kind of hours you work. It wouldn't be fair on either of you. I'm going to draw up a formal arrangement with Louis and Evelyn. Evelyn is his godmother, after all. I know they won't mind, and he would be best there, if anything happened to me.'

'Yes, I suppose you're right,' David said. He dropped his arm from around Sal's shoulder and his look of dejection was evident.

For a moment Sal wondered if she had made the right decision, but it was already too late.

'We can take care of ourselves, you know,' she said, defensive because of the hurt she knew she had inflicted.

David looked up sharply. 'I know that, for my sins,' he said, his anger flaring to meet hers. 'Keeping my promise to your father has not been easy.'

'My father?' The words slipped out before Sal could stop them.

David looked at her curiously. 'You know I promised him that I'd always take care of you. He, better than anyone, knew there was no love lost between you and your mother. The last time I saw him, before that wretched illness affected his mind, all he could talk about was your future happiness. He loved you so much. It's been a hell of a responsibility to try and step into his shoes.'

She began to cry, suddenly and unexpectedly, and there was no hope of hiding it from David. She turned away hurriedly, but he saw her face crumple before she did so. He put his arms around her and pulled her to him so that her head rested on his shoulder. This time she came willingly.

'I'm sorry, Sal, I'm the most tactless bastard alive. I know how much you loved your father.'

'It's not that,' Sal began between sobs.

'What then?' David drew away a little and looked at her, confused. 'What is it – what's wrong? I know there's something.'

'It's just that— '

'David, Mum.' Toby came running up, his face alight with pleasure. It sobered as he saw his mother's tears. 'What's wrong, Mum, what's happened?' He looked to David for reassurance.

'Nothing, old chap. It's just been a bit of an emotional twenty-four hours for your mother.'

Sal smiled at her son, and with a free arm drew him into the circle of the embrace, so that for a moment the three of them stood together, as in a tableau, linked by their need for comfort.

The following morning, Sal and Toby headed up the M40 towards Oxfordshire. David, on hearing of their intentions, had wanted to come too, feeling that a visit to her mother's house might well prove too much for Sal. She had been insistent, however, that she and Toby should go alone – confident that she should cope. Clearly, there was no way of persuading her otherwise.

The cottage felt somewhat eerie, in that it seemed so normal. Certainly it was impossible to believe that its occupant was dead. There were little touches everywhere – fresh flowers, a fire laid in the grate, the smell of furniture polish. Instinctively Toby reached for his mother's hand as they walked through the dark hallway into the sitting room. It was a bright, sunny room, but oddly sterile. It was too neat, too ordered, as if real life had not infiltrated the careful precision of the house. The cushions had been pounded into neat squares, the sofa covers smoothed, the magazines arranged symmetrically. Every room was the same. In the kitchen not even a coffee mug had been left to dry. It was a show-house. Suddenly, fleetingly, Sal wondered whether her mother had ever intended to come back.

That morning, before leaving for Oxfordshire, she had received a disturbing, but oddly touching, call from the taxi driver who had run her mother down. Still in his hospital bed, Charlie Edwards had managed to trace Sal's number and was ringing to say how sorry he was. He had sounded dreadful, truly appalled by Mrs Saunders' death. 'I should have slowed down for her,' he kept saying to Sal, 'but she was looking straight at me . . . she *must* have seen me.'

Letting go of Toby's hand, Sal wandered over to the kitchen window. The back garden, like the house, was neat and characterless – the lawn mown, the borders weeded, the first signs of spring already in evidence. Had her mother deliberately stepped in front of the cab? Certainly she was not a happy woman – never had been – but such an action made no sense. If Barbara had planned to kill herself, but wanted so desperately to tell Sal of her true identity, she would surely have done things the other way around. She had no way of knowing that she would survive being run over by a taxi cab long enough to tell her daughter her story. I'm being ludicrous, Sal thought to herself.

Toby was standing dejectedly in the middle of the

kitchen. 'Do you think Granny has any biscuits?' he asked. Sal grinned. The needs of a ten-year-old stomach took priority over any drama.

'I'll tell you what we'll do, Toby,' she said. 'You rummage for some biscuits and a drink, and I'll put the kettle on for coffee. While it's boiling, I'll just have a quick look through Granny's papers and then we'll sort out the heating and things like that. Then we'll find someone local to look after a key for us, and check the house from time to time.'

'What about lunch?' Toby asked mournfully.

'Two birds with one stone,' said Sal. 'The best place to find someone to help us is at the pub.' He brightened visibly.

Her mother's little rosewood desk stood in an alcove in the sitting room. Sal opened it cautiously, feeling oddly guilty. Her mother had been such a private woman; this seemed an intrusion. The contents of the desk were as neat and well-ordered as everything else in the house. There were a series of files, for house insurance, medical insurance, paid and unpaid bills . . . and simply nothing else. For a moment the strangeness of this did not dawn on Sal, such was her disappointment. While she had not expected instant success to substantiate her mother's story, the fact that there were no letters from friends or the usual jumble of papers – useful and useless – was extraordinary. She searched diligently again in the backs of the drawers – nothing. There was quite simply none of the paraphernalia associated with normal life. It was so clinical, almost as if her mother had expected somebody to go through her things, and wanted to be sure that no clue remained, other than the purely mundane. Suddenly Sal remembered the little safe that lived in her father's study upstairs.

'Just going upstairs, Toby,' she shouted, climbing the narrow staircase two at a time, gripped by a desperation to try and make sense of what had happened in the last forty-eight hours.

Colonel Saunders' room was oddly untouched, almost like a shrine to him. Sal had never lived in this cottage. Her parents had moved to it some years after she had left home, but the study layout was very similar to the room her father had occupied in the former family home. She could remember sitting on his knee while he read her stories and told her of his travels. Her anxiety momentarily forgotten, Sal stopped short in the room and gazed around at the familiar and comforting reminders – the hunting prints, the thick green corduroy curtains at the window, the old leather armchair, the numerous photographs of his regiment in different guises and in different locations.

The safe was where it had always stood, beside the desk. On her sixteenth birthday her father had given her a pearl necklace and earrings and had suggested that they be stored in the safe. He had shown her then where he kept the key – in an old school pencil box in the bottom drawer of his desk. In her anxiety, Sal was all fingers and thumbs. The desk was completely empty, except for the bottom drawer, where the pencil box lay in isolated splendour. She extracted the key and with shaking hands fitted it into the lock of the safe. The heavy door opened with a satisfactory clunk: there was nothing inside, except her mother's jewelry box.

For a moment Sal's disappointment was abated by the thought that there might be some papers inside the box – but on opening it, she found only a collection of rings, bracelets and necklaces. There was no room for any papers. It was extraordinary! There was no marriage certificate, no will, no death certificate for her father – nothing of any sort. The thought of a solicitor crossed her mind. Her mother had never mentioned one, and Sal had already been estranged from the family at the time of her father's death and so had not been directly involved in the winding up of his affairs. Suddenly she remembered Adrian Drummond, and the thought gave her renewed hope. Maybe all her mother's papers were lodged with the Swiss Federal Bank, or maybe he would be able to throw some light on the situation.

Sitting on the floor in her father's old study, her mind whirling, Sal abstractedly turned over the pieces of jewelry. There was a ruby ring, a diamond dress watch, two strings of pearls, a random collection of earrings . . . then a silver chain and pendant caught Sal's eye. She disentangled them and held the pendant up to the light. What she saw made her heart begin to pound and her mouth go dry. There was no mistaking the emblem on it. It was a *gusle* – the haunting, one-stringed instrument she had heard played several times. She had travelled extensively throughout Eastern Europe over the years and knew immediately the significance of the *gusle* – as the traditional national instrument of Yugoslavia, it was used again and again to accompany the old songs of that country's tragic past.

CHAPTER THREE

Adrian Drummond's office was like the man – small and unmemorable. Sal was early for the appointment, but he saw her immediately, fussing over her and offering her coffee she did not want. Since the discovery of the pendant the day before, her thoughts had been all over the place – one moment rejecting utterly her mother's story, and the next blowing up this one tentative clue into absolute proof to corroborate what she had been told. Her mother had never been abroad during the period Sal had known her – certainly never to Yugoslavia – so how could she have come by such a piece of jewelry? It had to give her story some credence . . . unless of course it was just a coincidence – a pretty trinket picked up somewhere, which by sheer chance carried the Yugoslavian emblem. In her mind Sal had quite decided that Adrian Drummond would solve her problems.

'I came in especially early this morning, Miss Saunders,' he began, looking suitably self-righteous. 'I wanted to double-check my understanding of your mother's position before I saw you.'

He paused, dramatically. Sal fought irritation.

'I'm afraid I have to tell you that sadly, you will not benefit in any way from your mother's association with this bank.'

Sal's irritation exploded. 'Mr Drummond, that's the least of my concerns! I'm fully financially independent. Whether or not I'm a beneficiary of my mother's esate is of no significance to me.'

Adrian Drummond frowned. 'I'm sorry, I must have misunderstood the situation. I assumed that would be your primary concern.'

Sal took a deep breath. 'Mr Drummond, I'm trying to solve a mystery, and I'm hoping that you'll be able to help me. Up until the moment of her death, I believed I knew my mother. Now it appears that she was something of an enigma, with a past I knew nothing about.'

As she talked, Sal studied Adrian Drummond's face with a journalist's eye. There was no register of emotion; he remained entirely inscrutable.

'For example,' Sal said, standing up and beginning to pace around the small room, 'it is inconceivable that my mother had a Swiss bank account. She was a very ordinary, conventional, middle-class Englishwoman living in the Cotswolds. True, I often wondered how she managed for money. I even offered to help her on occasions, but she would have none of it. However, the concept of her having anything as exotic as a Swiss bank account is ludicrous, yet clearly she did or I wouldn't be here.'

Still Adrian Drummond said nothing. Sal paused and swung around to face him. He almost caught his breath. She was a startlingly good-looking woman and powerful, too. He would have to watch his step.

After a moment, Sal continued: 'On her deathbed, my mother told me a story about her past which came as a complete shock. She told me that she had been married twice, firstly to a Yugoslavian KGB agent – my real father, would you believe? – and that he had made it possible for her to escape to this country when she discovered his true identity. I need to know whether this is true or not. Do you have any papers lodged here with the bank to help me verify, or otherwise, this story?'

Adrian Drummond shook his head. 'I regret not, Miss Saunders. We have nothing here.'

Sal collapsed into the chair. 'Then what on earth did my mother come and see you about? If there is no money in the account and no papers lodged with the bank, what did you two talk about?'

Drummond spoke slowly, taking time and care with his words, Sal noticed. 'Your mother was the sole beneficiary of a trust fund which was set up via our head office in Switzerland. She received a lump sum each quarter, part of which she used to live on, part of which she invested. The fund, however, terminates on her death.' He paused and then smiled slightly. 'It has been my privilege in recent years to advise her on her investments from time to time, and I imagine that these will be included in her estate and will come to you, Miss Saunders. I understand you're her only child.'

'You understand I'm her only child,' Sal echoed. 'Exactly *how* do you understand that?'

Adrian Drummond recoiled under the venom of Sal's question.

'Well, no reason really, other than it was only of you that she ever spoke.'

'She never mentioned a son?'

Just for the briefest of seconds, a flicker of recognition came into Adrian Drummond's eyes. Sal, who had been waiting for the moment, pounced. 'So you *do* know about my brother Georges! You *do* know about my mother's past. Who set up this trust fund? Was it my father?'

'Oh no,' said Adrian Drummond hurriedly. 'Colonel Saunders took a great interest in the investments, but— '

'I'm not referring to Colonel Saunders, and well you know it,' Sal interrupted. 'I'm speaking of my natural father – my Yugoslavian father.'

It was Adrian Drummond's turn to stand now. Slowly he got up from his desk and turned towards the window. 'I'm sorry, I can't help you. I'm afraid I don't know what you are talking about.'

'Then why can't you look me in the eye and tell me so?' Sal asked, her voice shaking with emotion.

He turned to face her. 'Miss Saunders, I'm a banker. I have administered your mother's trust fund over these many years on the strict instruction that the identity of the trustees remains anonymous.'

'All right, all right,' said Sal, 'so you're not going to tell me who set up the trust fund. I understand that, but you can at least tell me, if only by a wink or a nod, whether there's any truth in my mother's story.'

'I'm afraid I can tell you nothing.'

On impulse, the previous day, Sal had put the silver pendant around her neck. She pulled it out now from beneath her jersey.

'You see this, Mr Drummond?'

He squinted at the pendant, confused and agitated. 'Yes,' he said cautiously.

'This is the *gusle*, the national instrument of Yugoslavia. I found it yesterday in my mother's jewel box. This, Mr Drummond, is the only clue I have to suggest that my mother's story has any credence. Surely you can give me a little more to go on than this?'

'I can't, Miss Saunders.' He paused. His face was very pale, his eyes almost frightened. 'But does it matter now, so much?' he said after a moment. 'Your mother has sadly died, and the trust has died with her. You have your own life and your own future, you're still a young woman— '

'Don't patronise me,' Sal burst out. 'I don't think you understand the implications of all this. I was brought up by a man I adored, whom I believed was my father. It now appears that he was not, that someone else was – a man who apparently betrayed his country. It also seems that I may have a brother. I'm sure it's not asking too much of you, Mr Drummond, to appreciate the implications of all this from my point of view. *Suddenly I don't even know who I am.*'

Adrian Drummond's expression softened, and Sal seized on the change of mood. 'I don't know why I say this, but I have a feeling that you held my mother in some high regard.'

'That's very true. I greatly admired your mother, Miss Saunders.'

'Well, if that's the case, can't you help carry out her last wish? She refused treatment at the hospital – treatment that could very well have saved her life – because she wanted to tell me, wanted me to know, the story of my birth. You could say she died in the attempt. As her banker, her adviser, her trustee, whatever you are, don't you feel it's your duty to help her finish the job?'

'I would if I could,' said Adrian Drummond, 'but my hands are tied.'

'Rules can be broken,' Sal urged.

'Not in this case.'

The silence in the room was tense, but after a moment Sal stood up, recognising defeat. There was no more to be said. After many years of experience in journalism, she had learned that the most intransigent of people to deal with is the small-minded bureaucrat. Powerful men of vision and passionate belief can be surprisingly open-minded on occasions, even be persuaded to look again at their former decisions, their views, their ideals. But the true bureaucrat is immoveable. All he has in life is his set of rules. If he wavers from them, he is lost. The power of original thought is not his.

'I'll say good day to you then, Mr Drummond,' Sal

said, her voice shaking. By the time Adrian Drummond had struggled to his feet to form his reply, she was already out of his office and down the corridor.

He sat alone for a long time after she had left, unable to recall an occasion when he had been more upset or rattled by what had just taken place. He had made the right decision – the *only* decision, and yet if the young woman was right, if her mother had gone to such lengths, risking her own life to tell her daughter the truth, then surely, as she had suggested, he had a duty to complete the story. The girl was vulnerable, he was sure of that. Despite the tough veneer, there was an almost frightening insecurity . . . and small wonder. For the first time, he allowed himself to think critically of Barbara Saunders. Why hadn't she told her daughter the truth before? What harm could it have done, and what untold damage had been created by leaving this partial exposé until Salvena was a grown woman?

If only he could help. For a moment he wondered why he was in such a dilemma. The bank's rules, after all, were perfectly straightforward: to protect the customer at all costs. He had never questioned this wisdom before. In a flash he realised his mistake. For the first time ever, Adrian Drummond had allowed himself to become personally involved.

The funeral, by anyone's standards, was a bleak and dismal affair. David had wanted to come, but Sal refused.

'Funerals are grim at the best of times, and you and my mother loathed each other. I can't see the point.'

'The point,' David said, 'is to give you and Toby some support.'

'There are far better ways for you to spend your time, David. Why not fire a reporter or think up a new lottery? Something practical like that.'

David had been both hurt and irritated. She took her independence too far on occasions, he believed, both to her own detriment and Toby's, but he had known it was an argument he could not win.

So Sal and Toby made the journey to Horton-cum-Studley for the second time in a week, for the burial of Barbara Saunders. Apart from themselves there were half a dozen locals present, mostly elderly women, whom Sal assumed had been friends of her mother's, or perhaps had simply come along out of interest.

Barbara had not been a churchgoer, so the Vicar struggled in his address to sound as if he knew anything about the deceased. A chilly wind blew around the gravestones as the coffin was lowered into the ground. Toby, who was very pale and silent, clung to his mother's hand in a way he had not done for some years.

As Sal stepped forward to scatter earth on to the coffin, she had a last glimpse of the flowers that she and Toby had sent her mother – a bunch of white lilies, the flower of Bosnia. *Who were you?* The question seemed to hang in the air and for a moment Sal stood transfixed at the edge of the grave, staring down at the coffin, unaware that she was attracting curious glances. At last she stepped back and slipped her arm around Toby's shoulders.

'Are you all right, Mum?' he whispered. She nodded.

The Vicar finished his prayers and the mourners trooped away. At the lychgate Sal murmured her gratitude to everyone who had attended and shook hands with the Vicar. She asked if anyone would like to come back to Beehive Cottage, but they all declined. They did not know her, nor she them.

The Vicar, however, hovered behind, seeming to recognise a need in Sal. He turned to Toby. 'Look, my lad, why don't we give your mother a few minutes on her own here? It helps sometimes when you have lost someone close to you. You could come back to the vicarage with me. My children have all long grown up, but I've kept the train set in good working order in the hopes they'll produce grandchildren one day. Would you like to see it?' The vicar glanced at Sal, seeking approval. Toby did the same.

Sal nodded gratefully. 'Thank you, that would be lovely. You go with the Vicar, darling, and I'll be along in a few minutes.'

She walked alone back to the grave, taking a circuitous route around the back of the church. When she reached it, the grave-digger was already hard at work, filling in the hole. He stopped when he saw her, slightly embarrassed at the speed with which he was getting on with his job. 'Would you like me to go away and come back later?' he asked.

Sal glanced at the hole, now half-filled in. There was nothing left there for her. She shook her head. 'No, don't worry, it's OK.'

She turned and walked away across the graveyard

to where it met the fields beyond. There was a bench under an oak tree, a bank where crocuses were already in bloom. Sal sat down thankfully, leaning back against the rough wood. She closed her eyes for a few minutes, and then opened them again to stare out across the fields. The view calmed her.

It was during the funeral that Sal had finally and belatedly acknowledged how abnormal her mother's life had been. No true friends had attended and, of course, no relatives save for her and Toby. Her mother had always discouraged intimacy with people, always shied away from any potential friendship until, at the last, on her death, there had been no one to mourn her passing except, perhaps, Adrian Drummond. For a moment Sal felt a stab of guilt. She should have invited him, but would he have come? He had found their meeting too awkward; he would not have wanted to repeat it.

There were only three tiny shreds of evidence which substantiated her mother's story in any way. The first was the pendant – Sal fingered it at her neck for a moment. The second was the realisation that her mother had no friends at all, suggesting a desire to hide from the world which, if her story was true, was very understandable. The third was Adrian Drummond's reaction to her interrogation. He knew a lot more than he was telling – Sal's training told her that much. Yet, what point was there in pursuing these thoughts? Where could it lead her?

For the moment Sal tried to be rational, to imagine how she would handle it if the story were someone else's, but she couldn't do it. This was *her* story, moreover a story she did not really want to know. Her childhood memories were happy enough. Although the relationship with her mother was poor, she had been secure and comfortable. Now it was all blown apart, and she did not have any desire at all to pick up the pieces and see what was there. She might turn up unwanted details of her parents' lives – ugly facts – and her mind recoiled from the thought. *Who were you*? she whispered again. This woman had been her mother, yet had left her daughter no record of her life. At this thought, for the first time since her mother's death, Sal's eyes filled with tears. She cried silently, tidily, for some minutes, staring out across the fields through a blur.

As the tears dried on her face, her thoughts turned from Barbara to Georges, her long-lost brother. This, Sal realised, was the nub of the problem. Her mother was dead, her father – if he had really existed – was probably dead, too. But her brother, left behind when she and her mother fled . . . he was probably still alive, almost certainly so. Had he been exiled with his father to Russia, if that was his father's ultimate fate? Had he perhaps gone to live with his father's relations when his mother vanished? David had so accurately anticipated Toby's reaction to losing his grandmother, and as Sal sat there, she began to see that much of Toby's fear and insecurity was, in fact, her own. She had Toby, Toby had her, and that was it. She had never needed her family, not since as a rebellious teenager she had left home. But now, suddenly, their isolation appalled her. Maybe she had to pursue her story, not only to find Georges for his own sake, but also to give Toby an uncle and herself a brother.

What did it matter if she found out that her true father was a villain? There was good and bad in everyone, so would it be *so* shocking, *so* hurtful? She thought around the story for a moment or two, then pinpointed where her instinctive reluctance came from. It lay in the possibility of failure. To search for Georges, she knew, was going to open up a need in her that she had only just recognised existed. To expose that need, and then to fail, to be left with the uncertainty of not knowing who she was, with no other family in the world but Toby, seemed probably more than she could bear.

Normally, ever the optimist, someone well able to make a split-second decision, Sal found herself faced with uncertainty and indecision on a grand scale. 'Time,' she told herself aloud. 'I need time to think this through. I mustn't rush into it.' She looked around her, embarrassed suddenly in case someone had overheard her, but there was no one else in the cold and bleak graveyard that day.

The Reverend Alan Wilkins was a kind and sensitive soul. One look at the boy's mother, and he could see that she had been crying.

'Toby's entranced with the train set,' he said. 'Come along into the sitting room, my dear, and have a glass of sherry. I'm not going to ask you any embarrassing questions, but you look perished and miserable.'

Sal smiled at his warmth and followed him. His face did not look particularly old — he must once have been very good-looking, in an intelligent and gentle way — but he was stooped and as he poured them two enormous schooners of sherry, his hand shook. He splashed a little on the table. 'Oops, sorry. Parkinson's.'

'Oh, I'm sorry,' said Sal.

'Well, something's got to get me. They'll retire me soon, and at least Parkinson's gives them the excuse. I've had it for years — we're old friends.' He handed her the sherry. 'Come and sit down.'

A cheerful fire blazed in the little Victorian grate, either side of which were shabby, but clearly comfortable, armchairs. Sal sank down in one, grateful for the warmth and tranquility of the room. She took a tentative sip of her sherry. 'Delicious,' she sighed.

'Good.' The Reverend Wilkins eyed her benignly. 'It's a bright little chap you have,' he said.

'Yes, yes he is,' said Sal, her face lighting up at the mention of Toby.

'He doesn't seem unduly upset about his grandmother, but then I gather you didn't see much of each other.' It was simply a statement — there was no hint of criticism.

'No, that's right,' said Sal. 'My mother and I fell out some years ago and although we did attempt to meet on occasions in the intervening years, it was never a great success, I'm afraid.'

'She must have been fond of Toby, though,' the Reverend Wilkins suggested.

Sal shook her head. 'Not really. She never showed

much interest in him at all. In fact, they only met about half a dozen times in his entire life. It's strange, but then again perhaps it isn't, knowing her.'

'We don't choose our relations, you know.' The Vicar took a hefty swig from his glass. 'There's no need to feel guilty if your mother and you didn't see eye to eye. It takes two to make a relationship. Sad, but all part of life's rich pattern – so don't let it make you miserable.'

Sal smiled back at him, basking in his kindness. It suddenly felt good to talk. 'I imagine it's fairly normal to have regrets, though, isn't it?' She looked up and was rewarded by a nod of encouragement. 'Mother was a difficult woman, without a doubt, but I should have persevered. She had no one except Toby and me, you know. It wasn't right that she spent her last years alone. No one should be alone.' Something in the Vicar's expression made her forget her own problems for a moment. 'What about you?' she asked gently. 'Do you live alone here?'

'I do now,' he said. 'My three children are grown up, two married and one yet to be. My wife died of cancer eighteen months ago.'

'I'm so sorry,' said Sal.

'Yes, it was a blow. We were looking forward to retirement together. Still, live for today, that's all we can do, isn't it? I do miss her though, very much – more, strangely, as time goes on, not less.'

They sat in companionable silence for some minutes, until Toby appeared, flushed and excited at the door of the sitting room.

'Hi, Mum,' he said. 'It's the most fantastic train set, you'll have to come and see it before you go. If ever you write a bestseller, please can I have one just like this?'

'Bestseller?' Alan Wilkins stared at Sal for a moment. 'Of course, you're that newspaper girl, aren't you? I always read your column in the Record. It's very good. You really understand the problems of Eastern Europe, and the people. I was a fighter pilot in the war and worked very closely with the Poles. Marvellous chaps, very excitable, but so brave. You have a rare gift, my dear.'

'Thank you,' said Sal.

'Fancy, you being Barbara Saunders' daughter.' He grinned, his faded blue eyes twinkling. 'I can see why you two weren't close – chalk and cheese.'

'I'm afraid so,' said Sal, smiling back.

With difficulty he heaved himself to his feet and on impulse, encouraged by his interest, Sal said to him: 'Did you know my mother at all, anything about her – where she came from, that sort of thing?'

Alan Wilkins looked at her curiously, and so, Sal noticed, did Toby. 'No, not really, I never knew her at all. She wasn't a churchgoer, as I expect you know, and the once or twice I called on her she was very short and abrupt. In fact, she told me to go away the last time I tried to visit. She kept herself to herself, and was never involved in village activities. Besides, I can't think there's anything I could tell you that you wouldn't already know yourself. What were you wanting to find out, particularly?'

Sal tried to look casual. 'Oh, I don't know, nothing really.'

Alan Wilkins gave her a strange look. It seemed as if he was about to speak, but then apparently changed his mind. Instead, taking Toby's arm he said, 'Come on, my boy, lead us to the trains.'

CHAPTER FOUR

The Reverend Louis Noble loved the spring. Even this evening as he strode across the field towards home, the air dank from a day of tumultuous rain, he revelled in the squelching under his feet, the dripping from the trees. It was the smell he found so heady. There was an expectant smell coming from the hedgerows, the branches of the trees, the very earth itself. Things were about to happen – it was like a birth.

His thoughts strayed to the birth of his last child, Tamsin, his only daughter, blonde and beautiful, amazingly already four years old. The boys had been born in hospital, but Evelyn had endured enough institutionalised birth and, much against everyone's advice, had insisted on having her third child at home. The birth had been easy, in their own bed with the boys playing next door – it seemed so natural. The midwife had handed him the child immediately and it seemed to

him, even then, that she was different. She had none of
the crimson, screwed-up fury of most newborn babies
– certainly of his sons. She was a delicate pink, with
huge blue eyes that regarded him solemnly, and a tiny,
very distinctive face.

Louis remembered how he had gone over to the
window and looked up to the hills where he was
now walking. Dawn streaked the sky and, as he held
the baby, the sun suddenly burst over the horizon,
bathing the countryside in a golden light. To his eternal
embarrassment he had cried and at the time had seemed
quite unable to stop. Both his wife and the midwife had
been very understanding, but he had wished they would
go away. It had been the supreme emotional moment of
his life and he had not wanted to share it with anyone,
except Tamsin.

He reached the brow of the hill and called to heel
his Labrador, Jess. Below lay Hawkhead Farm, his
home. It was not a particularly prepossessing building
– a straggling pile of whitewashed stone which had
been chopped and changed, extended and converted
by generations of farmers dating back to the early
1700s. The Nobles were the first people not to farm
the land around it. The house had been acquired by
Louis' father as a working farm, but he had first rented
out the surrounding land and then sold it. The house
remained in the family though, and thanks to Evelyn's
skilful home-making had become a joy, a safe haven
for them all.

Most of their lives was spent in a dreary Victorian
terraced house close to Lambeth Palace, where Louis

worked, but whenever they could, even if only for a day, the Nobles took off for Hawkhead Farm. This weekend was a luxury, three whole days – a little extra leave since this time next week he would be in Russia. Louis thought of his impending trip with a mixture of excitement and apprehension. Would he succeed? It was God's will, he supposed, and yet he was not sure that God's will played much of a part in Eastern European politics. What was wrong with him? Why was he always challenging his faith these days? Once he had been so sure, but not now. Now the world seemed devoid of certainties.

Angry with himself, he began striding downhill towards home. Louis cut a dashing figure – tall, broad-shouldered, with a rather untidy shock of dark wavy hair. In deference to his West Country origins, he had pale skin, rosy cheeks and startlingly bright blue eyes. He was not strictly speaking good-looking, but he had a kind of rugged charm due mostly to the warmth and merriment of his expression. Unless dressed for the part, no one would have suspected him of being a clergyman. He just did not fit the pattern, which made it all the more surprising that his career had been so successful.

Details of the house began to take shape as he drew closer. A warm glow shone out from most of the windows and he could hear the shouts of the children playing in the garden. Then, screwing up his eyes to focus better, he saw Sal's red jeep parked slightly askew outside the front door. Typical Sal – he could imagine her coming up the drive too fast, throwing on the brakes and skidding to a halt outside the front door, pebbles flying in all directions. She would have run straight inside without bothering to knock, calling out their names. He smiled involuntarily. He had forgotten she was coming but it would add to the pleasure of the weekend.

Sal Saunders was Evelyn's oldest friend. They had been homesick and frightened at boarding school together at the age of eight. They were very different. Sal, with her commitment to her career, Evelyn, with her commitment to her home and children. He knew he should disapprove of Sal's lifestyle – her illegitimate child and the string of lovers who seemed to come and go in her life – but somehow he could not. She had a zest for living, an enthusiasm which he greatly admired and which he had to admit Evelyn did not possess. Sal always seemed so certain, so sure of herself but not in an arrogant way. She had obviously set herself a series of goals and was going to make damn sure she achieved them.

Evelyn always wished Sal would marry and settle down. Idly as he walked, Louis tried to picture Sal with a permanent man in tow. To his surprise he did not like the idea. It would remove the importance of his family in her life, he realised with regret. He liked his particular role – vaguely avuncular, her big brother. He knew their relationship brought her pleasure and comfort and this, he acknowledged now, was reciprocated. Things had not been right between him and Evelyn since Tamsin had been born, and yet it was hard to define why. Tamsin had been a much wanted child and was a joy to them both. Yet somehow he and Evelyn had drifted apart and their sex life, never tremendous, had become almost non-existent. Still, they were happy. Evelyn was his best friend and one could not ask more than to be married to one's best friend. He was blessed indeed. As to his relationship with Sal – it added a little spice, without being dangerous.

Standing by the kitchen sink, Sal gazed up the hill to where she could see the tiny figures of a man and a dog. She turned towards Evelyn. 'The Master returns, I think.'

Evelyn sighed. 'Louis does so love it here. It's a ridiculous thing to say, but sometimes I just wish we were ten years older so he could take premature retirement. Then we could stay here all the time, instead of living "over the shop" as we do at the moment.'

'That's a dreadful thing to say.' Sal was genuinely shocked. 'You can't wish your life away like that.'

'I know,' Evelyn said ruefully, 'but I'm just not cut out to be a career wife. All those dinners and functions we have to attend – I loathe it. A simple life around the Aga, that's for me.'

Sal smiled indulgently at her friend. Evelyn was still pretty, very pretty, but in recent years had let herself go. She was wearing no make-up, and her face was shiny and blotchy from the heat of the Aga. Her hair was scraped back into an untidy bun and she had on a loose skirt and clogs, topped by what appeared to be an old shirt of her husband's. She did have a weight problem, but the baggy clothes greatly accentuated it. Sal loved her just as she was, and she knew Louis did too, but she also knew that no one in a million years would suspect that the two women had been contemporaries at school. Evelyn looked a good ten years older than Sal.

'Another glass?' Sal held out the bottle.

'Why not,' said Evelyn. 'Drunk in charge of a roasting chicken – who cares!'

Sal had appeared at the door half an hour before, clutching a couple of bottles of champagne. They had toyed briefly with the idea of a cup of tea and abandoned it in favour of the champagne.

'What are we celebrating anyway?' Evelyn asked.

'I don't know,' said Sal. 'I should be in mourning really.'

Evelyn smiled at her sympathetically. 'It can't be easy losing one's mother. I'm lucky, I still have both my parents. I can't imagine it, it must be a . . .' she struggled for the word. '. . . a very *grown-up* feeling.'

Sal laughed. 'Yes, I suppose you're right – and very daunting, too. I'm in the front line now, next over the top and all that.'

'Oh, don't!' said Evelyn. 'Will you miss her?' She looked at Sal quizzically.

Sal said nothing and turned back to the window. Louis was recognisable now. He looked very happy, Sal thought, he and his dog, the wind tugging at his wild hair. 'Your husband looks as if he has a touch of the Heathcliffs today,' she said.

'You're evading the question, Sal.'

Sal turned to face her. 'I don't see how I can miss her exactly, but when I saw her again, I did have rather a shock.'

Somewhere on the journey, Sal had decided to tell Evelyn of her mother's revelation and to seek her advice. Now she found that once she started to talk, she could not stop. The words spilled out, tumbling over one another in her effort to tell Evelyn everything before Louis returned.

Evelyn was a good listener. She said not a word until Sal had finished. 'It's really shaken you, hasn't it?' she said at last.

Sal considered for a moment. 'Yes,' she admitted. 'Yes, I suppose it has. It shouldn't do, should it? I'm a grown woman, with a son. Who my father was really, is of no consequence.'

'Of course it is! Everyone needs to know who they are and where they came from, and besides which, there's your brother. Heaven knows, you and Toby have few enough relations – in fact, you haven't anyone except each other, and Toby's father, whoever he may be.' Evelyn paused pointedly.

It was a longstanding source of contention between them. Since girlhood there had been no secrets. They had told each other everything, except for this one detail. Sal had never revealed to Evelyn the identity of her son's father. Sal grinned. 'You never let up, do you?'

'Certainly not. I'll trap you into an exposé one day. Seriously though, Sal, there's something very comforting about a big family. Your brother is probably married with children of his own, which would give Toby cousins and you both blood relations, other than each other. You can't let it drop; you've got to try and find out some more. You've the right training for it and you're certainly in the right business.'

'Some days I think that too, but mostly I just don't feel I can pursue it,' said Sal.

Evelyn stared at her, genuinely bewildered. 'But you must.'

'No.'

'Why not?' Sal did not reply and with a sudden flash of intuition Evelyn stood up and came over to her friend, slipping an arm around her shoulders. 'It's because you're frightened of what you might find, isn't it?' Sal nodded, tears coming into her eyes. 'So much for our investigative journalist, winner of so many awards,' said Evelyn.

The gentle banter worked. Sal recovered herself, wiping her eyes on the back of her sleeve, like a child, angry at her weakness. 'I can't explain it properly,' she said, 'but I've lost my confidence, which is ridiculous because I'm still the same person I was before last Friday, aren't I? *Aren't* I, Evelyn?'

'Of course you are,' said Evelyn. 'You're just in a state of shock. In a few days I'm sure you'll feel differently. You'll begin to want to know more.'

'Maybe there's nothing more to know. My mother was close to death and confused – it's crazy to take her story seriously. She probably made up the whole thing.'

There was silence between the two women for a moment, for they both knew that Sal's words did not ring true.

* * *

Later that night, in bed, while Louis wrestled with *The Times*, Evelyn sat staring into space. Her silent preoccupation eventually got through to Louis.

'What's up, old girl?'

'Sal,' she said.

'Why, what's wrong with her? Oh, you mean her mother dying.'

'Sort of,' said Evelyn, and told Louis of Barbara Saunders' revelation.

'Poor Sal. Poor Barbara, come to that,' said Louis, when Evelyn had finished. 'I always suspected that woman had a past, she was such a strange person. Possibly she thought that if her true identity was ever revealed she might be killed – a hideous thought.'

'Yes,' said Evelyn. 'So not only does Sal not know who her father is, she doesn't know who her mother is either, does she? She must have been living in the UK under an assumed name. I wonder if Sal has thought of that.'

'Oh, Sal will have thought of that,' said Louis.

'I'm worried, Louis. I think it's all having a very bad effect on Sal, and I don't know how to help her.'

'In what way?' Louis finally relinquished his *Times*.

'It's hard to explain.' Evelyn sounded hesitant.

Louis took her hand and pulled her down beside him, her head resting on his shoulder. 'OK, tell me all.'

'It's serious, Louis,' said Evelyn.

'Why?' he asked, humouring her.

'Sal's always been very sure of herself. She's done

some odd things in her life, but she has never had time for any regrets or doubts. She's simply got on and done it.'

'I would agree with that,' said Louis, his voice heavy with irony.

'And now,' Evelyn was groping for the words, 'now all that self-assurance seems to have gone – overnight. It's really left her floundering, Louis.'

'She seemed fine to me,' he said. 'In fact, she was very good company during dinner tonight. You were both a bit the worse for wear, of course – all that champagne – but I thought she was on very good form. Looked very lovely, too, as usual.'

'She was brittle,' said Evelyn, 'almost desperate in her effort to be jolly. She's deeply unhappy at the moment and very confused.'

'Hmm,' said Louis. 'Well, it seems to me that the only way she's really going to come to terms with what's happened is to treat the whole story as a piece of investigative journalism. If she gets stuck into trying to unravel the mystery, she won't have time to be introspective.'

'I've already suggested that,' said Evelyn, 'but she's just not sure if she can face it. My pet theory, for what it's worth, is that she's afraid to know in case she turns up something unpleasant, which I suppose she's almost bound to do sooner or later. It all sounds a rather unsavoury story.'

'It would be good to find that brother of hers – for her and Toby.'

'I've suggested that as well,' said Evelyn.

They both laughed. 'You've really thought of everything, my darling, haven't you? So all you've got to do now is to persuade her actually to do it, and to find out the truth.'

'I'll try,' said Evelyn. 'I think it's so important not to let the whole thing fester. After all the years of stress and hard work, it could even be the trigger to something serious.'

'What are you suggesting,' said Louis, 'a nervous breakdown?'

'I don't know – maybe that's a bit dramatic, but something like that. She's going to need watching very carefully, and helping too. She may well have problems coming to terms with what she discovers.'

'Then,' said Louis, 'thank God she has a good friend like you.'

The next day was beautiful. The hint of spring had become a reality. The sun shone clear and bright and the crocuses, which had bravely pushed through frosty ground, opened wide now, basking in the warmth. It was a day on which it was impossible not to be happy.

They spent the morning in the garden with the children. The Noble boys, William and Sam, were younger than Toby but they were all great friends and had been from babyhood. Sal and Toby were family in everyone's eyes. It was easy and comfortable, the perfect antidote to the turmoil in Sal's soul and the insecurity in Toby's.

At lunchtime they went to the local pub and then

drove up on to the Downs for a walk with the dog.

'Toby and I ought to go home tonight,' Sal said, as she and Evelyn straggled behind the others.

'Good Lord, you can't do that. You must at least stay until after Sunday lunch.'

'I've got such a lot to do,' fretted Sal, 'things I need to sort out. You know me, ants in the pants and all that'

'I know you, all right, and you always have a lot to do,' said Evelyn, 'but you owe yourself this weekend. Go on – relax.'

'I can't,' said Sal. 'Sometimes, Evelyn, I wonder whether I'm in the right job.'

Evelyn could not believe her ears. 'But you love your job, Sal, it's your life.'

'Yes, and that's the problem. I hadn't realised until Mother died how insecure Toby's becoming, with me tearing around the world all the time. I ought to give it up, but I can't think what else to do, and I don't know how I'd cope without it. As you say, I do love my work.'

'And as I said yesterday, you're still in a state of shock,' said Evelyn firmly. 'You need a break. Couldn't you and Toby get away when term ends?'

'Perhaps,' said Sal.

'Well, come down again next weekend anyway,' said Evelyn.

'Oh, I couldn't,' said Sal. 'Poor old Louis needs some time alone with his family without me and Toby always being around.'

'Louis won't be here,' said Evelyn.

'Oh really, why not?'

For a moment Evelyn hesitated. Louis had sworn her to secrecy, yet the secret was safe with Sal — wasn't it? Just for a moment Evelyn was unsure. First, last and always Sal was a journalist, and yet had she not just expressed the desire to change her career? She was hardly in the mood to betray a friendship for the sake of a story. 'It's a secret,' she said. 'You mustn't tell a soul.'

'Scout's honour,' teased Sal. 'Don't tell me, there's going to be a bishops' conference in York! How can you stand the excitement?'

'Actually, it is quite exciting,' grinned Evelyn. 'He's going to Moscow.'

'Good Lord, whatever for?'

'You promise you'll keep this to yourself?' Evelyn repeated. 'Louis would kill me if he knew I'd let on.' Sal nodded. 'Well, he's going on the Archbishop's behalf to negotiate for the release of Gennadi Naidenov.'

Sal frowned. 'But surely that's the old boy who Gorbachov has already released from prison? I know he's been in and out of jail on and off for years as a supporter of the dissidents, but I'm sure he was in that batch Gorbachov released before Christmas to impress the West with his impersonation of Santa Claus.'

'Oh, so you know him,' said Evelyn, feeling a sudden note of disquiet.

'Well, know *of* him,' said Sal. 'Has he been imprisoned again?'

Evelyn shook her head. 'No, but he's causing something of problem. Now he's out in the big bad world again, he's almost changed sides. He keeps preaching against the sins of Capitalism.'

'I don't believe it,' said Sal. 'It doesn't make any sense.'

'I think it does in a way,' said Evelyn. 'Eastern Europe is your field, not mine, but he says that Communism in Russia is giving way to an even greater evil. At least in the good old hardline Communist days, there was no crime. Now there's a great deal, as I understand it, and Naidenov sees this as the greater evil.'

'I see,' said Sal slowly. 'So he's turning out to be an embarrassment to Gorbachov.'

'Something of an embarrassment to everyone,' said Evelyn. 'The Church of England, of course, have been campaigning for his release for years, and now he's out, he seems to be supporting the very people who put him in prison in the first place! As I understand it, Louis is being sent out to try and negotiate for Naidenov's release from the Soviet Union. The Archbishop is hoping that Louis will be able to bring him back personally.'

'Which will mean another gold star for Margaret Thatcher in forging relationships with Gorbachov, and one less obstacle in the way of Gorbachov's courtship of the West.'

'I hadn't realised that Louis had become so high-powered,' said Sal. 'This is real diplomatic stuff, with a touch of James Bond. I think I'll view him in a completely different light from now on.'

'This isn't his normal work.' Evelyn was slightly

irritated by Sal's manner. 'In fact, this is his first major
assignment. He's quite excited about it actually, but I
can't help feeling a bit apprehensive.'

'Why?' said Sal. 'It's safe enough, surely. People don't
disappear in Russia these days, especially high-profile
Anglican clergymen, trying to help Gorby.'

'Yes, I suppose you're right.' Evelyn gave her friend
a quick hug. 'So will you come down next weekend
and keep me company?

Sal considered for a moment. 'It depends what David
has in store for me when I get back to the office.'

So much for a change of career, Evelyn thought.

It would have been an irresistible story at any time.
Coming, as it did, when Sal's particular patch on the
globe, Eastern Europe, was becoming positively boring
with Gorbachov's increasing friendliness towards the
West, it was a story sent from heaven. All the way
home in the car to London, while Toby slept, Sal
turned the problem over and over in her mind. Evelyn
had told her of Louis' mission in strictest confidence
and certainly diplomatically it was not a story that
should be leaked for fear of jeopardising the whole
initiative. There had been no whispers in the press
circles about it. The information she had been given
was, without doubt, a good old-fashioned scoop –
hers for the taking. But to betray Evelyn's friendship –
that was another thing entirely. She tried to rationalise.
Maybe she could ask Louis if she could cover the story,
on the strict understanding that there would be a news
embargo, if he so wished. She thought this through

for a moment, then acknowledged that he would be in no position to give such authority. Lambeth Palace and/or the Foreign Office would be controlling media exposure, and clearly they had decided there should be none, at any rate until they had Naidenov safely in England. Should she confide in Evelyn, or rather, ask her permission? But Evelyn would do nothing without Louis' approval; her loyalty was unquestioning. So maybe she should just go ahead and do it . . .

She turned into the driveway of their house and drew up in front of the garage. She leant across and shook her son gently. 'Tobe, wake up darling, we're home.'

He opened sleepy eyes and smiled at her. 'We had a nice weekend, didn't we?' he said. 'I do love going to Louis and Evelyn's.'

'Me too,' said Sal, with a sinking heart. She could not do it, there was no way she could put their friendship on the line.

But the story would not go away. She saw Toby into bed, made herself a sandwich and paced around the house. Once or twice she thought of ringing David, but then decided against it.

She had to make the decision alone; Evelyn was *her* friend.

Sal thought back over the way their lives had interwoven. They had remained best friends at school, from eight to eighteen – no small achievement when girls' boarding schools are such a hotbed of intrigue and bitchiness, particularly in the teenage years. After school, Evelyn, always the studious one, had taken the sensible path. She had read History at Warwick

University, while Sal was getting pregnant and dabbling in journalism. Then Evelyn had gone on to teacher training college and met Louis. They had married very quickly, the fairytale couple – young, in love, decent, honest people, a white wedding with all the trimmings. It had been during this period that Evelyn and Sal had been most estranged, because their lives were so different. But once William, Evelyn's first son, had been born, they suddenly had the children in common and grew close again. The Nobles had proved to be wonderful friends.

Sal tried to look at it another way. Maybe as loyal friends they would understand. After all they, better than anyone, knew what a struggle it had been to raise Toby and keep a roof over her head while still fulfilling the demands of a job as a foreign correspondent. Surely they would not begrudge her this story? She could go and offer Louis a news embargo subject to Palace clearance, but then maybe the Palace would not give permission. If David had financed her trip to Moscow, his attitude would be to publish and be damned. A news embargo was a promise she simply could not make.

On impulse she rang her contact at Heathrow. It was after midnight, but Sal was lucky. She was still on duty. She called her back ten minutes later with information as to which flight Louis was catching to Moscow on Monday morning. Seats were still available on the plane. Sal did some more pacing. Perhaps that was a sign. At last, exhausted, she went to bed, but slept little. It was such a marvellous story, not just securing Naidenov's freedom, which in itself was very newsworthy, but the follow-ups – the human interest story, how he found the Western lifestyle, who he left behind. There was so much mileage in it.

She woke the next morning at five o'clock. Louis' flight left just before midday. Without allowing herself to think too hard, she rang Peter Blakeney, the photographer she usually used. 'Peter, are you working or anything at the moment?'

'Yes,' he answered morosely. 'Sleeping. What the hell do you mean by waking me up at this hour in the morning, Sal?'

'How do you feel about going to Moscow?'

'I hate the bloody place.'

'It's an interesting story.' She outlined it quickly, careful not to mention her personal connection with Louis.

'It sounds a goodie,' Peter admitted. 'There's nothing I'm working on that can't wait for a few days. Book me on the flight and I'll see you at Heathrow at ten-thirtyish. I wouldn't do this for anyone, you know.'

The phone went dead. So Peter had made the decision for her. Her heart hammering, she called Heathrow and booked their tickets with an open return. Then she dialled David's number.

'David, did I wake you?'

'Yes, you did,' he grumbled. 'What's up? It had better be important.'

Again, Sal outlined the story, only this time she had no choice but to admit that Evelyn had been her source.

'So, can Peter and I go?' Sal asked when she had finished.

'Yes, I suppose so,' said David.

'You don't sound very enthusiastic.'

'I'm enthusiastic about the story – who wouldn't be? I'm just worried about how this will affect you and the Nobles. Did you talk to them about Toby's guardianship, incidentally?'

'No, I didn't,' Sal admitted. 'I was going to on Sunday and then this story came up and I sort of funked it, I suppose.'

'Sal, are you sure you know what you're doing? You're very dependent on that family, they've been such good friends.'

'No, I don't know what I'm doing,' Sal told him. 'It's just that I need a good story, David, you know that better than anyone. I think if I explained it all to Louis once we're out there, he'll understand.'

'I hope you're right,' said David drily. 'You're certainly a good journalist – the job always comes first.'

'You're making it sound like a criticism,' said Sal.

'It's not intended to be. I just hope you've gauged this right. As your editor, I'm dead keen on this story. As your friend, it worries me.'

'Me too,' Sal said frankly. 'But I've made my decision, David, so I suppose I'll just have to live with it.'

After he put down the phone, David lay in bed staring at the ceiling, thinking of Sal. There was so much to admire about her. There was her courage, her enthusiasm, her professionalism – and, of course, her glorious good looks. The trouble was she always rushed her decisions, and that was where most of her mistakes in life had occurred. Take Toby – she had been much too young to have a baby. Firstly, she had got herself pregnant, heaven knows by whom, and then she'd rushed into the decision to have the baby rather than an abortion. Of course, Toby was a splendid child, always had been, and David was devoted to him, but the toll on his mother had been considerable. Life had been very tough trying to juggle a child and a career, particularly the sort of career that Sal enjoyed. Maybe the Nobles would understand that. He hoped so.

There was another thing, too. Something had happened to her around the period of her mother's death, he was sure of it. She was very tense and slightly out of control. It was just the time when she needed her friends.

CHAPTER FIVE

'It'll be raining,' said Peter morosely. 'It rains all the time there. Also it'll be cold, not a hint of spring, and dirty and ugly – and why don't they make these aircraft seats just a few inches further apart so I'm not kneecapped every time I move as much as a millimetre?'

'Because they have to make a profit and because most people aren't as big as you,' Sal replied tersely. 'Do you realise, we've been in the air for over an hour and you haven't stopped moaning?'

'It's just Moscow, Sal. It's a nightmare place, you know how much I hate it.'

'You didn't have to take the assignment.'

'Yes, I did. I wasn't going to let you go swanning off with any old Tom, Dick or Harry. The whole thing sounds dodgy to me; you need to be kept in check!' He looked at her and smiled, a big craggy man with a mop of curly brown hair and deep blue eyes, crinkled at the corners. He always reminded Sal of a favourite teddy bear and, of course, he was right – she would not have wanted to have anybody but him with her. She was still anxious, though without knowing quite why.

She glanced down the aisle. The back of Louis' head was unmistakable. It had been a risk, taking the same flight as him, but a large floppy hat and sunglasses had seen to it that he didn't recognise her. Besides which, of course, he wasn't looking for her. The thought made her feel sick with nerves. He wasn't looking for her because Evelyn had trusted her, and she had betrayed that trust. More than once during the flight so far, she had been tempted to go to Louis to confess what she had done and beg his forgiveness, to abort the trip, if that is what he insisted on. Yet something stopped her – professionalism, stubbornness, or a strong desire to avoid any form of confrontation, she was not sure which. Dragging her thoughts away from Evelyn and Louis, she turned to Peter. 'Suppose I order us some more wine, would that placate you a little?'

'A little,' he conceded, smiling. 'You know why I'm making such a fuss, Sal?' She shook her head. 'The place frightens me.'

Peter was always the same. He always had the ability to disarm. Sal could remember many difficult occasions when a remark from Peter had eased the tension and relieved her irritation. He was never predictable. Now his remark interested her.

'Why?' she asked. 'It never frightens me, and the last time I went, which was – let me see – about four or five months ago, Gorbachov's changes seemed to be having a positive effect. People were less nervous, more confident about talking to Western journalists than ever before.'

Peter said thoughtfully: From where I stand, it seems more like a tinder box to me, and what applies to Russia applies to the rest of Eastern Europe.' He shrugged his shoulders. 'When people had nothing, not even knowledge of the world outside their country, their lives were miserable but at least they didn't know any different. Now, with more access to the outside world, they're starting to recognise that they are the "have nots", and I think that's dangerous.'

Sal smiled. 'Quite a closet psychiatrist on the side, aren't you, Peter? Perhaps we should swap jobs.'

'You'd make a lovely photographer,' Peter replied, without rancour.

The stewardess arrived and Sal ordered more wine, careful to keep her voice low. She knew the husky quality of it was instantly recognisable.

As if reading her thoughts, Peter said: 'So when are you going to confront him? How long are you going to play this cloak and dagger game?'

'I don't know,' said Sal. 'I think I'd rather wait until he has taken delivery of the old boy. I think it's reasonable to assume it would be easier for him to talk to us once he has Naidenov.'

'This doesn't sound like the Sal we know and love. Your victims don't usually get this degree of concern for their well being.'

'Well, this one's different,' said Sal.

'Why?' Peter asked, refilling their glasses.

'He's actually a friend. His wife, Evelyn, is my very best friend, and she's Toby's godmother. We've known each other for ever.'

'Oh, so that's why you've been skulking in corners,' said Peter. 'I thought you were getting a bit paranoid about your public persona. I know I'm travelling with a celebrity, but I thought you were being a little over the top in assuming this churchman would think you were after him.'

Sal stuck her tongue out at him. 'Beast,' she said. 'You're not taking this seriously. It's been a hell of a decision. I just hope I've done the right thing.'

'You mean the hard woman of journalism has a heart?'

'Peter,' said Sal, genuinely hurt.

'I'm sorry.' He reached over and took her hand. 'Things have been a bit flat recently, haven't they, in your neck of the woods? If they're true friends, they're going to understand that. From what I've seen of him, he looks a kindly sort of bloke.' He grinned. 'And this friend of yours, Evelyn: if she's known you for as long as you say she has, she's going to know what a witch you are anyway, and won't expect anything less.'

Sal withdrew her hand abruptly, and cuffed Peter around the ear. 'Why the bloody hell do I put up with you?'

'Because I'm the best in the business,' he said disarmingly.

'True,' said Sal. 'But seriously, Peter, I'm glad you're here. The whole thing is a bit tricky.'

'Good heavens, she needs me,' smirked Peter. 'I'll drink to that.' He drank deeply and then grinned at Sal wickedly. 'Still,' he said, 'I'm glad he's your friend and not mine.'

Sal grimaced at him and returned to her newspaper, but the remark had disquieted her. After all these years of friendship, Louis would not mind, surely? They knew each other so well, they had helped each other out on many occasions. He might be a deeply religious man, but he was also a realist, very much in today's world and full of admiration when it came to her career – she knew that. OK, so this time he was on the receiving end, but sooner or later the story would make the press anyway. Surely, he would rather she told it than anyone.

Sal felt a sudden surge of self-pity. Why did every-body make it so hard for her simply to do her job? David and Peter with their criticism, Jenny, her house-keeper, silent with disapproval at breakfast because she was leaving Toby again, and Toby himself first pleading with her not to go and then when he realised that he could not shake her resolve, distant and cold. What was she supposed to do? If she didn't work, Jenny wouldn't have her job, Toby wouldn't have his school, his home and his toys, and David wouldn't have his story, nor Peter his assignment. Self-doubt was not normally a part of Sal's nature, but just for a moment she badly wanted to get up and run down the aisle of the plane and say, 'Louis, tell them I'm doing the right thing!' She bit her lip and forced herself back to the paper.

In front of her was a badly written article on Poland by a fellow journalist, Bill Jones, who had told her more than once that his expertise far outstripped her own when it came to Eastern Europe. Its sloppiness at least gave her some comfort, although her mind kept wandering.

She had made little progress in the last few days with her mother's story. Within hours of leaving Adrian Drummond's office, he had telephoned her. In the confusion of their meeting, he said, he had forgotten to give her the name of her mother's solicitors.

Green, Drake & Bodmin were an old-fashioned firm based in cramped and gloomy offices just off the Broad in Oxford. Temporarily elated at the prospect of some concrete information, Sal's hopes were almost immediately dashed. Mr Drake informed her that they were responsible for her mother's estate, but nothing more. Barbara Saunders had left everything to her only daughter – the house and contents, some stocks and shares worth about thirty thousand pounds, and between five and six thousand pound cash in the bank. Everything was well-documented, efficient and completely impersonal. The solicitors held no other documents and were reasonably confident that Barbara had been represented by no other firm. Another dead end. Was she relieved or disappointed? It was hard to tell.

As they touched down at Moscow airport, Sal felt the familiar surge of adrenalin she always experienced at the beginning of a story. 'Peter, I'll carry your bags – you follow and find out which hotel he's going to.'

Peter looked at her quizzically. 'Ah, so I'm Dr Watson to your Sherlock, am I? I hadn't realised that this was going to be my role.'

'Shut up and just do it, and don't lose him, for God's sake.'

Peter smirked at her. 'As you wish. Just be careful how you handle my camera.'

Sal hung back as the plane disgorged its contents into baggage collection. Peter joined her ten minutes later as she waited in the passport queue.

'Intourist,' he said triumphantly.

Sal's face fell. 'Oh, I was hoping for the Intercontinental.'

'Well, now we know where he is, surely we don't have to stay at the same hotel?'

'We most certainly do. How far ahead is he?'

'Oh, he'll be well on his way now. He had no baggage, and there was a driver waiting for him.'

Sal frowned. 'So how did you— ?'

'I asked the driver. I got there first. He was holding up a card with Louis' name.'

'Not very discreet for a sleuth,' Sal said, frowning.

'Sorry if I'm not coming up to your expectations,' said Peter.

Sal grinned. 'You and the hotel, both.'

The receptionist at the Intourist was able to confirm that Louis had checked in and was even sufficiently obliging, after the exchange of a few dollars, to tell them that his room number was 47. The bad news was that the hotel was full; even after a few more dollars, the best he could offer was a twin-bedded room with a shower that did not work.

'When can you get it working?' Peter asked with studied patience.

The man shrugged. 'Today – maybe tomorrow.'

Sal sighed. 'No shower and you snore – what a start!'

'I don't snore.'

'You do,' said Sal.

The receptionist looked from one to the other. 'Do you wish to take it?'

'Yes,' they said in unison.

While Peter filled out the booking form, Sal had a chance to study the lobby and its occupants. It was an incredibly busy place, full of people waiting, people meeting, people talking, arguing – a continual buzz, like a railway station in the rush hour. Suddenly Sal noticed a group of young girls sitting together, talking and smoking. It was obvious what they were. Sal studied them. Some of the girls seemed so young, in their early teens. They were horrendously over made-up, but this could not disguise their youth. Sal watched, fascinated, as a businessman shook hands with a colleague by the front door and then wrestled his way to the news-stand and bought a newspaper. He then approached the group, selected a girl who looked as though she was no more than fifteen, and the two of them moved towards the elevator. He had bought a paper and he had bought a woman . . . there was no more preamble or fuss with one than with the other. Sal realised with surprise that she was deeply shocked. It was the blatancy of it – the *normality* of it, and the extreme youth of the girls. It was all deeply disturbing.

When Sal pointed out the group to Peter as they made their way to the elevator, he shrugged his shoulders. 'Perhaps the old priest has a point. Certainly it's not a sight one would have seen in Moscow until recently.

'It's so extreme,' said Sal as they entered the lift. 'One moment vice is non-existent, the next it's so intrusive, and it's all happened so quickly.'

'Far be it from me to tell you how to do your job,' said Peter, 'but if I were you, I'd build this decline of morals into your article. I think it's rather interesting. As I said on the plane, make people aware that they are the "have nots" and they grab at whatever they can get.'

The room was tiny and airless, and it was not just the shower that did not work. Neither did the basin nor the loo.

'I'm hating this already. I told you Moscow was crap,' groaned Peter. 'Which bed do you want?'

'The one by the window,' said Sal.

'That's the one I want.'

'Tough.'

Peter regarded her in silence for a moment. 'So, where do we go from here?' he said eventually.

'I suppose I'm just going to have to wait downstairs and see what happens. Presumably Louis will have a meeting at the Kremlin and then, with any luck, he'll collect the old boy straight away. Whether he's going to bring him back to the hotel, I don't know, so I'll have to keep as close an eye on him as I can.'

'You make this sound like a one-woman crusade. What do you want me to do?' Peter asked.

'I suppose we could work in shifts.'

'OK.' Peter collapsed on the bed. 'You take the first one – I'm knackered.'

'I'm glad to see the age of chivalry isn't dead,' Sal said.

In truth she was glad to be handling it herself. Instinct told her that Louis would make contact right away. He was not the sort of man to hang about and presumably would be anxious to ensure the old man's freedom as quickly as possible.

She found the perfect dark corner, partly hidden by a pillar, but nevertheless affording a good view of the front door and the main elevator. With a newspaper at the ready and her large felt hat covering the giveaway white-blonde hair, she settled in to wait, hoping desperately she would be able to catch sight of Louis in the throng.

She did not have to wait long. Within a few minutes of her arrival, the lift doors opened and Louis seemed to explode out of them. He strode across the foyer and then stopped, staring around him. His eyes rested on her. She raised the paper hurriedly. With a few strides he stood in front of her. 'Sal, what the bloody hell do you think you're doing?'

The unecclesiastical language and the vehemence of his tone were even more surprising than the fact that he had recognised her. She lowered the paper and looked up at him, smiling nervously. 'Don't be angry, Louis. This is just too good a story to miss. I'm sure you understand.'

'I do *not* understand,' he bellowed. 'How could you betray Evelyn's friendship? I just can't believe it of you. She's in such a state.'

'How did you know I was here?' said Sal, very much taken aback.

'I rang Evelyn as soon as I got in, just to check that everyone was all right, and she told me.'

Sal stood up, Louis still towered over her. She had never seen him angry before – certainly not this angry and certainly never with her. 'How did she find out?'

'She knows,' Louis thundered, 'because unlike you she's a decent friend. She rang your home this morning to see if you'd had a safe journey back home, and to ask you to come down next weekend. She spoke to Jenny who told her you were flying to Moscow and she didn't need to be much of a clairvoyant to realise that you'd betrayed her trust.'

Damn, Sal thought, she should have warned Jenny, but the hostility she had received at the hands of both housekeeper and son had muddied her thinking. 'Look Louis, somebody's going to write this story so it might as well be me. At least you know I'll do it sympathetically from whatever angle you want.'

'It doesn't need doing at all!' Louis thundered. 'There is to be no publicity, none at all. It's a very delicate matter.'

'Why?' said Sal.

'The name of the man I'm collecting is the Reverend Gennadi Naidenov.'

'I know,' said Sal, 'and I know that once he was a very hot property, but Gennadi Naidenov is an old man now. I know he caused the Kremlin a lot of problems when he was younger, but that's all past. It's just a nice story – it shows Gorbachov is recognising the need for greater openness and— '

'Sal, it's not that simple. Just take my word for it,' Louis advised her tersely. 'Gennadi Naidenov has to be got out quickly and discreetly, for Gorbachov's sake, for the British Government's sake and most of all, for his own sake.'

'Why?' Sal asked.

'None of your damn business. Just catch a plane back to Heathrow. If I can't persuade you to leave for decency's sake, then maybe it will help if I tell you that I'm not going to give you a story. You're wasting your time here.'

'I'm sorry Louis,' said Sal. 'I can't leave now.'

'What do you mean, can't? Won't is more like it.'

Sal shook her head. 'The paper have paid for me and Peter to come out here. We can't go back without a story, so you have to give me something.'

'I have to give you nothing. Who's Peter?'

'My photographer – you know, the one I've told you about many times. I've used him on— '

'Yes, yes,' said Louis, glancing at his watch. 'I'm late, I'll have to go.'

'Where to?' Sal asked immediately.

'I'm not telling you that. I'm not telling you anything. Now leave me alone!

Louis turned on his heel and strode out of the foyer. In normal circumstances Sal would have gone straight after him – but this time she hesitated. She had recognised something in his expression that she had never expected to see there. He was clearly furious at her presence, but there was something else, too. *He was frightened*. Louis, the big reassuring man of God – always so calm, generous to a fault, and above all supremely confident in what he was doing and where he was going. But not this time, Sal thought, certainly not this time.

The shock made Sal resume her seat. For the moment, she did not feel up to facing Peter again. Why was Louis frightened? What was he not telling her? Sal thought back to her conversation with Evelyn. Were there any clues there? Naidenov had been preaching against the rising crime rate. Was it possible that he'd had a run-in with some sort of organised crime racket, someone who was threatening his life? It seemed so unlikely for a man who had to be well into his seventies.

Sal glanced around the foyer. The number of prostitutes had increased if anything, as it was now late afternoon. Again Sal was struck by the blatant display of their trade. Certainly it did not appear that this was a city where vice was something to be ashamed of any more. If Naidenov was talking about crime and violence, prostitution and drugs on a big scale, then he had to be talking about the Mafia, and it was well known that the Mafia did not take kindly to its critics.

Suddenly, all the doubts and guilt that Sal had experienced in her betrayal of Evelyn left her. Louis sensed that he was in some sort of danger, or at least that Gennadi Naidenov was, and Sal trusted his instinct. Peter was right, Moscow had always been a frightening place, and it remained that way. Maybe the secret policemen were not so much in evidence, but if organised crime was spiralling out of control, then Louis Noble had every reason to be scared, and perhaps it was just as well she was there.

The handover was brief and without any formal ceremony. Louis was disappointed; he had expected more. He had simply reported to a room in the Government offices and within a few minutes, his charge was literally delivered to him: Gennadi Naidenov – priest, poet, dissident and now, apparently, self-appointed politician. He was a small man with sparse white hair and a grey unhealthy complexion, hook nose and a mouth which was far too wide and generous in such a small face. Only his eyes made him special – deep brown, bright like a robin's, darting here and there, interested in everything.

The two men shook hands politely, but spoke not a word until they were escorted to the front door of the building. In his pocket Louis had the passport and visa which would release the old man from the USSR for the first time in his life. By his side, the man in question, tiny, only reaching his shoulder, stood stooped and leaning heavily on a stick.

'Well,' said Louis, a little too heartily, 'how does it feel to be a free man, Mr Naidenov?'

'I don't know,' he replied. 'Not yet. I know I shouldn't be leaving, I know that, but I suppose I have no choice.' He gave Louis a penetrating look.

'I'm not a politician,' said Louis, 'but it seems to me that as both sides want it, and you've undoubtedly earned it, a little peace and quiet in England would do you no harm.'

The old man shook his head. 'It's too soon.'

A taxi cruised past. Louis hailed it and ushered the old man inside. 'We're going back to my hotel,' he explained. 'Our flight isn't booked until the day after tomorrow, so it'll be necessary to spend two nights at the hotel. I hope this will be all right.'

'It is good,' the old man nodded. 'There is someone to whom I have to say goodbye.'

They sat in silence as the taxi negotiated the potholed road, jarring its passengers this way and that. If they had known the handover would be so easy, they could have flown out the same day, Louis thought. Two days in Moscow with this old man was a worrying prospect.

He turned to Naidenov. 'I'll have to look after you very carefully while we're still in Moscow. I understand that you may have some enemies.'

The old man shrugged his shoulders. 'Maybe. It is of no consequence.'

'It is to me,' said Louis quietly. 'I have to keep you safe.'

'As you wish.'

His apparent disinterest in his own safety came as no surprise to Louis. This man had led a life in which there had been no room for self-interest. It was hard to understand why he now represented any real threat. He was just a tired old man, a little cantankerous perhaps, almost a cripple. It was hard to understand the fuss.

At the hotel they arranged to meet again at dinner. Naidenov was tired, he said, and needed time alone. Tomorrow they would take a short journey to say goodbye to his special friend. Louis was to go, too – he would be interested, Naidenov said. Louis agreed reluctantly. He felt very much on edge.

Louis' nagging concern as to the safety of the old man was further heightened by a sense of disorientation. It was his first visit to an Eastern-bloc country and he could not believe that people were living as they were. He could see poverty all around him, the squalor, the hardship. He knew it was not how a man of God should react, but all he wanted to do was to go home.

With an afternoon to kill Louis knew he should have gone sightseeing, but instead he chose to shut himself away in his hotel room and pretend to catch up on some paperwork. It was crazy to miss the opportunity of seeing something of Moscow, but part of his reluctance to go out was the thought of meeting Sal again. He was, he realised as he paced up and down his hotel room, unspeakably hurt by her actions. All three of them, he, Sal and Evelyn, had often laughed at her ruthless exploits in pursuit of a story, but never in a million years had it occurred to him that she would apply the same rules to him and Evelyn. As far as he was concerned, Sal was family, and the betrayal was absolute. He minded for Evelyn, whose hurt was palpable down the telephone line. He also minded for Sal, feeling somehow that she had sold her soul for a story. In his mind he tried to make excuses for her, but could think of none.

By dinner Louis was seething with frustration. He knew that his inability to relax, to meditate – to be a thinker rather than a doer – was one of his main problems. He was a man of action, rather than of the pen, as had been pointed out to him by his superiors on many occasions. It was why, in a way, he was better suited to life in a parish. You could get things done, make things happen, dash about and see people. Attached to Lambeth Palace, where diplomacy and politics seemed the order of the day, he felt stifled.

Gennadi Naidenov looked almost dapper. He had dressed for dinner and Louis found it oddly touching. He had brought with him only one battered suitcase and from this, clearly, his suit had emerged, for it was crumpled and shabby. He wore it, though, with elegance and a certain panache and Louis, temporarily forgetting his frustrations, felt for the first time a quickening of interest in the old man. Here was someone who was so certain about his life, who had suffered terribly for what he had believed in, but by all accounts, had never waivered. Louis envied such commitment. Increasingly the modern church made him wonder at his own faith and calling, and he longed for a sense of conviction above anything.

They ordered food and wine and Louis found his

curiosity getting the better of him. 'Please don't answer this, if you'd rather not,' he said, 'but I understand from my superiors that you are unpopular with various factions. I don't understand this. I thought Gorbachov no longer considers you an enemy of the State, and certainly there was no trouble today in obtaining your release.'

Gennadi smiled ironically, his lined monkey-face creasing into private amusement. He took so long to answer that Louis assumed he was not going to do so. When he did speak, his voice was weary. 'For years Russia has been in the grips of a tyranny the world condemned – Communism. Now at last, with the assistance of Mikhail Gorbachov, we are being allowed to join the rest of the human race – in some ways, at least. Everything Western is considered wonderful – your music, your clothes, your hamburgers, your chips . . . also your drink, your drugs, your prostitution. Now we even copy your crime rate. There used to be no crime at all in Moscow – it was a safe city. It is a safe city no longer.'

'So what are you saying?' said Louis.

'That we're exchanging one form of tyranny for another. That as we are allowed to become more Western, we are picking up more of the bad habits than the good, aided and abetted, of course, by the Mafia.'

'The Mafia?' Louis said. 'My boss didn't mention them. I thought that particular form of organised crime belonged in Sicily.'

'The Mafia are all over Eastern Europe; they run

everything. This place is corrupt, a cesspit. The old ways were wrong, but this new way will destroy the Soviet Union. It will not survive. I forsee civil war — terrible times.'

Louis shook his head in disbelief. 'But in the UK we see this move by Gorbachov as nothing but good — the end of the Cold War, the removal of the nuclear threat — all these things now seem possible. Surely that's good?'

'Good for you, maybe. For us, no. After years of repression and misery, to suddenly be handed the so-called trappings of Capitalism is like giving a starving man too much food. He'll gorge himself until he is sick. Thus will it be here. Drink has always been a problem for the Russian — vodka, plum brandy . . .' Gennadi smiled. 'Drink certainly is a vice we recognise, but drugs — no, prostitution — no, and violent crime — certainly not. Every day on the streets of Moscow now, people are murdered, houses are looted, and there is — how do you call it? — mugging. The Mafia have a thriving prostitution business which is aimed not just at the tourists, but at the local Muscovites, and today's young people are falling prey to that most evil plague of all — drugs. The effect on our society is already terrible: families are breaking up, we now have an AIDS problem. Meanwhile, the Mafia grow richer. They are starting to control everything, just like the secret police before them. I am very fearful.'

'What you say makes perfect sense to me,' said Louis. 'We have seen what vice and violence has done to America and to Europe too, up to a point. You are trying to stop the same thing happening here. I cannot understand why your views are so unpopular, and if they are, with whom?'

The wine arrived and Louis poured it. They drank in silence for a moment, Louis now more comfortable in the old man's presence.

'Why, with the Mafia, of course! I preach against them, I expose them for what they are. I try to turn the people away from the corruption. Our Government doesn't like it, and your Government doesn't like it but most of all, the Mafia don't like it. That's why they all want me out of here.' He smiled feebly. 'And after all these years, the irony is I no longer want to go.'

'You don't want to leave Moscow?'

The old man shook his head. 'There's no need for me to go now. They have released me from prison, I have my own apartment, my life is here. If . . .' he smiled again '. . . if I had, how do you say, kept my mouth shut, I would have been allowed to go about my business in peace, but then, when have I ever done that? I cannot change now. I see what's happening to our young people and I have to speak. I cannot remain silent.'

'And so you're an embarrassment to everyone,' said Louis.

'That is it precisely. Gorbachov is trying to sell the new improved Soviet Union to the world by offering greater freedom for all. You know his wife, Raisa, she is a quarter Jewish. Traditionally we Russians hate the Jews, but Gorbachov tells the world his wife is a quarter Jewish and so there must be no more persecution of the

Jews. It is all a fairy story – what you call "window dressing". Then I come along and say, "No, what is happening is bad." Your Government is angry too, and the Americans. They want Gorbachov to move in the direction in which he's going and to embrace Western ideals. They don't want me telling the world that there's a different side to the story, a dark side.'

Louis refilled Gennadi's glass. 'So, what happens when you come to England? Are you going to stop preaching?'

'No, of course not!' said Gennadi. 'It'll be as you people say, "a new lease of life" for me. The press in Moscow are still heavily censored. In the UK, I believe, there's no such censorship. I will be able to talk openly about what is happening here. It does not seem much of a privilege to you, I know, for you cannot understand the wonderful thing it is, the freedom of the press.'

'Do they know this is your intention?'

'Who do you mean by "they"?' Gennadi asked him.

'Everyone – the Government, the Mafia.'

The old man shrugged his shoulders. 'I don't know, but they know me, and while I have breath in my body – I talk.'

'I'm surprised they're letting you loose. You're going to be . . .' he looked at his distinguished charge affectionately '. . . quite a celebrity, once you're safely in the UK.'

'If I get there. I, too, wonder why they are releasing me. In Moscow they have control over me; if I go too far I can always be rearrested, or I can meet with a convenient little accident. But once I am out of the country, once I am in the UK, I am no longer in their control. I can publish what I like, do what I like. I have to say, my friend, that their releasing me makes no sense at all, which is why I wonder if I shall ever see London.'

'I'm going to make sure you do,' Louis promised him. 'After what you've told me, we're not leaving this hotel until we go to the airport.'

'Ah, that's where you're wrong,' said Gennadi. 'Tomorrow, I have to go out.'

As he spoke, Louis looked up and saw Sal walking across the restaurant in his direction. She looked lovely, wearing a tiny black dress which showed off her figure. She was closely followed by a scruffy-looking young man, whom Louis assumed to be the photographer. A pleasant-enough face, but what a mess. He looked as though he slept in his clothes. The old man followed Louis' gaze.

'What a beautiful woman,' he said.

'Ah,' said Louis, 'now she can be one of your earliest targets. That's Salvena Saunders – she's a journalist.'

'Oh, I know Salvena Saunders,' said Gennadi.

'You do?'

'Well, no, not personally. I had no idea she was such an extraordinary-looking woman, but I've read her articles for years. She's quite a specialist on Eastern Europe. She understands us, which is rare in a Western journalist.'

'She may be a good journalist,' said Louis, 'but she's not much of a friend.' His voice was bitter.

'She's your friend?'

'*Was* my friend,' said Louis. 'I'm not so sure now.'

The old man threw back his head and laughed. 'My dear Mr Noble, if you are lucky enough to have that wonderful woman for a friend, you should get down on your knees every night and thank God.'

'I'm married,' said Louis stiffly. 'Happily married.'

'That's good,' said Gennadi, 'but you are still a man, or has the Church of England deprived you of your manhood?' Louis was shocked. It was hard to believe that this little man was a priest. His disapproval must have shown. 'Ah, I see. Louis . . . I may call you Louis?' Louis nodded. 'You have spent too much time with those appalling bishops of yours, so serious, so pompous, so sure of themselves. Jesus Christ would not have liked them, you know.'

Despite himself, Louis smiled. 'You seem to know a lot about the Church of England.'

'I have a superficial knowledge of most religions,' said Gennadi. 'They interest me.'

'Naturally.'

'The world is full of so many diverse and wonderful gods. If one was not born into a specific religion, it would be almost impossible to choose one's god, I think. I am a Christian, you know. I was born a Christian. It cost my father his life – his Christianity – and my mother her sanity. Some people never learn, so I, too, held to my Christian beliefs and they have brought me great comfort and great anguish. The irony is that bearing in mind what my faith has cost me, I dislike much of the Christian doctrine, and as for the Church of England and its Bishops . . .' he waved his hand in a dismissive gesture '. . . they indulge in political games and try to make self-important major issues out of nothing. Meanwhile, their Church is bleeding to death. Every year they lose more of their flock. The British way of life, the ideals, the values, are slipping through their fingers and the Church is doing nothing to help. *Nothing.*'

'Exactly,' said Louis, his eyes suddenly alight with enthusiasm.

'Ah, my friend, I have struck a chord with you. I thought you were not like them, very British and – how do you say – strait-laced, but a man, I think, who likes to see things done, not talked about.'

'Yes,' said Louis, 'that's me and you're right. More and more these days I question my religion, my calling, what direction I'm going in, and why. I have very little in common with my colleagues at Lambeth Palace. They drive me witless sometimes, no – often.' Louis smiled. 'I shouldn't be telling you all this.

'Indeed, you should, and as an old man, let me give you a piece of advice.'

'I'd appreciate it,' said Louis.

'Do not let the English Church, with all its cant and stupefying pomposity, deflect you from your own calling. I can see you are a good man – no saint, but then who of us is? I sense you have deeply-held beliefs, to which you must cling. That does not mean that you necessarily have to follow the Church's doctrine to the letter. Be your own man and then you will find peace of mind.' Gennadi suddenly grinned wickedly. 'Before you deflect me with theological discussion, I would just like to put on the record, Louis, that when we finish our meal, I would like an introduction to your friend, Salvena Saunders.' He glanced in the direction of Sal. 'Beautiful,' he whispered. 'Now, tell me about your life.'

Louis tried to make the meal last as long as possible, by rambling through his life history. To have to introduce Gennadi to Sal was a nightmare, playing right into her hands. She would be much amused by it.

The old man, though, knew exactly what was going on. 'You're dawdling . . . is that the right word? Dawdling over your coffee, Louis. I want to meet the lady, and I want to meet her now.'

The two men rose and went towards Sal's table. Sal saw them and smiled sweetly. Louis could have killed her. 'Sal,' he said, 'may I present the Reverend Gennadi Naidenov.'

'You certainly may,' said Sal. 'This is a great honour.' She took his hand. 'I'm Salvena Saunders, and this is my colleague, Peter Blakeney.'

Peter rose to his feet. 'Would you care to join us for a drink, sir?' he asked Gennadi.

'I would be enchanted.' He shot Louis a mischievous look. Louis did not dare open his mouth. Sal summoned a waiter and in an instant, cognac and glasses arrived and two chairs. Louis noticed the fawning waiters, which infuriated him still further. Gennadi observed all this with pleasure.

'We didn't get this service, did we, Louis?' he laughed. 'Tell me, why are you in Moscow, Miss Saunders?'

'To see you, of course,' said Sal. Louis could not believe her gall. She was neither embarrassed, nor apologetic.

Gennadi was delighted. 'So, I'm the story you're after. How wonderful, I can't believe my luck. Is it really true? I thought there was supposed to be a news blackout.' He looked to Louis for confirmation.

'There is,' said Louis, through gritted teeth. 'Unfortunately my wife is an old friend of Sal's and she let slip that I was coming out here to collect you.'

'Ah,' said Gennadi, eyebrows raised in mock consternation. 'A betrayed friendship, how terrible! Does this mean that I cannot speak with this wonderful woman?'

'You can speak to whoever you like,' said Louis. 'I'm past caring.' His rudeness silenced them all for a moment. 'Look,' he stammered, 'I'm sorry. I'm just not sure what sort of threat you're under, how much danger you're in. I suppose I'm not cut out to be a minder, and it worries me. Sal trying to cover the story is just another threat, that's all.'

'It is not for much longer, my friend,' Gennadi said gently.

'Tell me exactly why your life might be in danger,' Sal said, the instant professional.

'Ah,' said Gennadi, 'is this an interview?'

'It can be if you wish.'

Gennadi hesitated. 'I'm tired, and I've already told all this to Louis. Why don't we meet tomorrow, and I'll tell you why I'm such a nuisance to everyone – particularly the Mafia. There, does that whet your appetite?'

Sal smiled. 'It certainly does. Would you join me for lunch?'

'No, I can't do that, we're going out tomorrow morning.'

'But I just said— ' protested Louis.

'I know what you just said, but my oldest friend lives not far from here, in a bad district of the city. You will find it interesting. I tell you, Louis, if I do not see her, I shall not be catching that plane.'

Sal grinned. 'That sounds like a definite threat, Louis. I should take him seriously.'

'Oh, I'm certainly doing that,' sighed Louis, finally allowing himself a smile.

'So shall we meet later in the afternoon, four o'clock, perhaps?' Sal suggested.

'Yes, that would be good,' nodded Gennadi. 'I shall look forward to it. In the bar perhaps.'

Sal and Peter watched the ill-matched couple leaving the restaurant. Louis, so broad and tall, Gennadi, so frail and small.

'It's strange,' Sal said, 'but if you were to ask me which of those two was the happy man, I'd have no hesitation in telling you.'

'Gennadi every time,' said Peter.

'Exactly. His life has been a nightmare — KGB interrogations, Siberia, truth drugs. He's spent far more of his life in prison than out of it, and yet he is at peace. He possesses the gift of inner contentment.'

'Well, he's found his chosen path through life, hasn't he?' said Peter. 'He knows what he's doing, where he's going, and in a strange way, it's hard not to envy him.'

Sal laughed at him. 'But you know what you're doing and where you're going, Peter, surely?'

'I certainly do not. Since my career seems to be inexorably linked to yours, I never know whether I'm on my head or my heels from one moment to the next.'

'You know what I mean,' said Sal. 'You're happy in your work and there appears to have been a long string of devoted women in your life. What more do you want?'

'A wife, kid – the full bit, I suppose,' said Peter.

Sal stared at him, incredulous. 'Good heavens, I would never have thought you were like that. Footloose and fancy free, a woman in every port, or is it in every darkroom? That's how I see you.'

'Then it just goes to show you don't really know me at all,' Peter said, his expression surprisingly serious.

CHAPTER SIX

K aragodina Gorlov was beautiful. By her own admission she was nearer seventy than sixty, and she looked her age, yet her face still made men catch their breath. It had been a hard life, spent amongst the dissidents, resulting in several periods in prison and great poverty. A tough, compassionate woman, she had dedicated her life to helping the persecuted, the victims. She was as near a saint as made no difference and it showed. At least, this is how Gennadi had described her to Louis in the cab on the way to her apartment.

There was a tranquillity about her, a sweetness of expression, which immediately enslaved Louis. Her skin, though lined, still had a beautiful peachy bloom to it. Her hair, white now, must once have been blonde. She must indeed have been a great beauty, Louis thought.

She settled them down in the tiny sitting room of her

flat, offered Louis some coffee and then addressed herself to Gennadi, a great fountain of Russian pouring out
of her, excitedly, angrily – several times she pounded
the table. Gennadi tried to appease her with words but
she would not listen. At last he rose and gently kissed
her on the lips. Apparently mollified, she disappeared
into the kitchen, mumbling to herself.

Louis was amused. 'Good heavens, what on earth
had you done to deserve that?'

Gennadi smiled. 'She is upset. She thought I was
leaving for England without saying goodbye.'

Louis looked at him shrewdly. 'I imagine this is a
woman to whom it is not easy to say goodbye.'

'No,' Gennadi said. There was a silence between
them for a moment. 'We met while we were both
still at school.' His eyes met Louis', the pain there an
agony to witness. 'I have loved her ever since – all my
life. There has never been another woman.'

'But you never married?'

Gennadi shook his head. 'It would not have been
right. I could not have supported her as a husband
should. It would have been bad if we'd had children.
We were not meant to live lives like other people, with
homes and families. It does not mean that I do not
often wish we were.' He shrugged his shoulders and
smiled sadly.

Karagodina bustled into the room carrying a tray on
which was a spotless linen mat, three coffee cups and
three glasses.

'What are you talking about?' she asked suspi-
ciously.

'About you and me, and why we never married.'

'Oh, that,' Karagodina laughed and slapped him gently across the head. 'Because I would not have him, Mr Noble. He is impossible. He thinks too much, talks too much – how could I have lived with that, tell me?' Her smile and the warmth in her eyes belied her words.

Gennadi retaliated. 'And you think I would have had you? There are many prettier girls I would have chosen before you if I had taken a fancy to marriage. Tell me,' his expression was suddenly serious, 'how are your children?'

'Not too bad,' Karagodina answered. 'Some of them are doing quite well.' She left the room again.

'Children? I thought you said you didn't have any?' Louis asked.

'Ah, not *her* children, exactly. Girls, young girls from the streets.'

'Beggars, you mean?' Louis asked.

Gennadi shook his head wearily. 'Child prostitutes – little girls forced into prostitution by their parents. This area is notorious for them.'

Louis was appalled. 'And Karagodina, she tries to stop them?'

Gennadi looked surprised. 'No, no, she cannot stop them, there is no other way most of them can live. Now and again, yes, she has helped one or two escape the life. There was a very clever one. She managed to find some tuition for her and I think she went to university. And another one, a little one – I think she was nine – she managed to have her adopted.'

'Nine years old?' Louis was horrified.

'Oh yes,' said Gennadi, 'many start at nine, some even younger. They begin when their parents think they are ready.'

'You mean . . . you mean their parents are a party to this?'

'For many families in this area, there is no alternative for their daughters. That, or starve. It is run by the Mafia, of course. So now do you wonder why I speak out against them?'

At that moment Karagodina re-entered the room. 'Ah, Kara,' said Gennadi, 'I have just been telling Louis about your children.'

Karagodina smiled. 'My life's work,' she said. 'Not much, but then maybe something.' She poured the coffee into exquisite little Turkish coffee cups and then filled the three glasses with thick purple liquid.

'If you cannot stop them, and their way of life,' said Louis, 'isn't it very disheartening, very upsetting?'

Karagodina looked at him. 'It is not my job to stop them, nor to moralise. I wonder, Mr Noble, what you would be prepared to do faced with starvation. What I try to do is to make their lives a little easier. I have three apartments in this block. The girls may not bring their clients here; it is a haven for them. They come here to rest, to eat, to talk, and I look after their medical needs. When they become pregnant, I ensure they have a proper abortion, not one that will kill them. When they become sick from infection, I have a source at the hospital who gives me antibiotics. I do not always succeed. Most often I fail. Last week, one of my little girls had her throat cut. No reason – her client wanted an extra thrill, I suppose. Sometimes, they are mutilated, tortured to death, gang-raped. The little ones seem to bring out the brutality in men. Occasionally though, when God smiles, I am able to change their lives, like my little Anya.'

'The nine-year-old?'

'Yes,' Karagodina's face broke into a smile. 'She is in France now. She has an adopted Russian mother and a French father. He came here with his wife on a visit to her relatives, they heard about what I did and ended up by taking little Anya home with them and adopting her. The scars have healed, they say, the mental ones as well as the physical. She is at school, twelve now, doing well. But Anya is rare – one of the lucky ones. Most will be dead by twenty.'

'Dead?'

'We have AIDS now. Also, a girl's life, that sort of girl, is worth very little. But then, Moscow is not alone – this applies everywhere in the world, does it not? Girls who sell their bodies are the lowest form of life.'

'I suppose so,' said Louis.

'Anyway, enough of my children for today. To you, my old friend,' she raised her glass to Gennadi, and he to her in silent toast.

As Louis watched, it suddenly dawned on him that these two old friends – these lovers, as surely they must have been – were never going to meet again. This was their final parting. They began speaking quietly in Russian. Louis sipped his coffee and tried to imagine what it would be like to say goodbye for ever to Evelyn.

Surprisingly, he found he could not make the equation. He loved Evelyn, of course he did, and they shared the children, whom he adored. But there was a passion between these two people, old as they were, which he recognised that he and Evelyn had never shared.

It was an extraordinary revelation that two elderly people who had touched each other once, only briefly, in a chaste kiss, could generate between them such magnetic tension, such . . . yes, *sexuality*. He knew that he and Evelyn had settled for a comfortable life, rather than one highly charged with emotion, but the price they had paid was never to know the exquisite highs and lows that could be experienced between a man and a woman. Never before had he seen what he had missed so graphically portrayed, and between two such unlikely people. He did not know whether to thank them, or to envy them. He cleared his throat and they both stopped talking and looked at him. 'I feel I should leave you alone,' he said. 'Why don't I wait outside for you to make your goodbyes in private?'

'No, no,' they both said.

'Please do not feel that you have to be polite,' Louis insisted.

'It is not politeness,' Gennadi told him. 'It would not be good for us to be alone; your presence helps us. Alone, this parting would be too hard.'

'He is right,' Karagodina declared, 'and we should know, we who have said goodbye for ever so many times. Mr Noble, I have watched this old man being dragged away by the KGB from this apartment, and many others like it, more times than I can remember.

Each time I have known it is possible that he will not see another dawn, and yet each time, in the end, he has come back to me – older, uglier, and more difficult to please . . . but he always comes back. But this time – no, never.'

Her words hovered in the air. Then, as if responding to some hideous cue, the silence was broken by a terrible crash. There followed a thump, then the sound of splitting wood, and the flimsy door of the apartment simply flew inwards, crashing to the floor by the table at which they sat. Three men burst in. Two made for Louis, dragging him to his feet and forcing his arms behind his back. The third went straight for Gennadi, pulling him to his feet and then kicking him viciously in the crutch, so that the old man doubled up in pain and fell to the floor. Karagodina began to scream. One of the men holding Louis shouted at her, and she stopped abruptly, her eyes wide with terror, her face waxen.

'What's happening, what's going on?' Louis shouted.

'No speak,' came a gruff voice behind him. Louis began to struggle.

Karagodina shouted at him: 'Do not resist – they will kill you.'

Louis stopped struggling. The third man had Gennadi on his feet. The old man's face was twisted with pain.

'Come,' his captor growled. He dragged the old man towards the entrance to the flat. Louis, too, was being hauled along. He forced his head over his shoulder. Karagodina simply stood, staring out of the ruins of her flat.

'Who are they?' Louis shouted. One of the men

punched him in the side of the face. For a moment he almost lost consciousness, but as he was bundled out of the apartment door, he heard Karagodina's voice barely above a whisper. 'Mafia,' she said.

They were forced down the concrete stairs of the apartment block and literally hurled into the back seat of a waiting car.

Louis tried to keep his wits about him. He should have noticed what sort of car it was, but he was still in such a state of shock, he felt enfeebled. It was like some ghastly 'B' movie, too dramatic, too violently out of context to be real. Yet it was only too real. He and Gennadi were squashed tightly together. There was one man sitting either side of them, and another in the front seat next to the driver. They began hurtling through the back streets at a crazy speed, oblivious of the pot-holes.

'Where are you taking us?' Louis said. 'I demand to know. I think you should be aware that I'm a member of the British Government, and this is a flagrant— '

'Quiet,' said the man in the front seat. 'We know exactly who you are, Mr Noble. It is your misfortune that you chose to nursemaid such a man as this.' He turned and spat directly into Gennadi's face. Gennadi was too weak even to wipe away the saliva.

'I'm taking him to England,' Louis said. 'He's an old man; he can do no one any harm. Let us go, or at least let *him* go.'

'Do not be so naïve.' The man in front turned full around to face Louis. For the first time Louis met his eyes, and what he saw there filled him with horror. It was a face devoid of all normal human feeling – there was cold hatred there and violence, but nothing else. At that moment Louis knew they were lost.

He tried anyway, his voice sounding strange even to his own ears. 'I don't think your boss is going to like the fuss this will cause at international level if anything happens to Mr Naidenov. It will be very bad publicity for your organisation. Let me take him to England. I repeat: he'll do you no harm there.'

'You are a stupid man. He will do us very much damage. In the UK you have free press; he will talk and talk. He is the enemy of our organisation.'

'But— ' Louis protested.

'*Silence*!' The man swung around again, a revolver pointing directly between Louis' eyes. The gesture was so dramatic – ludicrous, even – that for a moment Louis almost laughed aloud. Then the horror of their situation began to seep into his bones. They were going to die; they were both going to die.

Salvena Saunders was not by nature a patient person, and that afternoon at the Intourist Hotel, she was particularly edgy and nervous, for no reason she could define. She had agreed to meet Gennadi Naidenov at four o'clock: it was now half-past five. There was no sign of him and neither he, nor Louis, had returned to the hotel. She had checked, and their keys were still in Reception. In desperation she sought out Peter, who was asleep in bed, a magazine over his face and an open vodka bottle on the bedside table.

'Peter, you slob!' Sal shook him awake, half amused,

half angry. 'Supposing I needed you in a hurry. What use are you going to be to me like this?'

'I'm fine,' said Peter, rubbing his eyes and struggling into a sitting position. 'One has to do something to while away the time, and sampling the local produce seems politically correct.' He eyed the vodka bottle appreciatively. He looked tousled, flushed and suddenly very young.

'I'm worried,' said Sal, sitting down on the bed beside him. 'Naidenov hasn't turned up for his interview.'

'Perhaps he's had a change of heart,' Peter suggested. 'After all, we are treading on fairly delicate political ground here. That's why I suggested we photographed him up here, rather than in the bar, to avoid attracting attention.' He nodded across the room to where his equipment was set up ready before a chair. Sal smiled. Despite his apparently casual approach to life, Peter was a true professional. His pictures would be good, too – would capture some aspect of Gennadi's character which the naked eye invariably missed.

'He's not in his room, either,' Sal said, standing up and beginning to pace about. 'The receptionist said that he and Louis checked out straight after lunch. They took a cab to a district called Lyubertsy. She seemed to think it was funny – I don't know why.'

'I do,' said Peter, laughing. 'It's an area well-known for prostitutes. I imagine the receptionist didn't consider Louis and Gennadi to be typical clients.'

Sal joined in his laughter. 'Two churchmen – one ancient and the other one heavily married – I agree it hardly seems an appropriate place for them to visit.

You're not seriously suggesting that they've gone to sample the local delights, are you?'

'Didn't Gennadi mention that he had to say goodbye to someone?'

'Yes,' Sal remembered. 'Perhaps the old devil has a regular woman in his life.'

'And why not?' said Peter. 'No one would have had time to marry the poor bastard, he wasn't out of prison long enough. One can hardly blame him for sowing a few wild oats when he had the chance, even if he is a man of the cloth.'

'Seriously, Peter, something could have happened to them. When you said that Moscow frightened you these days I dismissed the idea, putting it down to one of your grumbles, but even though I've hardly gone out of the hotel, I agree with you.'

'Good Lord,' said Peter, 'that has to be a one-off!'

'Oh, do belt up,' said Sal. 'I'm serious. A year or two ago Moscow was as it had always been − a very repressed place, alive with whispers, everyone looking over their shoulder, but in its own way it had a structure. If you didn't upset the State, the State didn't upset you. Now, there's definitely something different about the atmosphere. It's starting to feel more like Chicago. Being Russia, though, everything is always more extreme, and I doubt if they have many resources to cope with a crime wave. Thank God that Gennadi is a highly intelligent man. He may be old, and I think he looks like a wizened little pixie, but somewhere above that enormous nose there is a fantastic brain ticking away. Have you ever read his books?'

Peter shook his head.

'They're wonderful,' Sal enthused. 'Everything that has happened here during his lifetime, he has predicted. He has real vision – and I think he is right to be so alarmed for his country. What we're seeing here is only the tip of the iceberg. Eastern Europe is a sitting duck for organised crime. Gennadi's a lone voice at the moment, but if people start to listen to him, there might still be time to do something about it. If I was the Mafia, I'd consider him a real threat, wouldn't you?'

'I hear what you say, Sal, but I can't see the Mafia blowing him away. Adverse publicity would do them no good at all. In fact, Gennadi's death would probably light a torch to the message he's been trying to portray in life.'

'Good Lord, Peter, that's a bit poetic for you, isn't it?'

Peter blushed slightly. 'I like that old man, Sal. I hope we get the chance to know him better.'

Sal smiled at him. 'I do, too. That's why I'm so worried. If they're not back in another hour, I'm going to start making official enquiries,' she decided.

'I think you need to be a little careful about that, Sal,' Peter cautioned. 'You've already gatecrashed on a fairly sensitive situation. We've no idea how hush-hush this whole venture is. To go to the police, for example, could be embarrassing for everybody.'

Sal frowned. 'Not if I concentrated my enquiries on Louis.'

'It's still dangerous, in my view,' said Peter. 'Maybe the old boy simply forgot his appointment with you.'

'Louis wouldn't have done.'

'Maybe not, but would Louis have reminded him,' said Peter, 'bearing in mind he's not exactly pleased with you and your assignment? If Gennadi didn't remember off his own bat, Louis would have to be an extremely holy person to remind him.'

'That's just it, he is,' sighed Sal. 'He's brimful of integrity, is old Louis.'

'You've changed your tune,' said Peter. 'Last night you were spitting blood at the mere mention of his name. Now, suddenly, he's flavour of the month.'

'It's not that,' said Sal. 'It's just that he's my friend, a very old friend, and he's behaving out of character, and I'm worried.'

By seven o'clock there was still no sign of them. 'I know what I'll do,' Sal said to Peter. By now they were in the hotel bar. 'I'll settle for an honourable compromise. Instead of the police, why don't I ring the British Embassy?'

'They'll have all gone home,' Peter told her gloomily. 'I've yet to visit a British Embassy anywhere in the world where anybody works past five o'clock.'

'There must be an emergency number,' Sal persisted. 'I'll nip upstairs and give it a try.'

After an exhausting number of referrals, Sal found herself speaking to a vice-consul.

'You'll have been informed about the visit of Louis Noble to collect the Reverend Gennadi Naidenov,' she began.

'I'm sorry, madam, I don't know what you're talking about.'

'Listen,' said Sal, instantly irritated. 'I'm a journalist. My name is Salvena Saunders of the *Daily Record*, but in this particular instance, I'm not after a story. I'm very concerned because the two men have disappeared.'

There was a slight pause. 'How do you mean . . . disappeared?'

'Well, they were due back at the Intourist Hotel, where I'm calling from, at four o'clock. I had a meeting planned with Naidenov for that time but he didn't turn up, and they're still not back in the hotel. They're now three and a half hours late. I've since discovered they visited a district named Lyubertsy, a seamy area, apparently. Anything could have happened to them!'

'Miss Saunders, these men have not necessarily disappeared, they are merely three and a half hours late for an interview with you.' The voice was icy with sarcasm. 'It seems to me quite probable that they've decided not to talk to the press at this stage, and I can't say that I blame them. It may even be that they've changed hotels to avoid you.' Immediately the telephone went dead.

Sal slammed down the receiver. 'Bloody pompous twit!'

She sat glaring at the offending instrument. Something was wrong: she knew it in her bones. Peter was still heavily entrenched in the bar downstairs. On impulse she dialled Reception, and asked to be put through to the local Chief of Police. The receptionist was reluctant. What was wrong? he wanted to know. Sal simply said that it was a private matter and could he please find someone at the police station who could speak English. After a lengthy wait, she was put through to a deep-voiced Russian, whose English was far from good and who sounded either drunk or half-asleep – perhaps both. She went through the whole thing again, and the reaction she received was one of uncontrollable mirth.

'If your friends are in Lyubertsy district, you should not be surprised if they are not home until morning. You have nothing to worry about. All will be well, it's not a problem.'

She returned to the bar to find Peter, now severely drunk and trying unsuccessfully to chat up the barmaid.

'I've rung the British Embassy and the police,' she said. 'Neither are prepared to help. What are we going to do, Peter?'

Peter focused on her, just. 'Nothing. Go to bed and forget about it. In the morning, they'll be here.'

'They won't,' said Sal, looking at him with despair. 'There has to be someone, somewhere, who's going to listen to what I'm saying. I know something's wrong. Something's terribly wrong.'

The cellar was damp and evil-smelling; water dripped from the walls. One tiny chink of light came from what looked like a dislodged manhole cover high above them. They had been thrown down the cellar steps. Both were bruised and bloody, but neither had any broken bones. They had been left without explanation. When they had recovered sufficiently and checked their surroundings, they sat huddled together on the floor, both for comfort and warmth.

'Karagodina said they are the Mafia. Is it true?' Louis asked.

The old man's voice was little more than a whisper and his breathing was bad. 'I fear so, my friend. I am sorry that you have become involved in this. You are a young man and I would not have wished it.'

Louis swallowed hard. 'Are they going to kill us?'

'I can see no other reason for kidnapping us.'

'A ransom, maybe?'

'No, not for me, at any rate. I am an enemy of the Mafia. Thank God they did not harm Karagodina.'

'They won't go back there?' Louis asked.

'No, no, they'd have brought her with us if they'd wanted her. She is safe, God bless her.'

'What do we do now?' Louis felt like a child lost in an unknown world. The fear was almost tangible, the air seemed to smell of it.

'We wait – we wait to learn our fate.' Through the gloom Louis searched Gennadi's face. He was completely calm, which Louis found terrifying – not at all reassuring. It was as if he had already given up.

They did not have to wait long. Only two men reappeared, the man who had sat in the front of the car and the driver – at least it looked like him, Louis could not be sure. He was trying to remember details, but shock and fear were muddling everything in his head. The ringleader was short and squat with a heavy black moustache, but despite his short stature, he looked powerful. He also carried a revolver in a casual way, which somehow was far more menacing than if he had been actually pointing it at them.

'My name is Victor,' he said. 'This is my colleague, Anton, and this is all you need to know. You are Gennadi Naidenov, am I right?'

The old man stumbled to his feet. 'You know that I am,' he said.

Victor turned to Louis. 'And you are the Reverend Louis Noble, the special ambassador who has come to collect this piece of garbage to take to the UK.'

'The Reverend Naidenov is in my care,' Louis said quietly.

'"In my care" – do you hear that, Anton?' The man threw back his head and laughed. 'Well, Mr Noble, we will show you how we deal with men such as this.'

There was no warning. The man, Victor, levelled his pistol at Gennadi and shot him once in the groin and again in the stomach. The old man screamed and fell forwards, a gush of blood spurting from his abdomen. Louis sprang forwards, but Anton was already there with a blow to the stomach, like a sledgehammer, and then to the jaw. He fell back against the wall, crashing his skull as he did so. The killer came and stood over him.

'He is not dead yet, your little priest. We did not want him to die quickly, but slowly and painfully. It will take him several hours, it will not be pleasant and that is good, that is excellent. You will die also, but first we must arrange a little accident for you. As you said, we would not like you to become a diplomatic incident.' He laughed, and turning, the two men left the cellar.

Victor had been wrong about one thing. God, in His mercy, allowed Gennadi only half an hour of suffering, but it was the longest half hour of Louis' life. Again and again the old man screamed in agony. He kept vomiting blood and on each occasion Louis prayed the spasms would kill him, but somehow they did not. He rambled incoherently in Russian, and more than once Louis caught the name of Karagodina. Only at the very end did he look Louis in the eye, as the big man cradled the tiny broken body in his arms.

'Farewell, my friend,' he whispered; then lost consciousness, and a few moments later Louis could no longer find a pulse. He did what he could. He shut the old man's eyes and arranged his body, drenched in blood, as best he could. He had used his own jacket, shirt and vest to try and staunch Gennadi's wounds. Now he stood up and walked away from the body, to lean for a moment against a wall. Although he knew the room was cold, his body was burning, as if in a fever. He pressed his bare back against the rough, slimy stone. The pain of the dank cold penetrated his skin, easing for a moment the agony in his soul. Such barbarity was beyond him. If they had to shoot him, why had they not done so cleanly – with a single bullet to the head, ending his life at least with some dignity. But that was not their way.

For the first time since the men had left, Louis thought of his own fate and found himself shuddering with fear. He glanced over at the pathetic body of Gennadi. The old man's pain had staved off his own terror, but now he was left alone to face 'his little accident'. Of course, his body could not be found shot. What would they do? Throw him into the river, throw him under a car? Death did not frighten him, but the manner of it was another matter entirely. He thought of Evelyn, of the weekend he had spent Hawkhead Farm – amazingly, only three days before. He remembered striding across the fields, the wind in his hair, with such a sense of well-being. How could it be that he'd had no premonition of what was to come? How could a man, within days, be facing death and not see it coming? He had been apprehensive about the trip, he remembered, but never in his worst nightmares had he thought of this. His concerns had been simply about the handling of a tricky diplomatic exercise.

Suddenly the thought crept into his mind that maybe it had all been a setup, that maybe the Russians had handed over the old man knowing this would happen. Maybe it was the easiest way to dispose of him, while he was in Louis' care. From nowhere, tears of anguish and remorse began to flow down Louis' cheeks. What an idiot he had been – so confident, so arrogant. Why had he not sensed that something was wrong? For a moment he wondered whether Gennadi had foreseen their fate, but instinctively felt he had not. He had been a good man, Louis was sure. He knew Louis had a wife and children; he would not have put his life in danger intentionally, would he? Louis glanced again towards the body. There were suddenly so many questions he wanted to ask the Reverend Naidenov. Questions which in their time together had never occurred to him.

He allowed himself to slide to the floor, where he sat hugging his knees, like a child. The cold was beginning to reach into his bones now, and he began to shudder and shake. He felt so helpless. There was nothing he could do and no one in the world to help him. Then he remembered Sal, and the thought of her brought a momentary flare of hope. He tried to concentrate his mind. She had arranged to meet Gennadi that very afternoon, hadn't she? The meeting must have been some hours ago. Louis tried to peer at his watch, but it was smeared with blood that he could not bring himself to wipe off, and in any event, the light was not good enough to see by. How would Sal react to the missed appointment? Would she just imagine that Gennadi had changed his mind, or that he, Louis, had talked the old man out of it? Sal – he had always had a soft spot for her, and as Gennadi had rightly pointed out, she was so attractive, so vivacious, such good fun. And now she was the only one who could save him. They had always been linked through Evelyn but now, suddenly, their relationship was on a one-to-one basis, fused by the incredible melodrama of his situation. He gazed at his surroundings and briefly at Gennadi's body. It was all unbelievably terrible – and yet it was happening to him.

After a few minutes' thought, Louis decided it was pointless putting any faith in Sal. There was no way she could ever find him. She would try, bless her, once she realised something was wrong, but how long would that take? Too long: he was going to have to face his fate alone. Was this some sort of test of his faith? he wondered. If so, he would fail it. He felt anger at his God – he should have been prepared for this. He tried to pray, muttering to himself, and then shouting out loud. The familiar words brought a little comfort, but only because they were familiar: *they meant nothing*.

He was forty-four years old, and he was going to die, most likely in an agonising way. He was not ready, not ready at all. It was too soon . . . much, much too soon.

CHAPTER SEVEN

Lev Grishin had promised himself an early night. Yet barely had he lowered himself into his ice-cold bed, than he heard the telephone in the hall. Cursing, he stumbled out of bed and felt his way down the stairs. The hall was freezing and unlit. He fumbled for the telephone.

'Lev, is that you?'

The English voice threw him for a moment. Then he recognised who it was and all his bad temper faded. 'Sal! Hello, where are you?'

'In Moscow and needing your help.'

'You're here, great! When did you get in?'

'Earlier today,' Sal lied. She knew she should have called him before. They had worked closely together for years, but she had been so preoccupied with Louis' story that contacting Lev had not occurred to her until now.

'Look,' she went on, 'I don't want to explain over the telephone, but I think we've got some trouble here and I need your help. Could you get a cab and come over to the Intourist?'

'Yes, of course,' said Lev. 'You mean, now?'

'Could you bear it?'

He looked at his watch. It was eleven o'clock and he had not been to bed for nearly twenty-two hours.

'It's not something I'd do for everyone, but for you, Sal – I'll see you in half an hour.'

Lev dressed quickly and was soon bucketing his way across town in his ancient car. He was fascinated by Sal's call. He could not remember an occasion when she had needed help before.

Lev Grishin had always played the party line. He reported for the *Journalist Literaturnaya* exactly what was required of him. However, he fed the truth of what was behind these stories to Sal for her to publish in the Western world, where he felt the truth should be known. This act of defiance salved his conscience, and one way or another he felt he owed Sal a great deal. Plenty of commissions had found their way into his pocket over the years, which had lifted his standard of living from the most basic to something almost acceptable. Above all, his voice was heard across the world, although no one but Sal and her editor knew it.

She was waiting for him in the hotel lobby. Lev kissed her on both cheeks and regarded her solemnly. There was a tension in her face which worried him. 'What's wrong?' he asked.

'Let me tell you upstairs,' Sal said firmly.

In the bedroom Peter, who had sobered up, poured vodka, and the three of them raised their glasses in a silent toast.

'It's good to see you again, Lev,' said Peter. 'It's been too long.'

'Cut the crap, will you,' said Sal. 'I've got this feeling that time is running out.'

Lev glanced around the room, studied Sal's face for a moment and then beckoned them both to the door. In the passageway outside, he smiled sadly at their puzzled expressions. 'Is this sensitive?' he asked. 'Politically, I mean?' His voice was barely above a whisper.

'Probably,' said Sal.

'Then we talk downstairs. Your room is likely to be bugged.'

Sal and Peter stared at one another, appalled, and then followed Lev to the lift, Sal cursing herself privately for her stupidity. How could she have been so naïve? Obviously they were being bugged. Desperately she thought through her various conversations with Peter, her mind jumbled with worry and fatigue.

When they reached the bar, while Peter ordered soft drinks, Sal quickly told Lev the story. He listened in silence until she had finished.

'I think,' he said at last, 'that you are right to be concerned. It is well known in this city that Naidenov is playing a dangerous game – a very dangerous game. Everything he says is correct, of course: Moscow has changed out of all recognition in the last few months. Streets are no longer safe to walk in. Rape is now common and so is mugging, often by gangs of young people, searching for money to buy drugs. Murder has become an everyday matter. There are many different Mafia factions, all fighting for space to peddle their particular vice – they regularly fight each other. One day last week, five young men and a woman died in some such dispute. The men were known drug-dealers, and the woman too, I suspect. Their bodies were left lying in the gutter. They were not just dead, but mutilated.'

Lev smiled tiredly. 'I am accustomed to violence, Sal, you know that, but this sickened me. If this is what the West has to offer us, I do not want it, and neither do most of the citizens of Moscow. Naidenov, as he has always done, has touched the pulse of the people. He is saying what we want to hear. Yes, we *do* want to become a part of Europe. Yes, we *do* want to embrace the twenty-first century. And yes, we *do* want to be free from the tyranny of Communism, but this price of violence is too high.' Self-consciously Lev wiped a tear from his eyes.

Sal, too, was close to crying. 'And you're sure the Mafia are behind most of this, as Gennadi suggests?' she asked at last.

'Oh yes,' said Lev. 'The Mafia are sweeping across Eastern Europe. This is their new playground, and I can see what bad news Naidenov's big mouth is to them and their plans. He carries much respect, that little man, across the world. Am I right?' Sal nodded. 'So when he gets to the UK, people will listen to what he has to say, and maybe – who knows – maybe they will act. Maybe even Gorbachov will take his head from out of the clouds and see what is happening to his people! I think if Naidenov is missing, then the Mafia probably already have him, and your friend too. I am sorry to tell you this.'

'I think you could be right,' Peter said.

'So you're prepared to believe what Lev has to say,' Sal burst out furiously. 'Why the hell were you so negative all evening when I was trying to help them? You've probably cost them their lives, Peter. Why did you need to wait for Lev to tell you what I've instinctively known in here all along?' She put her hand to her chest, tears now starting out of her eyes.

Peter sighed heavily. 'Because I'm a slow-witted photographer, and it's taken me a while to appreciate the problem. I'm sorry, Sal.'

'It's not me you should be saying sorry to,' she gulped.

Lev looked from one to the other. 'Come,' he said, 'you two must not fight. You say they took a cab to Lyubertsy district? I have a feeling that I know where they'll have gone, who they went to see. Come on, let's get going! Peter, can you bring a camera – a discreet one? We might need it.'

In Lev's car they travelled across town. The streets were so dark and empty, it was impossible to believe that this was a capital city, and the time still well before midnight. Sal shivered beside Lev. Her instinct to contact him had been right. He had both the local knowledge and the global understanding to recognise the danger of Gennadi's position. Yet were they doing the right thing now, taking the law into their own hands? The scene that Lev painted of Moscow today was a terrifying one. In most situations, Sal reckoned that her position as a journalist protected her . . . but against the Mafia? She had promised Toby that she would not put herself into dangerous situations, yet here she was, careering across the Moscow streets – to do what? Two journalists and a photographer, attempting a rescue bid. It was madness.

'Lev, don't you think we should go to the police?' she asked.

He shrugged. 'We could try if you wish, but I'm sure they would do nothing. This is not something in which they would want to get involved. And in any event, they would immediately contact the Kremlin, and I've a feeling the Kremlin would choose to ignore everything.'

'What do you mean?' said Sal. 'Surely they wouldn't want this diplomatic mission to go wrong. The whole idea was to make it a goodwill gesture, as between Gorbachov and Thatcher.'

'I don't know,' said Lev. 'I am only guessing, but maybe the Kremlin planned this to happen, or in any event, hoped that it might. Think about it: on the one hand it appears that Gorbachov has conceded to Thatcher's request and has handed the old man into the care of her envoy. Then the two men stray into a dangerous part of the city, are kidnapped and killed by the Mafia. That is not the Kremlin's fault: it is perhaps the envoy's fault. The outcome, though, is to silence Gennadi for good. Does Gorbachov really want him telling the world that his dream of a new USSR is not as wonderful as he would have you believe? It seems to me that the little man is everyone's enemy. Everyone, that is, except the people. And, of course, traditionally in the Soviet Union, the people do not count.'

'Jesus,' granted Peter. 'What a cesspit this place is. I'm sorry, Lev, but—'

'It's OK, my friend,' said Lev. 'I happen to agree with you.' He gave a hollow laugh.

'So you really reckon the police would do nothing?'

'Not without reference to the Kremlin, and that will take time. And Sal is right: Naidenov and this Mr Noble do not have time.'

'Then we had better do what we can to help them ourselves,' Sal heard herself say.

'Exactly,' Lev replied.

The streets were becoming seamier, more derelict. Sal stared out of the window, her heart thumping against her breastbone. Toby . . . she had promised him, and yet what could she do? She thought of Evelyn, of her three children, of Hawkhead Farm and its cosy kitchen. How would Evelyn feel if she did nothing to try and help Louis? How many years of friendship did they share, how many times had Evelyn sat up half the night with Sal, listening to her problems, helping again and again with Toby when Sal was first forced to work away from home.

There was another issue, too. Sal had betrayed Evelyn's confidence, and here was an opportunity to vindicate that decision. She bit her lip, fighting back tears. If she died, what would become of Toby? Would he ever trust anyone again? An arm slipped around her shoulders and Peter drew her close to him. 'Sal, Lev and

I don't have kids. Let's find a cab to drop you back at the hotel.'

Sal looked up at him, grateful for the warmth of his body next to hers and his ability, as always, to get inside her head and know what she was thinking. 'Peter, I couldn't do that. You know I couldn't.'

'But why not?' said Lev. 'We have a journalist and a photographer here, we don't need two journalists, do we?'

'I just couldn't. Louis is my friend and this is my assignment.'

'I want you to promise me that if things get really rough and I say you're to stay out of it, you'll do as you're told,' Peter said severely.

'I can't promise that,' said Sal. 'We'll just work together as we've always done, feel our way and hope for the best.' She grinned suddenly, the old Sal returning. 'Bloody hell, we should be all right. We are rescuing two priests, after all. God has to be on our side, doesn't He?'

Both men smiled warmly at her. 'There's my girl,' said Peter. 'Now where the hell are you taking us Lev?'

'Wait and see,' the Russian said. 'I do not want to raise your hopes. It is – how do you say – a hunch I am working on.'

They pulled into a side street in front of a squat concrete block of flats.

'Peter, you stay in the car, I don't want it stolen. I'll lock the doors for your safety,' said Lev. 'Sal, you come with me.'

They climbed two flights of stairs, concrete, soulless, with a strong stench of urine. They walked along a corridor. Lev suddenly let out a low whistle. He had stopped in front of the door to one of the flats. Planks of wood were nailed across it. He stood staring at it for a moment. Sal looked puzzled.

'What does this mean?'

'I'll tell you in a moment,' said Lev. 'We'll try and wake up a neighbour.' He began hammering on the door adjacent to the broken one. For a long time there was silence, then he started shouting in Russian and eventually a light appeared. An old man opened the door, his face dark with terror. He spoke rapidly, Lev replied and Sal saw him visibly relax. He called out over his shoulder and a moment later they were being ushered inside.

The tiny sitting room was almost bare, save for a table at which sat an elderly, white-haired woman. She was crying noiselessly and from her ravaged face it was clear that she had been crying for some time. The conversation flew back and forth. The two men seemed to be questioning the woman, who answered between sobs.

'What's happening?' Sal whispered.

'Wait,' said Lev. 'I'll tell you in a minute.'

The neighbour shuffled off and came back with a bottle and glasses. He poured them all a drink. The weeping woman shook her head, but kindly he put an arm around her shoulder and guided the glass to her lips.

'Plum brandy?' Sal asked, knowing it to be the

Russians' answer to every crisis and every celebration.

'Of course,' said Lev. 'Now let me explain what's happening. The apartment next door belongs to this lady here, Karagodina Gorlov. I thought it was likely that Naidenov would want to say goodbye to her, since she has been his woman for many years. I'm afraid I was right. Naidenov and your friend Louis *did* come to her flat, but were kidnapped by a Mafia gang while they were there. As you saw, they broke down the door.

'Oh my God, Lev!' Sal panicked. 'So it's true. What the hell do we do?'

'We're just discussing that now,' Lev said, his voice reassuringly calm. 'This fellow has a friend who is a private investigator. He'll work for anyone who can pay him.' He smiled. 'The old man believes that his friend may be able to help us find out where the gang have taken Naidenov and your friend. Wait, we will talk some more.'

The talk raged backwards and forwards for nearly half an hour while Sal tried desperately to control her frustration. 'We must do something,' she kept saying, but nobody listened. Eventually a telephone call was made and ten minutes later a dapper little man in a shiny navy-blue suit arrived at the door: this was the investigator. He listened intently to Lev as he told the story, then he began talking excitedly.

'What is he saying?' Sal begged.

'The local Mafia here are the Rudenko gang, who come from the Ukraine. This man knows them well, knows where they operate. I, too, have come across them. They are dangerous people, Sal. Prostitution is their main livelihood but they also operate a very effective hit squad.'

The rest of the conversation flowed over Sal. She sat rigid in her chair, the alcohol before her untouched. *The Rudenko gang hit squad.* Louis was probably already dead. For a moment she closed her eyes. What was Lev going to suggest they do? Normally the decisions which took her into danger were snap decisions – she and Peter in the thick of some situation deciding whether to go with it or to pull out. This was different; the way ahead was being discussed clinically by people she had never met before – people who might well be sending her and Peter to their deaths.

What sort of chance did they stand, trying to take on the Mafia anyway? It was all too ridiculous – the stuff of bad movies. She wanted desperately to be home with Toby in good old reliable England. Yet even as she formulated the thought, it occurred to her that she was only half-English; that the other half, her Eastern European blood, should be called on at such a moment. She had more in common with these people than simply their apparent desire to save the two men.

She looked around at their faces as they talked. Her Russian was very limited, yet she felt comfortable in the presence of these people. The excitable way they talked, their words tumbling out one on top of the other, was the way she herself spoke: she was one of them, and needed to be at this moment. She looked at the glass in front of her and raised it to her lips, swallowing back its contents in one go. The liquid burned a welcome trail down her throat into the pit of her stomach. She caught sight of the other woman watching her. She smiled at Karagodina Gorlov and was rewarded by a smile in return — sad, but touching. Suddenly things seemed to be happening. The shiny-suited little man was writing down addresses on a piece of paper.

'OK,' said Lev, standing up abruptly. 'It is time we go.' He began shaking hands with everyone.

'Wait.' The voice was surprisingly strong and steady, and came from the old woman sitting at the table. She smiled again through her tears, directly at Sal. 'You must not go — you must stay here with us,' she said in excellent English. 'It is too dangerous for a woman.'

'I have to go,' said Sal.

'Is the big priest your husband?'

Sal shook her head. 'No, just a friend, but I am a journalist and this is my story. I have to be there.'

The old woman was not satisfied. She pointed at the piece of paper on which was apparently written three addresses. 'These are, I think you would say, safe houses for the Mafia. The Rudenki may be at any one of them. You could be shot or worse. They do terrible things to women. No, it is too dangerous for you.' She turned to Lev. 'You must not let her go.'

Lev looked at Sal questioningly. Sal shook her head. 'I'm sorry, Lev. I'm coming.'

Lev shrugged. 'She is used to danger. She will be all right, and we will try and bring your Gennadi back to you.'

At the mention of his name, Karagodina's eyes filled with tears again. 'Thank you,' she said simply.

Sal had completely forgotten Peter, still huddled in the back of the car. 'Every nocturnal weirdo in Moscow has peered through the window at me tonight,' he grumbled. 'What took you so long?'

'Peter, they've been kidnapped by a Mafia gang,' Sal said.

'Shit!' said Peter.

Lev decided to check out the addresses in reverse order, simply because the last one on the list was the nearest. Afterwards they realised that if his chance decision had been different, it could well have cost them all their lives.

They drove cautiously through the darkened streets.

'Can't we go any faster?' Sal fretted. She was desperate with fear. She kept thinking of what they could be doing to Louis – death, torture; her mind reeled.

'I don't want to draw attention to us. There are very few cars on the streets at this time of night, as you can see.'

Sal peered at her watch. It was now half-past one. There were no cars and no people, apart from the occasional shadowy figure, but then heat and light always had been at a premium in Moscow and was not to be squandered.

'It's here, somewhere.' Lev turned into a tiny side street where the buildings were crumbling; most seemed derelict.

'No one can live here,' Sal protested.

'Exactly,' said Lev. 'If this is where the Mafia take their victims, they are hardly going to want people around.'

'We should have called in the police,' said Peter.

'They wouldn't believe us,' said Sal, and she could hear the fear in her own voice. 'And as Lev said, by the time they did, it would be too late. It still may be.'

Peter reached out and took her hand, squeezing it in the dark. 'It'll be all right,' he said, but his words rang hollow. They had suddenly become caught up in a mad world and without a doubt, both knew they were right to be terrified. Lev suddenly braked, throwing Peter and Sal forwards.

'What is it?' Sal said, trying not to scream.

'This is the place,' Lev told them. 'Has anyone a torch?'

'Yes,' said Peter.

'Come on then,' Lev instructed, 'and quick.'

'What if the Mafia are still there?'

'There are no other cars in the street,' Lev whispered. 'Wait a moment, I'm not sure we can get out down at the bottom of the road. I'll turn the car around, so if Louis and Gennadi are here we can get them out quickly. We're only about ten minutes from the city centre.'

He did a three-point turn as noiselessly as possible and then switched off the engine. There was no sound – just the beating of their own hearts.

'I'm terrified,' whispered Sal. Suddenly all thoughts of Louis and Evelyn fled from her mind – they were simply not relevant. Toby filled her thoughts. She was never going to see him again, she was going to die here in this terrible place, her promise to her only child broken, blighting his life for ever. She wanted to run away. She was trembling from head to foot.

'Stay here, Sal, please,' Lev said.

'No,' Sal whispered. 'Come on, I'm ready.'

They climbed out of the car. 'Your torch, Peter, come on,' Lev urged. 'Do you have your camera?'

Peter nodded. 'I might even be able to take a picture if I could stop shaking,' he muttered.

They ran up several steps to a dilapidated front door. Lev turned the handle, and much to their surprise, it opened. Inside there was a hallway and more stairs going up. There were also doors leading off at either side of the hall.

'We'd better start checking the rooms, one at a time and we'd better stay together,' Lev hissed.

'Why don't we just call his name?' Sal whispered.

'Because then we'll have the Mafia around our necks,' Peter said. 'Don't be a silly girl.'

'If he's being guarded, we're in trouble anyway,' said Sal, 'but if he's alone, we're wasting time.'

There was a moment's silence.

'Go on then,' Lev said, 'he'll recognise your voice.'

'Louis!' Sal shouted. 'Louis, are you here? It's Sal.' Her voice echoed around the empty building. They stood frozen to the spot, expecting running footsteps, guns, voices, but there was nothing but silence.

'*Louis!*' Sal bawled in desperation. 'Louis – can you hear me? It's me, Sal. Where are you?'

Again there was nothing. Somewhere they could hear a dripping tap and now, perhaps in response to Sal's voice, some distance away, the sound of a barking dog.

'I think we should go,' said Lev. 'There is no need to check the building. If he was here, he'd answer.'

'Unless he's being prevented from doing so,' said Sal.

'I still think we should call in the police,' said Peter. 'We're out of our depth. What would we do now if a load of thugs burst in on us? We're behaving irresponsibly, and I can't believe we're helping Louis or Gennadi either.'

'You're right,' said Lev. 'The Police Headquarters is only a short distance from here. Let's go and tell our story and see if they can help. We can give them these addresses, can't we?'

Gingerly, they retraced their steps to the front door. As they stood in the doorway, Sal turned and called once more: 'Louis, Louis, can you hear me? Please answer.'

From almost beneath their feet they heard a muffled sound. They all jumped, Sal clutching at Peter.

A croaked, 'Who's there?' came wafting up through the floorboards.

'Is that you, Louis? It's me, Sal! Where are you?'

'I'm . . . I'm in the cellar, I think.'

'Where's the door?'

'I don't know.'

'You must do,' Sal said. 'Oh, it's all right.' Stairs led outside down from the pavement. 'I can see it. Come on, quick.'

Peter sprinted down the basement steps with the torch. Sal followed more gingerly, feeling her way in the dark.

'It's padlocked,' Lev said as he joined them, his voice now edged with panic.

'But we can break the chain,' said Peter. 'Think, Lev – have you anything in the car we could use?'

'A starting handle, I'll fetch it,' said Lev. 'Give me your torch.'

Peter and Sal were left alone in the darkness for what seemed an eternity.

'Louis, can you hear me? Are you OK?' Sal asked urgently.

There was a pause. 'Yes, but they've killed Gennadi.' Sal stifled a scream. Peter reached for her in the darkness and held her to him. 'And they're coming back for me. Soon, I think, Sal. It could be any moment.' His voice was strangely calm, almost dreamlike. Used as she was to witnessing violence around the world, Sal recognised it as a symptom of shock.

Suddenly Lev was beside them again.

'Here, give the handle to me,' Peter ordered. 'Hold the torch and stand well back.'

'They've killed Gennadi,' Sal said in a half-sob to Lev.

'What? When?'

'I don't know. Louis just said.'

'Shut up. Give me some space.' Peter bent his powerful body over the chain, now pulled taut, and wrenched. The chain held, but the wood on the side of the doorway began to split. 'Hold the damn torch higher,' Peter screamed.

It took three more tries before the chain came away from the doorpost. Peter flung open the door, panting from his exertions, and they shone the torch inside. Louis was standing directly in front of them. He was naked to the waist and covered in blood. His eyes were staring at them wildly, trying to focus on them beyond the torchlight. Sal ran to him and grabbed his hand. His arm was limp. It seemed almost lifeless. 'Louis, come on quick or we'll all be killed.' *Toby, oh Toby*. Sal tugged at Louis' hand, willing him to move.

'Where's Gennadi?' Lev asked.

'Over there,' Louis said brokenly.

Peter shone the torch on to the pathetic body, lying crumpled on the ground.

'They shot him in the groin and the stomach, so that he would die painfully and slowly.' Louis' words were spoken without emotion.

'Come on, everyone,' said Sal. 'For Christ's sake, we must get out of here.'

'Just one photograph,' Lev said to Peter. 'Just one — that's all we need.'

'Shine the torch on that wall there — it'll bounce the light back off it,' said Peter. A moment later it was done.

'We go,' said Lev.

'What about Gennadi?' said Louis.

'We can't do anything for him now — we have his photograph,' said Lev. 'Come on.'

'But I can't just leave him there,' said Louis.

'All right,' said Lev brutally, 'then we'll have to leave you with him. We've risked our lives to get you out, but we're not doing the same for a dead man.'

'Louis, please,' said Sal, desperately trying to reach

him in his trance-like state. 'Think of Evelyn and the children. Gennadi is dead – you can't do anything for him now.' She gripped his hand, and after a moment's resistance he followed her to the car, like a sleepwalker, and she bundled his huge frame into the back seat. In seconds, they were speeding off down the road.

'Should you check your speed?' Peter said nervously to Lev. 'You don't want to draw attention to us, remember.'

'You're right, of course,' said Lev, and slowed down. 'We won't be safe for another few minutes yet.'

'What will happen when they realise that Louis has gone?' Sal asked fearfully. 'Won't they try and get him back?'

Lev shook his head. 'That's another good reason for leaving Gennadi's body. It will never occur to them that we had a photographer with us. They will dispose of the body and assume there is no evidence. Louis' statement alone would not be enough, and in any event, if my theory is right, there won't be much of an enquiry. The photograph, of course, changes everything. Do you think it will come out OK, Peter?'

'Well, I'm not in the habit of taking photographs in the pitch dark, but I think I've got something and of course I can play around in the lab.'

'Peter's the best in the business,' said Sal. 'If anybody can get that shot, it'll be him.' She stared out of the car window. 'We're back near the hotel, aren't we?'

'Yes, this is Marx's Prospekt. The Intourist is just around the corner,' said Lev.

'Thank God,' said Peter.

'Amen to that,' breathed Sal. She sat back in her seat and for the first time since they had left the hotel, she allowed herself to believe that they might be going to live. She glanced at Louis. He was sitting bolt upright and silent, staring straight ahead of him, entirely unapproachable. They had put Lev's old car rug around his shoulders to keep him warm, which made him look extremely bizarre.

Sal reached out and touched his hand.

'Are you all right, Louis?'

He did not reply. Well, at least he was safe, and so were they all. Her mind travelled back over the events of the last half hour and suddenly the irresponsibility of their actions hit her with full force. They could so easily have been murdered, too. The sight of Gennadi's body . . . she would remember it always.

She must never put Toby's happiness on the line again. If only they were not so entirely alone, if only they had some other family. And it was in that moment, shocked, exhausted and highly emotional, that Sal made her decision. She would search for Georges. It was not right to deny either herself or her son the chance of an extended family, and for Georges, too, it could be important. She wondered fleetingly whether it was what her mother had wanted her to do, if only they could have talked some more. Imagining that it was her mother's last wish, she was surprised how much comfort the thought gave her.

'We're here,' Lev shouted.

'Peter,' said Sal, 'can you take your jacket off? We've got to get Louis into the hotel somehow, without drawing too much attention to ourselves.'

'Yes, of course.' Peter struggled out of his anorak and handed it to her.

Sal turned to Louis. 'Come on, put this on,' she said. 'It'll keep you warm, too.'

He said nothing, simply sat staring ahead of him.

Sal began dressing him like a child. He did not resist her, but nor did he help.

'What's wrong with him?' said Peter, watching Sal's efforts from the front seat.

'Shock, I think,' said Sal.

Lev parked the car. 'I suggest the three of you catch the first available flight in the morning,' he said. 'Don't worry about trying to get to London, just get out of Moscow — Paris, anywhere.'

'OK,' said Sal. 'I'll fix that, while you two take Louis upstairs.' She approached the sleepy receptionist. 'Could I have the keys for numbers forty-six and a hundred and twenty, please?'

'Oh — Mr Noble, he has returned?'

'Yes,' said Sal. She indicated the three men crossing the foyer behind her. 'He's had a little too much to drink, I fear.'

'A good evening?' The man laughed.

'Oh, yes,' Sal agreed.

She went across to the three men and handed them the keys. 'I'll organise some sandwiches and drinks down here, shall I?' she said.

'Good idea,' said Lev, 'and then we can work out a

plan. How long will it take for you to know if that photograph is any good, Peter?'

'There's nothing I can do about it until I get back to London, not safely. I haven't the equipment here, unless there's a developer we can trust.'

'No, you are right. I am being impatient, it is probably better to trust no one,' said Lev after a moment. 'What you have got is – how do you say? – a very hot potato.'

Sal organised plane tickets for a flight leaving at ten o'clock the following morning for Frankfurt, and then ordered beer and sandwiches to be delivered to the bar.

The food had just appeared when Lev and Peter returned.

'How is he?' she asked.

Both men shrugged their shoulders. 'We left him in his room. He said he'd be down in a few minutes, but he's away with the fairies,' said Peter.

'That's hardly surprising, is it?' said Sal.

'No, I suppose not,' Peter agreed. 'It must be quite a blow to a holy person's faith, seeing at first-hand Man's inhumanity to Man.'

'I hadn't thought of it like that,' said Sal. 'By the way, I've booked us tickets for tomorrow morning. There's a flight just after ten to Frankfurt.'

'Good,' said Lev. 'I did not want to say too much in front of Louis because I felt he had suffered enough, but I think it is very important that you leave the country as quickly as possible. Driving home I was thinking about the police, about whether to report

Gennadi's death to them, but I believe it would be wrong.'

'Why?' Sal asked.

'I am not sure exactly.' He hesitated, glancing over his shoulder nervously. 'If I am right, Sal, if Louis was actually set up and the Kremlin were actually a party to Gennadi's murder, or at any rate were prepared to turn a blind eye, then the whole thing could get very messy. Louis might even get charged with Gennadi's murder.'

'Oh, surely not!' Sal was shocked. 'That would cause an international incident, and that's the last thing anybody wants.'

'Possibly,' said Lev, 'but I do not think it is a risk worth taking. Gennadi is dead, no one can help him now. The important thing is to get you three and that photograph out of the country as fast as possible. I may be wrong about the Mafia. Louis may not in fact be safe from them, I do not know. All my instincts say that you cannot leave the country soon enough.'

'I couldn't agree more,' said Peter.

Lev smiled. 'I will be glad when you are safely home. Now, how are we going to handle this story? I want it told, Sal. Gennadi was a good man, a good friend to the people and he must not die anonymously. The world must know that he is dead and how he died.'

'I agree,' said Sal. 'I won't risk writing it until we're on the plane, then we'll just have to pray that Peter's photograph will back up my story. I'll also get a formal interview from Louis on the plane.'

'You think he will co-operate?' said Peter.

'I'd have thought so. I mean, clearly he'd formed quite an attachment to the old man, in that he didn't want to leave his body in the cellar. He's certainly going to want to see justice done.'

Lev gave a bitter laugh. 'Justice won't be done. The men who murdered Gennadi tonight, will murder someone else tomorrow.'

'What about his friend – the old lady?' Sal said suddenly.

'I, too, have been thinking of Karagodina,' said Lev. 'I'll go back to her flat now and tell her what's happened.'

'She'll be devastated,' said Sal, her eyes suddenly filling with tears. The strain was starting to take its toll.

'She was expecting it,' Lev said quietly. 'She's been expecting it all her life. She has always known that one day someone would take Gennadi from her, and when they did, it would be with violence.'

'They've been friends a long time?'

'Friends, and lovers too, all their adult lives, I think.'

'How amazing,' said Sal. She began questioning Lev about Karagodina's background, but Lev shook his head.

'You cannot mention her in your article. Her life may well be in danger as it is, but if you turn her into some sort of folk-hero, she'll be doomed. She runs a hostel for child prostitutes, that is her life's work. She doesn't try and stop their way of life, she couldn't, she just cares for them. In a way, the Mafia probably feel her presence is no bad thing – the children are fitter to work and live longer.'

'That's so cynical,' Sal protested.

'It's real life, Moscow-style,' said Lev, and rose wearily from his chair. 'I must leave you two now. It is one more adventure that we've been through together, my dear Sal. More dangerous than most – sadder than most.'

Sal stood up and embraced him. The little man was very emotional and close to tears.

'Thank you, Lev. You saved Louis' life tonight, without a doubt.'

'What will you do with the knowledge you have?' said Peter. 'Presumably there's nothing you can write about.'

'Absolutely not,' said Lev, 'not if I value my life. Still, it stays up here . . .' he pointed to his forehead '. . . filed away. One day I will be able to tell this story.'

'Will you write it down somewhere?' Sal asked with professional curiosity.

Lev shook his head. 'I dare not, but all these things I remember, they are held in my head and in my heart. God bless you both and do a good job for Gennadi.'

'We will,' said Sal.

Peter shook Lev's hand and they watched as he hurried away. 'That's a good man,' said Peter, collapsing again into his chair. 'God, Sal, that was our all-time dodgiest assignment. Have you ever been so terrified in your life?'

Sal looked at him and smiled. 'No, I don't think I have,' she said. 'Still, we got him, he's safe and it's one hell of a story.'

'Yes,' said Peter, 'subject to my photograph. Shit,

I hope I've got it. If I'd only had just a few more moments.'

'If we'd taken a few more moments, old thing, we might have been dead.'

They stared at one another, the reality of her words sinking in.

'I'd better go and see how Louis is,' Sal said finally.

'You don't think it would be better to leave him on his own?'

'No,' said Sal. 'I do know him very well, remember. It's not like being comforted by a stranger. I have to see how he is. He might like to call Evelyn.'

'So you reckon he'll have forgiven you?'

'I sincerely hope so – I've got to interview him tomorrow.'

Peter laughed out loud. 'You are incorrigible – first, last and always the journalist. Right then, you go and soften up the poor bugger, I'm off to bed. Could I just remind you that we have a plane to catch in . . .' he squinted at his watch '. . . six hours' time.'

'I'm not likely to forget *that*,' said Sal. 'See you later!'

'Come in quietly, please,' Peter yawned. 'Don't you dare wake me up.'

She watched with affection as Peter walked across the bar towards the lifts. For all his doubts and derision earlier on, it had actually been Peter who had set Louis free. He was 'a good man in a crisis' – an expression her father had favoured. She smiled at the memory, then her heart missed a beat – he hadn't been her father, only the man who had brought her up. Would she ever know the truth, she wondered, and would it ever stop hurting?

From the remnants of their meal, Sal made up a plate of sandwiches, and picked up a couple of bottles of beer. She walked across the darkened foyer and took the elevator to Louis' room. She knocked on the door, but there was no reply. She tried again; still silence. Turning the handle, she found it unlocked and walked in.

Louis was sitting on the bed with his back to her. He had started to put on a shirt, but had stopped, apparently defeated by the task. His head was in his hands and he was shaking uncontrollably. Without a moment's hesitation Sal set down the tray and ran to his side. She sat down beside him on the bed and quickly put her arms around him, as one would a hurt child. His chest was bare, his skin ice-cold – the shaking seemed to be tearing him apart. She pulled him tightly to her, laying her head on his chest, trying at once to warm and to comfort him. Gradually the violence of his trembling eased, and as it did so, Sal became increasingly conscious of her cheek against his chest, of his skin against hers. Working on instinct, without any conscious thought of the implications of what she was doing, she began stroking his back, pressing herself ever closer to him. At first it was no more than an extension of the comfort she was trying to bring, but gradually she became aware of a change in herself and sensed it, too, in Louis. There was a building of tension between them. Her face was burning against the coolness of his skin. It never occurred to her to stop stroking him – it never occurred to her to move away. It was Louis who suddenly let out an exclamation and, seizing her shoulders, pushed her away from him, holding her at arm's length, staring into her eyes as though he had just woken from a dream.

'You'd better stop this, Sal,' he murmured. Sal stared back. This man was her friend, her dear friend and he needed help. Instinctively she reached up and took his face in her hands and kissed him on the mouth. At first his lips were stiff and closed, and then they opened to hers, hot and demanding. They fell backwards on the bed, kissing as if they would never stop.

Suddenly, Louis pushed her aside a second time. He groaned. 'Sal, we have to understand why this is happening to us.' He struggled to sit up, his eyes large and troubled, staring down at her with unmistakable longing.

Sal sat up, too. What had happened? This was Evelyn's husband! 'I'm so sorry, Louis,' she stammered. 'I just want to help. What you've been through in the last few hours . . . I just can't imagine. Seeing that old man shot, and then expecting to be killed yourself.' She began to weep; exhaustion and the unexpected passion of their kisses had destroyed her self-control.

Louis reached out and took her in his arms. 'Don't cry, Sal. Please, don't cry. It's all right, it's over now.'

'It's me who's supposed to be comforting you,' Sal managed a shaky laugh. 'I was just so frightened, Louis. I knew something terrible had happened as soon as Gennadi didn't turn up for his interview. I thought you were dead, and I couldn't find anyone who would take me seriously. Nobody would help. They just thought that you'd gone to the red-light district for some fun. Everyone thought it was a joke. I was frantic.'

'Did I really matter that much to you?'

Sal withdrew a little from his embrace and met his eyes, her sudden desire for him obliterating all reason. 'It seems so,' she said softly.

'Oh Sal,' Louis' voice was hoarse with emotion. 'How am I going to resist you?'

'You mustn't— ' Sal began, but within seconds they were clinging together again as if their lives depended upon it. With a sharp thrill, Sal realised that this time she was the seducer, not the seduced, but she did not care. Instead, the knowledge filled her with an incredible sense of power which heightened her desire. All rational thought had left her, all guilt, all doubts.

She undid the rest of Louis' shirt buttons and slowly opened his shirt. The dark hairs on his chest had a sprinkling of silver and ended just under his ribcage. She leant forward and slid her tongue from the hollow at the base of his throat down his chest, to where the line ended. Louis groaned and when she found his nipples, the touch of her tongue made him jump as though he had been shot. She slowly undid his trousers and pulled them down. He did not help, but nor did he put up any resistance. She removed his underpants. His penis was rigid against his stomach – there was a small pearl of moisture on the tip and Sal leaned forward and licked it off gently.

Louis' eyes snapped open. 'Oh Sal,' he gasped, and pulled her on top of him. She helped him take off her clothes and when he rolled on top of her she gave a deep sigh and handed over control to his newly-found male dominance. He kissed her face and neck. He took her nipples in his mouth and sucked like a newborn who has just found the breast. When he finally entered her Sal felt as though her whole body had dissolved and there was nothing except this burning centre of her that was filled with hot hard sweetness.

She contracted her vaginal muscles and squeezed hard. Louis' eyes shot open in surprise. 'What are you doing to me, Sal?' he murmured. She did not answer, but simply reached for his face and kissed him, and as she took in his tongue she bit it gently and was thrilled to feel the telltale throb of his penis inside her. She moved to his throat and then on to his ears, biting, licking and sucking. She suddenly felt in control again.

'Tell me it feels good. I want to hear you say it,' she whispered.

'It feels so good,' he moaned. Sal felt he was so close to coming now, that she could not risk losing that incredible sensation of climaxing together.

'Move with me, Louis,' she said, and started to grind her pelvis into him. They moved together, quicker, faster, until he cried out and came, pumping inside her. She moaned his name over and over, as the exquisite spasms of pleasure coursed through her.

They lay cuddled together in silence for a long while, afraid that the spell would break. At last, they drew away a little and gazed into each other's eyes. Oh God, thought Sal, he regrets it.

Louis opened his mouth to speak. 'I didn't know — I had no idea.'

'What?' Sal whispered. She was terrified now, terrified of what he would think of her, yet to her amazement, there were tears in his eyes.

'I just didn't know that making love could be like that. There's only been one woman, you see, no one but— ' He couldn't say Evelyn's name, but the thought of her ran like a current between them. Instinctively they drew further apart.

'Don't think badly of me,' Sal said. 'I couldn't bear it if you despised me for what has happened. It began so innocently, Louis, you must believe that. I just wanted— '

He reached out and put a finger across her lips. 'I know . . . I know,' he said gently. 'It wasn't supposed to happen, it should never, never have happened and yet, my love, I can't find it in my heart to regret it.'

At his words, tears sprang into Sal's eyes. 'Do you really mean that?' she asked.

'Yes. How could I feel any differently?'

Sal stood up and began searching for her clothes. 'I'd better go back to our room. Peter will be wondering what on earth has happened to me.'

'You mean . . . you're sharing a room with Peter Blakeney?' Louis' voice was strangled.

Seeing the expression on his face, Sal went back to the bed and sat beside him, taking one of his hands in hers.

'Not like that, Louis! What must you think of me, that I'm some little tart who moves from man to man, without a thought? There hasn't been anyone in my life for a very long time. I don't make a habit of this, you know.'

Louis' expression relaxed slightly. 'But why are you sharing a room with Peter?'

'Because the hotel was full, silly. We wanted to stay in the same hotel as you to cover the story as easily as possible, but when we arrived there was no room. However, after a little persuasion in the form of a few dollars, they gave us a room on the top floor – with a broken shower and loo,' she added with a grimace. 'You see, Louis, Peter and I have been together in more situations than you could possibly imagine. We've slept on pavements, in barns, in the back of cars, we shared a bunk on a British Railway pullman once, and believe me, that's no joke, but there's nothing between us – there never has been. He's like my little brother. He's a damn good photographer but he's more than that – he's a good companion, a wonderful colleague and we wouldn't have mananged tonight without him. You know, technically, it was he who saved your life.'

'I realise that,' said Louis, 'but don't go back to your room tonight – not tonight. We only have this one night together and I can't bear for you to go – not now, not after what's happened.' Sal began to protest. 'Are you worried what Peter will think? Will he cause any trouble?' Louis asked anxiously.

'No, of course not,' said Sal. 'I'm just frightened about where this will lead us.'

'Don't let's think about it tonight,' said Louis. 'Tonight is ours, what's left of it.'

It was the point at which they could have ended it, for even then it was not too late to pretend that their lovemaking had been a shock reaction to what had happened. At that moment Sal had neither the strength nor the wish to resist the pleading in Louis' eyes. In the months that lay ahead she was to draw a little comfort from the knowledge that it was Louis who had ultimately taken the lead, Louis who had insisted that they stay together all night . . . and therefore Louis who had sealed their fate.

CHAPTER EIGHT

The flight home held no reality for Louis at all. In the past twenty-four hours he had experienced the strongest emotions he had ever felt in his entire life. He had witnessed barbaric violence and death, he had experienced terror . . . and love. The carefully constructed fabric of his life was in tatters. He was in love with Salvena Saunders, of that there was no doubt in his mind. Their glorious lovemaking, coming as it did to a warm and close friendship, fuelled by the horrors of what he had witnessed, was a lethal cocktail. He recognised it as such, but felt powerless to alter or regret anything. The fact remained that he was happy. Yet it was terrible to be happy when he had betrayed Evelyn, happy when he had witnessed a good old man die a terrible death, happy when he had denied the teachings of his Christian faith.

He glanced now at Sal, who sat in the seat opposite

him across the aisle. Her head was bent and a frown of concentration played on her face as she wrote furiously. Not for Sal the lap-top computer, Louis was pleased to see, but a battered old notebook. She was telling his story — his and Gennadi's. Maybe when he saw it in print, maybe then he would believe that it had happened. He shook his head as if to clear it and Sal, sensing his scrutiny, looked up at him and smiled.

'How are you feeling?' she asked quietly.

'More than a little disorientated,' Louis admitted with a smile.

'I'm not surprised,' Sal answered. 'It's been quite a memorable twenty-four hours, one way or another.'

Louis glanced nervously at Peter, who was sitting beside Sal and appeared to be asleep. Louis relaxed a little.

'What are you going to do when we get to London?' Sal asked.

'In the circumstances, I think I'd better go straight to Lambeth Palace. I'll ring the office from Frankfurt.' He stared at Sal. 'What are we going to do?' he whispered, hoping that no one could hear him but her. 'I can't bear the idea of being apart from you. We have to meet again soon, if only to discuss what happens next.'

She chose to ignore him. Evelyn dominated her thoughts. She was still exhausted and in no state to make a decision. 'I can't stop thinking about Karagodina Gorlov,' she said sadly.

Louis frowned. For a moment the name was familiar but unplaceable.

'Gennadi's ladyfriend,' Sal prompted.

'Oh yes,' said Louis, disappointed by the change of subject. 'What an extraordinary woman – wonderful, deeply committed to her work and of course to— ' he hesitated, 'to Gennadi. Sal, we should have told her what happened. We should have gone to see her.'

'Don't be ridiculous,' said Sal. 'That is one part of the city we couldn't go back to. Lev went straight on to see her after leaving us at the hotel. He was going to tell her everything – except how Gennadi died.'

Louis stared into Sal's eyes. Their expressions were both full of pain. 'What was he going to say?'

'That Gennadi died swiftly and cleanly.'

'Is that what you're saying in your report?'

'No, of course not.'

'Then she'll learn the truth.'

'Maybe,' Sal said, 'maybe not. In any event, as the days pass she will become stronger and more able to cope.'

'Still, it's a risk. Perhaps to spare her feelings . . .'

'Louis,' interrupted Sal, 'think straight. I have to tell the story as it was. The world has to know how Gennadi Naidenov died. All his life he was fighting for the man in the street, never for himself, never for his own ends. He deserved a few years of peace in England, not that horrible, violent death in that awful cellar. It is vitally important that people are shown what an enormous grip the Mafia are beginning to have in Russia and in Eastern Europe generally.'

'I don't suppose I'm going to be too popular either at the Palace or with the Government,' Louis said.

'Basically, I've messed things up all round. I should never have let Gennadi out of the hotel.'

'Were you given a brief along those lines?' Sal asked.

'No, I wasn't. I wasn't led to believe that Gennadi's life was in any danger at all. I was only warned that there might be some difficulty in removing him from the country – that the red tape, although allegedly sorted out in advance, might be tiresome. Certainly, there was no hint that his life would be threatened, although unaccountably I did feel very nervous. No, it was Gennadi himself who told me about the danger he was in. I should have refused his visit to Karagodina. If only I had!'

'Oh Louis, how could you have done that?'

'I couldn't today,' Louis said quietly, 'but maybe I could have yesterday.'

'What does that mean?'

Louis met Sal's eye and held her gaze. 'Yesterday I didn't know about true love – today I do. It's as simple as that. Today I understand why he would have risked anything, everything, to say goodbye to Karagodina.'

Sal said nothing, but her eyes filled with tears. Louis reached out across the aisle, took Sal's hand for a moment and squeezed it, releasing it hurriedly when a stewardess approached.

Sal leaned back in her seat. Her article was drafted, and she would tidy it up when she reached the office. At the moment her mind was too confused to continue. How could she have made love to Louis, not just once, as a reaction to the horror of what they had both witnessed, but again and again during the few hours they had been together. His need of her had seemed to be insatiable, and she had more than reciprocated. He was such a strange mixture. There was a child-like innocence about him in some respects yet, during the night, as his confidence had grown he had proved to be a marvellously inventive lover. There had been no time to think, no time to consider anything or anyone but the passion of their lovemaking. But now, now all Sal could think of was Evelyn – her loyal, wonderful friend, whom she had betrayed in the most terrible way. Surely there could be nothing worse that one woman could do to another than take her husband! She shook her head slightly as if to ward off the pain. No, she had not taken Evelyn's husband, she would never take Louis away from Evelyn, even if she could. But even as she tried in her own mind to use this as an excuse, Sal knew that the damage was already done. She recognised that she had lit a fuse in Louis, opened him up to a sensual world he had not known existed, until now.

She glanced at him. He had been watching her, she realised, and she saw the hunger in his eyes – *he wanted her now*. To her dismay, she felt the heat rise in her own body, and she was embarrassed by the strength of her own feelings.

Louis grinned, and leaned over to murmur: 'What have you done to me, you wicked woman. I could tear your clothes off right now.'

'Louis,' said Sal, smiling, trying to lighten the mood, 'I don't think it would be very good for your image. "Senior Churchman Ravages Woman On Plane".'

Louis smiled back. 'I don't think anything that's happened to me in the last twenty-four hours has been particularly good for my image.'

'Oh, I don't know,' said Sal wickedly. Their eyes met and held. It was Sal who looked away first, pretending to read her notebook. This had got to stop! She could not continue to deceive Evelyn, it was just not possible. They had to end it, pretend it had never happened. Even as she formed the thought, however, she doubted her own resolve.

At Frankfurt airport, weary and still more than a little traumatised, the three of them made their way to a British Airways desk. The news was bad. There were only two seats left on the next flight to Heathrow, boarding in a hour's time. The next flight was not for four hours.

'I'll catch the later flight,' offered Peter. 'You two have pressing reasons to be back.'

'No,' said Louis. 'I think you two should go on ahead. The important thing is to land your story.'

Sal smiled teasingly. 'I shouldn't say this, but I can't resist it, Louis. You have slightly changed your tune so far as the media is concerned.'

'A lot has happened to change my mind on a number of issues in the last twenty-four hours,' Louis said evenly.

Peter looked from one to the other. Clearly something had happened the night before. Sal had not returned to their room until the following morning, and now there was an almost physical tension between them. Surely Sal could not have fallen for such a man

— Louis Noble had absolutely *no* sense of humour. A regular bloke, certainly, but not right for Sal.

'Well, it's up to you guys,' Peter said slightly impatiently. 'Clearly, Sal needs to get back on the first flight. I can go with her or wait — whichever you want.'

'You go with her,' Louis said, 'but thank you for the offer.'

Having booked their flights, Peter, sensing he was somewhat superfluous to requirements, suggested coffee and a brandy in the bar. Having organised everyone — for suddenly Sal and Louis seemed incapable of organising themselves — he found the need to make some urgent telephone calls and left them alone. As soon as he was out of earshot, Sal turned to Louis, her dark brown eyes serious, her expression hard to read. 'So this must be the end then, mustn't it?'

Louis stared back. 'I don't think it can be. I would like to believe that last night was a kind of kick reaction to what had happened.' He paused. 'Certainly, without the catalyst of the night's dramas, I imagine it would never have occurred. Now it has, though, I realise I've loved you for years but never known it. We can't just pretend it never happened.'

'But you wanted us on different flights,' Sal persisted. 'It suggests a parting of the ways. It has to be right, Louis. We must never hurt Evelyn.'

He reached out and took Sal's hand. 'Different flights was all about the press. As you spoke to your editor this morning, I assumed there might be reporters at Heathrow to meet us. I just couldn't handle it at the moment.'

'Don't worry, there'll be no reporters. This is the *Record*'s scoop,' Sal said lightly.

'I feel so vulnerable. I've had no experience of this sort of thing. I keep feeling that everyone knows about us.'

Sal grinned. 'They probably do, the way you're holding my hand and gazing into my eyes.' He dropped her hand immediately. 'It was a joke, Louis. Nobody cares a toss here,' Sal said gently. She picked up her brandy and swirled the golden liquid around in the bowl of the glass. 'I could handle it far easier if you were married to any other woman in the world but Evelyn.'

'Yes, of course,' said Louis. 'The dreadful thing is that I haven't felt guilty, and I haven't given her so much as a thought – or the children. I'm supposed to be a professional Christian. Maybe I'm just a professional hypocrite.'

'Don't be too hard on yourself,' said Sal. 'There's only so much you can take on board at any one time. You've seen a man die in horrible circumstances. You've lived with the subsequent terror of assuming the same thing was going to happen to you. Then the woman you thought of as no more than your wife's best friend, suddenly becomes your lover.' Sal smiled. 'It's been a big day for Louis Noble.'

'It may have been a big day for Louis Noble, but it doesn't bear too much scrutiny. I have betrayed everything I believe in, my God, my Christian beliefs and my marriage vows, and I seem to have done it with such ease. All these years I've been not only trying to be a good Christian myself, but persuading others to do the same — and then in the space of just a few hours I abandon everything I've ever believed in. And what's more extraordinary, with no regret. How can that be, Sal? How can I be that flippant about my life's work?'

'Evelyn said to me the other day that you weren't very happy in your job.'

'A job is one thing, my faith quite another. It's true I'm not happy at Lambeth Palace. I don't like the political clergy, I don't like all the backbiting and bitching that goes on there. Far more time is spent jostling for position than thinking of ways of bringing the Church up to date and making it a useful tool in today's society. The Church used to be so powerful, now it's meaningless. I want to do something tangible, Sal. I want to be able to come home at night and feel that I've achieved something, helped someone — but all that happens is that we have interminable meetings about nothing.'

'Your job took an unexpected turn this week, though, didn't it?' said Sal.

'You're laughing at me.'

'Well yes, I suppose I am, but how can I resist it? You've just explained to me that you have no job satisfaction, so how do you get your kicks then, Mr Noble?'

'I love you,' Louis said. 'I love the way you can laugh at life, I simply love everything about you. I don't know where we go from here, but I know I have to see you again, Sal. I want you again and again, I want you now.' He smiled deep into her eyes. 'I can't believe I'm saying this, it doesn't sound like me at all.'

Sal took his face in her hands and kissed him. The moment their lips touched, their bodies were suddenly taut with desire, and this instant reaction took Sal by surprise. She pulled away almost as if she had been burnt.

'It's powerful,' she whispered, 'this thing we have, Louis.'

He nodded. 'The stuff of the devil,' he murmured.

'Can love really be of the devil?' Sal asked.

'Illicit love, yes.'

Sal hesitated. 'I had an affair with another married man once, many years ago. He was the first man in my life, the first man I really cared about, who cared about me. I was only a teenager – I didn't tell anyone, not even Evelyn.'

'What happened?' Louis said, feeling a ludicrous stab of jealousy and fury that there should have been anyone in Sal's life before him.

'He went back to his wife,' Sal said quietly. 'He had responsibilities. He did the right thing.'

'And has he stayed with his wife?'

'They divorced some years later, five or six years, I think.'

'And did you two get together again?'

Sal shook her head. 'No, there'd been too much pain already. I couldn't have gone through it again.'

'Not even when he was free?'

'No.'

Louis was silent for a moment, digesting the information. 'And do you think you were responsible for the break-up of his marriage?'

'No,' said Sal. 'No, I don't. There was something intrinsically wrong with the relationship in the first place, and it finally just fell apart at the seams without much help from anyone.'

'I don't think Evelyn and I are like that,' Louis said quietly.

'Neither do I,' said Sal. 'Neither do I, Louis.'

They sat in silence for several moments, both thinking of Evelyn, both trying unsuccessfully to come to terms with what they had done.

'Where's Peter?' Louis asked after a while.

'I said I'd meet him in the departure lounge,' said Sal. 'I think he was just being tactful, leaving us alone.'

'Then he knows about us?' Louis looked appalled.

'I presume so,' said Sal. 'He was already up and getting dressed when I got back to our room this morning. That coupled with the fact that you and I have been behaving pretty strangely, must make it fairly obvious . . . but don't worry, Louis. Peter would never say anything to anyone.'

'I hope you're not going to get serious about that chap,' Peter remarked as the plane began taxiing down the runway. Sal looked sharply at him. He grinned back. There was no malice in his voice, nor in his eyes.

'Why do you say that?

'Because's not for you, Sal. I know he's married and he's in the Church and all that, which heaven knows is problem enough, but I'm not looking to morality. It's just that he is rather a bore.'

'He's not a bore,' said Sal hotly. 'He's been a good friend for years, remember.'

'No, he hasn't, not really,' Peter disagreed. 'It's his wife who's been your friend. I bet if you were to spend an ordinary day in his company, you'd be yawning your head off in a couple of hours.'

'I don't think so.' And Sal blushed slightly at the memory of the previous night.

Peter picked up the innuendo. 'Well, once the sex thing has died down, I mean . . .'

Sal's blush deepened. 'Peter, you won't say anything to anyone, will you?'

'I find that deeply insulting,' he returned, only half-joking. 'Of course I won't. Honestly Sal, what kind of person do you think I am?'

'I think you're the kind of person who would never say anything to anyone. In fact, I told Louis as much a few minutes ago.'

'But you had to check, though?' Peter sighed. 'Your secret is safe with me – you know that, old girl. But, seriously, remember what I said. This Louis guy spells nothing but trouble. Apart from being fearfully dull, he also has an awful lot to lose if your relationship ever becomes public knowledge. There's not just his marriage, but I presume his career and his calling, whatever that means. Are you a Christian, Sal?'

'I suppose so – in a way, like most people,' said Sal. 'I like the comfort of religion. I like listening to the same words being said no matter where I am in the world, hearing the same hymns. I suppose too, it provides a code for living, although having said that, I must have broken just about every Commandment in the book.'

'Several times, I shouldn't wonder,' said Peter drily.

'Oh come on,' objected Sal. 'What about you? You're no saint.'

'I never said I was, dear girl – never said I was. Ah, thank God, we're taking off – now let's have a drink.'

It was late afternoon when Sal burst into David Thorson's office. He looked up from his work and studied her for a moment. She looked very tired and was dressed casually in sweatshirt and jeans. Somehow, though, she still managed to look as if she had just stepped out of a shower. He laid down his pen and stood up slowly and came around the desk to meet her.

'One of your more dramatic adventures, I think,' he said seriously. 'Thank God you're all right.' He kissed the top of her head and held her for a moment. 'Your copy's ready, I hope.'

Sal laughed. 'That didn't take long.'

'What didn't?' David asked.

'Expressing concern for the staff's well-being, before getting down to the nitty gritty.'

'For you, my darling, I've cleared the front page. It's all yours, if the story's as good as it sounds.'

'I'd have expected nothing less,' said Sal, relieved that he had instantly grasped the importance of what she had to tell. On top of a sleepless night and a tiring plane journey, not to mention the emotional dramas surrounding Louis, she had feared having a fight on her hands to make sure the story had enough prominence.

'It is an awful story, David,' she said, sitting down on a chair and handing him her notebook. 'You can't work in Eastern Europe without realising that the Mafia is gaining a fairly strong grip, but I'd no idea of the extent of their involvement in Moscow. I mean, what real harm would Naidenov have done? His life was nearly over.'

'You liked him?' David asked.

'Very much, but I say that only instinctively. I didn't have more than a few minutes' conversation with him as it turned out. There was a sincerity and a tranquillity about him. Maybe that was why he infuriated his persecutors so much. Nothing seemed to ruffle him; nothing could disturb his beliefs. I felt . . . overawed in his presence. I'm sorry if this sounds melodramatic, but he's probably the nearest I've come to meeting a saint.' She paused. 'Peter's developing his film now. We should have a shot of the body, as I mentioned on the phone.'

'And where does Louis Noble fit into all of this?' David enquired. 'Was he co-operative, so far as you were concerned?'

'Yes, Louis is co-operative,' Sal said carefully.

'You and Peter saved his life, I gather. If you hadn't been there, if you hadn't pursued the story, he'd be dead now. That's about the size of it, isn't it?' David scanned Sal's copy as he talked. He looked over the top of his reading glasses at Sal and was surprised to see her shifting uneasily in her seat, avoiding his eyes. 'That is right, isn't it?' he said, observing her shrewdly.

'Yes, yes, that's right.'

'Don't tell me you're suddenly getting a twinge of conscience about betraying a friend's confidence. Surely now, Louis and Evelyn are just damned grateful you were there.'

'I suppose so,' said Sal.

'Is there something I don't know, something else you should be telling me?' His persistence was uncanny.

'No,' said Sal firmly. 'Nothing at all. Louis is as anxious as Peter and I that the story should be told so that Gennadi hasn't died in vain. I just wish we could have Karagodina's story too.' And, at David's look of incomprehension, Sal told him briefly everything she knew about Karagodina Gorlov and her work.

'I think we should run it,' he decided.

'No – absolutely not. I promised Lev, and I know Gennadi would not have wanted her to have the exposure. It's too dangerous for her.'

'But if we exposed her to the world's press, there's no way the Mafia are going to run the risk of bumping her off.'

'Oh, don't be so naïve, David. They might not do it this week or next week, but in the next few months they'll get their revenge, whether they poison her soup, or run her down in the street. Sometimes, you lot make me sick.'

'By "you lot", I assume you're talking about us desk-bound editors?'

'Something like that,' said Sal. 'You don't know

anything about the real world — you just read about it in the newspapers.'

'Dear me, I think a night's sleep is called for,' said David mildly. 'How's Toby?'

Sal glanced up at him. 'I don't know. I haven't had a chance to ring home yet.'

'Then I suggest you do, and when you've done that, go home and make a fuss of him. You do worry me, Sal.' He walked over to the window of his office and made a great play of adjusting the blinds.

'Why?' Sal said challengingly.

'You could have been killed in that cellar. What would have happened to Toby then?'

'I wasn't killed. I'm all right, I'm here and I'm going home to him any moment.'

David turned to face her, his expression sad and troubled. 'I'm your editor, and you're one of the best journalists I've ever worked with — you know that, I've told you many times. This story is typical of you. Not only have you waded right in there, got involved to the extent that our readers will feel that they rescued Louis along with you, but you've told it so well. I've only glanced at your copy, but it's all there — the passion, the terror. But one of these days, my love, you're going to come unstuck, and I just wish you weren't the single parent of a young boy with no other living relative in the world.'

'So what do you want me to do?' said Sal. 'Resign, and start contributing to the weekly women's page?'

'I know that's not realistic. It's just that when I heard what had happened, what you and Peter had been up to, I was frightened for you. That's all. I'm a human being, you know.'

Sal stood up and smiled warmly. 'Now, that *is* a piece of news I didn't know before! I think we should cancel my story and make the front page lead with "*David Thorson is a Human Being*".'

'Get out of here,' said David, with a laugh, 'and give Toby a squeeze from me, will you?'

She blew him a kiss as she left the room. He stood staring at the closed door of his office for several moments before returning to his desk and sitting down heavily. He had always known that he would never be emotionally free from Salvena Saunders and the knowledge did not worry him. He welcomed it, the caring for her, the intimacy and camaraderie they shared. Of late, though, she had worried him. There was something bugging her, he was sure of that, and it seemed to have happened around the period of her mother's death. Normally she told him everything, but this time she was definitely holding something back. Something had undermined her confidence; somehow she seemed less in control, more vulnerable. When he thought of her in that cellar, his blood ran cold. What an extraordinary woman she was. There had been no fuss or hysterics, she had taken the whole thing in her stride, but then that had always been her way. He wondered where her strength came from, the near-loveless childhood perhaps, throwing her entirely on her own resources. Still though, despite her bravery and self-control, he felt that her air of confidence was barely skin deep. What he needed to know was *why*.

*   *   *

Toby's Easter holidays were not proving to be a success. His mother had promised they would go away somewhere, but it had never happened. His friends from school all seemed to be on holiday. His best friend James was in the Caribbean on his father's yacht, but Toby had done nothing more exciting than mooch around the house and he'd had enough of it.

The call from his mother's office to say she would soon be home had bouyed him up and he had decided to mend the puncture on his bike. Something had gone wrong, though. The kit had not worked properly and the tyre would not hold. He looked at the bike now, standing upside down in the entrance to the garage, the tyre as flat as a pancake. Everything was useless. It was a surprisingly hot April and he wanted to be out of London, almost anywhere but where he was.

There was a familiar toot on the horn, and his mother's red Jeep swept into the small driveway. Despite his mood he was pleased to see her, but he could not camouflage the resentment he felt as she jumped from the car and ran towards him.

'Tobe, darling, how are you?' He breathed in Chanel No 5, and felt the familiar embrace. It was so easy for her apparently to walk in and out of his life.

'How are you?' she repeated, searching his face. 'You've grown, I swear it, in just a week. Why the gloomy look?'

'I can't fix the puncture on my bike,' he said sulkily.

'Don't worry, darling. We'll take it down to the shop tomorrow.'

'Why can't we fix it together?' said Toby.

'Because I don't know anything about mending punctures,' said Sal, 'and in any case, I'm absolutely knackered. I was in Moscow this morning, Toby. Give me a break.'

He dragged himself away from her embrace and shuffled off towards the bike. She watched him for a second. 'I'll just tell Jenny I'm back, and then I'll put the kettle on. Come in and tell me what you've been up to.'

He did not reply, and when he heard the front door slam he aimed a vicious kick at his bike and sent it reeling across the garage floor.

'How are things, Jenny?' Sal collapsed at the kitchen table.

'OK,' said Jenny. 'A cup of tea?'

'Yes, please. How's Toby? He seems a bit down.'

'He's been like that all the holiday. You must have noticed.' There was no obvious hint of criticism in Jenny's voice, but something was not right.

'What are you saying, Jenny, that he's unhappy at the moment?'

'Well, he's not happy – put it like that.'

Sal had the beginnings of a headache and she was suddenly exhausted and drained. She was not up to this. 'He has this lovely home, plenty of toys, a garden, schoolfriends and you to look after him when I can't.'

'His friends are all away at the moment,' said Jenny flatly. 'Like his Mum.'

Sal looked up sharply at the remark. Jenny had turned her back and was making a fuss of preparing tea. It was not like her to be critical, she was normally so supportive.

Jenny had been with Sal and Toby since Toby was two years old. Up until then, Sal had employed a professional nanny to look after her son while she worked. But at two, when he had started playgroup, she had looked for someone different — more of a companion for her and Toby, more of a housekeeper than a nanny.

Jenny Menzies had been raised in Edinburgh. An early marriage had gone wrong, leaving her childless and she had come to London seeking a new start. It appeared that Sal and Toby fulfilled her definition of a new start, although at times Sal worried about her. She was still a young woman, only in her early thirties and had dedicated the last six years of her life to them, with no hint of a boyfriend, and few close girlfriends. She seemed to Sal to lead a very sterile life, but she was normally very good company, had a wicked sense of humour and loved a drink. At parties she had established quite a reputation among Sal's friends. After a few glasses of wine, she became a brilliant impressionist, very funny and imaginative. Equally though, Sal was sure that while Jenny was in sole charge of Toby, she never touched a drop. She was loyal, hardworking, reliable and usually uncritical.

'I'm sorry you feel I'm giving Toby such a lousy time.' There was a challenge in Sal's voice.

Jenny turned to face her. She was not a pretty woman, but her curly brown hair and freckled open face had a certain charm. Now it was creased with concern. 'It's not just that Toby is having a miserable holiday. He took his grandmother's death quite badly, you know. I think he feels it has left him vulnerable. If only you two could go away for a few days. I do my best, but I'm no substitute for you – you're his mother. Couldn't you take him with you on one of your assignments?'

Sal shook her head. 'It's simply not done, Jenny. You know that.'

'I do know a child deserves an occasional holiday with his parents, whatever job they do,' said Jenny evenly.

At that moment Toby came through the back door, slamming it none too quietly behind him.

'Hello, darling,' said Sal. 'Come and sit, and have a cup of tea and tell me all about what you've been doing.'

'There's nothing to tell,' said Toby. 'I'm going up to my room.' He slouched across the kitchen and both women listened to his footsteps trudging up the stairs.

By the time the phone call came through that night, Sal was exhausted and depressed. Jenny had gone to her room two hours before. Sal had made a desperate attempt to talk to Toby, but he had simply shut her out. He sat on his bed watching television, and when she offered him first tea and then supper, he said he wasn't hungry. Like all mothers and children, there had been ups and downs between them, but Sal had never experienced any real difficulty communicating with him before. She found his new mood disconcerting.

Was it puberty? she wondered. Surely he was a little young for that. It was one of the few occasions when Sal wished there was an active father-figure in their lives, someone with whom she could talk through her worries, someone Toby could look to, besides herself.

She was sitting over the remains of a chicken sandwich and a glass of wine, drifting in and out of an uneasy doze when the telephone made her jump. 'Sal, it's David here.'

'Hello, David. Did the picture develop OK?'

There was a moment's hesitation. 'Yes, it did and very well too.'

'Oh great!' said Sal.

'No Sal, I'm afraid it's not great. There's a news embargo placed on the story and it's come from the top. We're not going to run it.'

'You have to be joking,' breathed Sal.

'I'm not.'

'Jesus Christ – can't you ignore them?'

'Don't be silly Sal, you know how it works. We're forbidden to run the story now or at any time in the future. We've had to send your copy, plus photographs, to the powers that be. I suppose in their own way, they'll probably do some good in that they'll be seen at high level. Sadly, though, your story is not going to sell newspapers and nor are the public going to be aware of what happened to that poor little bugger, Naidenov. God, what a mess they made of him, didn't they?'

'Yes,' said Sal, scarcely able to take in what he said. 'Look, David, I can't believe this. Does Louis know about it?'

'I presume so. I imagine this is a decision made between Lambeth Palace, Downing Street and MI5.'

'He's going to be absolutely furious. He established a relationship with the man, he was there – good God, he was with him when he died! He's not going to stand for this.'

'To be perfectly honest,' said David wearily, 'I don't think it matters a shit whether Louis approves or not. There's no way anybody is budging on this. I spent an hour arguing the toss with everybody I could think off. I went in the backdoor, confronting the thing full on, spoke to all the people who matter. Believe me, I've pulled out all the stops for you, Sal, because I truly believe this story of yours should be told.'

'I know you'll have done everything that could be done, David, and thank you,' Sal said. 'I just can't believe they can do that. It's so immoral – I suppose it's an arse-licking Gorby exercise.'

'I myself can't help wondering whether it wasn't a setup,' David said after a pause.

'How do you mean?'

'Well, think it through. I'm not going to say any more than this, as walls have ears, but why wasn't Louis advised of the security risk?'

'Good God,' said Sal, 'Lev said as much, but I thought he was being melodramatic.'

'Enough, I said,' cautioned David. 'We'll discuss it in further detail some time, but not right now, OK?'

'I'll see you tomorrow then,' said Sal heavily. 'I just can't bear it – it's one of the best stories ever.'

'Not tomorrow,' David told her. 'Take a few days off

with Toby and come back after the weekend. There's nothing much going on here, anyway.'

'OK,' said Sal.

'How is he, by the way?'

'A bit morose.'

'Shall I invite myself to Sunday lunch?'

'I think you should do that,' said Sal.

'I'll look forward to it.'

Sal replaced the receiver and sat hunched over the phone for a long time, her mind in turmoil. Then slowly, deliberately, with a shaking hand, she picked up the telephone and dialled Evelyn and Louis' number.

CHAPTER NINE

'Sal, I'm so grateful.' Evelyn's voice was full of warmth, the way it had always been for Sal, over decades.

'Don't be silly, Evelyn.' By contrast Sal's voice was strained, almost impatient.

'But for you and your photographer, Louis would have been killed. I just can't believe it – thank heavens I didn't know what was going on until it was all over. I didn't like him going to Russia. Eastern Europe frightens me, it always has. I suppose it's because of all the stories you've told us over the years, but I never thought . . .' her voice trailed off. Sal could tell she was close to tears.

'Evelyn, I'm so sorry I betrayed your trust,' Sal said shakily. 'It was unforgivable of me. You must have been so angry.'

'I don't mind admitting I was bloody angry initially

that you'd used the information I gave you, but as it turned out, thank heavens you did. I keep thinking about that. If I hadn't told you about Louis' assignment, he'd be dead. Forget it, Sal. Maybe the fates intervened to save Louis, or maybe even his God, who knows. Either way, this is definitely a case of the end justifying the means.'

'Is he there?' Sal asked. She couldn't bear talking to Evelyn another moment. 'Only we have a problem with the story.'

'Yes, of course he's here. Actually he's asleep, but I'll wake him up if it's important.'

'I think it is – I'm sorry,' Sal said.

There was a slight pause. 'You sound odd,' Evelyn said. 'Is there anything wrong?'

'No,' said Sal, too quickly. 'No, I'm just tired. It's been a crazy couple of days.'

'I should think it has,' said Evelyn. 'Hold on a moment.'

There was a lengthy silence while presumably Evelyn went to wake Louis. Sal imagined Evelyn leaning over the bed shaking him gently awake, his dark head on the pillow. What was he dreaming of, who was he thinking of, as he struggled up through the layers of sleep? Sal tried to push away the image. The whole situation was such a complete nightmare. There could be no worse form of betrayal than making love to your best friend's husband. Evelyn was so good, so trusting, such a wonderful friend. How could she do this to her? It *had* to stop.

Louis' voice was thick with sleep, but the formality

of his tone made it clear that the call was a strain for him, too. 'Louis here, Sal. How can I help you?'

'They've axed the story, Louis. Did you know?'

There was silence for a moment. 'I don't know what you mean,' he said.

'They've placed an embargo on it – the Government, Lambeth Palace, whoever. My editor is not allowed to print it, and nor will any other newspaper be allowed to run it. Peter's photograph and my copy have been sent to the Foreign Office, and that's an end of it. The public are never going to know how Gennadi Naidenov died.'

'I don't believe this, Sal. Are you sure?' Louis sounded as if he thought he was still dreaming.

'I've just put the phone down from my editor,' said Sal. 'There's absolutely no doubt about it, and believe me, David Thorson is a top man with marvellous contacts. He's been in the business so long there's nobody he doesn't know, and he's much respected. The Government often use him to leak a story because they know he'll do it accurately. He has tremendous integrity. You can be sure if there was anything anyone could have done, David would have done it.'

'This is monstrous!' exploded Louis. 'I can't believe this can happen. It makes us no better than the Russians.'

'You're probably right,' said Sal, 'but there's absolutely nothing we can do.'

'There has to be,' said Louis. 'I'll get on to my office right away . . . Oh no, there'll be nobody there now. In the morning then, I'll find out what the hell is going on. We can't sit back and take this, Sal.'

'I think we have to,' said Sal.

'That doesn't sound like you. Where's your fighting spirit?'

'Louis, I've been in the business a long time. It's no good bashing one's head against a brick wall. Let's just hope that our recent experiences have at least made the Government aware that the Mafia are becoming a force to be reckoned with in the Soviet Union.'

'But what is their motive? I don't understand why the story can't be told.'

'David says he'll talk to me about that, but I think I can hazard a guess,' said Sal.

'And what would your guess be?' Louis challenged.

'Simply that Gennadi's death would be bad publicity for the Gorbachov regime. Thatcher and the Western powers are all fawning over Gorbachov at the moment and are anxious to present him as Mr Clean. Gennadi's death would do his image no good at all.'

'It's absolutely monstrous,' repeated Louis. 'I'm not prepared to let it rest here. Look, can we meet tomorrow?' He stumbled over the words for a moment, and Sal felt her heart miss a beat.

'Yes, all right. What sort of time?'

'Lunchtime. Can you suggest somewhere?'

'What about Julie's, in Holland Park Avenue. It'll be quiet if we go early and it will give us a chance to talk in peace.'

'Twelve-thirty, then?'

'Yes,' said Sal. 'I'll be there.'

*   *   *

By the time Sal reached Julie's the following afternoon, she was armed with the full details of David's theory and was bristling with rage.

Louis was already in the restaurant when she arrived. He looked tired, very pale and grim. He rose, and she approached the table and kissed him chastely on the cheek.

'How are you, Louis?' she asked.

'Not good. And you?'

'Angry. How did you get on?'

'The Palace say they know nothing, other than the fact it's been decided the story is not in the best interests of East-West relationships. I couldn't get any further than that. When I suggested that perhaps we were acting immorally by suppressing the story, I was simply told that we were not politicians and that it was not up to us to interfere.'

'That's rich! I'm so fed up with the way the senior clergy are playing politics these days. Here's a legitimate reason for them to become involved and they back off. Sorry, Louis, but the Church makes me sick sometimes.'

'I'm inclined to agree,' Louis said sadly.

'And that's not all,' Sal burst out, eager to share her outrage. 'I think you were set up.'

'What do you mean, exactly?'

The waitress arrived and Sal ordered a bottle of wine and waited until she had gone.

'You were advised, weren't you, that there might be a problem of a purely bureaucratic nature – good old

red tape getting in the way of having Gennadi released?'
Louis nodded. 'You were told nothing, though, of there
being any risk to his life or, indeed, to yours?'

'No, I wasn't.'

'Instead, when you arrived in Moscow, he was
released into your care immediately. The next thing
you know, you're at the mercy of the Mafia. David's
theory, for what it's worth, is that it's exactly what
both Governments meant to happen. They wanted
Gennadi conveniently disposed of, by someone other
than themselves, of course.'

'Both Governments?' said Louis, appalled. 'You
really mean our Government, as well as Moscow?' Sal
nodded. 'But that's outrageous! So you're suggesting
that I was expendable, too?'

'I think that's being a touch dramatic,' Sal said with
a wry smile. 'I don't expect they imagined you'd be
involved.'

'But they must have known it was possible. How
on earth would they have explained it if I'd been
killed too?'

'They would have slapped a news embargo on that
too,' said Sal. 'Evelyn would have been fed a series of
platitudes and a pension. Of course, they had reckoned
without me!'

'How do you mean?' Louis asked, puzzled.

'They weren't to know that we were friends. If you
had been killed and I hadn't been involved in the
mission, I'd have been tearing around trying to get
at the truth, and with my contacts in Moscow, I'd
probably have got to the bottom of things.'

'But what difference would it have made?' Louis said. 'You still wouldn't have been able to print what you found.'

'That's certainly possible,' said Sal. The wine arrived and she poured out two glasses. Louis took a gulp of his, distractedly running a hand through his thick hair.

'Sal, how can we be so corrupt? I thought the Brits were supposed to be an honourable bunch.'

'I think you have to look at the whole thing in context,' said Sal. 'The Soviet Union, under Mikhail Gorbachov, has moved a very long way towards the West. Many of the dangers associated with the Cold War seem to be at an end. The big three – Gorbachov, Thatcher and Reagan – genuinely seem to have struck up a relationship which could destroy the threat of nuclear war for ever – certainly on a grand, world-war scale. They don't want anything to upset the applecart and are prepared to go to any lengths to protect the progress they've made.'

'But it's so immoral!' Louis said. He was almost shouting and people at adjoining tables glanced in his direction.

'Maybe it is,' agreed Sal, 'but supposing this tenuous relationship between the leaders broke down. Supposing things went wrong, back to the bad old days of Brezhnev – it doesn't bear thinking of. OK, so it has cost one old man's life, a good life, but well worth sacrificing for the sake of the accord which is building up. Believe me, I'm as angry as you – I had been given the front page for this story – but I can see the argument for the other side.'

'Is that all you can think about – your career?'

'No,' said Sal evenly. 'No, it's not, but equally the embargo doesn't surprise or shock me.'

'Well, I think it should,' said Louis hotly. 'If more journalists made a fuss about this sort of thing, the Government wouldn't be able to exercise their control in this way. We're supposed to have a free press, after all.'

'And we have,' said Sal, 'usually, but sometimes in the interests of national security, stories have to be suppressed. Come on Louis, calm down. Let's eat something.'

'I couldn't eat a thing.'

'What do you want to do then?' Sal asked.

'I want to take you to bed,' said Louis.

They faced each other across the king-sized bed and their eyes locked. They both started to remove their clothes, and in moments they were naked.

'Come here and kiss me,' said Sal, and he came round the bed with his arms outstretched, pulling her to him with a sigh.

'I love you, Sal,' he said.

She looked up into his face and saw the mixture of desire and torture in his eyes. 'Just kiss me, Louis,' she whispered.

It was as though her mouth was a magnet that drew his lips to it against his will. Her mouth opened under his; she bit his tongue, he bit back. Their kiss became more and more passionate until they were moving against each other in a frenzy. Louis suddenly pulled away, picked Sal up and threw her on the bed. He entered her straight away and although she cried out in surprise, she was more than ready for him. He came almost immediately, shouting her name again and again, then lay on top of her, shaking with the ferocity of his climax. 'I'm sorry, Sal,' he whispered in her ear.

Sal just smiled, pushed him over on to his back and knelt astride him. He closed his eyes as she started to kiss him, slowly and softly. With licks, sucks and gentle bites she covered his body, starting at his throat and ending at his groin. He had already started to harden as she licked the length of his penis. When he could stand no more and begged her to stop, she quickly moved on top of him, impaling herself on his penis. She sat on his hips for a moment to enjoy the feeling of him inside her; he felt so right. She opened her eyes to find him looking at her; she smiled and slowly rotated her hips. She kept moving slowly, wanting to prolong their lovemaking for as long as possible.

Louis reached for her hips and pulled her gently off and up, towards his mouth. With her knees each side of his head she positioned herself over his face. At first he just looked at her and ran his thumb over her clitoris, then he started to lick her gently but firmly, keeping up a steady rhythm while she groaned above him, not daring to move too much in case he could not reach her and the amazing sensation would stop. She came suddenly with such force that she collapsed beside him, shaking and crying. He brushed the hair from her face and kissed her, then as the kiss deepened he rolled her over and entered her. They lay without moving, all their feelings centred in the kiss. She started to run her fingers up and down his back. He shivered and said, 'Sal, I want to make this last for ever.'

He moved slowly, pulling himself right out and pausing before plunging into her again. She whimpered as he came out and sighed as he thrust into her. She looked at his face, transformed by passion. He had the look of someone primitive and savage and she found that his expression excited her. He pushed her legs wider apart and came to his knees, lifting her ankles until they rested on his shoulders. When he thrust into her, she cried out in a mixture of pain and pleasure. He hesitated, but she cried, 'No, don't stop! Please don't stop!'

He began to move more quickly and she could feel herself coming, starting with small waves of pleasure and building, building. . . . She climaxed, her eyes wide, staring at his face and shrieking his name. He lowered her legs, bent down and kissed her face all over.

When she finally gained control of her senses she realised he was still hard. She smiled at him. 'My turn now,' she said as she pushed him on to his back and climbed on top. She slowly started to rotate her pelvis. He closed his eyes and his breathing quickened as she settled into a rhythm; alternating rotations with lifts of her body, sliding herself up and down, round and round until she could feel him start to come. She slowed down, not enough to stop his climax, but just enough to prolong and intensify it. His head thrashed from side to side on the pillow and when he was finished he went completely limp until she kissed his mouth and he opened his eyes and folded her in his arms.

The sun had gone down by the time they woke. Sal clambered out of bed and peered out of the window of the hotel into which they had booked.

'Louis, it's after seven! I'll have to ring home, my housekeeper is supposed to go off duty at six. What time did you tell Evelyn you'd be home?'

Louis simply lay back on the pillow and smiled at her. 'Come here,' he whispered.

'No,' said Sal. 'Come on, we have to be sensible.'

'How can I be sensible, with you looking like that? Come here – please.'

In the end they told their respective families that they would be home late. Jenny and Evelyn, both equally longsuffering, accepted it without question. Then they made love again, slowly and gently, utterly familiar with one another now. Later they dressed and went down to the hotel restaurant for dinner. They ate ravenously.

During the meal Sal was uncharacteristically quiet. When the coffee arrived, Louis reached out and took her hand. 'What's wrong, darling?'

'Oh come on, Louis, you know what's wrong,' she replied. 'I can't bear the way we're deceiving Evelyn like this. When you telephoned her just now, I could hardly endure it. It's such an awful thing to do to one's best friend. It's an awful thing to do to any woman.'

Louis squeezed her hand. 'Sal, we didn't go in search of this, it just happened.'

'But we could have stopped it,' Sal argued. 'We could have stopped it after Moscow, accepted that it was just a reaction to the drama of the moment – it didn't have to go on.'

'Is that all you still really think it is?' Louis asked. There was hurt in his eyes.

'No, of course not,' said Sal. 'Do you think I would have ended up in your bed this afternoon unless I felt a great deal more than that? It's just that I don't understand this thing between us, Louis. I recognise it's very powerful and it frightens me. I'm doing something I know is wrong, but I seem to be powerless to stop it. Is that how you feel?'

Louis stirred his coffee cup in silence for a moment. 'Well, of course I know it's wrong. Heaven's above, with my particular calling I should be more aware of the rights and wrongs of this than you. I should also be suffering more from divided loyalties. Evelyn may be your best friend, but she is my wife and what I'm doing to her is unforgivable. And yet . . .' he looked up and met Sal's eye '. . . and yet, Sal, I don't feel guilty. In fact, I don't feel any sort of remorse. I'm quite sure that if we hadn't got together, I would have gone to my grave not knowing what true love was all about, and maybe because of that, I'm justifying in my mind what we're doing – I don't know.'

'But there is no justification,' Sal said. 'If Evelyn found out what was going on between us she would be desperately unhappy and hurt and betrayed twice over. How can you possibly justify that?'

'I can't,' Louis admitted. 'I suppose I feel in such a complete state of turmoil at the moment, it's hard to believe in anything much. The shock of what happened in Moscow, that poor man dying in such a terrible way . . .' For a moment his expression twisted in pain at the mention of Gennadi's death. 'And then this thing with us, set against a general disillusion I've been experiencing concerning the direction in which the Church is moving . . . it's all come together to such an extent I no longer seem to know what is right or wrong. I just feel that there is a query in my life about every aspect of it – my faith, my sense of right and wrong, my marriage . . .'

'But you and Evelyn have a good marriage,' Sal said quietly. 'I know that, I've watched it evolve over the years.'

Louis sighed. 'Well, I suppose we have, yes, but it can't be that wonderful or I wouldn't be so much in love with you.'

'Our relationship could simply be based on good sex,' Sal suggested.

Louis shook his head. 'Don't speak of it like that,' he said. 'Don't debase it. It's much, much more than that, and you know it.'

Sal bit her lip. 'Yes, I suppose it is. But Louis, whatever sort of future we have, it cannot be at the expense of Evelyn's happiness. Can we please agree about that?' Louis nodded; they were both close to tears.

It was a conversation which was repeated many times during the summer that followed. Again and again Sal tried to end the affair, but Louis always destroyed her resolve. His need of her seemed to increase each time they met. It was heady stuff, and Sal, with no other emotional ties in her life except for Toby, could not resist him. For appearance's sake twice she and Toby visited Evelyn while Louis was away on a conference. It was an agony to try and behave normally. For all her faults, Sal was essentially an honest person and she felt as if betraying Evelyn was quite literally destroying her.

By the end of the summer, she'd had enough. She badly needed a break from Louis and his endless demands. The urge to learn the truth of her origins was never out of her mind these days, and so she resolved to tackle both problems at the same time.

She invited David Thorson to Sunday lunch on a balmy autumn day. The weather was so warm that they had lunch in Sal's little walled garden and afterwards walked in the park. Toby had been asked to sleep over with a schoolfriend and was collected about six o'clock.

'Are you doing anything this evening?' Sal asked when they had waved him off.

David shook his head. 'No, not especially. Why, would you like me to take you out to dinner?'

'No, let's have some supper here,' said Sal. 'I've got a favour to ask you.'

'Oh, I see,' said David, 'so I've been softened up all day, have I?'

'Something like that,' said Sal. She made a pasta and salad. The evening was still warm and again they sat outside as the sun set.

'You're very lucky with this house,' said David. 'You have the illusion of not being in London at all, here in this garden. The trees blot out just about everything.'

'Except for the background noise,' said Sal.

'What are you going to do about your mother's house? Are you going to sell it? You haven't been down to Horton-cum-Studley much this summer, have you?'

'I don't really know, David. I never lived there, so it's not like my home. On the other hand, a cottage in the country would be nice and I don't need to sell it for financial reasons. I thought I'd just wait and see – which brings me neatly to my favour. I wondered if I could have a few days off – a week at the most.'

'Of course,' said David. 'So you're going to take Toby on a holiday – wonderful.'

'Well, actually, no,' said Sal. 'I want to go to Yugoslavia, to do some research.'

'What for?' asked David. 'For heaven's sake, Sal, take that boy away and get some roses in his cheeks before the school term starts.'

'This is something I have to do alone,' said Sal, 'and I feel I need to do it now.'

'Surely you can take Toby with you.'

'I can't,' said Sal.

'Why not?'

'The new school year starts on Wednesday, and in any event, I'm not sure he should be involved in what I'm doing.'

'Good Lord!' said David. 'That sounds intriguing.'

Unable to talk properly to Evelyn any more, Sal had already reached the conclusion that it was time to take David into her confidence. Haltingly, she told the story of her mother's deathbed scene. David listened carefully, asked a few questions, and when she had finished he commented, 'I think you should take Toby into your confidence. Tell him all about it, involve him in the search. After all, it's his family too.'

'I think he's too young,' said Sal.

'Come on, he's not a baby. He's ten, he can more than cope with this.'

'I disagree,' said Sal. 'Look, you yourself recognised how insecure my mother's death would make him, and you were right. If he's still feeling like that, to start introducing doubts as to who he really is can't be sensible. I mean, my name may not even be Saunders by right. If so, then neither is Toby's.'

'Yes, I suppose you're right,' said David thoughtfully. 'It's certainly silly to stir up the boy if there proves to be no truth in the whole thing. But the association with the bank, the interest you've always shown in Eastern Europe, and even your name – it does seem to stack up, doesn't it?'

'Yes, it does,' said Sal. 'Do you know, I haven't said this to anybody, David, or barely even admitted it to myself, but when my mother told me, although I was shocked, there was some element that was like a kind of foreknowledge. She was telling me something I already knew.'

David stared at Sal. 'You certainly don't have the typical English-rose appearance. You're really far too exotic to have been bred on these shores.'

Sal laughed. 'Then you'll let me go?'

'Yes. But what will you do with Toby?'

'He can stay with Jenny during the week and go down to Evelyn and Louis at the weekend, I suppose,' said Sal. 'It seems the best place for him.' The words came easily, yet as she thought through the implications of what she was doing, she was appalled. Asking the woman she was betraying to care of her son – sending him to her lover's home. Dusk, luckily, hid from David the expression on her face.

'It must be extraordinary for you to consider the possibility of suddenly having a brother and, I suppose, a father too.'

Sal looked up at him quickly, grateful for his under-standing. 'Yes, yes, it is,' she said. 'I don't expect my—. Oh David, I can't say the word "father". Tim was my father.' She was suddenly close to tears. David moved his chair so it was beside hers and slipped an arm around her shoulder. She leaned her head against him for a moment.

'Tim was your father, no one can take that away from you, or him. He really loved you, Sal, I know that – and if he loved you knowing that you were not his own flesh and blood, then that makes your relationship all the more special, doesn't it?'

'Yes, I suppose it does.' Sal smiled wanly. 'I'll call him my mother's first husband. If my mother's first husband was, as she said, a great deal older than her, the chances are he is dead from natural causes – that is, assuming he survived as a spy in Belgrade. My mother found out what he was up to. For all we know, others may have too. He may well have been shot as a traitor.'

'And your brother?'

Sal's expression softened. 'My brother's another thing entirely,' she said. She stood up and began pacing around the small garden. 'David, you're going to think this is really weird, but I'm sure he's alive, and I'm sure I'm meant to find him. I have to admit that it has become something of an obsession in the last few months, which is why having taken the decision to try and find out more, I want to get on with it — now, before I lose my courage.'

'I can understand that,' said David. 'I wonder what sort of chap he is? He's almost certainly married with a family of his own. It would be wonderful for Toby to have relations, as well as for you, of course.'

'Yes, I've thought about that as well,' said Sal, 'and I've tried to picture my brother in my mind. I suppose I've built him up to be someone very special. He certainly was as far as my mother was concerned. She clearly loved him very much. She died with his name on her lips, you know.'

'And did that hurt you?' David asked. Sal came and sat down beside him again and considered this question. 'No,' she said. 'You see, you can't miss something you've never had.'

'What do you mean?' David asked.

'A mother's love,' Sal said. 'I realise now why she never loved me and it has helped in some respects. Georges, her son, was everything to her and she had to give him up. I suspect she never forgave me for not being him.'

It was Sal's fifth night of dining alone in her Belgrade hotel and she was weary — weary of the apparent futility of her search and of her own company. The decision to come to Yugoslavia had been useful in one respect. It had helped her to clarify her feelings about Louis. The affair had to end. Quite apart from her terrible guilt regarding Evelyn, she was not even sure any more that she really loved Louis. She loved him as a friend, of course — but as a lover? Within a day or two of being away from him and his endless telephone calls, Sal had acknowledged that what really attracted her to him was his need of her. He had been a man dying of thirst in a desert and she was, for want of a cliché, the oasis. Whatever had gone wrong with his and Evelyn's sex life, if indeed it had ever been right, must have happened some time ago. Since then, because of his position and his beliefs, he had been trapped in a life of apparent near-celibacy. Then Sal had unleashed in him something over which he seemed to have little or no control — and that excited her. But that was certainly not reason enough to cause Evelyn any unhappiness. The affair had to be ended as soon as she returned to London, which she would do the day after tomorrow — or perhaps even tomorrow, since the progress in her search had been nil.

She had concentrated on the records office in Belgrade, because, clearly, if her father had been involved in the Government, as her mother had suggested, then they would have been based in Belgrade. However, a search through the births, marriages and deaths registers had shown nothing, largely because she did not know what she was looking for. Initially she had concentrated on her own birth, assuming that her Christian name, at least, was accurate, since it was clearly Yugoslavian, and that her mother had probably kept her daughter's original date of birth. But the search had proved fruitless. There was no baby Salvena born in Belgrade around her own date of birth. Then she had pursued her parents' marriage, convinced that her mother's name, Barbara, would be easy to find amongst mainly Yugoslavian names. There was nothing. Finally, she had tried searching for her brother's birth. He had been eight, her mother had told her, at the time of her own birth. She had looked back for babies born with the name of Georges eight years before her own year of birth. There were a number, of course, but none of them with a mother or father who was obviously recognisable.

She had visited the city's maternity hospital in the hope of finding old records, but with no success, and the following day had decided to visit the main schools in Belgrade in her search for Georges. It was so difficult to make any sort of progress without a surname – and it was so easy to become disheartened – and she could not ignore the nagging doubt in the back of her mind that in fact there was no truth in the story. She and her mother had not only never been close, Sal was sure that her mother had been jealous of her relationship with her father, Tim. Maybe her mother, in the last few moments of life had chosen to sow the seeds of a story to discredit her relationship with Tim Saunders. It was a terrible thought and Sal hated herself for thinking it, but it still astounded her that in all the years she had lived with her mother, there had never been a hint of a former life in Yugoslavia. Suddenly, Sal wondered if Tim himself had ever known (assuming the story was true) or whether Barbara had literally carried the burden of the truth alone until she was dying. Somehow Sal felt that if the story was true, it was in character for Barbara to lie about her past even to her husband. She was such a private person. Clearly, Tim knew he was not her father but what, if anything else, had he known?

She sat drinking coffee, staring out into the Belgrade night. She felt no desire to go out. Belgrade depressed her. Of course, compared with most of Eastern Europe it was a wonderful city, so cosmopolitan, so full of life, but it was drab architecturally and oddly sterile.

Her rambling thoughts were interrupted by the arrival of a receptionist. 'Miss Saunders?'

Sal nodded. 'Yes.'

'There's a fax arrived for you. I thought you might like it.'

'Oh, thank you.' Sal took the message. It was from Judy, her secretary.

'Mr Adrian Drummond telephoned today. He said it was urgent and personal and that I was to try and contact you. Otherwise, all quiet on the Western Front. Have fun. Judy.'

Adrian Drummond . . . for a moment Sal could not place the name and then suddenly she remembered — he was her mother's banker. So why was he getting in touch after all these months? He had so firmly slammed the door. For the first time in the last five weary days, Sal felt a surge of excitement. Maybe, just maybe, he was going to help her after all. She looked at her watch with impatience. It would be at least twelve hours before she could telephone him. Still, it was the first positive thing to have happened since her search began.

'Mr Drummond, this is Salvena Saunders.'

'Ah, Miss Saunders, how good of you to ring. I hope I haven't disturbed your holiday.'

'No, no,' said Sal impatiently. 'What is it? Have you been able to find out any information for me?'

'Not exactly,' said Adrian Drummond, 'but this may be of help. You will be aware that probate has now been finalised. I should be dealing with your solicitor over this really, but now your mother's affairs have been wound up, it appears that there is a safety deposit box at our head office in Zürich, which your mother left with specific instructions for you to have.'

'What does it contain?' Sal asked.

'I've absolutely no idea. No one is allowed to open it but yourself. I wouldn't imagine there is anything of any great value in there because we were very much a party to any major expenses your mother made, but it may offer some clues.'

'I'm in Belgrade at the moment.'

'So I gather,' said Adrian Drummond.

'I've been trying to track down my birth records, but without success. What I'll do is to fly from here to Zürich. Can you give me details of where I should go?'

*   *   *

The head office of the Swiss Federal Bank was sumptuous indeed. Sal still found it extraordinary that her obviously conventional mother could be involved with a Swiss bank. She was ushered into a private room, given coffee and eventually a kindly elderly man appeared, reverently carrying a small battered box.

'Would you like to be left alone now?'

Sal nodded. Her mouth was dry, her heart pounding. Ceremoniously the little man handed Sal the key and withdrew discreetly. For a long moment Sal stared at the metal box. In it, she was sure, she would find the truth one way or another to her mother's story. Slowly she turned the key and opened the box. Nervously she peered inside. It contained a large red jewelry box, beside which lay an envelope. Sal lifted out the jewelry box, and opened it. It contained jewellery she had never seen her mother wear. There was a beautiful set of pearls, a diamond choker, a dress-watch, and a tiny, delicate diamond tiara with matching necklace and bracelet. It was fascinating, extraordinary, but not really what Sal wanted to see.

With trembling hands, she reached for the envelope and opened it carefully. Out fell two birth certificates, one instantly recognisable as her own. She had been born Salvena Kovic. The date of birth was, indeed, her own – 3 October 1955, and she had been born in Zagreb. The second certificate was that of Georges Borislav Kovic, born in Belgrade on 27 August 1947. In both cases the parents were shown as Serge and Marie Kovic. For a moment the name Marie threw

Sal completely. Her mother's name had been Barbara – the idea that even this was false was for some reason deeply disturbing.

For a long moment Sal stared at the two birth certificates, particularly at Georges'. Clearly, during her search in Belgrade she must have found his registration of birth, but without having any idea as to his surname, she had not recognised it. She looked again in the envelope. All that remained was a photograph. She pulled it out. It was of a family group: a man, a woman and a small boy, aged four or five. The boy was instantly recognisable – his features were so similar to her mother's and her own. He was smiling, happy, sitting between his parents, one arm thrown across his father's knee. Her mother looked the same yet completely different. She was younger than Sal had ever remembered her, of course, but it was her expression which astounded Sal. She looked so carefree, so joyful – a completely different woman from the one she later became.

Sal turned her attention to the man. Her father was a good-looking man, with high cheekbones, pale hair, and almond-shaped dark eyes. She stared at the face. The nose was aquiline, the mouth firm and generous, but there was a slight weakness around the jawline. It was a terrifying moment. This was a face she instinctively did not like, and yet in it she could recognise many of her own features. She gazed for a long, long time at the little family – *her family* – and then began to weep, tears pouring down her face as if they would never stop. It was how the bank official found her when he returned to check up on her progress.

For twenty-four hours following her discovery at the bank, Sal lay in her hotel room in Zürich, trying to digest what had happened to her life – trying to come to terms with the fact that without a doubt now, her mother's story was true. There was so much for her to come to terms with. The most distressing was the fact that the man, Tim Saunders, who had loved her like a daughter, was not her father. Yet there had never been a hint of it. He had been selfless in his love for her, proud of her, supportive, bringing colour to her life when her mother's drab world threatened to overshadow her completely. And then, there was her mother. Sal went over again and again in her mind her mother's story. Clearly she had come to England, doubtful as to whether they would be allowed to survive, and that fear of her past being uncovered had haunted Marie Kovic/Barbara Saunders all her life. It accounted for her reluctance to make friends, to allow Sal to bring friends home, to mix with people at all. Anonymity was her God – she wanted to be as faceless as possible. Now, at last, Sal understood why. She began to feel sympathy for her mother, and with the sympathy came guilt. She lay on her hotel bed for hours upon end, alternately crying or staring at the ceiling. Her life would never be the same again. She was quite simply another person from the child and young woman she had been. As the fog began to clear from her mind, Sal could think of only one thing. *She had to find Georges*. It was now not only a quest, but an obsession.

Within hours of her decision she was on a plane back to Belgrade. She began simply by looking in the telephone book for his name. She visited every conceivable official, the missing person's bureau, housing lists, she even called on the British Embassy in the hopes that they might be able to help her – Georges, after all, was half-British. But it was as if he had never been. He had been born in the city – she found his registration of birth – but then he seemed to have disappeared.

Of her father, there was equally no record, but that did not surprise her. If he was a KGB agent, then presumably he would have gone to live in Russia at some point, maybe taking his son with him. Where to start? Back to Moscow again? The thought did not appeal, and in any event how likely was it that she would find him? In a moment of horrifying clarity, she suddenly realised that even the name Kovic could be false. She now knew she had never been truly Salvena Saunders, but that did not mean necessarily that she had been Salvena Kovic, either. Her father could have operated under a false name. Her sense of disorientation was total. Alone with no one to talk to, she wondered if she was going mad.

After one of her fruitless sessions, she returned to her hotel to see there was a call from Jenny. Instantly alarmed, she telephoned home.

'Is something wrong with Toby?' she asked.

'Yes, he has bronchitis. It started out as flu, but now it's moved on to his chest. The real problem is that he's missing his mother. You said you'd be away for a few days, Sal. It's nearly two weeks now and the boy needs you back here.'

'I know, I know,' said Sal. 'Look, let me speak to him and I'll catch a flight tomorrow.'

It was a relief to have to go home. Toby needed her and with his need came a sense of reality. If she was no one else, she was in reality Toby's mother. On the flight home Sal made several important decisions. She was going to tell Toby everything she had discovered concerning their background. Now that her mother's story was confirmed, maybe it would help give him some security. After all, somewhere he might have an uncle, even a grandfather. She also resolved to keep her promise and spend more time at home, and to end her affair with Louis — however difficult that might prove.

Toby looked dreadful. 'How long has he been like this?' she asked Jenny.

'Only a day or so. I've had the doctor out to him and he's on antibiotics. The doctor's not sure they're going to do any good, though. He says we just have to sit it out and keep steaming him.'

Toby croaked a laugh from the bed. 'It's ghastly, she keeps pointing the electric kettle at me and covering me in steam.'

'Poor Toby,' said Sal, hugging him, 'and poor Jenny too. Are you exhausted?'

'Just a wee bit — it's good to have you home.'

'I have lots to tell you,' Sal said, 'but I'd better ring into the office first.'

'Things are hotting up in East Germany,' David said,

when Sal rang into the office. 'I'd like you out there in the next few days – say by the weekend, at any rate.'

'David, I can't. I've only just got back from Yugoslavia.'

'That was holiday and this is work. There's talk of the Wall coming down.'

'Oh, come on,' said Sal. 'Pigs might fly.'

'Something is going to happen. Haven't you been reading the papers, Sal?'

'No, I haven't. I've been chasing relations, and trying to come to terms with what I've learnt.'

'Any luck?' Sal told him briefly of her discoveries. 'I'm sorry this is such a difficult time for you,' said David, 'but duty calls. Spend a couple of days with Toby, and then I want you out there. You should have taken him to Yugoslavia, like I suggested, and then he wouldn't have caught that dreadful bug.'

Having settled Toby for the night, Sal found Jenny cleaning up in the kitchen. They shared so much – their daily lives, the loving and caring for Toby. That Jenny loved Toby was without question; it was not simply a job. Sal knew the time had come to offer Jenny an explanation for her absence and surprisingly, as she poured two glasses of wine and invited Jenny to sit at the kitchen table with her, she found she was glad of the opportunity to unburden her thoughts. It was a role that normally would have been fulfilled by Evelyn – the thought made her sick to the stomach.

'Jenny,' she began, 'you know I told you I was going out to Yugoslavia to do some research?' Jenny sipped her wine and nodded. 'It was true, but not the whole truth.' As quickly and dispassionately as possible she told Jenny the whole story, from her mother's deathbed revelation to the discovery of the safety deposit box.

When she finished Jenny put out her hand and patted her awkwardly on the arm. She was not one for physical demonstration. 'You poor wee thing, what a lot to cope with. No wonder you look so tired and pale. It must be a very strange feeling to learn that you're not who you thought you were.'

'That's it exactly,' said Sal, 'and of course I may not even be Salvena Kovic. My father – if he *was* a spy – may have used a false name, in which case heaven knows who I am!'

'Sal,' said Jenny gently, 'it is just a name. You are who you are. The person inside is the same. People change their names all the time – when they get married, when they get unmarried – it's not a big deal. Salvena Saunders, Salvena Kovic, what does it matter? You're you, you're Toby's mother, you're my very demanding boss, you're one of the best journalists in the country – bloody hard to live with at times and perfectly charming at others. All that stays the same. There's no need to fuss yourself about it.'

Jenny's down-to-earth approach was just what Sal needed to hear. Half-laughing, half-crying, she fetched the wine bottle from the fridge and topped up their glasses. 'Jenny, you're marvellous. What on earth would Toby and I do without you?'

'I do not know,' said Jenny cheerfully. 'Are you going to tell Toby?'

'Yes, I am.'

'I'm glad, he'll be pleased. Who knows, perhaps

your brother is impossibly good-looking and has an unhealthy fetish for small, dumpy Glaswegian women who won't see thirty again.'

'Well, if he has,' said Sal, 'he'll be a jolly sensible chap.'

Feeling a lot better, Sal was digging herself in for a quiet evening at home with a mountain of mail, when the phone rang. It was Louis. 'I hear you're back in England, Sal. I must see you.'

'How on earth did you find out?' Sal said, instantly feeling a sense of claustrophobia.

'I've been ringing into the paper every day.'

'Louis, are you all right?' His voice sounded ragged, almost hysterical.

'No, I'm not, I've missed you dreadfully. I need to see you, Sal, and we need to decide about our future.'

'We don't have a future,' Sal said wearily. 'Your future lies with Evelyn and your children, we've been through it a hundred times.'

'I'm sorry, I just can't accept that, not after what's happened to us. Please meet me, Sal.'

'I can't at the moment. Toby's ill, he has bronchitis.'

'By the end of the week, then – Friday, for dinner. I shall be in London. Can we meet at Julie's as usual? Please, Sal. You owe me this.'

'All right,' said Sal. 'I'll see you then.'

Toby made very slow progress over the next couple of days, but was much more cheerful in himself, Jenny assured Sal. Nonetheless, it seemed to be a vicious bug and by Friday morning Sal was sure she had caught it too. She woke to a headache, a sore throat and streaming eyes, and the thought of going off to East Germany appalled her. In normal circumstances she would not have hesitated to cancel her dinner with Louis, but she was desperate now to end their relationship before Evelyn found out. She had not been in touch with her since her return from Yugoslavia, when once Evelyn would have been the first person she would contact. Evelyn had to be wondering what had happened to their friendship and worse still, why. It was vital, she knew, to act quickly.

Louis' appearance frightened her. He had lost more weight just in the fortnight they had been apart. There was a haunted look about him. He was restless, agitated and did not seem able to stay on the same subject for more than a moment. It was a shock to realise just how much he had changed. Anxious to keep off the subject of their relationship initially, she started to tell him about the safety deposit box. He listened politely, but she could tell that he wasn't really interested.

'I've been given some leave,' he said. 'A month's paid holiday to think things through.'

'What things?' asked Sal, horrified. 'You don't mean you and me?'

'Oh no, I haven't mentioned us to my superiors. I still can't stop thinking about Gennadi, about the way he died and the fact that no one knows about it. It's so wrong. Are you sure no one would publish his story, Sal? Perhaps we could try again. After all these months, the powers that be might not feel so strongly.'

'No, Louis. Look, we've been through all this. I

know how difficult it was for you because you were the one who was with him, but you have to move on from things, you can't just dwell on them. Gennadi is dead and in a better place where no one can hurt him now.'

The banal words fell on stony ground. 'Do you know what I'd really like to do?' said Louis. Sal shook her head.

'I'd like to give up my job, give up my family, my home and my mortgage. I'd like to go off with you somewhere, a croft in Scotland, a cottage in the Scilly Isles . . . I don't know, somewhere like that. I'd like to grow things, till the soil and stop thinking, stop questioning, find some peace.'

'That's all very admirable,' said Sal gently, 'but the woman you should be doing it with is Evelyn, not me. By all means, give up your career, give up your home, Evelyn wouldn't care as long as she was with you and the children. Why not do something mad and start a new life? It's probably what you both need, but count me out of it.'

'I can't count you out of it,' said Louis desperately. 'You're the major part of it now, a part of me. Sal, I told Evelyn I was at a conference tonight and wouldn't be back until the morning. Can I stay at your place?'

'No, of course you can't,' said Sal. 'What if Toby or Jenny saw you?'

'I could just come in for coffee, and if Jenny is in bed I could stay a few hours. I'll leave in the morning long before anyone wakes up . . . please. I can't go home, not after I've said I was at a conference.'

'You could stay in a hotel,' said Sal. Her mind was confused. She knew she had to end things — if only she didn't feel so ill.

'Please, Sal, I have to be with you,' he begged.

Her head was aching and she could not eat the meal being placed in front of her. Her chest felt constricted and she was suddenly desperately cold. She could not argue, she hadn't the strength. She just agreed that he could come back home with her.

Jenny spotted the problem the moment they walked through the front door. 'Sal, have you got Toby's bug?'

'I think I must have,' said Sal.

Louis looked at her, surprised. 'Aren't you feeling well?'

'No, I'm not really.'

'It was kind of you to see her home, Mr Noble,' said Jenny. 'I'd better get her up to bed. Help yourself to a coffee or something, I'm sure you know where it all is.'

Sal could have kissed her. Like a child she was led away up to the safety of her bedroom. Jenny sat her on the bed and produced a thermometer. 'Let's take your temperature, Lassie,' she said. Sal sat obediently with the thermometer in her mouth. Now she came to think about it, she really did feel terrible.

'A hundred and four,' said Jenny. 'No wonder. Which are you at the moment, hot or cold?'

'Both — first one and then the other.'

'Snuggle down into bed and I'll get you a hot drink.'

'How's Toby?'

'He's fine, he's sleeping. He had a bit of a coughing fit earlier, but he's fine. You're our number one worry now.'

'Jenny, you're magic. I don't say it often enough, do I?' Sal looked at her and smiled.

'No, you don't,' said Jenny. 'Not nearly often enough. The trouble is, I suspect, that you're being so kind to me because you're delirious.'

Sal stuck out her tongue. 'Oh Jenny, one more favour. Can you get rid of Louis?'

'No problem, but don't you want him to come up and say goodbye?'

'Absolutely not. He's been in a bit of a state ever since our do in Moscow. I just can't cope with him tonight, Jenny.'

'Leave it to me — he'll be out of the door in ten minutes if he's got himself a coffee — five if he hasn't.'

'God bless you,' said Sal, sinking back on to the pillow.

Things became very confused. There were dreams, dreams of her father shouting at her mother, with the shadowy figure of her brother always just out of reach. Then the body of Gennadi in the cellar and Louis, dead too. She was aware vaguely of Jenny and of Toby, looking white-faced, of her trying to ask how he was, but it proving too difficult. There was a tightening band around her chest, a doctor, and then amazingly a group of people inserting drips into her arm and telling her she was going to be all right . . . an ambulance, then hospital, then oblivion.

She was alone when she woke up. She had no idea where she was, which heightened the sense of disorientation which had been growing over recent days, even before her illness. It did not greatly worry her. She lay, gazing up at the ceiling. There was no window, it was a cubicle, rather than a room. It was too hot and the smell was unmistakable. A hospital – normally she hated all institutions, but strangely now she felt oddly calm and relaxed. She lay and waited and after a while a nurse arrived.

'Well done, Mrs Saunders,' she said. 'Glad to see you're back with us. You gave us all a nasty fright.'

'What's happened to me?' Sal asked.

'Pneumonia, that and an attack of asthma.'

'I haven't had asthma since I was a child.' Sal found it difficult to speak; breathing was intensely painful.

'I expect the pneumonia brought it on. We're lucky to have you, you know. If the ambulance who came to fetch you hadn't been armed with an experienced paramedic, we would have lost you for sure. Anyway, you're all right now and your son and housekeeper are out there fretting. Would you see them just for a few minutes, or don't you feel up to it yet?'

'No, of course I'd like to see them,' said Sal.

Toby and Jenny were soon ushered in. Toby still looked very pale. 'Mum!' He ran forward and put his head on her chest, carefully avoiding the drips.

'It's OK Toby, I'm fine now.' Sal managed to put an arm around him.

'You gave us a real scare,' said Jenny. 'Especially this boy. How long had you been feeling ill?'

'Not long – a day or two,' said Sal. 'I suppose I was just worn out, what with one thing and another.'

'Well, you've got to start taking more care of yourself, or we're going to insist on it, aren't we, Tobe?'

Toby sat down on the chair beside his mother. 'It's all my fault,' he said mournfully. 'It was my horrid bug you got.'

'Of course it wasn't your fault. I've been tearing around too much lately, Toby. We're going to have a more ordered life from now on, I promise you.'

'We certainly are,' said Jenny. 'No one is going to let you do anything for weeks, judging by how your doctor has been muttering.'

They went after a while and, exhausted, Sal fell into an uneasy sleep. When she woke again, to her horror Evelyn was sitting by her bed.

'I just heard about you, and came straight here,' she said. 'How are you feeling?'

'A bit groggy,' said Sal.

'You are a silly idiot. How did you get yourself in this state?'

Sal shrugged her shoulders.

'As soon as you're ready to leave hospital, you must come down to Hawkhead and stay with Louis and me. Bring Toby, of course – and Jenny too, if you like.'

'No,' Sal said, too quickly.

'Why ever not?'

'Because . . . because I need to be in my own home, because I've missed so much work already and I have to be near the paper. Thank you, Evelyn, I'd love to come when I'm stronger, but I must go home when I'm discharged.'

'Well, I'm going to be fierce and insist you come to me.'

'Please, Evelyn,' Sal said. She was close to desperation.

Evelyn stared at her strangely. 'Have I done something to upset you?'

'No, of course you haven't,' said Sal.

'It's just that you seem to have been avoiding me over the last few months. You haven't been down to see us since before . . .' Sal could see her searching her mind '. . . since before your trip to Moscow. I keep wondering why it is. Louis wasn't too awful to you, was he, when he discovered you'd decided to cover his trip?'

'No, no,' said Sal, 'of course he wasn't. He was obviously angry to start with, but in the end everything was fine.'

'And you know how we both feel about it, Sal. I was angry, too, at the time – of course I was, because I felt you'd betrayed my trust, but then I thought about it, and after all it is your job. As things turned out, thank heavens you did go. I've said it to you before: Louis owes his life to you, so how can there be any hard feelings on our side? I just want to put all that behind us and get back to normal. The kids and I are really missing you and Toby.'

'And we're missing you.' Sal realised as she spoke that it was no less than the truth.

'Then come and stay, as soon as you leave hospital.'

'No,' said Sal. 'Not at the moment. I will come, and bring Toby for a weekend really soon, but it's just not practical now, what with school and everything.' Her voice tailed off.

'Oh Sal, I wish you'd come.' To her horror Evelyn began to cry.

'What's wrong?' Sal asked, reaching out a hand and taking Evelyn's.

'I'm sorry. I don't want to burden you with my problem when you're so ill. Forget it — I'll go.'

'No,' said Sal. 'Tell me, what is it?'

'It's Louis. Ever since he got back from Moscow . . . I know it was a terrible experience, but he's just so awful. He shouts at the children, he shouts at me, it's honestly become a relief when he's not in the house. He's just not like himself at all.'

Sal closed her eyes, as if to ward off this new piece of information. She knew she just could not cope.

'I'm sorry, Sal,' said Evelyn. 'It's not fair on you, you're so ill.'

Sal tried to rally. 'It was a difficult time for him, Evelyn. The barbaric killing of an old man is not a good thing to face at any time, but when you're an academic Christian, like Louis, it must be very difficult to rationalise.'

'He's not just an academic Christian,' Evelyn said. 'He's a very religious man.'

'I know that,' said Sal. 'His belief is both emotional and academic, and so I imagine he feels assailed on all sides by what he witnessed. He feels his faith has been betrayed by society's lack of interest, I suppose.'

'Is that what he's told you?' Evelyn said.

Sal thought carefully. 'No . . . no, it isn't. It's just what I expect has happened. Maybe he ought to have some sort of post-trauma counselling.'

'I've suggested that,' said Evelyn. 'He won't hear of it. He's hardly ever at home now, Sal. It's awful, I just don't know what he's up to and I don't know what to do to help him. You couldn't talk to him, could you?'

Sal took a deep breath. 'I could try,' she heard herself say.

She was still reeling from Evelyn's visit when Louis arrived.

'I saw Evelyn leave, so I knew it was safe to come up.'

'Louis, I can't handle any kind of conversation with you right now,' said Sal.

'It's all right. I just wanted to say I'm sorry for the other evening. There was me trundling on about my own problems and I had no idea you were so ill.'

'Nor me,' said Sal. 'Listen, you're making Evelyn very unhappy.'

'What's she said?' Louis asked defensively. 'I'm doing my best.'

'Can't you see that this is a hopeless situation,' Sal said. 'Here we are, you're both confiding in me and yet I'm the one who's causing all the trouble! We've got to end this, Louis. We've got to agree never to see each other again, except within the confines of a family gathering.'

'I can't do that, Sal. I'm sorry.'

'And I can't talk about it any more now,' said Sal. 'Somehow, though, you'll have to persuade Evelyn that I shouldn't come and stay with you when I come out of hospital. At the moment she's absolutely determined it's what should happen, and I have to say that in different circumstances it's just what I need. You'll have to talk her out of it, Louis.' She shut her eyes firmly and then opened them again to find him staring at her like a madman. She gathered her last remaining strength. 'I love you, Louis, but I also love Evelyn and I've loved Evelyn a very long time. Today I stared her unhappiness in the face. I saw what it meant to her to lose you, and I'm not prepared to be a party to it. If you decide your marriage is over, that's up to you, but never, never for one moment think that there is any chance of a life with me. My loyalty is to Evelyn – it has to be, it always will be – and there is nothing anyone can say or do that will change my mind, especially you.'

He stared at her in silence for a moment, and then turning, he shambled out of the room like an old man.

'You've had too many visitors,' the nurse said moments later.

'I agree,' said Sal.

'Right then,' she said. 'No more until tomorrow, unless it's your son.'

'Thanks,' said Sal weakly. 'You can make it no visitors except my son for a week if you like.'

'Oh, we'll have you out of here before then. Don't worry.'

The days dragged by. Sal was released from hospital and returned to a home full of flowers. There were solicitous cards, letters and phone calls. It was all too much. She felt so weak, unable to do anything, the least exertion leaving her helpless again.

Toby was wonderful. Somehow his mother's illness had brought out the best in him.

Sal used the unusual amount of time she had with Toby to talk through very carefully the details of their origins. She told him about his grandmother's final exposé, and of her search in Yugoslavia. 'I'm sorry I didn't tell you before I went, Toby, but I didn't want to stir you up and then find that the whole thing wasn't true.'

'I understand, it's OK,' he said and he did. He was growing up.

Toby's understanding was the highspot – everything else in Sal's life was a shambles, particularly her career. For the day she had been admitted to hospital, the Berlin Wall had come down. David had been so busy covering the story with less experienced reporters than Sal, that it was nearly two weeks after the collapse of Communism in Eastern Europe had begun before he managed to get to see her. 'Stirring times,' he said, having deposited a kiss on her forehead, a bunch of grapes and a bottle of brandy on the table before her.

'I can't believe I'm missing this,' Sal said. 'I'm so desperately sorry, but it would be more than my life was worth to try and catch a flight, let alone cover a story. I think even passport control would be too much for me at the moment.'

'It's OK,' said David. 'I wouldn't have let you go. I have got it covered – not as well as if you were doing it, but well enough. And Peter's been out there, so I'm getting the pics. Everything's fine, truly.'

'It's not,' said Sal peevishly. 'I've spent all these years faithfully recording the story of these countries crushed by a regime, exploited and plundered, and now suddenly it's all at an end, and I'm not there to witness it. It's ghastly, David. It's like some sort of moral retribution.'

'Why, have you been doing something particularly bad?'

'No,' said Sal hastily. 'Well, no more than usual, I suppose.'

'The extraordinary thing is that it seems to be all happening without any real bloodshed,' said David. 'Right across Eastern Europe, Communism is collapsing and democracies are being established and there's not been a shot fired in anger.'

'The Ceauşescus won't give up without a struggle,' Sal said. 'Mark my words, there'll be trouble in Romania.'

'You think so? That's interesting. It's not what people seem to think. They see him as toady to Russia, with no real clout of his own.'

'Well, they're wrong,' said Sal. 'Nicolae Ceauşescu will not give up Romania – he will have to have it taken away from him.'

'If you're right, maybe you'll be well enough to cover it.'

'It's only another couple of weeks they reckon, before I'm fully operational,' said Sal.

David studied her for a moment. She was still startlingly good-looking, but there was an ethereal quality about her that had not been there before. She had lost a great deal of weight and was very pale, her skin almost translucent, and for the first time in his life the word 'vulnerable' came into his mind when thinking of Sal.

'You need cosseting,' he said tenderly. 'There hasn't been a man in your life for some time, has there? It's about time there was.'

'Mind your own business,' said Sal. For the first time since he'd arrived, the old Sal was back.

'I'm right though,' said David, 'and if there's no man in tow to cheer you up, I don't see why on earth you don't take yourself off to the country, to Evelyn and Louis'.'

'What I've decided instead,' said Sal, reacting entirely on the spur of the moment to deflect David, 'is to take ourselves off to our own place in the country this weekend.'

'To your mother's house?' said David. 'What a good idea.'

'Oh, and another thing. When's Peter back from Berlin?'

'He's back now.'

'I'll give him a ring,' she said. 'I must hear all about it first-hand.'

'He was furious that you weren't there,' said David. 'You're a good team, you two.'

'The best,' said Sal.

'You're getting better, before my very eyes.'

'Talking to you is making me feel better. I want to be back in harness as soon as possible.'

November was a busy month for Sal. There were so many stories coming out of Eastern Europe, but she kept her promise to Toby, and if she did go away, it was only for twenty-four hours at a time. She gained in strength daily. Still always at the back of her mind was the unfinished search for Georges, but it was something that would have to wait. There was a living to be earned, a son to support, and she and Toby were spending more and more weekends at the cottage. Luckily it never occurred to Toby to query why they went to Louis and Evelyn's less than before, and he certainly did not seem to mind. When they went to the cottage they tended to take a schoolfriend, and Toby seemed to revel in having a place of his own in the country. They turned her father's old study into a playroom. They redecorated and reorganised until Beehive Cottage began to feel like a home from home. It was somewhere that Jenny never came, and without discussing it, Sal felt sure that Toby felt as she did, that this was their private place. He loved Jenny dearly, but Jenny being around always meant that his mother was absent. In the cottage they were always together.

Louis continued to harass Sal with phone calls. She managed to avoid seeing him, but the phone calls persisted, and there were letters, too. Finally one day in the first week of December, Louis telephoned her at work.

'Sal, I've got to see you. I've made a decision – I'm leaving Evelyn and I'm going to have to tell her why.'

'Don't be ridiculous, Louis, there's nothing to tell her.'

'But there is. I know you won't have me, but I can't go on living a lie. I love you, not Evelyn.'

Clearly, Sal could avoid the issue no longer. She was busy at lunchtime and so they agreed to meet in the evening, at the Gay Hussar in Soho. The venue was convenient for Sal, but it was a convenience for which they would all pay dearly.

Louis still looked dreadful, but this time, at least, Sal was well and felt more able to cope. She listened to his great tirade of problems. She felt enormous sympathy for him, but there was no spark left in their relationship so far as she was concerned, and she now wondered how there could ever have been. He was back to being Louis, husband of her best friend.

Sal knew that only she could stop him leaving Evelyn, and in the end she won. After what seemed like hours of arguing, she said the one thing which they both knew was true.

'Louis, if you go ahead and tell Evelyn everything, don't you see what you're doing? It is an act of gross self-indulgence. You are finding the pain of deception unbearable: so what do you do? No longer deceive? That would be the moral and sensible thing to do. But instead, you are hellbent on a course of destruction – to destroy your marriage, your children's stability, your career – and for what? So that you can share your pain around, dilute it so that those you love suffer with you. Is that the action of a Christian?'

'I'm not sure I am a Christian any more,' said Louis.

'So, because you saw one man shoot another, because you suddenly rediscovered sex, all moral principles are no longer relevant. Is that what you're saying?'

'No, of course not.'

'Louis, you say you love me. If you leave Evelyn, not only can you never come to me, but quite honestly I will despise you. Love walks hand in hand with respect. How can I respect a man with no moral courage? If you leave Evelyn, we will never meet again.'

'All right, I'll stay, and I'll try and make our marriage work if that's what you want, but please don't walk out of our lives. I couldn't bear not to see you. Can you come for Christmas like you usually do? I will be sensible, behave normally, I promise.'

'We're going down to our cottage in Oxfordshire for Christmas,' said Sal. 'But perhaps in the New Year.'

'I'll have to settle for that then, won't I?' He smiled endearingly, and just for a moment Sal felt her heart lurch. Peter had been right, he was not for her, even if he had been free, but he was very special in his way.

'I sound very hard, don't I?' Sal said suddenly. 'I do love you, Louis, always believe that. The thing we had, if we'd been single, free . . . it might have been something that would have lasted a lifetime. As it is, we've already made each other very unhappy and what we have to do now is to go for limited damage. We've suffered, but then we've deserved to suffer. Evelyn must not.'

'I know you're right,' Louis said gently. There were tears in their eyes. 'You're a good woman, Sal.' He laughed, the first genuine flash of humour she'd seen from him in months. 'I used to disapprove of you, you know. I thought your lifestyle was not a good influence on Evelyn — too many affairs, that sort of thing. God, what a stuffed-shirt I must have been!'

'And now?' said Sal, joining in the sudden lightening of mood with both joy and relief. 'And now?'

'As you said, we've made ourselves very unhappy, but we also made ourselves very happy too. I shall hold on to the crumb you've given me, that you did love me as something more than just your best friend's husband. The time we spent together — and I'm not just thinking about the sex — was wonderful. I've been an idiot. Instead of carping on about wanting more, I should have been grateful for what I've had. I love you too, Sal, I always will, and we'll manage it, you and I. I'm not saying I'll find it easy and we'll both find it strange to start with, but we can get back to where we were.'

'We can do it if it's what we both want to do,' Sal said.

'I know.' There was a silence between them. 'I've been so self-obsessed,' said Louis. 'I've never really taken on board the problems you've had to cope with in recent months. You must be going through something of an identity crisis at the moment with this story of your mother's. I don't know if it's any comfort or not, but please Sal, never feel alone, never feel lonely again. There will always be a part of me which will belong to you, but I promise I won't let it affect my relationship with my wife or my children. Still, if ever you need me . . .'

Instinctively Sal leaned forward and kissed him gently on the lips. Louis responded, but it was a gentle goodbye kiss, and they both understood it as such.

CHAPTER TEN

The nightmare began at precisely seven o'clock the following morning. Sal was in the shower, Jenny was getting breakfast and Toby was refusing to get out of bed. It was in all respects a standard morning, until Jenny arrived outside the bathroom door and said, 'Sal, you'd better come and have a look at these.'

There was no premonition, no feeling of doom. She breezed out of the bathroom to find Jenny carefully laying out newspapers on her bed. She took all the major dailies – it was her trade – but on that morning she would have given anything not to have done. She and Louis had made the front page with their final goodbye kiss in the *Sun*, and there was also reference to them on the front page of two other tabloids. Jenny was busy leafing through the others. They had worked together like this a hundred times, chasing a story, seeing what other papers had said about a subject, but never before had the subject been herself.

Sal reached for the *Daily Record*. On page four she had written a high-profile article on the problems facing Romania, after interviewing a number of Romanian refugees. That was the only mention of her in the paper. David would clearly have known of the story but mercifully vetoed it.

'Practice What You Preach', screamed one headline; 'Senior Lambeth Palace Envoy Enjoys A Night Out' ran another. Sal's practised eye skimmed down the column. It was all there, their trip to Moscow — not the details, of course, no one knew of those — but the alleged affair that had taken place ever since, even the fact that she and Evelyn had been at school together and that Evelyn was godmother to Toby. Toby in the gutter press — Sal flinched at the mention of his name: 'Toby, Salvena's son by an unknown father'. It made her sound like a whore.

'Is it true?' Jenny asked. 'I'm sorry to ask you Sal, but Toby's going to have to cope with this at school. I need to know on what basis I'm working.'

'It's sort of true,' Sal said. 'We did have a very brief fling in Moscow, but it's over.'

'It doesn't look like it from this photograph.'

'It's such a nightmare! Truly, Jenny, that was a farewell kiss. It's over. We'd planned to get the families together for the New Year. It was a stupid thing, Jenny, it should never have happened.'

'No, it shouldn't,' said Jenny evenly.

'Please,' Sal said, close to tears. 'Don't judge too harshly. The danger we were in – everything conspired . . .'

'I know, sorry. I'm just wondering how Toby's going to deal with this.'

Sal thought rapidly. 'I don't think we need go into it today. It's unlikely that most people will have read the papers before school. I'll start making some phone calls and try to get it stopped.'

'OK, we won't say anything to him at the moment if you're sure,' said Jenny. 'I just hope you're right.'

For once, Sal was not even thinking of Toby and how his schoolfriends would react. She shut the bedroom door on Jenny and as she began mechanically to dress, her mind was full of thoughts of Evelyn. The previous evening she had pleaded with Louis not to tell his wife what had happened, but that would have been infinitely preferable to Evelyn reading of her husband's infidelity in the press. For a moment she considered ringing Evelyn, but what could she say? She could not reassure her because everything the papers said was true. To apologise was pointless – it was so hopelessly inadequate. In fact, she had never felt so inadequate in her life before. She was out of control and she just did not know which way to turn.

Toby had barely left for school before the phone went. It was David, of course.

'What the bloody hell is going on, Sal?'

'I'm sorry. Can we stop the story?'

'I very much doubt it. When journalists turn on their own, for some reason they're usually particularly vicious. Is there anyone outside your house yet?'

'No, not yet.'

'There will be. You'd better come in here quickly. They're already waiting for you outside. Are you going to deny it?'

'I can't.'

'You could, if you've no witnesses. I suggest you get hold of Louis and work out a story – but leave home now. I don't want you holed up in your house with the paparazzi all round you, until we've spoken. I'll try and track down Louis for you.' His voice was cold. He was not being her friend, he was her boss whose only concern was to minimise the damage to his paper.

She did not argue. She told Jenny she would be in touch, and asked her not to answer the door or say a word over the telephone to journalists.

They were waiting outside the *Daily Record* offices; even TV crew were there in force. When they fired questions at her, she smiled and kept walking. She felt like a hunted animal.

In David's office, he poured her a mug of coffee and handed it to her. 'Bad news, I'm afraid. Your friend Louis Noble isn't going to deny it.'

'He must! let me speak to him, David. The only person who could possibly have any proof of an affair is Peter, and I know he won't say anything.'

'No, he won't. In fact he's already been on the phone

to ask if there's anything he can do to help. You may talk to Louis by all means, but I can assure you he won't budge.'

'Why?' asked Sal.

'He says he can't add lying to his list of sins. Something along those lines. He was very pompous, Sal. What on earth do you see in him?'

Sal ignored him. 'Did he say how Evelyn was?'

'Didn't mention her — too busy being a martyr. Answer the question, Sal: why the bloody hell did you do it?'

'I keep asking myself that. I can honestly say, David, with my hand on my heart, that before I went to Moscow on that trip, Louis was no more an object of desire in my life than Father Christmas. It was something to do with finding him in that cellar — the danger we were all in, the relief at getting him safely back to the hotel. We have . . . well, seen each other since but finally — and here's the irony of the whole thing — last night I persuaded him that we'd have to part company, and he agreed.'

'Why on earth go to such a high-profile restaurant? It's ridiculous!'

'I didn't think,' said Sal quietly.

'You're an idiot, my girl. You know it's a Mecca for gossip columnists.'

'I know. I suppose as far as I was concerned, the affair was over and because it was over, I didn't see the danger.'

'How can you be so naïve, after all your years in this game?'

'I don't know. I'm sorry,' she said hopelessly. 'Is there anything we can do to lessen the impact?'

'Nothing. I've rung round fellow editors, they're all apologetic, but they reckon this one will run and run. The only thing you can do is to get the hell out of it. I'm sending you to Romania tomorrow. I want you to stay until the revolution breaks. You were right, it's going to be any day now.'

'But what about Toby? I can't leave him to cope with all this on his own, and I'll have to be back for Christmas!'

'You'll be back when the revolution has broken.' He was implacable.

'At least give me another twenty-four hours, David. I don't know what sort of flak he's going to get at school.'

'With all due respect, Sal, you should have thought that out before you embarked on this thing. You may think I'm being very hard, but you've been such a fool. All these years we've painstakingly built up your credibility as a serious political journalist and it's not been easy. Young women – particularly good-looking young women – are usually relegated to family matters or the beauty page. You had it in you to be a good journalist, I knew it, and so between us we've capitalised on your skills to the point where you have a reputation second only to Kate Adie. And then you blow it, appearing suddenly no better than a cheap floozy.'

'I haven't blown it,' said Sal angrily. 'I had an affair, that's all. People do it all the time!'

'An affair with a married man is not good. An affair with a married man, who happens to be a senior ranking churchman, is worse. An affair with a married man who is a senior ranking churchman who also happens to be the husband of your best friend, stinks. People aren't going to like you for this, Sal. If they don't like you, they won't want to read what you have to say and they won't respect your opinions. I want you out of the country – I want you out so fast, it's not true. The fact that I'm giving you until tomorrow even is only out of consideration for Toby. If I had any sense, I'd send you to Bucharest today. Now go home and pack, pick up Toby from school and book yourselves into a hotel for the night. The flight to Bucharest goes tomorrow just before midday, Terminal Two, Heathrow. I've already booked your ticket and you'd better be on that flight if you want a job.'

'David, why are you being like this?'

'Because I cannot believe how you've let yourself down. I'm shocked, hurt and disappointed in you.'

Sal was fighting tears. 'I just can't bear you being like this. David, please try to understand. I've been very lonely recently and ever since my mother died I've been feeling odd, not at one with myself. It's very hard to explain.' Tears were rolling down her face. 'I suppose I felt comfortable with Louis because he was such an old friend. I know there's no excuse for how I behaved – God knows, I'm aware of that. Please don't be too harsh on me, it's the final straw.'

'I just don't want to hear any more of this,' said David quietly. 'If you're feeling sorry for anyone right now, it should be Evelyn.'

'Well, of course that's who I'm feeling sorry for,' exploded Sal. 'She was the first person in my thoughts the moment this broke, but you're not making things any easier.'

'Who said they need to be easy?'

'You're always saying you're my friend as well as my boss, that you'll always be there for me and Toby. Well, here's an occasion when we really need you.'

'And I'm acting in your best interests,' David said. 'Now get the hell out of my sight before I lose my temper.'

Sal fled from the office. Unable to face the newsroom, she left by the back entrance of the building. She was in luck; there was no one in sight. She took a taxi home, ran the gauntlet of journalists outside her front door and forced her way in.

Jenny was grim-faced in the kitchen. 'I never was too keen on your profession – even less so, now. They ring the doorbell, they bang on the windows. They knew you weren't here, but I guess they want access so they can photograph your bed or your knickers, or something. It's hell!'

'We're leaving,' said Sal. 'I'm off to collect Toby from school.'

'That's the other thing,' said Jenny. 'The school has been on the telephone. The Headmistress wants to see you. Toby's already getting some flak.'

'Oh God, and I've got to go to Bucharest tomorrow.'

Jenny was making coffee. She slammed the coffee mug down on the table, spilling it everywhere. 'There's no way you can go abroad now. You can't possibly leave him with all this going on.'

'I either go to Bucharest, or I have no job. David has made that absolutely clear.'

'He can't do that. David's so fond of Toby.'

'I tried, Jenny, but he insists. He wants me out of the way.'

'Can't you take Toby with you?'

'Don't be daft. There's about to be a revolution there.'

'Oh, great – that's all he needs. His mother's being called a tart all over the national press, and then she flies off, not only leaving him to face the music alone, but heading straight into a war.'

'I'm sorry, Jenny. I just don't know what else to do.' Tears began to flow down Sal's cheeks again. 'I can't afford to lose my job. I'm not going to get another now, am I? Then bang goes your job, bang goes this house, bang goes Toby's whole life. I haven't had a decent story for months. I missed the Wall through being ill. Even without the scandal, I need to land some good copy or I'm going to be out on my ear anyway.'

'I know,' said Jenny comfortingly. 'It's just that it's always the same: Toby's the one who suffers. When he broke his arm, when he fell out with his best friend, when he had chicken pox, when his grandmother died . . . *you weren't there*.'

'But you were, Jenny.' Sal looked at her through her tears. 'And you will be, won't you?'

'Oh yes,' sighed Jenny. 'I'll be here – God help me. Come on then, let's pack some things. How long should Toby and I stay in the hotel?'

'Three or four days should do it. They'll have a new victim by the weekend,' said Sal.

Miss Jane Wheatley was an excellent headmistress – no one could deny that. She had dedicated her life to her children. It was a big job, running a prep and pre-prep school which sent its pupils on to Eton, Cheltenham, Radley and Benenden – every major public school. She maintained high standards for herself and for her pupils, and expected nothing less from their parents.

'Frankly, Miss Saunders, I could have done with a little notice of this scandal,' she said, sitting ramrod straight behind her desk.

Sal felt four and a half, rising five – certainly no older. 'So could I, Miss Wheatley.'

'This sort of thing is not good for the school.'

'The school, as I recall, has not been mentioned.' Sal tried to sound firm.

'No, but Toby has and, of course, a number of the pupils have picked it up. He's had a very hard time this morning, poor fellow.'

'For that I'm deeply sorry,' said Sal.

'I take it – and please don't answer this if you wish not to – but I take it the rumour has some foundation? I only ask, because I know that Toby has a very close relationship with the Nobles.'

'The rumour has foundation,' said Sal.

'Yes, well . . .' Miss Wheatley cleared her throat. 'The thing is to minimise the impact so far as your son is concerned. Do you expect there to be more in the papers tomorrow morning?'

'I suspect so,' said Sal. 'My paper is sending me abroad; they feel it would be best to get me out of the country.'

'Leaving Toby to cope with it on his own?'

'Not on his own,' said Sal patiently. 'Jenny will be there.'

'Ah yes, the paid help.'

Sal bit her lip to avoid rising to the bait. 'I've booked them into White's Hotel. They've gone in under Jenny's name, so there's absolutely no way the press will ever find them there. I've suggested to Jenny that they stay there until the weekend, and David Thorson, my editor, will run a story tomorrow saying that I've gone to Bucharest. That should take the heat off things.'

'For you, yes, but presumably not for the Nobles.'

Sal flinched at this. 'I was going to pick Toby up now, if that's all right,' she said quietly.

'Yes, that might be best. In fact, if you're taking Toby out of school, I think I may have a word with his fellow pupils, tell them you're going away and explain how difficult it is for Toby. Why are you going to Bucharest?'

'There's about to be a revolution,' said Sal.

'Good.'

Sal stared at Miss Wheatley. 'What do you mean?'

Miss Wheatley smiled, a wintry smile, but a genuine one. 'I can turn you into something of a heroine in their eyes – going into battle, that sort of thing.'

'You're wonderful,' said Sal.

'I don't condone what you've done, Miss Saunders, but my job is to protect Toby and I will do so in your absence – you can be sure of that.'

Sal felt unexpected tears come into her eyes. She stood up quickly. 'Thank you – thank you very much.' She walked to the door. 'Oh, and Miss Saunders.'

'Yes?'

'I know this can't be easy for you. Take care of yourself.'

Toby did not acknowledge his mother when he came out of the form. He simply scooped up his satchel and his blazer and followed her out of the school. She had expected nothing less. Jenny was at the hotel, already unpacking. She loaded Toby into the car and drove to the Serpentine. It was a cold, crisp day, but the sun was shining. It looked beautiful.

'Where do I start?' she said.

'I don't want to know anything about it,' Toby said, 'except to ask one question.'

'Go ahead,' said Sal.

'Is it true?'

'Yes,' said Sal, 'but it's over. That photograph – I don't know if you saw it?'

'Oh yes, I saw it,' said Toby.

'That was Louis and me saying goodbye.'

'A funny sort of goodbye.'

'Toby, I know it was wrong, but I never really told you about Moscow. Peter, you know, the photographer Peter, he and I found Louis in a cellar with a murdered man. The Mafia were coming back to kill him — Louis, that is. It was very dangerous. We were all frightened to death and it brought Louis and me closer together.'

'I don't want to hear about it. You know what you're being called at school? A prostitute, a slag — my mother!'

'I know, but it will stop now. Miss Wheatley is going to talk to them.'

'Will the papers stop?'

'No, not immediately. They'll probably carry the story for another couple of days and then there will be somebody else to persecute.'

'And what about Evelyn and Louis? What's going to happen to them? Are they going to get divorced? What's going to happen to the children?'

'I hope they won't get divorced, Toby, but that, of course, is up to them.'

'But if they do, it'll be your fault. You'll have broken up their family.'

'Yes, I suppose so.'

'I hate you for this.' He began to cry. Sal went to put an arm around him, but he shrugged her off. 'I've never known what it's like to have a proper family,' Toby said between sobs, 'but at least Louis and Evelyn showed me how a family could be — they made me feel a part of theirs when you were away. And now that's all over. You've ruined it for them, and you've ruined it for me. I wondered why we kept going to the cottage instead of to the Nobles'.'

'But you like Granny's cottage.'

'Yes, I do, but I like being part of the family more — and now I'll never be able to go to Hawkhead Farm again. Will I? *Will I?*'

'I don't know,' said Sal, 'but I suppose probably not.'

'Sometimes I hate you,' choked Toby.

'Sometimes you're right to,' said Sal, and began to cry too. After a while, she drove back to the hotel, carefully — aware that she was in no fit state to be driving at all. Toby sat slumped beside her.

'David's sending me to Bucharest tomorrow,' she said.

'Where's Bucharest?'

'Romania.'

'Where's Romania?'

'Eastern Europe, sort of near Yugoslavia and Hungary — south of Russia.'

'So you're leaving just like that.'

'David didn't give me any choice.'

'I don't believe that. David's always on my side.'

'I think he is on this occasion too,' said Sal. 'He knows that the best way to stop the story is for me to be out of the country. We're going to stay at White's Hotel for a while. You'll like it, it's nice. Jenny's already there. You and she are going to stay there for a few days until the fuss dies down, and I'll be back as soon as I can.'

'Will you be back for Christmas?'

'That's five days away. I'd have thought so.'

'It doesn't matter anyway. We won't be spending Christmas with the Nobles, so it won't make much difference whether you're there or not.'

CHAPTER ELEVEN

T he *Daily Record* was not ungenerous with its
expense allowances. Normally when travelling
to Eastern Europe Sal flew with British Airways via
Frankfurt. However, today, because of the unholy
rush to get her out of the country, she was flying
with Romanian Airways, Tarom.

Romania was the only major country in Eastern
Europe which Sal had not visited. She had tried to enter
the country a few years previously, but her visa had
been refused. Nicolae Ceauşescu, Romania's despot
dictator, did not like potentially unfriendly journalists
reporting on his antics, and more especially, talking
to his people. This time, however, there appeared to
be no problem and David had said she would find
a number of familiar faces at the Intercontinental in
Bucharest, all come to view the possible takeover.
In normal circumstances Sal would have found this

comforting, but now the prospect of facing fellow journalists embarrassed her.

She was sitting gloomily in the departure lounge at Heathrow, desperate about leaving Toby, desperate about what the scandal was doing to Evelyn, and trying to avoid the bookstall for fear of glimpsing another incriminating headline, when a familiar figure came striding towards her.

'Peter!' She jumped up, ran to him and threw her arms round his neck.

'My goodness, I don't usually get this much of a welcome!'

'I'm so pleased to see you. David said that you couldn't come.'

'He was playing safe in case he couldn't find a replacement. I was on a job up North, studying miners' unrest, but he found another photographer to handle it and . . . here I am. Not that I'm really equipped to be in the company of such a notorious woman.' He looked at her, grinning.

'Oh shut up,' she said. 'It's been a ghastly couple of days.'

'I'm sure it has.'

'I've been trying to steel myself to see how they've handled the story today, but I can't face it.'

'Would you like me to go and take a look?'

'Yes,' said Sal. 'But don't bring me any of the papers, will you. I don't want to read about it.'

'No, of course not.'

'But don't lie either.'

'I won't,' he promised solemnly. He was back a few

moments later. 'Don't worry, you're not front page. It seems that you and your love life are simply *not* that interesting.'

'Was there much inside the papers?'

'I didn't look, and I'm not going to. The point is, if you're not front page today, you're on the way out. You know that as well as I do. Come on, Sal, I'm going to buy you a coffee, a croissant and a large brandy – it's the last decent meal we're going to get, so I'm told.'

There were only five people including themselves on the Tarom flight to Bucharest that day. As Sal knew, Romanians were rarely allowed out of their own country and so there were none of them on the flight. The other passengers were two French journalists and a shady-looking American, who described himself as a businessman. The plane seemed, quite literally, to be falling to bits. The seats were all sorts of different colours and styles, put in higgledy-piggledy down the aisle. Lunch, served by a sullen young woman, consisted of a stale roll and a piece of extremely suspect salami, and soapy cheese curling up at the corners. This was accompanied by warm red wine, which was surprisingly good. The American glanced across at Peter and Sal as they picked their way through the meal.

'This is your standard fare from now on,' he said. 'In fact, I'd go so far as to say this is the best Romanian meal you'll have.'

'Assuming the plane makes it,' said Peter.

'It's OK – it is a well-known fact that Romanian pilots are the best in the world.'

'Really?' said Sal.

'Oh yes.' The man let out a great guffaw of laughter. 'They have to be, to fly these heaps of rust!'

They talked little until they had nearly arrived at Bucharest. Sal was exhausted, but at last it was she who raised again the subject of Louis. 'David told me you had rung him to offer your help when the Louis story broke.'

Peter was characteristically self-effacing. 'It just occurred to me that if you decided to go the route of denying everything, I could at least corroborate the story. I imagine I was your only potential witness.'

'Yes,' said Sal. 'I would have done that like a shot, but Louis was hellbent on admitting everything. Still, maybe he was right. Evelyn wouldn't have believed us anyway.'

'Who's Evelyn?' Peter asked.

'Louis' wife, my best friend – my *former* best friend.'

'Oops, I'd forgotten about that,' said Peter. 'I still don't know what you saw in him, Sal, I really don't.'

'Well, right now, neither do I,' said Sal.

Peter smiled at her, squeezed her hand. 'I expect David gave you a hard time, did he?'

'Yes, very,' Sal admitted, 'and so did my housekeeper and Toby's headmistress, not to mention Toby himself. I know it's all my fault and I don't deserve any sympathy, but it's such a mess. All the people I thought were my friends, suddenly don't seem to be any more.'

'I'm still your friend,' said Peter, bending forward and kissing her forehead.

'Thank you, Peter.' Sal felt tears coming into her eyes.

'Oh no, don't start blubbing,' he ordered. 'If there's one thing I can't stand it's blubbing women. Knowing you, you could do it very prettily, but let's do without it, shall we?'

'Beast,' said Sal, smiling at him.

'That's better, that's the first smile I've seen since we met. Look, my advice for what it's worth is that everyone will forget about it very quickly. Not you, of course, you'll remember the hurt, but everyone else.'

'Except Evelyn,' Sal said haltingly. 'She's not going to get over it quickly. I wanted to ring her, but I didn't know what to say.'

'I think you're probably right not to,' said Peter. 'Not for a few days anyway. Let the dust settle, let her and Louis do some talking to decide what sort of future they have.'

'If their marriage breaks up, it will be all my fault. They have such lovely children and a lovely home – I don't know how I could have done it, Peter.'

'Look, it's done and you can't undo it. Put your heart and soul into this revolution as only you know how. When we get home will be time enough to face the music again, and with a bit of luck, everything will have blown over. One proviso, though. I'm putting you on a strict diet.'

'What do you mean?' Sal asked.

'No married men in Romania, right?'

'I agree,' said Sal.

*   *   *

It was snowing when they landed at Bucharest, and clearly had been for some time. They were ushered into the airport building which was grey and freezing. Soldiers, looking not much older than Toby, stood around, guns slung carelessly over their shoulders. One approached Sal and Peter, fingering his gun nervously. 'Cigarette, please.' Sal, who never travelled through Eastern Europe without a caseload of booty, hauled a packet of cigarettes out of her handbag and gave it to the boy, who was pathetically grateful. There was no trouble at Passport Control. Secretly Sal had been hoping that they would be turned away, so that she could go home to Toby.

In the building beyond Immigration it was again bitterly cold. The ancient baggage carousels stood still. Sal approached what appeared to be an airport official. 'Our baggage,' she asked. He shrugged. She tried German.

He answered in English. 'The machinery is frozen. We are bringing the baggage by hand. You must wait.'

It took nearly two hours, by which time Peter and Sal felt frozen solid. The strain of the last couple of days, the bitter cold and the uneasy feeling in the air around the airport heightened Sal's sense of apprehension. 'I can smell trouble,' she murmured.

'Me too,' said Peter. 'I keep fantasising about my flat – sitting in front of the fire with a good book and a glass of whisky.'

'Don't,' said Sal.

There was a lot of shouting and men began running

up and down the defunct rack, hauling suitcases. At last their luck had changed, for theirs were among the first few to appear. Outside the airport they headed for the first taxi.

'Intercontinental Hotel, please,' said Peter to the driver.

'I will try,' he said. 'There is a big rally in Parliament Square. It may be difficult to reach the hotel, but I shall drive via the back streets.'

'Your English is very good,' said Sal, settling into the back seat.

'I speak many languages – French, Italian, German. One day I will leave Romania. I will go to university and study modern languages.

'What's your name?' Sal asked.

'Andre.'

'Andre, would you like to help us in the next few days? We need a regular taxi driver who can show us Bucharest.'

'Are you journalists?'

'Yes.'

'OK. You pay in dollars?'

'Right,' said Peter. 'What shall we say, twenty-five dollars a day?'

'No, too much. Ten.'

Sal and Peter exchanged a look. A strange man indeed in an impoverished country, to turn down money.

The trip to Bucharest was hair-raising. Snow was packed tight on the road to a depth of perhaps seven or eight inches. There was sleet and wind, and the visibility was nil. Andre drove at top speed. If he had been forced to apply the brakes, they would have been across the road in seconds and, no doubt, straight into the path of one of the heavy lorries thundering along the opposite side.

'Do you think we were right in our choice of taxi driver?' Peter whispered to Sal.

'He has to be a good driver,' she hissed back, 'or he'd be dead, rather like the pilots.'

The rally was mercifully over by the time they arrived. After the dark drabness of the city streets, the Intercontinental shone like a beacon. It was warm, too. They checked in and were making their way across the foyer, when a large man erupted into their path.

'Sal! I thought it wouldn't be long before you appeared.' It was Ed James, an American journalist who, like Sal, specialised in Eastern Europe. They had met many times over the years in many extraordinary circumstances.

'Ed, how long have you been here?' They embraced.

Ed shook Peter's hand. 'A couple of days. Things are really hotting up – they've been shooting people in Timisoara, you know.'

'What's Timisoara?' Peter asked.

'It's where the protests to Ceauşescu's regime began,' Sal explained. 'A priest named Pastor Tokeş started it. They say he and his followers have been burning pictures of Ceauşescu, but there's been no real violence yet.'

'That, folks, was yesterday,' said Ed. 'The Securitate,

Ceaușescu's secret police, have been shooting children today.'

'Oh my God,' said Sal. 'Can we get out there?'

'I don't think we need to,' said Ed. 'The revolution's coming here, to Bucharest. I can feel it. There's a big rally tomorrow and I think that will be the beginning of the end. Sleep well tonight. I guess you'll have none tomorrow.'

The morning of 21 December 1989 dawned cold but bright. Sal dressed warmly. Years of coping with Eastern European winters had taught her never to underestimate their ferocity. On top of thermals she wore a shirt and a jersey, tights, thick trousers, woolly boots and a coat. To this she added a scarf and the obligatory fur hat. In the foyer of the Intercontinental she met Peter, similarly clad.

'Come on,' she said. 'We must hurry, or we'll miss the Old Cobbler. The rally starts in fifteen minutes.'

He frowned at her. 'Old Cobbler?'

'That's what they call Ceaușescu. It's what he started out as, you know – a humble cobbler. I don't think he's got the brains to be much more. It's his wife, Elena, who's the driving force.'

'It's always the same,' Peter lamented. 'Bloody bossy women.'

'That's right,' said Sal, with a grin. 'So get a move on. We'll have to walk, but it's not far.'

'I didn't realise that you'd been to Romania before,' Peter said.

'I haven't, but I did my homework overnight. You've heard of Ceauşescu's palace?'

'Dimly,' said Peter.

They went through the revolving doors of the hotel and the cold outside hit them with a tangible force.

'I've got a hip-flask,' said Peter, taking Sal's arm.

'Just as well,' she said.

They walked into Parliament Square and took the road towards the palace. Crowds were heading in the same direction.

'We should see the palace in a moment,' said Sal. Thousands of homes were destroyed to create it. It's monstrous, apparently.'

And so it was. An avenue of gleaming white buildings culminated in an enormous semicircle of stone: a huge building on one side, a slightly smaller one on the other.

'His and Hers palaces, I believe,' Sal said.

The crowds were all around them now. 'We're going to have to find somewhere I can get a decent picture,' Peter fretted. 'If we're not careful we're going to get hemmed in. I'd better start flashing my press pass about.'

'I don't think you should,' Sal warned him. 'With the threat of Timisoara, I shouldn't imagine the Securitate would be too keen on this particular rally being photographed, until they see how it goes. Look, they're everywhere.' And so they were. Grim-faced young men, batons in their hands, guns slung casually over their shoulders, eyes darting around.

Fighting the crowds, holding tight to one another

for fear of getting lost, they at last made it into Palace Square, which was full of people carrying banners, all the same, all depicting a youthful, smiling Ceauşescu. Everyone was looking up towards the balcony. Inching their way forwards, Peter and Sal got as close to the front as they could. There were microphones all around the Square: voices screamed from them, apparently chanting slogans.

'This is a very well-oiled propaganda machine, isn't it?' Peter said in her ear.

'They've had enough practice,' she replied drily.

Suddenly, above them, figures appeared on the balcony: a number of men, and just one woman. There were cheers and shouts as a small man, clearly Ceauşescu, moved forward to address them. He waved enthusiastically at the crowd, as did the woman beside him, but suddenly Sal realised that the shouting and cheering was only coming from the front of the crowd. The vast majority, indeed the people standing all around them, were silent. Peter was already hard at work, a telephoto lens trained on the balcony.

'What's he look like?' Sal asked, but Peter was too busy to reply.

The man began to speak. Sal had no idea what he was saying, but she fancied neither did anyone else: the microphone was distorting the sound. There was an eerie silence in the crowd now, a strange paralysing stillness. There was menace there, too – and suddenly, close to her, Sal heard the word 'Timisoara', half-whispered, half-spoken. Like wind through the trees, the sound gathered momentum. 'Timisoara,

Timisoara!' Ceauşescu faltered in his speech and then
carried on, trying to make himself heard above the
shouting and booing which now completely drowned
his voice.

'It's happening!' Sal said to Peter. 'And we're here.
The revolution – this is it, Peter! They'd never, never
have dared do this before.'

Now the cry had changed. '*Jos Ceauşescu*! *Jos
Ceauşescu*!' The old man continued with his waivering
speech, but now the crowd had turned on those
holding the banners and began tearing them down.
Peter paused. He stopped photographing the balcony
and was now concentrating on individuals, zooming
in on this one and that, catching expressions: of
rage, disbelief, uncertainty, terror . . . and slowly,
miraculously, hope.

'What if these guys start shooting? Do you think we'd
better get out of here?' he shouted to Sal.

Sal did not hear him. She was totally caught up in this
country and its sudden desperate bid for freedom.

'Isn't it wonderful, Peter?' She clutched his arm.
'This is history in the making. Look at them all. At
last they've had the courage to rise up and it's going
to work – I know it.'

The crowd began to move. From around the square
more people arrived, calling excitedly to one another.
Others started to head back towards Parliament Square.

'Come on, we need to dispatch this anyway,' said
Peter, 'and I want you out of here.' Half-dragging Sal,
and being carried along with the crowd, Peter began
walking in the general direction of the hotel. Suddenly

there was a rumble behind them. Armed personnel carriers were edging forwards from in front of the palace, driving the crowd away. People were trying to stop them, others falling in their path and being crushed.

'Come on!' bawled Peter. 'We're getting out of here – now!'

Parliament Square was also now crammed with people. Peter and Sal had to fight their way back to the hotel. Ed James was already struggling with the telephones in the foyer. 'I told you,' he shouted at Sal. 'They've done it! He'll never survive this, I'm sure of it.'

'I hope you're right,' said Sal. 'I just can't believe we saw it happen!'

For the next two days Peter and Sal toiled in the streets, faithfully recording what they saw. On the night of 22 December they witnessed a mother and her toddler being mown down by the high-velocity rifles of the Securitate guards. Peter photographed the dead bodies, which clung together in death as they had done in life. His picture appeared in newspapers across the world. It typified all the evil of Ceauşescu's rule. He had preyed on the innocent, destroyed and terrorised their lives and made them prisoners in their own country. He had plundered their wealth so that he could live in decadence while they tried to survive in abject poverty.

By Christmas Day it was all over. At eleven-thirty on Christmas morning, for the first time in nearly forty years, carols were being broadcast in Bucharest, and the trial of Nicolae Ceauşescu and his wife Elena had begun.

The trial was held in secret, but before it took place Sal had managed to bribe and bully her way into the palace. With their faithful taxi driver Andre acting as interpreter, they had been allowed two minutes with Elena. The dictator's wife was not sorry for what had happened. Her eyes were steely cold. Sal found this image of womanhood terrifying. Clearly she was mad. She had been charged with the death of sixty thousand people and the theft of a billion dollars. 'These are very serious accusations,' Sal suggested.

'You are foreign, you know nothing,' Elena replied. 'We have given our people everything. We have sacrificed our lives for the greater Romania. This is all a mistake, it will be over soon.' Even in her madness, Sal could see that she did not believe the words, but there was no fear, just absolute confidence that she was right.

Sal was not allowed near Ceauşescu himself but was hurried away. At that moment she could not know the enormity of the scoop she had achieved. For just over two hours later, Nicolae and Elena Ceauşescu were taken outside, put against a wall and shot dead by a three-man firing squad. Apparently there had been so many people volunteering to take part in the execution, that it had been necessary to draw lots. Sal had the last interview and Peter the last photographs of Elena Ceauşescu during her lifetime.

With their despatches made, they collapsed in the

hotel bar, drinking brandy. The atmosphere was extra-ordinary, the jubilation immense, but Bucharest was still a very dangerous place to be.

'They've decapitated the monster,' Sal said to Peter, 'but one feels that there's still life in the body that remains. I don't think they're going to destroy the Securitate that easily.' Peter agreed.

It had been an amazing day but that night Sal went to bed with a heavy heart. She had tried repeatedly to get a line through to England to wish Toby a Happy Christmas, but none had been available. She wanted to reassure him that she was safe. Some of the headlines in the papers would almost certainly frighten him. What if Toby thought she was in real danger? Images of Elena's dead-fish expression, the mother and child lying in the gutter, of Toby alone on Christmas Day, flashed through Sal's mind as she tried to sleep.

The following morning Bucharest was awash with stories. A torture chamber had been found in the palace. Nicu, Nicolae and Elena's son, had been arrested, along with his sister, Zoia-Elena. Nicu was professed to be a monster, who would tour Bucharest picking up pretty girls and taking them back to his house, where he had a rape room. He did not follow his parents into instant execution, but a trial would follow shortly.

Still the fighting continued: the Army versus the Securitate forces. During the day a Belgian TV reporter was killed and the news broadcast around the world. Desperately Sal tried to get through to Toby, but could get no reply from the house.

'Where are they?' Sal asked Peter desperately.

'Don't worry,' said Peter, 'they're bound to be staying with someone over the holiday.'

'I've got to speak to him. He'll think I've abandoned him.'

'I expect it's David who has sorted him out,' said Peter.

'I'm not sure of David any more.'

It was early in the morning of 27 December that the phone rang by Sal's bed. She picked it up to hear David's voice.

'David, thank God!'

'Sal, you've done one hell of a job. It's time to come home.'

'But there are so many stories here,' she objected.

'I know, but you've done your bit – more than your bit. I wouldn't be surprised if you don't get some award for that interview with Elena. I'm very proud of you.'

'Thank you, David.' Fleetingly Sal remembered their last meeting and dismissed it. 'Look, I'm desperate about Toby. I couldn't even speak to him on Christmas Day. The lines were all unobtainable.'

'Hang on a minute,' said David. A second or two later Toby's voice came on the phone.

'Toby, where are you?'

'I'm staying with David at the moment,' he said, sounding very grown-up. 'Me and Jenny both are. We had Christmas with him, it was great.'

'Oh, I'm so pleased, darling – and I'm so sorry I wasn't with you.'

'It's OK. David explained all about it. I understand.

He says you are very brave and that you're the best journalist in the world.'

'He said that? He must have been drunk,' giggled Sal tearfully.

'Oh, he was,' Toby admitted with the candour of childhood.

'Darling, David says it's all right for me to come home. The airport was still closed yesterday, but they think it might be open tomorrow. I'll get home just as soon as I can.'

'OK, Mum. See you.'

'Thank you, David,' said Sal, when he came back on the line. 'You're a true friend.'

'I try to be,' he said, 'though it isn't always easy. How are you coping with the aftermath of the problem we won't speak about now?' Clearly Toby was still in the room.

'OK,' said Sal, realising with a shock that not for one minute had she given a thought to Louis. Only Evelyn haunted her. She felt a tug of guilt, but nothing more – the events in Bucharest had completely overwhelmed her.

'I was just telling Toby,' she said, anxious to change the subject, 'that the airport was still closed yesterday, but I'll try and get a flight out tomorrow, if not the day after. Can Peter come home too?'

'Absolutely, you guys need a break. We'll send someone else out towards the end of the week.'

It was another cold day, bright but sunny. Taking a notebook and not sure what she was looking for, Sal left the hotel alone and started wandering through the streets. The tension was still there, but it was low-key now and there was a definite carnival feel in the air in strange contrast to the buildings, pockmarked by bullets. Sal walked and watched. Still the necessities of the day had to be dealt with, despite the momentous thing that had happened to this country. There were long queues for bread, for meat, for vegetables. Few people looked well, or prosperous. Most looked clearly undernourished. Children running in the streets were often barefoot, pitifully thin and inadequately clothed, despite the freezing conditions.

This was Eastern Europe at its very worst, locked in a sort of timewarp of another century. Dickens would have been perfectly at home in these streets, perhaps even a little shocked at the appalling state of the people. Sal was used to seeing squalor and deprivation whether in Russia, Poland, Hungary, Bulgaria or East Germany, but nothing on this scale. The shops were a sham, there was nothing in them. Ahead of her she saw an old woman in faded peasant clothes, a headscarf tied around her neck. She carried with her a bundle, something reverently wrapped up in a dirty cloth. She kept looking around her surreptitiously, which was what attracted Sal to her in the first place. What was she looking for? Suddenly, without warning, she knelt down on the pavement, on the edge of a street corner, and very carefully opened the dirty cloth. Inside lay a wrinkled swede, half a dozen mangy-looking carrots and two onions. Immediately there was a crowd around her; money and goods changed hands with lightning speed. People sped away with an onion here, two carrots there . . . Her produce gone, the old woman stood up stiffly and slowly counted her money before putting it deep in the pocket of her apron. Then she shuffled off out of sight. It was so depressing.

So caught up had she been in the events in Romania over the last few days that Sal had thought of no one except Toby and, with a deep pain, Evelyn. Now, suddenly, Georges came into her mind. She had built up a picture of her brother, married with a charming wife and two children, living in the suburbs of Belgrade or possibly out in the country. All at once the darker side of Eastern Europe seemed to engulf her. Perhaps life had not been good to him, after all. Perhaps he was a beggar on the streets, or at best like these people bustling past her, struggling to find the next meal. Of course, conditions in Yugoslavia were infinitely better than in Romania, but the underlying malaise was still there. Under the Communist regime, ordinary people undoubtedly suffered.

'*Where are you Georges*?' Unwittingly, she had spoken the words out loud. She must find him, now that she knew the story was true, now that Toby also knew; they must search together. Standing alone in that strange Bucharest street, the coldness seeping into her bones, Sal knew there would be no real peace of mind for her until Georges was found.

On the spur of the moment she took a tram, not knowing where she was going, just wanting to get a sight of the city which, because of the fighting, had been impossible before. The tram lurched its way along. In repose, the people sitting around her still wore the beaten look of citizens living under a dictatorship. Would the new administration betray them again, or was there really hope for the future? Sal wondered.

The tram disgorged its load, Sal with it. She looked around her: the sign on the street told her she was in Sector 4. She began to walk aimlessly, but making careful mental notes as she did so.

Suddenly, behind her she heard the now familiar crack of gunfire. Around her people scurried into doorways. Sal ducked into a side street and hurried down it. The houses on either side had a kind of faded elegance. Once they must have been lovely, now they were falling apart. The gunfire came again. She felt no fear, for off the main street it seemed safe enough, but she stopped and listened intently to see in which direction it was moving. It was then she heard the other sound – the babble of chattering children. Curious, she turned the corner ahead and stopped, staring in disbelief.

Before her were great iron gates, heavily netted over with rusting wire, enclosing a ramshackle garden of sorts containing a few broken-looking swings. A large group of perhaps fifty children were huddled against the gate, peering through it, clearly listening also to the sound of the gunfire. They appeared totally unafraid, just excited. Then they saw Sal and called to her. The word 'Mama, Mama,' was the only one she recognised. She went to them, smiling. They held out their hands, poked their fingers through the wire to touch her. They looked terrible. Their complexions were deathly white, grey almost, and they all had the same shaven heads. On first sight, Sal assumed they were all boys but some, she could see, wore tattered skirts or dresses. Several had open sores and the smell was terrible. One little child, of perhaps no more than four, pushed his hand through the gate to catch at her coat and in so doing gouged a channel down his arm from the jagged barbed wire. Blood began to pour from the wound. She knelt down, trying gently to push his arm back, but he had not even seemed to notice what had happened to him. He just smiled and nodded, stroking the material of her coat.

Who were these children?

'Does anyone speak English?' she said. No one answered. 'Parlez-vous français?' Nothing. They were asking for things now, clamouring. From the dilapidated building behind, a woman appeared, dressed in a dirty white overall. She shouted at the children, and even above their excited chatter, her voice was loud and harsh. They fell silent immediately. She beckoned to them, and with backward glances at Sal, they ran towards the house, some of the bigger ones picking up the little ones as they went. Sal stared after them. The woman glared at her, remonstrated with the children, pushing them through the door, cuffing one and then another. Then she followed them in and slammed the door shut.

Sal looked more closely at the empty garden. There was glass all over the paths where the children had been playing, also rubbish and clearly human excrement. Who were they? Was it a school? No, it couldn't be.

The white faces, the dark eyes, the filthy rags they wore, their smell, the sores . . . the obvious suffering was indescribable. For a moment Sal was tempted to go and knock on the door but then she thought better of it. She needed Peter and she needed an interpreter. Gunfire forgotten, she turned and almost ran back to the main street, hailing the first taxi she could find to take her back to the hotel.

The journey gave her a different perspective of the city. The squalor of the people and the streets had been so evident to Sal as she had walked among them but now, from the snug back seat of the taxi, Bucharest seemed a far more cheerful place. They passed tanks with smiling soldiers aboard. People swarmed all over the tanks, women and children with gifts of precious flowers, bread and wine. There was a great deal of animation in the air. Groups were gathered together on street corners, talking excitedly to one another. From many buildings flags were flying – the Romanian flag with a hole cut out of its centre.

As they drove through Palace Square, Sal could see that looting of Ceauşescu's grotesque palace was already underway. Or was it really looting? she mused. No, it was simply the repossession of items which rightly belonged to the people. Young men were up on the balcony throwing pictures and books down into the square. It was hard to believe that things had happened so quickly; that this one man and his evil regime had kept the entire nation in prison and that now, miraculously, they were free!

Sal's thoughts returned with a jolt to the children she

had seen behind the wire. Had she overreacted? Here she was, chasing across town in pursuit of . . . what? They were a ragged, miserable-looking little band, agreed – but then most of the children in Bucharest were like that. And yet these were different: she knew in her heart they were different. Something told her that here was a story worth telling.

She glanced at her watch. Peter had arranged for them to catch the flight at eight o'clock the following morning, and it was still only midday; there was the whole afternoon to pursue the story.

Miraculously Peter was in his room. 'Peter,' she said urgently, 'can you come with me now? I think I may have a story. I'll tell you all about it on the way there.'

He was lying on his bed, glass of wine in hand, apparently staring into space. 'We're going home tomorrow, Sal, remember?

'Of course I do, but this could be important! I've got a gut feeling about it.

'I'm a bit short on film,' said Peter. 'Still, let's have a go. God help me but I've learnt to trust your gut feelings. You're not going to get me shot, are you?'

'No, no, nothing like that. Where's Andre?'

'I don't know. I'll give him a call and see if he's at home.'

Andre was, and ten minutes later he picked them up at the hotel. 'Where do I take you?' he asked.

'Sector Four,' said Sal.

'It's a big area. Do you know which part?'

'I think if you follow the main tramlines I'll be able to tell you. I couldn't find a street name.'

'So what's all this about?' Peter said as they sat in the back of the cab, he intent on loading cameras.

'There was this group of children,' Sal began. 'I can't explain it, they were half-starved with ragged clothes. They were sort of caged in what could laughingly be described as a play area, they were freezing most of them, covered in sores, and their skin— ' she stopped for a moment and shuddered. 'They looked as if they hadn't been outside for months.'

'Well – who are they?' Peter asked.

'That's it, I don't know. A woman saw me and ushered them inside. She looked like a nurse or something.'

'Is it a school, perhaps?'

'No, no,' said Sal. 'It wasn't a school.'

'So why are we going there?' Peter asked, reasonably enough.

'I don't know that either,' Sal admitted. 'I just know that we have to.'

They found the right street surprisingly easily. Andre looked a little apprehensive as they drew up outside the tatty-looking building. 'What is this place?' he asked.

'I don't know,' said Sal. 'That's what I want to find out. Will you come in and interpret for us?

'Yes, of course. Who lives here?'

'I don't know that either – yet,' said Sal.

Andre stared at her, shrugged his shoulders and heaved open the heavy iron gates. The three of them walked up a wide concrete path which was covered in rubble and litter. On one side a few scrawny chickens pecked away at the frozen earth. When they reached the building they could hear no sound.

'Well, the children aren't here now,' said Peter. 'You'd hear them.'

Ahead of them was a doorway with stairs leading straight up into the main body of the building. On their right were some grimy windows. Sal rubbed away at them with her hand, but the windows were frozen. She peered in. 'Peter, it looks as if there are cots in there. Come and look.'

Peter joined her. 'Rows of them,' he said.

'Let's go inside,' said Sal. 'I have a bad feeling about this place.' She hurried to the door and the two men followed. In the hallway, instead of going up the stairs, she darted off to the right, heading towards the room she had seen through the glass. The air was foul with the stench of urine, of human decay. The smell got stronger. She walked down a short passageway, either side of which was piled high with dirty linen. At the end was a mesh door. She opened it . . . and walked into Hell.

On either side of her, as far as she could see, was row upon row of iron cots, most of which were rusted through and held together with pieces of string or dirty rags. In each was a child, some quite large, others tiny, almost newborn. Although there were perhaps sixty children in the room, there was a terrible eerie silence, to such an extent that for a moment Sal wondered if they were dead, until, as she stood there, she heard

the odd cough or muffled groan, a slight shift in the
position of one child or another. Peter was standing
beside her.

'Oh, my God,' he said, 'what is this place?'

They did not know it then, but they had discovered
the orphanages of Romania.

CHAPTER TWELVE

Afterwards she was to wonder why she had felt no sense of revulsion. Horror, yes, compassion, of course, and a kind of desperate anger that twisted at her gut.

She walked towards the nearest cot. A baby of indeterminate age lay there, his big brown eyes huge in his ashen face. There appeared to be no bedding. The mattress, split all down one side, was filthy and smelt terrible. The child was dressed in a jersey and some soiled cotton dungarees, which must once have been white. His feet were bare, his clothes sodden with urine. He was shaking, presumably from cold for the room was unheated. She instinctively held out her arms and joyously, he held out his in return. She scooped up the pathetic bundle, holding his body against hers to warm it. There was blood on her coat from the sores on his head. She did not notice. She just held the little body to her, desperate to give comfort.

At this, a slight stirring rippled through the room. One or two children stood up. One of them reached out to her from across the room. 'Mama,' he called. 'Mama.' As he spoke the word, there was a chorus from other children. Sal turned to Peter and Andre, tears springing into her eyes and pouring down her face. She clutched the baby in her arms. 'Who are these children?' she whispered.

Andre shook his head. 'I think it must be an orphanage. Shall I go and find out?' Sal nodded. Meanwhile, Peter began moving between the cots, holding a hand here, stroking a limb there. Some of the children responded, others shrank from him. Sal simply stood where she was, holding the tiny child to her breast. He was quite tall, she realised, but his body was so emaciated that she was afraid to hold him too tightly for fear that something would break. It was like cuddling a sparrow.

The door burst open and a hard-faced woman stepped inside. Sal instantly disliked her. She had blonde dyed hair and was heavily made-up. A woman perhaps in her forties, her eyes calculating.

'Who are you? What you do here?' she demanded in broken English.

'You speak English,' Sal said. 'Good.'

'A little. You go away, you must not be here.'

Sal ignored her and looked at Andre, who had come in behind her. 'Who is this woman, Andre?'

'She is the principal here. This is the orphanage Luca.

She says there are many such places in the city. These children either have no parents, or their parents have abandoned them.'

Sal stared at the woman. 'But this is no way to treat them! These children don't have enough food or clothes. Many of them are obviously ill, and look at their bedding. Ugh! It all needs replacing. This child . . .' she was still clutching the little boy '. . . this child is so cold, he will die.'

The woman must have caught the gist of Sal's words. 'We can do nothing,' she shouted. 'You leave now.'

Sal looked at Andre. 'We must do something to help these children. Can you ask the Principal if we may have a talk with her – go to her office, perhaps?'

Andre had a rapid conversation with the woman. Suddenly her manner changed. She smiled at Sal and pointed towards the door, indicating that they should go together. Sal looked at the child in her arms. He had gone to sleep. Very gently she laid him back in his stinking cot. He stirred, but mercifully did not wake. Peter was beside her. 'You go and talk to that old bitch. I'm going to find some food for these kids. I just can't stand it.'

'Where will you go?'

'I don't know – back to the hotel, I suppose.'

'The little boy I was holding had very dry skin,' Sal said. 'He may be dehydrated. Perhaps you should get some juice or something, even water would do.'

'OK,' said Peter. 'I'll try and find some milk, too. God, this is awful, Sal.'

In all their adventures together, Sal had never seen him so moved. There were tears in his eyes – again, something she had rarely seen. 'This is the worst yet, isn't it?' she said, putting a hand on his arm.

'I've never seen anything like this,' he agreed.

They threaded their way through dark corridors until they came to a pleasant area where two or three women, wearing what appeared to be nurse's uniforms, were sitting around a table playing cards. The room was warm and well-lit, and the remains of a Christmas tree stood in one corner. Sal stopped and stared at the women. 'Andre, ask the Principal who these women are.'

Andre obliged. 'They are the children's nurses,' he reported.

'Then what in God's name are they doing sitting here playing cards when those children are starving to death?'

'I don't know,' Andre said. He was suddenly very reserved, almost sullen.

They were shown into an attractive office, where they sat down and Andre handed round the inevitable cigarettes.

'Can you begin by asking her name,' Sal requested, but the woman had already understood. 'My name is Ana Popescu,' she said.

Sal introduced herself and Andre. 'How many children do you have here, Mrs Popescu?'

Andre translated. 'Two hundred, maybe two hundred and fifty. Some arrived yesterday from another orphanage,' he explained.

'And how many other orphanages are there, and are they all like this?' Sal asked.

'Many orphanages,' the reply came back. 'Many here in Bucharest, and in the country. The biggest is orphanage Number One – there are six or seven hundred children there.'

'In this condition?' Sal asked.

The woman became angry. 'What do you expect us to do?' was the reply. 'We have no money, we have no food, we have no clothes for the children. We have an hour of electricity a day – we cannot keep all the rooms warm or the clothes washed.'

Sal thought for a moment. 'Look,' she said. 'What you need is help. Through my newspaper I can tell the world about these orphanages. If you let me write about you, then I will be able to find help – toys, clothes, food, medical supplies – everything these children need.'

'She will talk,' Andre told Sal after a moment's conversation, 'but she wants to know how much money she will get.'

Sal had to fight her sense of revulsion. The Principal was clearly more interested in what she was going to get out of it, than helping the children in her care. 'Fifty dollars, some perfume and cigarettes,' said Sal.

'It's too much,' said Andre.

But Ana had heard. 'Fifty dollar, fifty dollar, yes, I do it,' she said enthusiastically, and so for the next hour Sal heard Ana's story and then toured the orphanage.

She saw the most harrowing sights she had ever seen in her entire life, like the child, aged perhaps eight or nine, desperately thin, who was tied down naked in his cot by his arms and legs with filthy bandages. 'He is mad. We had to do this or he would hurt himself,' was the explanation.

There were children covered in sores, smeared with their own vomit and excrement, and others, particularly babies, who were obviously close to death. Many of them called out weakly to Sal as she went from room to room, her despair mounting. Some just sat, swaying in a corner of their cot, or continually scratching at a sore. One tiny child was beating his head rhythmically against the bars of the cot, over and over again. There was a deep dent and an open wound on his head, and yet he was oblivious to the pain.

'Why is he doing that?' Sal asked, tears streaming down her face.

'I do not know,' Ana said, turning away. Sal stared after her. There was no compassion, no involvement. This woman was allegedly in charge of all these children, and yet to her their feelings were of no consequence. It was as if they were not human. As Sal and Andre stumbled after Ana down the long corridor back to her office, Sal realised that she was as shocked by this woman's chilling attitude to the children, as she was by the terrible state of the orphans in her care.

Back in the relative comfort of the office, Sal decided on a more aggressive stance. 'It seems, Mrs Popescu, that you do not care for these children.'

The expression on Ana's face became instantly hostile. 'How can I care for them? How could any one woman care for them? There are too many.' She shrugged. 'Their families do not care for them

– so why should I? I have a family of my own.'
As Andre translated this statement, he kept his eyes
averted from Sal's.

'I can't believe any woman can feel like this. You
are a mother yourself?' She stared at Ana while Andre
made the translation.

'I am a mother,' Ana replied, 'but I would never
put my child in an orphanage. These children are no
good. Many of them are gypsies or illegitimate, or
their mothers are prostitutes, with too many children
already.'

'Does that mean that they should not have the chance
of a good life?' Sal retorted.

Anger was flaring between the two women. Mercifully they were interrupted by the arrival of Peter. With
him was a man and a woman Sal did not recognise.

'This is Sadie and Martin Harris,' Peter said. Sadie
was a small vivacious blonde of about thirty-five;
Martin, obviously older, was dressed in an expensive
suit. 'They're from the States,' Peter added as they all
shook hands.

'We're over here,' Martin said, 'because I'm thinking
of setting up a company in Romania. I've just heard
about this place from your colleague. Mrs Popescu,
my wife and I have helped bring over some stuff for
your children. There are a couple of guys unloading it
right now.'

Andre translated for Ana, then they all went down to
the entrance of the orphanage, where two taxi drivers
were disgorging the contents of their car boots. There
were biscuits and milk, fruit, cheese, chocolate.

'Where did you get all this?' Sal said to Peter, amazed. 'The shops are empty!'

'I simply plundered the hotel kitchen,' he told her. 'I hope David's feeling generous when he sees my expense account but there was nowhere else I was going to get it in Bucharest at the moment. Oh, and incidentally, I've got some brandy and cigarettes for Ana to keep her quiet. Do you want to give them to her?'

'I think I'd better,' said Sal. 'Ana and I were about to go ballistic when mercifully you arrived and it might be something of a peace-offering. Peter, she says there are orphanages like this all over Bucharest – all over Romania. We must get this story out quickly and organise some aid. There are some terrible cases in there. There's this little boy . . .' But Sal couldn't go on. Peter put an arm around her and drew her to him. She rested her head on his shoulder, drawing comfort from him. She could smell the tweed of his jacket – it felt normal, English, reassuring in a world gone mad.

'We've done a lot of stories together,' Peter said quietly. 'We've done some good, we've inadvertently messed up people's lives on occasions, we've had some dramas and saved a life I suppose, in the case of Louis Noble, but we've never, never had an opportunity that is more worthwhile than this one. We have to make the world understand what's going on here, Sal.' There was a break in his voice as he spoke.

'You're a good man, Peter,' Sal said gently.

'I don't know about that,' he said, 'but I know that what I've seen today I will carry with me to my grave.'

'Me too,' said Sal.

'Now, let's be practical. I don't think we want pictures of the food being distributed to the kids – that would be wrong. What we need are photographs of them as they are now. You have the story?'

'Oh yes,' said Sal.

'OK, then you divert Ana with the brandy and cigarettes, while I get a few shots.'

'The little boy I wanted to tell you about,' Sal said. 'I'll show you where he is. He's tied down in his cot. They say he's mad, but his eyes aren't – his eyes are those of a trapped animal.'

Peter took the picture of the boy whose name, they later learned, was Radu. This was a picture that was to be shown again and again in relation to the horror of Romania's orphanages. It travelled the world symbolising the suffering of the children. It was a miracle it was such a good picture, for as Peter pressed the shutter, he could see nothing. His eyes were blinded by tears.

The hotel bar was stuffy after the cold of the street and the orphanage, but the little group sitting around empty wine bottles did not notice it. They felt ship-wrecked, washed to safety after struggling in Hell. Martin, Sadie and Andre had spent all afternoon at the orphanage distributing food and trying to make a layman's assessment of what the children needed most. Sal and Peter had returned to the hotel to file their stories before going back to the orphanage to help.

David, initially, had not been enormously enthusiastic. 'You need to come home, Sal. Don't worry about the Louis thing, it's completely blown over. I know I was hard on you at the time, but I don't think it's done any lasting damage, either to you or to the paper.'

Yes, but what about Louis' marriage, Sal thought but said nothing, not wanting to antagonise David. She had to get across to him the gravity of what she had discovered. She went through it slowly and carefully. The phone was cut off in mid-conversation and it took her an hour's frustrated dialling to get through again. All the while she was desperate he would not understand.

'Just wait until you see the pictures, David. They will say more than my copy ever can. Tomorrow we're going to orphanage Number One, and we'll try to discover how many of these places there are in Bucharest and around. There could be millions of children, certainly hundreds of thousands in this condition. I want you to launch an appeal through the newspaper immediately. They need everything.'

In the end he caught her enthusiasm. 'What about Toby?' he said. 'I've told him you were coming home tomorrow.'

'Toby will understand if you explain it to him. He's a very caring person. Show him the pictures too, they're horrific, but he's old enough to understand. Say that I'll try and call him tomorrow.'

'OK. I'll give you a week on this story and then you really *must* come home – both of you.'

By the time they gathered in the bar, Martin and

Sadie had contacted friends in America who were sending out nappies, creams and medicines for the children. Peter had spoken to an old schoolfriend of his who was now a doctor at the John Radcliffe Hospital in Oxford. He, too, had promised to plunder the medical stores and see what he could have flown out on an immediate basis. Sal thought of Evelyn and felt hopeless and impotent. Evelyn would have been marvellous, with her love of children. She wouldn't have hesitated to lean heavily on her Church contacts, and would have worked tirelessly to raise money and collect clothes and toys for the children. Clearly the priority was food and medicines, but clothes and something to do had to follow – and quickly.

They talked a little as they sat around in the bar. Martin told them about his machine-tool business, which he hoped would bring some prosperity to Bucharest. Sadie told them about her three children back home. Peter and Sal explained their backgrounds and families. Only Andre was uncharacteristically silent.

'What's wrong?' Sal asked when Martin and Peter had gone to the bar for more wine.

'I feel so ashamed.'

'Of what?' Sal asked.

'Of the orphanage – that children in my country should be living like this. You see, you have to believe me, Sal, I had no idea. No one does, I think.' Most unexpectedly he began to cry. Sal put an arm around his shoulders and he leaned against her, like a child. 'I live in Sector Four, less than a kilometer from that place – yet I did not know it was there. I have heard of orphanage Number One, but not this one. I have never been to any of them. People do not visit orphanages in our country.'

'But why do so many people put their children in these homes? Are all those children really orphans?' Sal asked.

Andre made an effort to pull himself together. Peter and Martin had returned to the table and wine was poured out all round.

'You must understand what has been going on in my country,' Andre began. 'The Old Cobbler – Ceauşescu – he wanted women to have many children. It is against the law to make an abortion. So many children are born that people do not want them and cannot feed them, so they go into orphanages. This pleased Ceauşescu. He was hoping to build an army from these young citizens, who would know no other mother and father than the State, than Nicolae and Elena Ceauşescu.'

'That is terrible,' said Sal, but Andre was warming to his theme now, anxious to try and justify what he had seen.

'Women are dismissed from their jobs if they have an abortion. Also it is difficult for them to care for their children when they are sick. Women are not permitted to leave their work.'

'So,' Sal said, 'if a mother has a child with medical problems, she will put that child into an orphanage?'

'Most likely, because she cannot care for the child herself at home. She must work – and who would look after the child all day? It is difficult for you to understand, maybe?'

'Yes and no,' said Sal.

Andre struggled. 'There is a tradition of orphanages in this country. It began, as all bad things do, with the gypsies.' At the mention of their name he literally snarled with contempt. 'The gypsies traditionally put their children in orphanages at birth and then, when they are old enough to work, they take them out. Now everyone has to use the orphanages, once they have too many children.'

'But why are those places so terrible?' said Sal.

'Because the orphans are "at the bottom of the pile", as you would say.'

'He's right,' said Peter. 'In a country where nobody has anything much, it's hardly surprising that the orphans have nothing at all.'

Eventually everyone except Peter and Sal left the bar.

'How are you feeling?' Peter asked.

'Dreadful,' said Sal.

'At least we're trying to do something,' Peter suggested.

'I know. It's just that however much aid we bring in, however many tons of food and medical supplies, no matter how many toys and clothes, those children still aren't going to have the "mama" they keep calling for. Why do they do that?' She began to cry.

'I don't know,' said Peter, taking a handkerchief from his pocket and handing it to her. 'I suppose it's just an instinctive thing. After all, it's the first word that every child learns – Mummy, Mum, Mother, Mama, Mommy – it's the same the world over.'

'I just can't bear it,' said Sal. 'I just want to scoop them all up and take them home and love them and love them.'

'I feel the same,' Peter said. 'I really do. Until now I've always been fond of children, but . . .' his voice tailed off.

'It was strange, wasn't it, what Andre said,' Sal reminded him, blowing her nose and trying to pull herself together.

'What do you mean?' Peter asked.

'About him not knowing that that orphanage existed, although he lives so near by. After the war the Germans insisted that they didn't know about the concentration camps. In our media-obsessed world we think that's a very tall story, but I'm sure Andre was telling the truth. I suppose when your information is controlled, handed out only in the form of propaganda, it's quite possible not to know what's going on, on your doorstep. There are a lot of similarities, aren't there, between Hitler and Ceauşescu? Certainly this idea of breeding a totally loyal army is terrifyingly familiar.'

'Do you know one of the things that really got to me?' said Peter. 'Those children could have been your's or mine. They were so European looking. Good God, we're less than a thousand miles from London and all this has been going on. We're living in the same continent and yet nobody knew about Romania's children.'

'They'll know about them now,' said Sal, tears coming into her eyes again.

'Yes, by God,' said Peter, 'they will.'

'The test will come, though, after the media interest dies down. Will anyone still care?'

The next day passed in a haze for Sal. Orphanage Number One surpassed her worst nightmares. She had spent the previous night tossing and turning, images of the children coming into her mind again and again. But in the cold light of day and in the reality of orphanage Number One, her dreams paled into insignificance.

The orphanage was a big one, with over 700 inmates. Conditions were worse here, and most of the children seemed to be desperately ill, thin and weak. She was told that Hepatitis A and B were rife, malnutrition too, but there seemed to be an extra and deadly element afflicting these children, who seemed more dead than alive. It wasn't long before that element was given a name – AIDS.

The days blurred together. Sal and Peter worked from dawn until dusk, their reports and pictures filling the newspapers. It was not until the following weekend that Sal had a chance for a long conversation with David. Communication was still very difficult; phone lines were like gold dust and liable to be cut off at any moment. At last though, at two in the morning, Sal put a call through to David's home and was successful.

'Sorry to wake you up, but it's the first time I've been able to get through to you.'

'It's OK,' he said sleepily. 'Hang on, let me turn on the light so I can hear myself think.'

'Be quick,' said Sal. 'We could be cut off any moment.'

'Sorry. Now before we start talking about the paper, let's talk about Toby. He's starting to miss you. He's spent the whole of Christmas without you, and tomorrow is New Year's Eve.'

'Is it?' said Sal. 'I'd forgotten.'

'I know this whole thing must be awful for you – and by the way, our circulation's gone through the roof – but I think it's time you came home. Even if you go back to Bucharest again soon, you still need to come home for a few days, for Toby's sake and for your own. After all, it's not so long since you were very ill, and you must be absolutely on your knees by now.'

'Oh David, it's such a nightmare!' Sal told him passionately. 'These children have nothing and no one – no hope, no future – and it's going to be years before Romania sorts herself out. The children we've seen will be dead or terribly warped adults by then.'

'I disagree,' said David, 'And that's partly why I want you to come home. There are a lot of people in the UK and, I imagine, across the rest of Europe, wanting to adopt your children. It's not a clever solution in the long-term – taking children away from their country of origin – but in the circumstances it's got to be the only answer.'

'If the Romanian Government will allow it,' said Sal.

'That's what I want you to find out – whether they will allow overseas adoption, and when you have the answer to that I want you to come home, Sal – and I mean it.'

'What are you doing for New Year's Eve?' Sal asked hesitantly.

'Don't worry, it's not a question of what I'm doing for New Year's Eve, it's a question of what me, Toby and Jenny are doing. We're going out to supper and a movie, and then we'll see in the New Year at home. Your boy's OK, Sal, but it has been too long this time and things aren't helped by the fact that you're something of a household name back here at the moment.'

'I'll do as you ask,' said Sal. 'We'll plan for coming home on the second, and thanks . . . about New Year's Eve, I mean.'

Adoption . . . yes, it was an option for some, Sal thought as she put down the phone, but there were so many and for some of them, she knew instinctively that it was already too late.

The last day of 1989, which for Sal had been a very mixed year, began with a visit to a home for irrecuperables a few kilometres outside Bucharest. One of the doctors at orphanage Luca had told her of this place, where children who were either physically or mentally disabled were sent; because there was no room for them in ordinary society.

As Andre drove Peter and Sal out of Bucharest, the three were strangely silent. Sal and Peter had by now formed a close bond with their interpreter. Their experiences of the past few days had sobered them; the jokes and the drinking that had been a part of their earlier days had stopped, and somehow they knew that today was going to represent the culmination of all the suffering they had witnessed to date.

The countryside became pretty. There was no snow,

but a heavy frost the night before had made everything white – every twig, every leaf etched out. The area became hilly as they drove closer to the Carpathian Mountains. The little town, when they reached it, was very quaint, like something out of a fairy tale – houses with Alpine roofs, cobbled streets. The orphanage stood just outside the village and was built like a fort, with a huge door.

'This really is like Dracula's Castle,' Peter said, trying unsuccessfully to lighten the mood.

In the cobbled courtyard beyond the door was a strangely eerie atmosphere. Andre went to investigate and returned with a sullen-looking man in stained overalls. Andre looked very pale. 'Sal, you must not go in here – this is not a place for a woman. Peter will take the photographs – you stay here.'

'No,' said Sal. 'I'm sorry but I can't do that, Andre.'

'It is not— ' He began to cry. 'Forgive me, but I do not think I can go back in.'

'Come on, old girl,' said Peter, taking Sal's arm. 'Tell this guy to show us around, Andre. We understand how you feel. Wait for us here.'

They could never have envisaged this degree of human suffering. Few of the children here wore any clothes at all, although conditions were freezing. Most were tied to their beds, or just tied to the floor, their bodies skeletal, the whole nightmare place reeking of sewage. Most of the children were too far gone even to notice Peter and Sal as they stumbled through the wards. Now and again a child would lunge at them, shrieking with terror, shock, joy – it was impossible to tell. Peter took his photographs while Sal stood by helplessly. These children were beyond comfort. They had been incarcerated here in the hopes that eventually they would die and cease to be a drain on the State. Peter and Sal saw no staff the whole time they were there, other than the morose man who showed them the way. At the end of their tour they gave him dollars and cigarettes and he shuffled away into the bowels of the building.

Outside, they found Andre talking animatedly to an elderly woman dressed in an old-fashioned peasant's dress and pinafore, her grey hair tied back in a scarf. Her face was careworn and lined, but kindly. Andre beckoned them over. 'This is Eleanor, a nurse here,' Andre said. 'She has been telling me about the children. It is awful.'

'Yes, it is,' Sal said. She was in a state of shock. 'More awful than anything I've seen, ever.'

'No,' Andre said, 'you do not understand me. Some of the children when they come are not mad, they simply become mad by being here.'

'How do you mean?' Sal asked.

'At three years old they are assessed. There are certain tests they have to pass in the eyes of the orphanage authorities. They must be trained to use the lavatories, they must be able to walk and to talk. If they cannot do these things they are sent here, or to another place like this – a home for irrecuperables.'

'But most of the children we have seen in the orphanages are way behind in their development! I very much doubt that many of them could achieve the milestones you mention,' Sal objected.

'Exactly,' said Andre. 'In addition, Eleanor knows of many children who have come here, who either are just a little slow or maybe have some small physical defect,' he shrugged. 'A foot damaged at birth – how would you call this?'

'A club foot,' Peter said.

'A club foot, that sort of thing. She says it breaks her heart, but there is nothing she can do. They have very little food, just some soup. Many die. They are all cold now, but there are not enough clothes.'

'There are not any clothes,' said Sal. 'Tell her, Andre, tell her we will help. She must have faith that we will be back.'

Andre nodded and relayed the message. The old woman raised her head and looked at Sal, deep into her eyes. For the first time since her arrival at Bucharest Sal felt a real bond of caring with someone. They stared at one another and something passed between them. The old woman trusted Sal, believed she would come back, and she was right to do so.

The Intercontinental Hotel was celebrating that night. 1989 – the year Romania would never forget – was at an end, while 1990 was a year full of promise: the Ceauşescus dead, Communism at an end, a free country with free people.

Andre made his excuses and left, saying he would be spending the night with his family. He had told them little of his background, other than that he had a wife and two sons, and that night he seemed anxious to be with them. Sal and Peter were in no mood to celebrate. They decided to have dinner in the formal Hotel restaurant, as opposed to the snack bar where they usually went. It transpired that there was a dinner-dance on. They secured a little table as far from the band as they could manage and drank steadily while they waited for indifferent food and suffered, cheerfully enough, the terrible service.

'So how has 1989 been for you?' Peter asked, raising his glass to Sal.

'Definitely curate's egg,' said Sal, 'but I think the bad parts outweigh the good. And you?'

'About the same.'

'We never talk, do we, Peter?' Sal said suddenly. 'About our personal lives. I know your views on just about every subject on earth, but I know nothing about your women or how you live your life.'

Peter smiled at her, a twinkle in his eye. 'Well, not all of us make the headlines where our romances are concerned, you know.'

'Shut up,' said Sal.

'Are you missing him?'

Sal thought of Louis for a moment. 'No,' she said. 'I should be, of course, but these children . . . The orphanage problem has blown everything else out of my mind. It's an extraordinary, terrible way to end a year.'

Without planning in any way to do so, she found herself telling Peter about her mother, the discovery of her origins and her abortive search to date.

'I can't explain why exactly,' said Peter, 'but I'm not at all surprised. In fact, I would go so far as to say you don't even look English – that's meant to be a compliment, by the way.'

Sal laughed. 'A lot of people have said that and I suppose I'm getting used to the idea. It's my brother who haunts me. My father, you see, is probably dead, but my brother is only eight years older than me . . .' she bit her lip.

Peter reached out and took her hand across the table. 'You'll find him,' he said. 'You're like a dog with a bone when you get a story. You won't let go of it.'

'It's different, though, when it's someone else's story – much easier. A part of me wants to know more, another part of me is afraid to. My father must have been, well, not a very pleasant sort of person, to be a spy, to lead a double life . . .' her voice tailed off. 'And now that I have his photograph, the awful thing is that he looks like me. Or should I say, I look like *him*. He has such a cruel face.' She shuddered.

Peter squeezed her hand. 'I can assure you, Sal, that you do *not* have a cruel face.'

He was grinning at her and she smiled back. 'You're so good for me, you always make me laugh at myself.'

'Well, someone has to,' said Peter.

'What are your parents like?' Sal asked suddenly.

'Both dead, I'm afraid,' he said. 'My father was killed just after the war. It was very sad, really. He was in mine-sweepers. He survived the war, came home on leave in 1945, which is when I was conceived, and then returned to his ship to help in the clean-up of the Mediterranean. A great many ships were lost in that period, I gather. I suppose without an enemy people became careless. Anyway, his ship was blown to bits and I was born about three months after his death.'

'Your poor mother,' said Sal.

'Yes.'

'And are you an only child?'

Peter nodded. 'Yes. I had a splendid relationship with my mother. She was a good woman who dedicated her life to raising me on a small Naval pension. She was never overprotective or demanding. When I got a place at university and left home for the first time, she was genuinely pleased, not thinking of herself and how lonely she'd be.'

'She sounds wonderful,' said Sal.

'Yes, she was,' said Peter. 'She died two years ago of cancer. Even in that, she was determined not to be a trouble to anyone. A thoroughly decent person.'

'So your wife, when you find one, has quite a lot to live up to?'

'I hadn't thought of it like that,' said Peter, 'but perhaps you're right. Certainly, I never seem able to make a commitment to anyone.'

'It's strange, isn't it,' said Sal, 'but we're both alone in the world, without parents or brothers and sisters, or serious partners.'

'Lost souls,' said Peter sagely.

'We'd better stop this or we'll start feeling sorry for ourselves,' said Sal. 'Could we raise a glass to Toby, who may not be starving, who may have a nice home and all the creature comforts that go with it, but he's still seeing in the New Year without his mother. To Toby.' Both sipped their champagne.

'Tell me to mind my own business but who is his father, Sal?' Peter asked suddenly.

Sal was instantly on the defensive. 'Why do you ask?'

'I don't know, I just wondered. He doesn't seem to figure in your life, or in Toby's — at least, you never mention him. Does he play any part in the boy's life?'

'No,' said Sal. 'I've lost touch with him.'

'That's a bit hard on Toby, isn't it?'

'I don't think so,' said Sal. 'He doesn't seem to miss a father. In fact, once or twice when I have talked it through with him, he's not even been interested.'

'That may change,' Peter told her. 'My mother always tried to keep my father's image alive for me. I had his picture on the wall in my bedroom, that sort of thing, and his medals. But it meant nothing to me really, until I was a teenager. I suppose then, fumbling around between boyhood and manhood, I needed a role-model and there wasn't one available to me. I became obsessed about how it would have been if he'd lived, what sort of relationship we'd have had.'

Sal stared at him. 'Do you think that's really going to happen to Toby?'

'I don't know,' said Peter. 'I'm only telling you what happened to me, but maybe it's something you should bear in mind.'

'So many problems,' Sal said, almost to herself. 'Sometimes . . .' her voice trailed off.

'Sometimes what?' Peter said softly.

'Forget it,' said Sal. 'In any event, what possible problems could I have, compared with Romania's orphan children?'

'It certainly does put one's life into perspective,' Peter agreed. 'Let's hope to God that what we're doing is going to make a difference to them.'

'I'll drink to that,' said Sal.

A figure suddenly loomed up at their table. 'Excuse me, are you English?'

Sal looked up into the eyes of an extraordinarily attractive man: dark, with wild curly hair, deep brown eyes you could drown in, tall and broad and with a smile that made her feel weak at the knees. 'Yes, we're English,' she said.

'I was wondering, madam, whether you would care to dance with me, if your partner has no objection?'

Peter looked from one to the other and smiled ruefully. The chemistry was there for all to see. 'I'm not her partner,' he said. 'I'm her colleague and I'm just off to bed. A dance would do her good.' He stood up.

'Peter, where are you going?' Sal said, in panic.

Peter grinned. 'Have a good time – raise my glass to you at midnight.'

'Don't go,' Sal said, genuinely alarmed at the thought of being left with this complete stranger.

'I'm not playing gooseberry,' said Peter. 'See you around.'

Sal stared at his departing back and then looked up at her new companion.

'I'm sorry,' he said, shrugging his shoulders and

grinning. 'No, I am *not* sorry. I have sent him away and I am glad. Now, would you like to dance or would you prefer to have a drink?'

'I think I'd rather have a drink,' said Sal. 'It's been a long day.'

The man clicked his fingers and a waiter appeared. They ordered drinks.

'Let me introduce myself,' he said. 'My name is Cristian Popa. I am a lawyer, a good lawyer.'

'Salvena Saunders,' Sal said, surprised at herself for using her full name. 'A journalist,' she grinned. 'A good journalist, I think.'

'Salvena. You're Yugoslavian then?'

'Partly, yes,' said Sal. 'How did you know?'

'I spent some years in Belgrade — three, no nearly four. So what has brought you to my country? The revolution, I assume?'

'In the beginning,' said Sal, 'but now it is your children.' And she gave him a description of what she had seen in the last few days.

'Every country has its orphanages,' Cristian said dismissively.

'Not like these, I can assure you.' Sal was firm. 'Not like these.'

Cristian shrugged his shoulders. 'What do you do with children no one wants?'

'You care for them!' Sal cried. 'You care for them properly until you can find someone who does want them.'

'There are many other, more important issues in Romania besides these children.'

'None more important than this,' said Sal quietly. 'Not to me, anyway.'

Cristian sighed. 'Do not let us talk of these things.'

'Very well,' said Sal, 'but before we stop, there is one thing you could do for me.'

'I would do anything for you,' Cristian said, his voice heavy with meaning, but his manner light and bantering.

'If you're a lawyer, can you find out whether it is possible for foreigners to adopt the children from your orphanages?'

'You want to adopt some children?' He looked astonished.

'Not me,' said Sal patiently, 'but there are a number of people who do.'

'I will find out for you,' Cristian promised.

'First thing in the morning?' Sal pressed.

'First thing in the morning. And now, Miss Salvena Saunders, I would like to have that dance.'

CHAPTER THIRTEEN

The following morning it was an effort for Sal even to lift her head off the pillow. Everything ached; her mind was foggy, her eyes unfocused. Initially, she assumed she was in the first stages of another attack of flu, but after a tepid bath, which was all the Intercontinental could offer, she realised there was nothing wrong with her but lack of sleep, too much wine and the stresses and strains of the previous ten days. She studied herself in the mirror. Her skin was pale and there were dark circles under her eyes. Make-up seemed to make not the slightest difference. Her hair was dry and seemed to fly in all directions, and trying to make herself presentable was an effort.

She decided to have breakfast in the restaurant downstairs and toyed with the idea of knocking on Peter's door first. Then she decided against it. She was not up to comments about her evening with Cristian.

In the restaurant she immediately spotted Sadie and Martin, the Americans who had helped them with the supply of food for orphanage Luca. Not having seen them for several days, she had assumed they had gone back to America. They were talking earnestly, heads close together.

'Hello,' said Sal. 'I thought you'd gone home.'

Sadie's bright complexion flushed warmer with apparent excitement. 'No, such a lot has been happening to us. Come and sit down and have breakfast with us.'

Sal scanned the restaurant. There was no sign of Peter. 'I'd love to,' she said, and drew up a chair.

'We've found this little girl,' Martin burst out, 'in orphanage Luca. Her mother's dead and her father is happy for her to be adopted. She's very ill – so pale and covered in sores – but she just loves being cuddled. Her name's Daniella. The papers are being drawn up now, and we think we'll be able to take her home in a few weeks. We're flying home today to organise the paperwork in the US.'

Sal's sluggish mind was suddenly alert. 'You're going to adopt her? You have a lawyer?'

Martin and Sadie seemed surprised by her sudden interest. Martin, his round open face suddenly wrinkled with concern, said: 'You don't think we're doing the wrong thing, do you? I mean, you think it's OK, morally?'

'Of course I do,' said Sal. 'I've been into five orphanages now and the state of the children in every one is pitiful. Any chance they have to get out has to be wonderful. No – please don't misunderstand me, I'm only interested because I gather that there are a number of couples in the UK who want to adopt, and I was anxious to know how it's done.'

Martin shrugged his shoulders. 'Provided you find a child who is eligible, I don't think it's a problem at all. We contacted our Embassy a couple of days back and they've been most helpful. We have a Romanian lawyer who's putting together the paperwork and we understand that our file then goes before Iliescu for his signature.'

'Iliescu – the new President?'

'He is the only one who can sign adoption papers at present, apparently.'

'So there's no judicial process?' Sal said.

'I believe not.'

Sadie suddenly put a hand on Sal's arm. 'I'm so worried. We have to go back to the States today in order to have a report prepared to show that we are suitable parents, but what will become of Daniella meanwhile? I'm just terrified. We have been feeding her every day and even taking her out with us, but now she'll be alone again. She'll think we've abandoned her.'

'How old is she?' Sal asked gently.

'Seventeen months, but she's more like a three-month-old baby in size. Still, she's very knowing. She expects us each day and when we don't come, what will she think? She's too young to understand.' At that point, Sadie broke down and cried.

Martin reached across and took her hand. 'It's only

for a few weeks, honey, and then she'll be safe for the rest of her life.'

Sadie looked at Sal. 'It's as if she knows that we're her last chance. She's so weak, and yet there's a brave spark there – she so wants to be happy and strong and well. When she thinks we've abandoned her, she'll give up.'

'She's only a baby, honey. She'll take each day as it comes.' Martin's words sounded hollow to both women.

'I'll look after her,' Sal heard herself say. 'At least for the next couple of days, then I should be able to find someone to take over from me. Don't worry. Let me fetch some coffee and then you can tell me all about her.'

It was an hour later before Sal finally extricated herself from Martin and Sadie. The contents of their bedroom had been moved into Sal's. With true American efficiency, they had obtained everything – baby milk and rusks, nappies and clothes, medicines and even a buggy.

'We visit at eleven, and again at six,' Sadie told Sal for the umpteenth time. 'You have to bribe the staff to let you see her, but not much – just a little coffee or a couple of cigarettes.'

'Don't worry,' Sal assured them.

'We'll go and see her now, on the way to the airport,' Martin said, 'so you'll visit this evening – is that really OK?'

'Yes,' said Sal, 'I promise.'

'And we'll call you tomorrow and see how she is.'

Sal waved them down in the lift, marvelling at their concern. They had three children at home, but somehow this little Romanian girl had woven her way into their hearts and they were not going to be happy again until she was safely home with them. She thought of Cristian. They had arranged to meet in the lobby at eleven, when he ought to have some news on the adoption process. She smiled at the thought of him – it had been an interesting evening.

Peter was in his room. 'Where have you been?' Sal asked. He had photographs laid out all over his bed.

'Take a look at these,' he said. They were the photographs of the previous day's visit to the home for irrecuperables. They stared at them together in silence for a moment.

'I just don't know how anyone is ever going to believe these,' Sal said. 'They're just too grotesque, too awful – yet maybe they will shock people into trying to do something.' She sat down on the bed. 'What are we going to do today, Peter? I promised that woman, Eleanor, that we'd be back. We must keep that promise.'

'I agree,' said Peter. 'I think we should try and persuade David to link the paper's name quite specifically to one or two institutions including this one. That way the readers will be able to see how their donations are used. There are several relief organisations setting up in the UK already, I'm told. I managed to get through to the picture desk today and they told me about it. They'll go mad when they see these pictures.'

'I think it's time we went back to London, you know,'

Sal told him. 'We can go on and on reporting about all this ad infinitum, but what we really need to do is ensure that something happens as a result. Have you heard about what Sadie and Martin are doing?'

Peter nodded. 'I bumped into them in the lobby last night.'

Sal sighed. 'I've just taken on the responsibility for their little girl. I've got to go and see Daniella tonight.'

'You're hopeless,' said Peter.

'Actually, I'm dreading it,' Sal confessed.

'Why particularly?'

'It's hard to explain. I suppose it's because orphanage Luca was the first one we saw – the one which had the major impact – and the fact that so far I've managed to distance myself from individual children.' Peter began to protest. 'No – I'm involved, of course I am, right up to my neck, but not on a one-to-one basis. The moment I start caring for this little girl, things will change. Does it make any sense?'

'I think so,' said Peter. 'But remember, little Daniella is one of the lucky ones. She's going to get adopted.'

'That guy you dumped me with last night, he's a lawyer. I'm meeting him at eleven o'clock. He's going to tell me whether foreigners will be allowed to adopt or not. It could make quite a difference if they are.'

'Oh yes,' said Peter grinning. 'How *was* last night, by the way?'

'You are rotten,' Sal said, slapping him lightly. 'Why did you get up and leave me just like that, with a perfect stranger? I thought we were going to see the New Year in together.'

Peter gave her a friendly squeeze. 'The chemistry zipping between you two was instant. It's why I haven't contacted you before, this morning – I didn't want to interrupt anything.'

'Do you seriously think that I'm the sort of person who would meet someone and jump straight into his bed?'

'I'm not sure,' said Peter. 'It was you who said there's so little we really know about each other, remember? What I *do* know is that what we're witnessing at the moment is very tough emotionally, particularly, I imagine, for a woman with a child. I thought you might be in need of comforting.'

'If I did,' said Sal, 'wouldn't it be better to have spent the evening with you, after all these years of friendship and shared experience?'

'Oh come on Sal, he's just your type – big and flamboyant.'

Sal relented. 'He is very attractive, but in answer to your next question, I sent him packing just after midnight.'

'It's only a matter of time, in my view,' said Peter sagely.

Cristian was already waiting for her when Sal reached the lobby. He stood up, a huge man yet surprisingly light on his feet as he raced across to meet her. He took her hand enthusiastically and kissed her on both cheeks. 'Ah Salvena, I'm so pleased to see you. I thought about you all night, you wonderful woman.'

'Steady on, Cristian,' said Sal, 'it's only eleven o'clock in the morning.'

'I know, I know.'

'Have you the information I need?'

'Yes, I have. Come, I will take you to the bar for a drink and tell you all I know.'

In the bar he ordered a bottle of wine. 'I hope you're not expecting me to drink half of that,' said Sal. 'I have to work this afternoon.'

'We shall see.' Cristian smiled at her. It was a heart-stopping smile, his eyes warm and brown. Peter was right, and yet what on earth was she doing, even looking at another man so soon after Louis?

She turned her mind firmly to the job in hand. 'About adoption.'

'Ah,' said Cristian, 'it's not a problem. The parents, if they are alive, must be happy for the child to be adopted. Then all that is necessary is for the parents' written consent to be signed before a notary. Then a small report has to be made on the social conditions of the family. Where the child is an orphan, it may be more difficult, but the director of the orphanage does have the power to grant permission to adopt.'

'Why is it more difficult?' queried Sal, puzzled. 'Surely it should be easier.'

'Orphanage directors are paid by the number of children they care for. One less child equals less money. It is necessary to offer some . . . compensation. You understand me?' He grinned wickedly.

Words failed Sal. To deny a child the chance of a
new life because of money seemed monstrous, but she
knew what he said was true. She had learned a great
deal about the Romanians in the last few weeks.

'What I can't understand,' Cristian said, interrupting
her thoughts, 'is why people should want to adopt these
children. Most of them are sick – they are no good. If
there are English people who want to adopt, why don't
they adopt children from their own country? Most of
the children in the orphanages are mad. They say, too,'
he lowered his voice, 'that there is AIDS in those places,
although I do not know if this is true.'

'It is true,' said Sal. She sighed and stared at Cristian
for a moment. He was not an unkind man, it was
clear to see from the laughter lines around his eyes
– indeed, he was surprisingly normal by Romanian
standards. It was understandable that so many people in this country seemed still to be paranoid and
clutched by fear; it was the legacy of the Ceauşescu
years and the Securitate's reign of terror. In addition, it appeared that, as in the case of Cristian,
there was very little room for compassion. When
you're fighting to survive, Sal mused, how can there
be compassion for others? How can I criticise the
orphanage director for not wanting to lose money?
Maybe her children are starving. To what lengths
would I go in order to protect Toby? I'd do anything,
she decided.

'Why are you staring at me like this?' Cristian
demanded, uncomfortable under her scrutiny.

'I'm sorry,' said Sal, 'it's such a hard thing to

explain. Please don't think that I'm being critical, but in Romania there is very little kindness.'

Cristian was instantly serious. 'Go on,' he said.

'I understand, or sort of understand, why this is. Life has been so hard for you, you have not had time to consider the feelings of others very much. The people who want to adopt these children – and there are people now from all over the world wishing to do so – are doing it out of a sense of caring, of love. They cannot bear to see these children suffer and want to do something personally about it.'

Cristian was silent for a moment, then he raised his glass and drank deeply. 'I do not think,' he said after a moment, 'that we Romanians like each other very much, and I think perhaps that this was one of the strengths of Ceauşescu. He turned us against ourselves; he did not want us to like or trust one another. If we had done so, we would have united and turned against him. He was a man of no education, you know, but he was clever – very, very clever. I worked for him quite closely for a while, until I had my own private revolution.'

Sal was fascinated. 'I don't understand. Please explain.'

Cristian refilled their glasses. 'I was taught to be a good Party member. My father, like me, was a lawyer, but he worked only for the State. At school I joined all of Ceauşescu's youth bands. I was a model schoolboy and believed passionately in the Ceauşescus and what they were doing. I could not understand it when my parents criticised them, which they did very occasionally, whispering in their own home, but still looking over their shoulders. I did well at school and studied law, and when I became a lawyer, because of my strong Party connections, I began working at the palace. Soon I was number two to Nicu, the Ceauşescus' son – the infamous one.'

'Was he really as bad as they say?'

'Oh yes,' Cristian said. 'At least as far as women were concerned. He would send his people out, you know, to drag women off the streets, then he'd rape them and return them. He was into drugs, he was bad. Decadent, is that right?'

'Yes,' said Sal, amazed at the man's breadth of English. 'Sorry,' she said, 'I interrupted. Go on with your story.'

'Because I was so trusted,' Cristian continued, 'I was sent abroad in a diplomatic capacity. Ceauşescu, you understand, was very nervous about who he sent out of this country, for fear that they would tell tales about him and how he ran Romania. He had to be absolutely certain that the people he sent were loyal only to him. He was sure of me. I went to a number of countries, at first only to those in Eastern Europe.'

'And that's how you came to be in Yugoslavia?' Sal said.

'Yes, I was in Belgrade for three years. Later I also spent a little time in London and in Paris, and what I saw there changed me.'

'In what way?' Sal asked.

'I saw what it meant to walk freely in the streets, to stop and talk to who you wish, with no fear. I saw what it was like to have a full belly, to see children run about laughing. I learned . . .' he hesitated '. . .

about freedom and I learned about self-respect. On my return from Paris I found Bucharest unbelievable. The contrast was extraordinary. I realised in the course of just one night, one sleepless night, that Ceauşescu was wrong, that what he was doing to Romania was destroying it, not creating a great and glorious country as he'd promised.'

'One night?' said Sal. 'You realised that in just one night?'

Cristian, normally so self-confident, looked uncertain. 'Yes,' he said. 'Why do you ask?'

'It's such an extraordinary intellectual leap,' said Sal.

'You're laughing at me,' Cristian was annoyed.

'Certainly not,' Sal denied. 'Here is a boy who's been brainwashed from the moment he first entered school to believe implicitly in the Ceauşescus, who's been taught to believe implicitly in everything they stand for, and yet you had the breadth of understanding to question and ultimately to condemn. I'm quite sure I would neither have had the mental agility nor, quite honestly, the courage.'

'Thank you,' said Cristian fervently, 'I didn't think you'd understand. It is difficult for people who've been born free to realise how hard it is.'

Sal smiled at him, anxious to relieve the tension. 'So what did you do?' she asked.

'To start with, nothing. What could I do? I was increasingly unhappy. In my job I saw things I would rather not see, did things I'd rather not do . . . and then my chance came.'

'What happened?' said Sal, completely caught up in the story.

'There is a dissident here, you may have heard of him, you may not. His name is Andre Keissler.'

'Of course I've heard of him,' said Sal. 'The poet — I've read much of his work.'

Cristian seemed surprised. 'Really?'

'I've spent most of my working life studying Eastern Europe,' Sal said. 'Andre Keissler is one of my heroes.'

'Then you will know that he was brought to court to be tried as a dissident, a year ago now.'

'Yes,' said Sal, 'and his sentence was surprisingly lenient — was it five or six years?'

'Six years,' said Cristian.

'Six years,' said Sal. 'I know everyone expected him to be condemned to death, or certainly to receive life imprisonment.'

Cristian smiled, and there was a note of pride in his voice. 'The reason he had such a small sentence was because of me. I represented him, I argued his case in court.'

'Wow!' said Sal. 'What on earth did the Ceauçescus think of that?'

'To start with, they thought it was very clever. They thought if one of their men was going to be representing Andre, there would be no problem in obtaining a death sentence, which is what they wanted. They were not pleased at his sentence, but I simply agreed with them. I said that I, too, was appalled that the case had not gone the way I had imagined, and that I was sorry.

They, of course, could not be bothered to read the court transcript and so I got away with it. Then, of course, their minds were on other things. They could see the way the tide was turning in Romania. It was not much but it was my own little revolution. Keissler is a clever man, he realised what was happening to me. I helped him and he helped me find myself. I went to the court this morning. I have filed for his immediate release and I am hoping that he will be out of prison in the next week or so.'

'I would like to meet him,' said Sal.

'Then, Miss Salvena Saunders, you shall do so.' Cristian smiled.

'So,' said Sal, 'coming back to you, how do you feel now, now that the Ceauçescus are dead?'

Cristian lit a cigarette, the fourth since their conversation had begun. It was hard to imagine a Romanian without a cigarette in his mouth, Sal thought. 'I am worried,' he said finally. 'I feel that we have tried to slay the dragon, and in doing so we have not done a good enough job.'

'That's what I said to Peter,' Sal told him. 'You have decapitated the monster but the body remains.'

'Exactly!' said Cristian. 'And I, like you, fear the body may grow a new head.'

Sal took a sip of her wine. 'You're saying that Ceauşescu's regime will live on?'

'Not Ceauşescu's, but I think the grip that Moscow holds over Romania will remain. I do not see us being a free country yet. We have taken the first step, but this is not the end. It is only the beginning.'

Sal smiled. 'You are a clever man, Cristian Popa.'

'Perhaps.' He reached out and took her hand. 'And so,' he said, 'back to where we started. When you tell me that I should understand why people want to rescue these dirty, diseased little children I am worried, because it shows that I have a long way to go to understand how the West feels and thinks. I cannot imagine wanting to take one of these children into my own home, even if my wife could not have children of her own.'

'Are you married?' It was a question that had not occurred to Sal before.

'No,' Cristian smiled. 'There has never been time, I have always been too busy. There have been girls, though.'

'I can imagine that,' said Sal. He was still holding her hand. She could feel the current between them and it was terrifyingly strong. If he felt it too, he gave no sign. He squeezed her hand and released it. 'So, help me with my education, and I will help you with your adoptions.'

'You mean you can organise them?'

'Yes, yes, it is not a problem. As I said, adoption papers are all signed by Iliescu at the moment and I know his assistant very well. He's a lawyer, too, who trained with me. He has told me that if I pass the adoption papers to him, he will make sure they are signed. You need to see your Embassy, I think, to find out what papers you need in the UK. I would come with you but they will not see me. The British Embassy do not have a very good reputation here in Bucharest – it seems they do not like Romanians any more than Romanians like themselves.'

'Really?' said Sal.

Cristian nodded. 'And now I shall take you to lunch.'

'No,' said Sal. 'I shall take *you* to lunch. You've been a great help to my paper, and the least we can do in return is to buy you a decent lunch.'

They got drunk, mildly, over lunch. Another bottle of wine plus brandy with their coffee. They talked of many things, of their parents, of their lives, and suddenly Sal found herself talking about her search for her brother. Cristian's interest quickened. 'I think I may be able to help you. I have some very good contacts in Belgrade. What details can you give me?'

'Very little,' said Sal. 'My father's name was Serge Kovic, he worked in the Government for Tito, I think, but originally he was an Army officer.' She balked at telling Cristian that her father was a traitor. She hurried on: 'He had two children, me and my brother, Georges. We, my mother and I, left Yugloslavia in 1955 I think. My mother's name was Marie, incidentally, and my brother was about eight at the time. I have his birth certificate and mine. If it would be helpful – in fact, I have them with me.' Sal took the envelope from the safe deposit box everywhere with her. The photograph had become particularly precious; she spent hours looking at it.

'If you could copy them,' said Cristian, 'and leave them with me, I will see what I can find out.'

'I've been through most of the records in Belgrade,

which is where Georges was born. I was born in Zagreb for some reason.'

'OK. Maybe if your father worked for the Government, your family's file is secret.' He hesitated. 'Still, it was all a long time ago. It may well be possible to gain access to the information now.'

'I would be very, very grateful,' said Sal. They smiled at one another.

'Sal!' Across the room Peter came hurrying towards them. 'I've just had a call from Martin and Sadie Harris on their way to the airport. There's a crisis at the orphanage.' He smiled at Cristian. 'Hello again.'

Cristian rose to his feet. 'May I introduce myself formally. My name is Cristian Popa.'

'Peter Blakeney,' said Peter. 'Look, I'm sorry to interrupt your lunch, but I think we'll have to do something. It's a national holiday, I understand, today being the first of January.'

Cristian nodded. 'Yes?'

'Well, all the orphanage staff are on holiday too. There is no one there to look after the children. They haven't been fed or cleaned up. Martin and Sadie said it's unbelievable, indescribable. There's just one old lady caretaker, who's doing nothing for the children. She's just sitting in the office.'

'How many children are at this orphanage?' Cristian asked.

'About two hundred and fifty,' said Sal. 'We'd better raid the hotel kitchen again, hadn't we?' She looked at Peter.

'Yes, but we can't go on like this, Sal. We've got

to get back home and make people understand what's going on here.'

'I'd like to come too, if I may,' said Cristian suddenly.

'I don't think you should,' Sal began.

'Look, Sal,' said Peter, clearly exasperated, 'we are in no position to turn away any offer of help.'

'But what about all the other orphanages?' Sal said.

'They'll all be the same, I imagine, but this one we know about.'

'My sister will come,' said Cristian, apparently caught up in the drama. 'I have a sister who has four children. She's a good mother. I will go and collect her and some of her friends.'

'Let's find some soap and towels and flannels,' said Sal. 'If we're going to do this job, let's try and do it properly.'

In the end they worked until two in the morning, washing, feeding, cuddling and talking to the children. Martin and Sadie were all for missing their flight, but Sal insisted that they caught it. 'The sooner you are home, the sooner you can come back and get Daniella out of here.'

She immediately understood their obsession with Daniella. She was a tiny pale-faced child, with huge blue eyes and blonde down on her head which had been cruelly razored. She looked very ill, but there was a brightness in her – certainly she had not given up on life.

Cristian's sister Marianna was very different from

her brother – small and slight, though with the same dark mane of hair and kind bright blue eyes. She and her two friends worked like Trojans. They were rougher with the children than Sal would have liked, but they got through the work, dealing with twice as many children as the rest of them could do.

When at last every child in the orphanage had been given a meal of sorts and cleaned up where possible, they staggered out into the street and climbed into Cristian's battered old car. In the hotel they ordered wine and all went straight to Sal's room.

Marianna had agreed to look after little Daniella until Martin and Sadie could return. She would take no money. 'I do this to redress my country's shame,' she said sternly. She did not possess her brother's humour.

After drinking the wine and loading Martin and Sadie's supplies into a taxi, Marianna and friends left them amid grateful thanks from everyone. Peter, too, went to bed, leaving Sal and Cristian alone. They sat awkwardly on the edge of Sal's bed.

'You know,' said Sal, 'for a man who professes to think very little of the orphanage children, you worked very hard today. In fact, for someone who has never had children of his own, you were remarkable.'

'I am learning,' Cristian said with sudden touching innocence. 'I could see that many of those children were not mad, and if properly fed and clothed they would be like anyone's child – your child, or mine. I can see that now.'

'They are being denied the chance of life, Cristian,'

Sal said. 'They're being made to suffer appalling degradation simply because their families cannot care for them. It's so wrong.'

Cristian smiled. 'That little girl, Daniella, she will be very pretty and very clever, a real character. She has not given up on her life – yes?'

'That's right,' Sal said, smiling. 'So is she the sort of little girl you could take home?'

'Not yet,' said Cristian. 'I cannot imagine taking another person's child into my home, but maybe you will teach me to think that I could.'

Sal stifled a yawn. Her eyes were aching with exhaustion, her back and shoulders were shouting in protest at all the children she had picked up and carried about.

'You go back to England tomorrow?'

'Yes,' said Sal wearily. 'If we can ever drag ourselves out of bed.'

'But you will be back?'

'Oh yes,' said Sal. 'Probably in about a week.'

'And if I give you my telephone number, you will contact me and I will meet your plane. I will try and find out about your brother while you are gone.'

'That would be very kind.'

He bent over and kissed her. Their lips met briefly. Even in her exhaustion, Sal's heart began hammering in her chest.

And then he was gone.

The following morning, numb with exhaustion and disorientation, Sal and Peter sat side by side staring out of the window as their plane climbed into the sky and circled once above Bucharest before heading west.

'Sum up Romania for me, Peter,' Sal asked.

Peter stared at her in silence for a moment. 'You're the journalist, I just take the pictures.'

'I want to know how you feel.'

Peter hesitated. 'Well, having seen what I've seen and experienced what I've experienced, I feel my life will never be quite the same again. Am I being melodramatic?'

Sal shook her head, tears coming into her eyes. 'I want to go home, of course I do, I'm missing Toby terribly and all of life's creature comforts but . . .'

'But a part of you is still down there?'

'Yes,' said Sal. She began to weep openly.

'Come on, Sal,' said Peter gently. 'This is not the tough old cookie I've come to know and love. You mustn't let it get to you like this.'

'I can't help it,' said Sal between sobs. 'Yesterday we helped two hundred children to have one meal in the space of twenty-four hours, but how many thousands of children across Romania had nothing, while the rest of the world celebrated the first day of the New Year? How many, Peter?'

Peter said nothing. He stared over Sal's head at the clouds scudding by, obliterating Bucharest.

'Like you,' Sal said, 'I've never been a particularly baby-orientated person. I mean, I don't coo over every pram I pass. In fact, children often drive me crackers. It's just that this is so terrible.'

As she spoke, a fresh bout of sobbing racked her

body. 'I feel so helpless. I want to help them so much – I want to give them a chance of life! I can't bear to live in a world where they're suffering so much, and I just don't know what else to do.'

'Sal,' said Peter, 'you've told the world about them, you've told the world in very dramatic style that no one can ignore. There is nothing more one human being could do than you have done.'

'Than *we* have done,' Sal said. 'This is a story where the pictures tell more than the copy.'

'In some instances, yes,' Peter agreed, 'but you've managed to portray the scale of the horror in a way I could never do. Look, if we're going to be any use to the children, we have to distance ourselves a little or we'll crack up under the strain and that'll be as bad as simply turning our backs on them.'

'I know you're right,' said Sal, wiping her eyes furiously. 'I'm sorry.'

'It's OK. Believe me, I understand.'

'I know you do,' sniffed Sal, blowing her nose hard. 'It's just that there will be no rest until we've really done something tangible about helping those children.'

'None,' Peter agreed. 'None at all.'

CHAPTER FOURTEEN

A t Heathrow, Sal and Peter wandered out to Arrivals. There was no one to meet either of them. Without needing to put their thoughts into words, they both recognised they were reluctant to pick up the threads of 'normal' life again. On the plane they had worked out a battle plan, drawing up a list of contacts whom they hoped would either give, or raise, money for the Romanian orphanages. This, together with the fund they hoped the *Daily Record* could raise, would at least make some contribution towards relieving the suffering. Somehow, though, it did not seem enough.

'Shall we have a brandy and coffee before we leave the airport?' Peter suggested.

Sal nodded. 'I should be getting back to my son.'

'Yes, you should,' said Peter, 'but just have a quick one.'

At the bar they found a table and collapsed. They

were both utterly exhausted. 'I suppose we're feeling guilty about opting out, flying home and leaving,' Peter said, trying to make sense of their mood.

'Yes,' said Sal, grateful for his understanding. 'You know what I'm afraid of? I'm afraid that the daily demands of our lives will just overwhelm us – and that we'll forget just how awful it is.'

Peter reached across and took her hand. In the past there had not been much physical closeness between them, but Romania had changed all that. They needed the comfort. 'We've made sure that the world won't forget them. You heard what David said, he said that coverage has been immense.'

'Oh come on, Peter.' Sal released his hand and slumped back wearily in her chair. 'Today's media hype, that's all it is. To try and keep the momentum going will be impossible. What's that terrible expression? "Compassion fatigue". The punters can only take so much misery. Then they want coverage of the latest Royal scandal or who is favourite at Wimbledon.'

'Children are different,' Peter said.

'Yes, yes,' said Sal, 'children *are* different, and this is on such a huge scale that we'll be able to keep their interest for a while, but believe me, by this time next year it will be yesterday's news, and no one will want to know.'

'You're very cynical,' he told her.

'You know I'm only speaking the truth. There are so many young lives at stake – some already damaged beyond repair. Yes, some – like little Daniella – may have a chance of a new life, a chance to survive, but what about the rest? Normally . . .' She shut her eyes for a moment. She was close to tears again and wanted to control them. She took a deep breath. 'Normally when we inform our readers of a catastrophe, I feel that we have done our job. We've made them aware of what's happening and then left it up to them to think, feel, or do, whatever is appropriate.'

'But not in this case,' Peter said quietly.

'No,' said Sal. 'Not in this case. I feel that personally, I have to do more.'

'You're crying again.'

'I'm not.' She wiped the tears away hurriedly.

'Look, old girl, if it's any consolation I feel exactly the same. This one has got to me in a way that nothing else ever has, and God knows why. I'm not even a parent like you.'

'Thank you for reminding me,' said Sal shakily. 'Come on, we'd better drink up and go.'

The house seemed different somehow – lighter, airier, cleaner. She had only been away four weeks, but it felt much longer. She called out, but at first thought there was no one in. Then Jenny emerged from her bedroom upstairs. 'Sal!' she said. 'I'm glad you're home, very glad.' She came down the stairs, two at a time, her open round face full of friendship. The two women embraced.

'I'm sorry I left you alone for so long,' Sal said. 'How's Toby?'

'Coping,' said Jenny, 'just.' Her face clouded. 'I'm

sorry too,' she said. 'I've been meaning to write to you, but I didn't know the words and I didn't even know if you'd get the letter.'

'What about?' said Sal.

'To apologise for the way I behaved when you left. It was a time when you needed my support, not my criticism. Those children – what a nightmare you must have been through.'

'You read my reports then?'

'Devoured them, and so has the rest of the country. You can't turn on the television or the radio without someone talking about Romania and the children at the moment.'

'Thank God for that,' said Sal. 'Then perhaps somebody is going to do something about it.'

'Oh, they are already. Voluntary organisations have been set up all over the country to take stuff out. I'm surprised you haven't heard about it.'

'You don't hear anything about anything in Bucharest,' said Sal. 'That's wonderful, I'm so pleased.'

'And there are people who want to adopt the children, but I don't know if that's possible.'

'It seems as if it may be,' said Sal. 'Now, what's the time?' She looked at her watch. 'I'll put in a call to David, and then I'll go and collect Toby from school.' She started to walk towards the telephone.

'Sal.'

'Yes?'

'I think you may find Toby very difficult.'

Sal stopped short. 'In what way?'

'He's feeling very resentful. I've done my best, but

he's got it firmly into his head that he's pretty low on your priority list at the moment.'

'I suppose in a way he has been,' Sal admitted. 'I've missed him dreadfully, but I know he has a warm bed and plenty of food, good friends and you to care for him.'

'And a mother who seems to have forgotten he exists,' said Jenny. 'He loved your Christmas presents, but he would have given up the lot to have had you there in person.'

'I understand,' said Sal. 'What is it that he resents – just the time I've been away or my concern for all these children?'

'Not the children so much. He's proud of what you've done there,' said Jenny, 'but he's still very angry about your affair with Louis. He feels you behaved very badly, so far as Evelyn is concerned. He's very fond of her, you know.'

'Yes, he is,' said Sal.

'Of course he realises that your friendship with the Nobles is over. For him, particularly, it is like losing another part of his family. Next to you and me, the Nobles are the people closest to him . . . or they were. Looking at it from his point of view, you've alienated him from his best friends. Then you swan off to the other side of Europe and appear to expend all your maternal sympathy on other people's abandoned children.'

Sal let out a sigh. 'Where do I start, Jenny?'

'That, Sal, is up to you. He's your son. Now, if it's OK with you, I'm going out tonight. It's been a *long* four weeks. There's a shepherds pie in the fridge.'

'Yes, of course. Would you like a few days off?'

'I'll take the weekend off if I may, unless you're going abroad again.'

'I won't be going anywhere this weekend,' said Sal. 'I'm going to spend it with my son.'

'I'm very glad to hear it,' said Jenny.

There was already a group of mothers around the school gate when Sal arrived. She knew a few of them by sight, but nobody well, as she so rarely collected Toby herself. If she did, she was usually in a hurry so there had never been any time to make friends with the other mothers. Today, though, it was different. Her mind still full of her conversation with Jenny, she expected to wait alone by the gate as usual. Instead, as soon as they saw her, the other mums rushed to meet her, all talking at once.

'What can we do?' 'What's the best thing?' 'I've been digging out all my son's old clothes.' 'I'm collecting tins of baby food.' 'Is it money they need?' 'When are you going out there again?' Questions came thick and fast. David had been out when Sal had telephoned the office and she had made an appointment to see him early the following morning. She was therefore still largely unaware of the impact of her reportage. The warmth of these women touched her, their desire to help was so genuine. She began talking animatedly, suggesting that they co-ordinated with the paper and yes, they must arrange to send trucks out and yes, everything was needed – clothes, nappies, medicine, toys and above all, food. The circle of people around her increased. She handed out as many business cards as she had with her, telling them all to contact the office with details of what they had available.

She did not know how long he had been standing there. He stood apart from the group, watching her, his hands in his pockets. His fair hair was a little too long, and his head was tilted on one side, the gesture he always adopted when he was slightly embarrassed.

'Excuse me,' she cried out desperately, 'excuse me.' She fought her way through the crowd to where Toby stood. 'Hello, Tobe,' she said. 'I've missed you so much.' She went to put her arms around him but he moved slightly away so she could not reach him.

'Hi, Mum. Have you finished here or shall I wait in the car?'

'I've finished here,' she said. 'Come on.'

It was a cold afternoon, almost dark. Sal shivered involuntarily as she climbed into the car. She reached out and took Toby's hand. It was lifeless and unresponsive in hers. 'Toby, look at me.' Reluctantly he turned and met her eye. 'I'm really terribly sorry I've been away for so long, but these children . . .'

'Oh, I know all about them. I've read your reports. It's not that I mind.'

'If it's about Louis and Evelyn . . .?'

'I don't want to talk about that. Let's go home.'

Sal started the car and began to drive. She was silent for a moment or two, but was aware that if she was going to confront the issue at all, the car was the best place. At least she had him as a captive audience. 'What we did, Louis and I, was wrong,' Sal said.

'Of course it was wrong,' Toby burst out. 'I just can't think why you wanted to take him away from Evelyn and mess up everyone's lives.'

'I didn't want to take him away from Evelyn.'

'So why did you . . . Why did you . . .' He could not find the word. His voice tailed off, embarrassed.

'Why did I have an affair with him?'

'Yes.'

She glanced at him. He was now acutely embarrassed and blushing. It gave her a feeling of confidence, for he suddenly looked younger and more approachable. 'Toby, I never tell you much about my trips abroad, because sometimes they are quite dangerous and I don't want to worry you, but as I told you before I went away, the thing with Louis just happened because he had been in terrible danger.'

'What sort of danger?' Toby said, and Sal told him, without sparing any of the details, of Louis' brush with the Soviet Mafia and the death of Gennadi Naidenov. 'There's no excuse for what happened,' she concluded. 'It's just that we were far away from home and everything was so awful. I know it's not much of an excuse, but in the middle of all that, I wasn't thinking it through. I wasn't thinking "this is going to mess up Toby's friendship with the Nobles", I was just thinking "poor old Louis. My friend for a long time needs comfort".'

'You should have spent more time explaining it to me before you went away.'

'I know,' said Sal, 'but you see it's a problem all parents suffer from – not realising how grown-up their children are getting.'

'Well, it's hardly surprising you don't know how grown-up I'm getting. You're never here to see me grow!'

'That's not true, Toby.'

'It is.'

Sal felt tears in her eyes. Damn, Romania had changed her. She found tears came much more easily than they had done in the past. 'But what else am I to do, Toby? I have to work. It's not easy being a single parent.'

'Then perhaps you should never have had me.'

'Oh Toby, don't!' Tears were running down her face now. 'Look, you're the best thing that's ever happened to me. The only decent thing that's ever happened to me. It's just hard to please everyone.'

'David says that you could give it up. David says that you could get plenty of freelance work, now you're so well-known.'

'Oh, he did, did he? Well, he shouldn't interfere.'

'He was only trying to be kind,' said Toby. 'He knows how I hate you being away, and he was just telling me there was something you could do about it, if you wanted to. I don't care about the school and the clothes and the toys. I just want to have an ordinary life like everybody else. And why won't you tell me about my father?'

The question, when it came, was like a body blow. Sal was not up to it – it was all too much. She drove the car to the side of the road, put the hand-brake on and switched off the engine, then buried her head in her hands. 'Toby, do we have to go into this now?'

'It was you who wanted to talk.'

'I've told you before,' she said. 'I lost touch with your father. It was a silly thing – a one-night stand; it should never have happened. I'm very glad that it did, but I never kept in touch with him.'

'What was his name?' Toby said.

'I can't remember.'

'You can't remember the name of the father of your child? It can't have been very important to you then, can it?'

'Toby, I was very young and single, I didn't even have a job. The easy thing for me to do was to have an abortion, but I didn't. I had you because I really, really wanted you.'

'But why did you want me, when you're not prepared to spend time with me? You write about those children in Romania. You call them orphans. Well, I'm nearly an orphan.'

Sal began to cry in earnest, her head on the steering wheel, great sobs racking her body. 'I'm sorry, I'm sorry,' she murmured.

Toby looked at her aghast. He had never seen her like this. Tentatively he put out a hand and touched her arm. 'I'm sorry, Mum. I didn't mean . . .'

'It's all right,' she managed between sobs. 'You're quite right, Toby. I'm only upset because you're quite right.'

'I just get so lonely,' he confessed, tears coming into his eyes, too. 'Jenny's nice but—'

Instinctively mother and son turned to one another, and flung themselves into each other's arms. Holding him against her, he seemed suddenly so small and frail. It was not a conscious decision, but as the words came out, Sal knew she meant them. 'Tobe, I'll have to finish this job, see it through, this Romanian thing. I have to try and help these children. You understand that?' He nodded against her chest. 'After that, I swear to you I'll give it up – go freelance like David suggests.'

Toby drew away a little from the circle of her arms. 'Do you really promise that? Do you really mean it?'

'Yes.'

'We could go and live in the country,' Toby said. 'In Grandma's house.'

'Would you like that?' Sal said, astonished.

'Yes, I would, very much,' said Toby.

'But what about your friends and your school?'

'Oh, I don't care. I'll make new friends and I can go to the local school. That'll save money, won't it?'

'Yes, it will,' said Sal. 'I didn't know you were a country bumpkin at heart, my lad.'

'I just want us to have a normal family life,' he said simply.

'What about Jenny?' Sal asked. 'Shouldn't she come too?'

'No.'

Sal stared at him. 'I thought you liked her!'

'I do, she's great, but she's not my mother. If we're going to do this, then you must look after me, not

Jenny. I don't need much looking after now, anyway. It will probably be me looking after you.' He laughed. His face was tear-stained, but the strained, unhappy look had left him. Sal felt a sudden surge of excitement. He was right! It had taken her eleven-year-old son to sort out her life.

She took his hand in hers. 'Thank heavens I've got you, Toby. Without your good sense, God knows where I'd be.'

'Can we go down to the cottage this weekend?' he asked eagerly. 'We could work out who's going to have which room and where we'll put everything. And then you can sell our London house, and that'll help us out with money, won't it?'

Sal laughed. 'Absolutely. Perhaps you'd like to be my business manager as well.'

'No problem. Can we, though? Can we go to the cottage, or have you got to go away again?'

'I'm not going away this weekend, Toby. I'm going to spend it with you – and yes, of course we'll go down to the cottage.'

Sal arrived at David's office at nine-thirty sharp the following morning, having dropped Toby off at school. She was greeted by coffee and Buck's Fizz. He hugged her, as full of boyish enthusiasm as ever.

'What's all this in aid of?' Sal said, looking at the champagne.

David hesitated. 'You may feel this is in poor taste, but I had to mark the occasion in some way. The paper's circulation has beaten all records this week,

outstripped anything it's ever done before, even the
time we were running that sweepstake – and it's all
down to you, Sal.'

Sal froze for a moment. 'You're right, it *is* in bad
taste.' Then she turned and walked over to the window.
'I can't describe how those children are suffering,
David.'

'But you have, you've just described it to millions of
people. Aid and money is rolling in, Sal. We've had to
employ a dozen people just to cope with the post.'

'All the same . . .' her voice dropped away. David, from
his desk, watched her profile. She looked exhausted and
she was very pale and thin. She rallied. 'I so want this
campaign to be different. The problem isn't going to
disappear overnight. People are full of zeal now, but
will it last?'

'I don't know, I shouldn't think so,' said David
cheerfully, 'but let's at least take full advantage of our
punters' generosity while they're in the mood.'

'Oh, David.' Sal leaned forward and pressed her
forehead against the window, shoulders hunched, rigid
with tension. David had never seen her like this.

'Sal, what is it? What's wrong?' She did not answer.
He hurried to her side and put his arms around her,
drew her to him until her head was buried against his
shoulder. 'Stop frightening me,' he murmured into her
hair. 'Please tell me what's wrong. I can't bear it.'

For a moment she stood silently in the circle of
his arms, gaining comfort from his familiar presence.
Then, with a show of some of her old determination,
she released herself from his embrace and sat down in

front of his desk in a businesslike way. She reached for the cup of coffee he had poured her. Her hand was shaking, he noticed.

'I'm sorry, David, it's just everything. The Louis thing, Evelyn — I'm at a loss to know what to say or do as far as she is concerned. Have you heard anything about them, about their marriage?'

'Not a thing,' said David.

'And then Toby. I've been away from him for so long and it's all wrong. On top of it all I keep thinking about my brother. I want to find him so much, you see. Everything has just piled up, I'm sorry.'

'After this lot,' said David, 'I suggest you have a holiday. There's no need for you to go out to Romania again. We'll send someone else.'

Sal looked at him as if he was mad. 'David, you understand nothing, do you, nothing about this! I couldn't *not* go back. If you sacked me, I'd still be out there next week, doing what I could in the orphanages. This just isn't a story you can walk away from, this is different.'

'My circulation tells me it's different,' said David.

'Why does everything always come back to money?' Sal burst out.

'Because it's usually the truest indicator. Your story of the Romanian orphanages has sold more papers than I'd have believed possible and, as you say, that makes this story different. I'm trying to understand, Sal, but it's difficult for me because I haven't been there. I read what you write and look at Peter's pictures, and I've heard in the last few weeks your voice on the phone as you've become increasingly more involved and clearly more affected by what you've seen. But without seeing and touching first-hand, it is hard for me to understand exactly what you're going through.'

'I know,' said Sal. 'I'm being unfair.'

'You're certainly making an old man very upset and worried.' David grinned at her. 'So, are you going to accept a glass of Buck's Fizz — not to celebrate, mind, just to cheer us both up.'

'You're incorrigible,' said Sal.

'I try to be. Now listen, I have three potential adopters for you to take out on your next trip, assuming I accept that there's going to be a next trip. All three of them are Social Services approved. I want you to help them secure adoptions and follow their stories. If they each bring home a child, that will be three children saved. How many people can say they've saved the lives of three children? You'll be able to, Sal. It may not be much in the scale of things, but it's three precious little lives.'

Sal smiled, and walked over to perch on his desk. 'Why is it that you can always make me feel better? Why do you always know just what to say? Yes, I will have some of that champagne, please, and don't worry about the orange juice.'

'That's my girl,' said David. He poured two glasses. 'Here's to you and the *Daily Record*. What would we do without you?'

Sal, about to raise the glass to her lips, stopped. 'No,' she said, 'that's not a toast I'll drink to. To the orphaned children of Romania. Please God, may the world never forget them!'

They touched glasses and drank, David studying her face as they did so. She had changed so much. For the first time ever, he doubted her ability to cope. With first her illness, then the strain she had been under . . . it was hard to believe she was not going to snap. Was he right to think of sending her out to Romania again? As she said herself, she would go anyway and he knew it was not a hollow threat. Sal never said things she did not mean, besides which, there was a pioneering light in her eye. She was not going to abandon these children.

While David studied her, Sal's mind was reeling. Should she tell him of her decision to leave the paper? No, not yet. She would not renege on her promise to Toby, she was sure of that in her own mind, but she owed David a great deal and picking the right moment was important.

'You'll be glad to hear that it looks as if the Romanian Government will allow adoptions,' she said. 'There's an American couple who helped us the first day we discovered the orphanages – they are well on the way to adopting a little girl, and I've met a lawyer who claims to have the whole thing sussed out.'

'I thought I could rely on you. What's the new President like, Iliescu?'

'I don't know. No journalist has been allowed near him yet. He wants to get his feet under the table, but the lawyer I was speaking of has doubts about him.'

'What sort of doubts?'

'Well, as he described it to me, they have cut off the head of the monster by killing the Ceauşescus, but the beast lives on.'

'An ugly thought,' said David.

'It's an ugly place,' said Sal, 'but it could be so beautiful – the buildings, the people, the culture, the countryside . . . it is wonderful. It's appalling what that man did to the people, David. He took away their soul. I hope to God they can find it again.'

'Is it worse than other Eastern European countries, I wonder?' David asked.

'Yes, in a way. The people literally have nothing, and so soon after the revolution, they are still finding it difficult to shake off old habits. They're terrified of speaking to anyone, of speaking out of turn or being seen in the wrong place at the wrong time. Mind you, perhaps their worries are not ill-conceived. Rumour has it that the Secret Police are still very much in evidence.' Sal held out her glass for a top-up of champagne. 'The orphanages are terrible, but so is the way that ordinary people live, David. They queue for hours for everything, they make the Russian queues seem like nothing, and yet they're so proud and so hospitable. They're wonderful people, but how they came to let Ceauşescu run their lives, I just don't know. If ever a country deserves a helping hand, it's Romania.'

'Then we'll just have to see what we can do for her children,' said David quietly.

'I'll drink to that,' Sal said.

'Tell me, how are you and Toby?' David said. 'He's missed you a great deal.'

'He's fine,' said Sal, noncommital, not wanting to be drawn on the pact she and Toby had made. 'While we're changing the subject, what happened to the Louis story? Did it run for much longer after I left?'

'No.' David looked away, avoiding her eyes. 'It lasted about another twenty-four hours. I'm sorry if I was a bit rough on you Sal, but I knew if we got you out of the country and into the heart of a revolution, our colleagues would drop the matter. We may be bastards to one another in some respects, but you don't have a go at someone if she's out there risking her life.'

'I don't think we should turn on our own colleagues at all,' said Sal. 'I'd never write a derogatory piece about a fellow journalist.'

'I'm sorry but I don't agree with you. I don't think that's the right attitude at all,' said David. 'If we're being strictly ethical, we should write any story about anyone, if it's going to provide the readership with what they want.'

'Maybe, but I did feel hurt the way Jim Peters had a go at me in the *Sun*. I thought we were old chums. God knows, we've known each other for years.'

'All's fair in love, war and journalism,' David said.

'So it would seem,' sighed Sal. 'Toby read all about it, you know.'

'So I understand.' David got up and walked over to the window. 'Sal, now he's lost the Nobles, don't you think it's about time you told Toby who his father is?'

'So it was you who put the idea into his head,' Sal said, suddenly angry.

'No, it wasn't,' said David impatiently. 'We went for a walk on New Year's Day, and he asked me if I knew anything about his father. I said that I didn't, which is true. Then he got quite excitable and said he didn't feel that you had the right to keep the information from him. I have to say that I agree with him.'

'David, I've told you a hundred times, I never kept in touch with the father. It was just a stupid teenage party. I had too much to drink then wham, bam, thank you Mam, and he was gone.'

'Was he known to the person giving the party?'

'I don't know, I never asked.'

'Well, don't you think you should? Don't you think that even at this stage you should try and find out for Toby's sake.'

'And what happens when the poor bloke suddenly discovers that he has a son?' Sal said hotly. 'How is it going to affect his life? He's probably married with more children of his own. How's he going to feel, to suddenly have this wished upon him? It could do Toby a great deal more harm than good, if his father rejects him – as well he might.'

'It's up to you,' David said gently. 'I don't want to upset you, particularly when you've had such a rough time, but it's my belief that in a few years' time Toby is going to look for himself. It might be that you could save him a lot of grief if you made the initial contact. I'm sure he'll find his Dad – if that's what he decides to do. He has great tenacity, you know.'

'He might not find it that easy,' Sal said.

David came over and put an arm around her shoulders. 'Sorry, I shouldn't have mentioned it,' he said. 'Tell me about you. How do you feel about Louis now?'

Sal raised her eyes and met David's. They were clear and blue, and he had an oddly innocent expression for a middle-aged man, quite extraordinary for a newspaperman. 'I feel absolutely nothing, David, and that makes things even worse. Having caused all that pain I should at least be pining my heart out or something, but I feel nothing at all.'

David bent forward and kissed her gently on the cheek. 'I'm glad,' he murmured. 'He was not for you, that one. We'll find the right man for you yet, but sure as hell it isn't Louis Noble.'

'Well, it's good to know someone has taken over responsibility for the task,' said Sal with a smile.

'Evelyn, it's Sal.' Sal's voice shook with nerves and emotion.

'Yes,' said Evelyn, her voice cold.

'I'm ringing to say I'm sorry,' Sal said. 'I know it's not an adequate word, given all the circumstances. I just don't know what else to say, Evelyn.'

'You're right,' said Evelyn, 'it's not an adequate word. Hold on a moment, let me close the door.' There was the sound of her footsteps across the parquet floor, and then Sal heard her shut the hall door. She could envisage the scene, she knew the house so well. She ached with remorse.

'Hello.' Evelyn was back.

'It was such a stupid thing . . .' Sal began. 'It would never have happened but for— '

'Don't,' Evelyn broke in. 'I don't want to talk about it to you. If you use your imagination, I'm sure you'll understand why. In fact, Sal, I don't know that there's much point in us talking at all.'

'Please don't hang up on me,' Sal begged. 'Evelyn, of all the rotten things I've done in my life, and there've been a few, this is the most rotten. I know I've caused you a great deal of pain, I suppose what I'm trying to say is that it's caused me a great deal of pain, too. I don't want you to think that I've – if you like – got away with it.'

'So what am I supposed to do?' said Evelyn. 'Feel sorry for you?'

'No, no, of course not! How are you, anyway? How are things?'

'I'm sorry, Sal, I simply can't discuss anything with you. I don't want to talk about Louis, I don't want to talk about the children, and I certainly don't want to talk about myself.'

'I just wanted to know if you were all right,' Sal said.

'Well, of course I'm not all right. My best friend, the person I trusted most in the world, has had an affair with my husband. The affair in question changed him from a mild, easygoing man, happy with his lot, to a difficult, angry, deeply unhappy man with no sense of direction and a complete lack of faith, both in himself and for his chosen calling in life. His career is in ruins, so is our marriage, so is our family life. Don't tell me you're suffering as much as I am. Don't you *dare* tell me that.'

'I wasn't trying to— ' Sal began.

'This conversation is getting nowhere.' The phone went dead.

Sal held on to the receiver. For a moment she thought she was going to be sick. At last, breathing heavily, she replaced it and slid down the wall to end up on the floor, knees hunched up to her chest, like a child. This was how Jenny found her a few minutes later. The hotel bedroom was almost dark. Jenny peered at her through the gloom. 'Sal, what the hell are you doing?'

'I've just spoken to Evelyn,' Sal whimpered.

Jenny crouched down beside her. 'What did she say?'

'She said that Louis' career is in tatters and that their marriage is over and the family is in disarray and it's all my fault. Oh God, how can I have done such a dreadful thing to them all! I can't even cry, I don't seem to have any tears left. What sort of person am I?'

'Don't shout at me for being flippant,' said Jenny sympathetically, 'but it takes two to tango. You can't take all the blame; some of it has to rest with Louis.'

'He's such an innocent, though,' said Sal. 'Without a doubt it was me who seduced him, at any rate to start with. Am I shocking you?' Sal raised her head, and even in the gloom, Jenny was horrified by the sight of her ravaged face.

'No, you're not shocking me,' Jenny said. 'But why did you do it? Had you always been attracted to him?'

'No, never,' said Sal. 'I went to his room that night in Moscow, the night we rescued him, with no thought but to check up on him and see if he was all right. I thought he might want me to put through a call to Evelyn, or organise his clothes to be washed for the morning – they were covered in Gennadi's blood, you see. That was all, honestly. I swear to God, Jenny.'

'I believe you,' said Jenny.

'And then when I got there, he was in shock, I comforted him, and things just got out of hand. Then suddenly it was too late. We were both very disorientated, I suppose, by what had happened, but where we went wrong was carrying on with it. If we'd stopped it there, things would have been different.'

'But you didn't,' said Jenny.

'No, and now I've ruined all our lives. Oh Jenny, they were my best friends!'

'I'll ring David and get him to postpone your trip. You're in no fit state to go to Romania.'

'No, please don't. Quite honestly, at the moment it's the only thing keeping me going. Those children need me to be their voice. In helping them, at least I'm doing something worthwhile. It's not going to atone for what I've done, but it's something.'

'So how long are you going to go on punishing yourself?' Jenny asked. 'And remember, when you punish yourself, you punish Toby.'

'Not for much longer,' Sal said. 'I promise. I want some peace, Jenny, and I want to find my brother. I want to find my brother so badly.' And then came the tears. When she was spent, Jenny helped her up on to the bed and then sat with her for a long time, wondering what on earth the future held for all three of them. For one thing was certain: Sal could not go on as she was for much longer.

As the Tarom flight bucketed into the sky above Heathrow airport the following Wednesday, Sal at least felt happier about Toby. Their parting had been emotional, but they were much more confident of each other and their relationship and, of course, they shared the secret of Sal's retirement from the paper. Before the fateful call to Evelyn, they had spent a marvellous weekend at her mother's cottage, planning how they would live, what furniture would go and what would stay. They had even begun to partially clear out some of the rooms to the extent that by the end of the weekend it was already beginning to feel more like their home than her mother's. The tranquillity of the little village of Horton-cum-Studley, Sal found, brought her a peace of mind she had not expected so soon after Bucharest.

Being alone with Toby was good, too. They were so much alike, she realised. He was growing up so fast these days. Although she had always loved him more than anyone else, Sal came to see that she had not been in tune with his development for some years. Somewhere along the line the little boy had gone. What she had now was a stalwart companion and a good friend. She was desperate to keep it that way.

Sal glanced across the aisle at her fellow companions on the flight. Peter was with her, of course, morose and hungover, feeling, she suspected, much as she

did herself – needing to go back to Bucharest and
yet wishing he did not have to. With them were the
three potential adopters supplied by the *Daily Record*.
The paper was paying their fares and accommodation,
and in return Sal was to write their stories. As David
had promised, they had not been chosen at random.
All three had been trying to adopt a child for some
time and so had been passed by the Social Services as
suitable candidates. David and Sal were very anxious
that the whole affair should not look like 'a puppy for
Christmas' syndrome. These three women were deadly
serious about the commitment they were making. They
sat in a row now, clearly deep in thought as to what
lay ahead. They had talked only briefly, over a drink,
before boarding the plane, but Sal had instinctively
taken to all three of them, although they were very
different.

Margaret Johnson was in her early forties. She
already had grown-up children and was in the process
of applying to adopt an older child from the UK. Now,
suddenly, the plight of the children in Romania had
seemed more urgent to her and she had her husband's
full backing on this. She was a tall woman, quite a force
to be reckoned with – a strong, confident character.
There was a warmth about her though, and humour.
She was not a pretty woman, but her kind brown eyes
and lively expression gave her undoubted charm.

Diana Wainwright was a barrister in her early thirties, again rather high-powered and outspoken, but in a
much more disciplined way than Margaret. Three years
before, Diana and her husband had adopted a little boy

from Brazil. The experience had proved so traumatic that they had vowed never to adopt again. Romania had changed all that. She was beautifully groomed, an elegant woman, clearly very efficient. Sal found it hard to imagine her in an orphanage setting, and it worried her.

The youngest of the three, Jill Cookson, looked, frankly, terrified. She was only twenty-four and described herself to Sal as 'irrevocably infertile'. She and her husband were on the waiting list to adopt a baby, but they had been told it would be at least four years before there was any chance of adopting in the UK. Jill was very pretty, slight and fair, with large china-blue eyes which kept fixing on Sal with trust and awe. Sal prayed that her trust was justified.

It was an interesting mix. Watching them surreptitiously, Sal felt sure they had been chosen by David personally. His skill with people was rightly renowned. She already had three very different stories because of the contrast between the women.

Margaret Johnson was quite clearly going to Romania out of a sense of zeal. She had done her parenting, her children were grown-up, yet she wanted to do more to help a deprived child. Her motives were truly altruistic.

Diana Wainwright quite simply wanted a brother or sister for her young son. There was little sentiment attached to the plight of Romania's children, so far as she was concerned – but Sal could see no harm in that. She clearly adored her son – she would be a good mother, but for her Romania was simply a means to an end.

Sal was most drawn to Jill. She was not nearly so confident as the other two women. She'd had to carry the burden of knowing from an early age that she could never bear children. She still couldn't understand why her husband had been prepared to marry her in the circumstances, and now the chance of motherhood suddenly loomed. 'I went to Mothercare,' Jill had whispered to Sal. 'Your paper suggested that I should take out some basic clothes and food for a baby. I couldn't believe it was me doing the shopping. I couldn't believe that there might be someone for me out there.' Her pretty face flushed pink, her eyes filled with tears. Although in the full public glare of the Departure Lounge, Sal had wanted to throw her arms around her. There were going to be a lot of tears in the next few days.

She turned her attention to Peter. 'So how was your brief leave?' she asked.

'Ghastly,' said Peter. 'My mind was still in Bucharest and I was tearing around trying to co-ordinate a relief lorry to go out from my area. On top of it all, I had woman trouble.'

'Woman trouble you'd like to talk about?'

'No, not particularly,' said Peter. 'It's been bad enough living it, I don't think I could face going through it all again. Suffice to say, I think I'm going to become a monk.'

'You're in good company,' said Sal. 'I'm seriously thinking of giving up men.'

'You have to be joking!' Peter threw back his head and laughed.

'What makes you say that?' said Sal.

'Your Romanian friend, the lawyer Cristian, is undoubtedly the next victim – mark my words.'

'I don't like the way you say "next victim", and as it happens, you're completely wrong. I can't cope with any emotional entanglements at the moment. Certainly not with a crazy Romanian lawyer.'

'I bet he meets us at the airport,' Peter teased.

Sal had the grace to blush. 'Well, as a matter of fact he *is* meeting the plane.'

Peter grinned. 'Oh Sal, you're making me feel better already.'

'He's only meeting us at the airport,' Sal said sternly, 'because I have already telephoned him about our three charges. He's made an appointment for them to go to orphanage Number One tomorrow, and he wants to see their files tonight.'

'No comment,' smirked Peter.

'Maybe your mind lives permanently below your belt,' said Sal huffily, 'but it doesn't necessarily apply to the rest of us.'

'All right,' said Peter, taking her hand and squeezing it. 'I faithfully promise not to say "I told you so" when you and Cristian start gazing into each other's eyes.'

'What an infuriating man you are,' Sal said.

'I know,' said Peter smugly.

Cristian was indeed at the airport. Somehow he had managed to wangle his way to the wrong side of Passport Control and steered them through the Diplomatic Gate where their passports were hardly glanced at. Before they knew where they were, they were in a taxi.

'What's happened to our luggage?' Sal asked.

'I've left a friend at the airport. He will pick it up for you and bring it to the Intercontinental.'

It was very different from Peter and Sal's first arrival in Bucharest and Sal was grateful – both for her sake and for the three women with them, who, having fleetingly passed through Bucharest airport, already looked as if they had been hit over the head.

Sal sat in the front seat, next to Cristian, with Peter squashed in the back with the three women. As he started the engine Cristian turned one of his flashing smiles in Sal's direction. 'I have missed you. It has been too long.'

'It's been less than a week.'

'Still too long.' He kept his voice low. 'You are already very special to me, Salvena.'

Sal felt a rush of warmth at his words. 'Don't be ridiculous, Cristian,' she replied. 'We barely know each other.'

'I have some news for you,' he said, 'about your family.'

'What news?' Sal's heart was suddenly pounding.

'I'm not going to tell you now. It is quite, how do you say, complicated. We will talk to these ladies, I will see their files, and then we will go somewhere quietly, so I can explain.'

'Just tell me something now. I've waited so long for this: is my brother alive?' She held her breath.

'Later,' Cristian insisted. 'Trust me, it is better this way.'

Sal sat back in the seat, looking out at the darkened streets. What had he found out? Was it possible that he had located Georges' whereabouts? Had he been able to substantiate the story? She could hardly contain herself.

At last they reached the Intercontinental. Cristian arranged for them all to be booked into their rooms and then he ushered them into the ground-floor café. 'I will order you some food and wine,' he said, 'and then I will look at your files.'

'I think I'll leave you to it,' said Peter. 'Unless you want me. Do you, Sal?'

'No, no one is up to being photographed tonight.'

'The appointment tomorrow at the orphanage is for ten o'clock,' said Cristian. 'We will leave here at half-past nine, yes?'

'I'll be ready,' promised Peter. He glanced at the three women. 'I hope you all have a good night's sleep, though I doubt you will.'

Diana smiled. 'I doubt it too. I feel completely out of my depth already.'

'Don't worry,' said Peter. 'You'll find tomorrow very distressing, but very positive too. Please God, there are three children who tonight have no future, but by this time tomorrow, will have a loving family and a wonderful life ahead of them.'

At his words, Sal felt a lump in her throat. What was wrong with her? Her emotions seemed so near the surface. She glanced up at him – the untidy, shambolic figure who had been her friend in so many adventures. He was a nice man, a very special man. He caught her eye and smiled down. 'And you sleep well too,' he said, and winked. The kind thoughts instantly disappeared; Sal grimaced at his departing back.

The women's files, at a quick first glance, were all in order. 'I can see no problem at all,' said Cristian. 'First we must find your child, then seek Mother's consent, if she is alive. Then there will need to be a social report here in Romania. I put the file together and present it to Iliescu's office.'

'Supposing we found a child tomorrow,' Margaret said. 'How long would it take?'

'A week, maybe.'

'Only a week?'

'Provided there is no problem with parental consent, I can see no reason why you should not fly home in a week.' He glanced at them. 'All of you seek babies?'

'No,' said Margaret, 'I think I would like an older child.'

'And I don't mind,' said Diana Wainwright. 'My little boy is four. I would like a child younger than him, but it doesn't have to be a baby.'

'And sex?' Both women shrugged their shoulders.

'The important thing,' said Margaret, 'is to find a child who really needs help.'

Cristian gave a short, mirthless laugh. 'Believe me, madam, there will be no problem with that.' He turned his attention to Jill who, so far, had not said a word. 'What about you?'

'I have no children,' she said. 'I would like a baby, if possible.'

'Would you mind if I asked how old you are?' Cristian said.

'Twenty-four.'

'I think, maybe, it would be better if I took you to one of the maternity hospitals.'

Jill looked alarmed. 'Why?'

'There are many mothers who, when their babies are born, give them up straight away to the orphanage.' He hesitated. 'Mothers who cannot cope with their children and so do not take them home. I think maybe we could find such a baby for you, if you would be prepared to look after the child here at the hotel, while I sort out the paperwork for you.'

'Oh yes, yes,' said Jill, tears beginning to flow down her cheeks.

'I have just said something wrong?' Cristian asked, looking anxiously around.

'No,' said Sal. 'You've just said something right.'

CHAPTER FIFTEEN

'I'm taking you up to your room. You're tired, and in any event I want to talk to you in private.' Cristian was guiding Sal across the foyer of the hotel.

'What you have to tell me isn't going to be pleasant, is it?' Sal said. She had been full of apprehension ever since their brief conversation in the taxi.

'Not very,' said Cristian. 'Come on.'

They let themselves into her room. A bottle of champagne and two glasses stood by the bed. 'What's this for?' Sal asked.

'Champagne is good medicine,' Cristian told her. 'It lifts the spirits, and helps one to see things in perspective. Tonight I am your doctor as well as your lawyer.' He smiled at her; he really was a very attractive man.

Mindful of Peter's warning, Sal carefully avoided the bed and walked over to the large window, which took up the whole of one side of her room. She gazed out over the dim lights of Bucharest.

'As Peter said,' she said softly, 'there are three little children out there who, please God, are going to spend their last night unloved.'

Cristian joined her with two glasses, gave her one and slipped an arm around her shoulders. They both stared out into the night sky.

'I'm starting to understand,' he said. 'You are a good teacher. These children, they have as much right to life as you or I and these women you brought with you — they are good women, I can see.'

Sal remembered Martin and Sadie. 'How are things going with the Harris'?' she asked.

'Fine, fine. I took over the adoption, you know, and all the paperwork is completed,' he said. 'They are flying back here tomorrow. Once I have their file it should be very quick.'

'And Daniella?'

'She is doing very well. I have seen her several times. She is . . . how do you say? . . . good fun!'

Sal laughed. She took a sip of champagne and taking a deep breath said, 'I don't want to put this off any longer. Can you tell me everything you know?'

'Yes. Come and sit down.' He took her hand and they went and sat down opposite each other, on the two large beds dominating the room. 'I made my enquiries through my friends in Belgrade and I found out much information very easily. There was quite a scandal in Government circles at the time, and I was lucky. One of my friends — I cannot tell you his name because all this information is confidential – but his father actually worked with your father, so that made it a great deal easier. He was able to . . .' he hesitated.

'Put some flesh on the bones?' Sal suggested.

'Exactly. Your father was Serge Kovic.'

'Yes,' Sal nodded.

'He was a very clever man. He went to university in Belgrade and then to Cambridge, in England. He studied mathematics.'

'Cambridge – really? When would that have been?'

'Before the war. I cannot tell you the exact dates, but he was certainly in Cambridge for three or four years, and my friend believes it was there that he was recruited by the KGB. Did you know about this?'

'Yes,' admitted Sal. 'I was too ashamed to tell you that my father was a spy. I rather hoped you would disprove the story. Of course! He would have been up at Cambridge when it was literally a nursery for the KGB. Anthony Blunt, Burgess and Maclean – they would have all been there in the same period.'

'I do not know about such things,' said Cristian, 'but anyway he came back from Cambridge and joined the Army. He had a good war, his languages were particularly useful and he ended up in Cairo. It was there that he met your mother. I do not know any details about her, other than she was English. They married and he brought her to Belgrade. They lived in a very nice house in a smart part of the city and your father was given quite a responsible job in the Government. Because of his mathematical abilities, he helped Tito with the rebuilding of the economy.

He was well-known and liked. Your mother was very charming and apparently a very pretty woman.' For a moment Cristian hesitated, and smiled at Sal. Her face was very tense and he wanted to lighten the mood. 'It is not surprising that she was pretty . . .'

'Oh, stop it Cristian. Go on.'

Chastened, Cristian continued. 'My friend knows nothing more until July, 1955. Firstly it was reported that Serge Kovic's wife Marie and baby daughter Salvena had died of tuberculosis within a few weeks of one another. They had apparently been taken to a clinic in the mountains, but neither recovered. He received much sympathy at the time. He was left with one son, Georges, who was eight. My friend is not sure of the circumstances, but somehow not everyone was convinced. The whole affair of his wife and daughter's disappearance triggered off an enquiry, during which it was discovered that Serge was a traitor, that he had been passing secrets to Moscow for years. As I am sure you are aware, the relationship between Moscow and Tito was not an easy one. There was even a plot to assassinate Tito, you know – although I do not think your father was involved in that. Certainly though, he greatly damaged Tito's Government at a very crucial time, and over a long period – ten years. He was instantly deported to Moscow. He was lucky. The Yugoslavs do not take kindly to traitors. The only reason Tito did not execute him was because he did not want adverse publicity – he did not want it to be known that somebody whom he had trusted, thought of as a friend, was, in fact, a traitor. It spoilt his image, he felt. So your father was allowed to leave the country.'

'And Georges?'

Cristian reached for the bottle and filled up their glasses.

'He's dead, isn't he?' Sal said, her voice choked with emotion.

Cristian shook his head. 'I do not know. Serge tried to take the boy with him, but they would not allow it. It was Tito's punishment, you see. He would like to have killed your father. He could not, so he punished him in the only way he could think of – by keeping his son. After your father had been deported, the boy was sent to an orphanage.'

Sal gasped and clapped her hand over her mouth. 'Oh no!' she said. 'No, not an orphanage! What happened to him then? My God, what happened next? I can't bear it.'

Cristian shrugged his shoulders. 'That is the problem. My friend has searched for details of the boy. His father was positive that Georges was sent to an orphanage, but there is no orphanage, in the Belgrade area at any rate, which has any record of a Georges Kovic. It could be, of course, that they changed his name, or maybe they sent him to a children's home in a different part of the country.'

Sal was bent double over the bed, crying as though she would never stop.

'Don't, Salvena.' Cristian was beside her, putting his arms around her in a great bear hug. 'Don't, please don't cry. Georges did not die, that is the main thing.

He has probably grown up well and strong and has a family of his own.'

'Eight years old,' Sal sobbed. 'To learn here – in Bucharest, of all places on earth – that your brother was sent to an orphanage, it's a nightmare.'

'The orphanages will not have been like these here in Romania. They will have been much better.'

Sal raised a tearstained face and looked at him. 'How can you say that?'

'Because Yugoslavia is a better place than Romania. Tito saw to that.'

'Despite the best efforts of my father,' Sal managed to say, before breaking into sobs again.

Cristian cradled her in his arms, rocking her to and fro like a baby. 'Listen to me, my Salvena. I have been to several orphanages – thanks to you – over the last few days. The children who suffer most are the babies and very small ones, those who are not yet three. If they live beyond that age, sometimes they have quite a good life, even here in Romania. Georges was already eight, a big fellow. He would have made friends quickly. The life would have been hard, yes, but children are very, very resilient.'

'He was only eight, and he had lost his mother, baby sister and then his father. You said that he'd enjoyed a good standard of living. He'd have gone from a home with everything to an orphanage with nothing, and presumably he'd have carried with him his father's reputation. He was the son of a traitor! He may have been bullied in the orphanage. I can't bear this, Cristian. I just can't bear this.'

'If he is anything like his sister, he will be a strong man,' Cristian said. 'He will have been OK.'

'All the time I was growing up, he was in a home. No wonder my mother was half-mad: I can see that now. She was only half a person. Half of her was still in Yugoslavia with her son, and it's why she always resented me, because she always did.' Sal was rambling, but Cristian let her. 'She never really liked me, Cristian. I can understand her now. She saved me and lost Georges. I was just a baby, but she had spent eight years caring for Georges. She must have loved him so much, and then she had to lead this life in England, a sham, to protect our true identity, while all the time her son . . .' her words were interrupted by another spasm of crying.

Cristian held her tight. 'Maybe she never knew he was in an orphanage,' he suggested. 'Maybe she assumed that he was with your father. If so, it was better that way, don't you think?'

'Oh, she was bound to have known.'

'Why are you so sure?' said Cristian. 'She had to change her identity. It would have been dangerous to make any contact at all with Belgrade.'

'She was a mother,' said Sal. 'I have an eleven-year-old son. I couldn't have just walked out of his life without checking what was happening to him. She would have found a way. There would have been someone who would have given her reports on his progress, I'm sure of it. Oh, if only she'd told me.'

'She was trying to protect you. To protect you from this,' Cristian insisted.

'She could have shared it with me,' said Sal. 'Maybe together we could have found Georges. Now Tito is dead, it would have been safe for us to go back on holiday. We could have searched.'

'We have searched,' said Cristian, 'and we can find no trace. For all you know, your mother may well have tried to do the same thing. I think you must face it, Salvena, that you will never find your brother. I don't like to say this to you, but I think it is important that I do. My friend in Belgrade, he is a very high-ranking official, he has access to all records, and, as I told you, his father actually knew your father and knew the circumstances. If they cannot trace your brother, then I am afraid it is most unlikely that you will ever do so. I know this is hard for you, but I think you have to put the whole thing behind you. Who knows, maybe in the end he was allowed to join his father in Moscow.'

'Oh come on, Cristian,' Sal said. 'Everyone knows Tito could be a vicious man. As you said, what better way to punish my father than to deny him his son . . . I bet they did change Georges' name,' she said, the journalistic instinct suddenly fighting through her emotions. 'It makes sense. The KGB, after all, are very powerful and my father had been a good servant. Unless Tito changed Georges' identity, there would have been a risk that the KGB would kidnap him. It would have been the least they could do for my father. I bet he was put in an orphanage under an assumed name.'

'Maybe,' said Cristian. 'Maybe the KGB *did* kidnap him; maybe he grew up with your father.'

'What sort of man must my father have been?' Sal said suddenly, half to herself. 'How could he betray his country like that? Whatever one thought of Tito, however history judges him in the future, he gave the people of Yugoslavia a far better life than most of Eastern Europe, wouldn't you say?'

'Certainly better than Romania,' Cristian smiled ruefully, 'but then, almost everywhere is better than my country.'

'Seriously though, he stabilised the country, he resisted too much intervention from Moscow. I remember talking to someone in a bar in Zagreb some years ago, when I was following a story,' Sal told him. 'They described Yugoslav Communism as a very strange form of Communism because it allowed a sense of both moral and intellectual freedom. That's hardly Communism at all, is it, and they have Tito to thank for that.'

'If my friend is right,' said Cristian, relieved that Sal's crying had eased, 'then your father was recruited as a very young man, away from home and in a strange country. The KGB are very clever, we know that here in Romania.'

'But it's a horrible feeling, isn't it?' said Sal. 'To recognise that your father is a traitor.'

'You could try and find him, I suppose,' Cristian said. 'He may be still alive. Maybe he knows where Georges is.'

Sal shook her head. 'No, as you rightly say, the KGB are all-powerful. If he had so wanted, he could have made contact with my mother and me once he was out of Yugoslavia. He could even have invited us to join him.'

'Perhaps he did,' said Cristian.

'My mother did remarry,' Sal admitted.

'Really? When was that?'

'I don't know,' said Sal. 'Ridiculous, isn't it? There was this man, Tim Saunders, who was around all my life, as far as I was concerned. I believed he was my father – I loved him as my father. He was in the Army, too. He was away a great deal, but when he was there, he was marvellous. I had far more in common with him than my mother. People used to say that I looked like him – ironic, isn't it?'

'But there is no possibility that he was your father?'

'Oh no,' said Sal. 'No, he was an Englishman – very much so, and besides which, my mother told me when she was dying that he was not my real father. There were definitely two men in her life.'

'Are you feeling calmer now?' Cristian said.

'Yes, I suppose so. Sorry, I must look a sight.'

'You look wonderful,' said Cristian, and he wiped a tear away from under her eye.

'It's just what you said at the beginning,' Sal said.

'What was that?'

'You said that our disappearance, my mother's and mine, seemed to trigger off the enquiry that led to my father being discovered as a spy. What that means is that my mother and I were saved, and the price was Georges. I wonder why my father sent us out of the country. Do you think it was because he knew he was about to be discovered?'

'I imagine so.'

'But why didn't he send Georges as well? It doesn't make any sense.'

'I suppose Georges was such a Yugoslavian boy. Maybe he would have been too obvious in England. I do not know, I can only guess,' said Cristian.

'It just doesn't make sense,' repeated Sal, 'to leave a boy as young as eight behind. It's almost as if he was a kind of hostage, held so that my mother and I could escape.'

'I think you're letting your imagination take over,' said Cristian.

'I don't,' said Sal. 'Somehow I feel Georges was sacrificed for us. I feel it because of my mother. Her whole life was haunted, haunted by something, and now, of course, I know what it was.' She threw herself on the bed, drumming her fists on to the pillow and sobbing.

Cristian let her cry for a while, then gently massaged her back.

'I'm sorry,' Sal said. 'Just leave me, Cristian. I'll be all right in the morning, I promise. I just have to work my way through this.'

'I'm not leaving you,' Cristian said. 'I'm making love to you tonight. I'm going to drive the devils out of your head.'

Sal sat up abruptly and stared at him. 'No you're not, Cristian, you're really not. I like you very much, I'm very grateful for all the help you're giving, but— '

He put a finger over her lips and silently handed her another glass of champagne. 'We have something between us, which was there from the very first moment we met. I know you have just had a bad shock but you must not give in to it. I will drive the sad thoughts from your mind.'

'I can't cope with you as well as everything else, Cristian.'

'Salvena, you must trust me. I can help you.' He stared at her for a long time, his eyes a warm deep brown. There was kindness there, humour and something else – lust, love? She was mesmerised by his gaze, lost in the confusion of her emotions.

At last he took the glass from her hand and put it on the bedside table. He took her face in his hands and kissed her lips; their mouths opened and the kiss deepened. Sal felt the heat rising inside her as they fell back on the bed. Cristian broke away and sat up. 'Slowly, Sal. I want to take this very slowly.' He started to undress her, sliding her silk shirt from her shoulders. Finding her bra-less brought forth a crow of delight and he bent his head to lick round and round her nipples without actually touching them, making Sal draw in her breath with frustration. When he finally took one into his hot mouth and gently sucked on it, Sal let her breath out with a rush. She knew she hadn't mistaken the looks that passed between them. He was going to be expert at lovemaking.

He continued to undress her. As each new area of bare skin was revealed he would kiss and caress it until she was jumping every time his mouth touched her body. When she was totally naked he knelt over her and just looked, his eyes sweeping from her hair down to her feet, lingering on her breasts and pubic hair. He bent his head, parted her legs and kissed the soft inside of her thighs. Sal gasped with pleasure.

Cristian rose from the bed and removed his clothes. His body was tanned and muscular. He took the pillows from the bed and piled them up under her. 'Now, my dear,' he said, picking up the half-empty bottle, 'I'm going to drink champagne from your beautiful body.' He knelt down, putting his tongue against her clitoris and poured a gentle trickle of champagne down through her pubic hair. When it reached his tongue he lapped it up like a cat at a saucer of milk. He kept pouring, a little at a time and every so often he would stiffen his tongue and plunge it inside her, making Sal moan with pleasure.

When the champagne was almost finished, Sal started to climax. He plunged his tongue inside her and rubbed her clitoris with his thumb; her orgasm was amazing, very intense, leaving her trembling and shaking. She opened her eyes to find him sitting on the bed, grinning at her. 'Now it is your turn,' he said, pointing at his half-erect penis. 'What are you going to do with it?' he challenged.

'Sit right on the edge of the bed,' she ordered. When he was in position, she parted his legs and sat between them on the floor. Thank God the glasses were the old-fashioned saucer style, Sal thought, as she poured in what was left of the champagne and dipped his penis into the glass. She slid it into her mouth, sucking off the champagne and licking up the drops before they ran down her chin. His head was thrown back and his penis was slowly hardening – the combination of the cold champagne and Sal's hot mouth making sure the process was slow and immensely enjoyable. When he was fully erect and on the point of orgasm, Sal put the glass down on the floor. 'Do you want me to go on, or do you have something else in mind?' she asked.

'Don't stop, just don't stop,' he gasped. She slid his penis into her mouth and took his balls in her hand. She moved her mouth up and down and gently squeezed his balls at the same time. He came shouting and grunting. It was then she realised that he was still half-erect. Oh God, she thought, I've read about men like this, but I've never actually met one. He smiled at her. 'It will only go down when I come inside you. I have always found it a most satisfying attribute.'

She laughed at him. 'You are very wicked,' she said.

He reached out his hand and drew her to her feet. 'Lie down on your stomach and I will give you a special massage,' he said. Sal lay down on the bed with a shiver of anticipation. Cristian knelt over her and took his penis in his hand. When Sal felt it stroking down her back, her arms and legs, she could not believe the erotic sensation it gave. He varied the pace, but not the gentle pressure, and after some twenty minutes Sal found herself begging him to enter her. 'Please, please, come inside,' she pleaded.

On hearing this, he raised her up on all fours and entered her from behind. As she felt him thrust inside her, she let out a cry that was almost torn from her throat. He reached round her and took a breast in his hand, thumbing her nipple. He was moving slowly inside her, just rotating his hips gently — it was the most exquisite sensation. Sal was moaning and pushing herself back against him so she could feel him deeper inside her. He let go of her breast and moved his hand down to her clitoris and began to rub gently, at the same time picking up the pace and starting to thrust in and out of her more quickly. As he felt her begin to climax he grabbed her hips with both hands and powered into her. He came at the same time she did, shouting, 'Yes! Yes!' at the top of his voice. When he was finally spent they rolled over and lay in each others' arms.

The following morning Sal lay in bed for a long time. She felt extraordinary. Her mind was in a state of enormous confusion and yet her body felt wonderful. She thought of Cristian the night before and went weak at the memory of their lovemaking. He had left her in the early hours, saying that he still had paperwork to do before the morning.

She knew she should feel guilty at what had happened, and yet it had been so right for her. If he had left her earlier, she could not imagine how she would have coped. Now there was pain at the thought of what she had learned, but she was in control of it. She wondered how she could have allowed Cristian in her bed so soon after Louis. But then, as with Louis, it had been a reaction to the drama of the moment. Georges — her mind recoiled at the thought of his fate.

She struggled up into a sitting position and gazed

through the window, out over the city of Bucharest, grey and dreary in the morning light. To have discovered that her brother had been sent to an orphanage, that he had lived alone in an institution all during the early years of her babyhood and childhood, was terrible enough. But as she had said the previous night to Cristian, to learn it here, in Bucharest, was a double agony. Cristian was right, of course, Yugoslavia *was* different from Romania, but then so were children's homes and orphanages the world over in the mid-fifties. She thought of Toby at eight – three years ago – being suddenly plucked from his home and put into an institution. It did not bear thinking about. There were no tears now, just a terrible deep well of sadness, her grief compounded by the knowledge that she was unlikely now ever to find her brother.

Cristian had to be right. He had the best contacts and still had been unable to locate Georges. Her years in journalism had taught her the moment at which to let a story go, the moment when the possibility of being able to pursue it was outweighed by the effort involved. This was the case now. But she knew that the same rule could not apply in the case of Georges. What else she could possibly do, she was not sure, but she knew she would have to do something.

She glanced at her watch. It was seven-thirty. She would have a shower and then steel herself to cope with the emotions of the day ahead.

The courtyard leading to the entrance of orphanage Number One was surprisingly attractive. It was a cold, frosty morning. The sun glinted on the old stone, belying the horror inside.

'This doesn't look too bad,' Margaret Johnson said, a little heartily. Cristian had gone ahead. Peter and Sal exchanged glances, but said nothing. While they waited, Sal put her mind through a series of emotional hoops. With the knowledge she now had concerning Georges, she knew facing the inside of an orphanage was going to be hard – very hard indeed.

Cristian returned as the little group stood shivering in the cold. 'It is all fixed. One of the doctors will show your party around.' He put his hand on Sal's arm. 'Will you be all right here? I will ask Andre to run me around to the maternity home with Jill Cookson, and then send him straight back to be your interpreter.'

'That's fine,' said Sal. He smiled at her, a secret smile, a lover's smile. Sal was embarrassed for she could feel Peter's eyes upon them.

'Good luck,' Cristian said to the group. 'See you soon!' and was he gone in a great flurry.

'Damn!' said Peter, grinning.

'What's wrong?' asked Sal.

'I should have put money on it. I knew it was a completely gilt-edged bet. Still, I'm not going to say "I told you so"!'

'Oh, do be quiet, Peter,' said Sal, embarrassed. 'We've got more important things to think about right now.'

The interior of the building was almost as cold as the temperature outside. The visitors shivered as much from shock as from the cold. They moved from cot to cot, shaking their heads in disbelief, holding hands, cuddling children who wanted it, crying, talking to Sal and Peter with quick bursts of anger. Margaret, the big-hearted woman with her booming voice and easy confidence; Diana, the controlled, elegant barrister with her cool efficiency – completely disappeared. They became two stumbling, confused women who had walked into a Hell the memory of which would affect them for the rest of their lives. Every now and again they looked to one another for comfort, choking back tears. In a matter of just a few moments, Diana's beautiful navy-blue tweed coat was stained and creased from the children she had held, but clearly she neither noticed, nor cared.

Sal and Peter understood – they had been through it themselves. They found the women's grief, horror, despair, their ready tears and their emotions quite out of control, almost a relief. It indicated that their own reactions over the last few weeks had not been so strange.

When Andre returned, they began to talk to the doctor in charge. When she discovered that Margaret was not looking for a baby but an older child, she looked pleased and hurried her away. Sal and Peter followed. They were taken to a small ward in which a little boy of perhaps eighteen months stood defiantly at the end of his cot, his eyes bright and alert. When he saw that it was he who was being singled out for attention, the fierce expression softened. He shrieked with delight, throwing out his arms to Margaret to lift him up. She did so. 'How old is he? What is his name?' she asked, cuddling him to her.

'He is four. His name is Ion.'

'Four?' Margaret said. 'He can't be four, he's so tiny.'

'Yes, he is four.' The doctor consulted her records. 'He is a clever boy.'

'How long has he been in an orphanage?' Sal asked.

'Always,' the doctor replied. 'Not always here. He was in Number Six. He has a twin brother, but he is no good. You take this boy, Ion, he will be a strong boy. He has a good mind.'

'A twin?' Margaret said. 'Where is his twin?'

The doctor shrugged. 'I do not know. They were both at Number Six. Maybe the other boy is still there.'

'It's a boy? So they could be identical. Why on earth have they been separated? It's barbaric.' Tears were flowing down Margaret's face.

'As I say,' the doctor said, 'the other boy is no good. He has something wrong – his leg, I think.'

'They should still be together,' Margaret said angrily.

'Please,' Andre said quietly to Margaret. 'Don't upset the doctor.' He began talking to the doctor, calming the situation. Sal watched him, marvelling at the way he had developed in confidence and understanding since they had first met. Sal and Peter had been the first Western Europeans with whom Andre had ever had any contact. He turned suddenly to Margaret. 'Would you wish to adopt his twin, even if he is damaged?'

'Of course,' said Margaret. 'I couldn't possibly have one boy without the other. It would be quite wrong.'

Andre translated this. The doctor seemed annoyed. 'It is stupid,' she said directly to Margaret.

Margaret stared at Andre. 'Why does she say that?'

'She says there are so many children who are not damaged who need a home. It is foolish to take a child who has a problem, when you do not have to do so. She says if you want two boys, have this one and another. She will find you another in this orphanage of the same age – if that is what you want.'

Everyone stared at Andre aghast. 'No,' said Margaret. 'I will take this boy.' Ion was clinging to her and she cradled him as she spoke. 'Tell her, I will definitely take this boy, but I will also find his brother.' Andre translated, and the doctor shrugged her shoulders, dismissively.

'I can adopt Ion, can I?' Margaret said, already panicking.

There was more heated discussion. 'She says yes. She thinks you are mad, but she says yes to Ion. The father, she knows, is dead, and the mother – there will be no problem. She does not want the boy, she has never visited him. She lives here in Bucharest. She will not be difficult to find.'

Peter took photographs of Margaret and Ion, and then they left her alone. A practical woman, she had brought a mug of juice and some rusks. She took the little boy out into the corridor, so that the other children would not see and he sat on her lap contentedly, resting against her shoulder, eating his rusk and drinking his drink.

Sal had found Margaret rather strident, but now, watching her with the child, she could see that the woman was a natural with children. Ion trusted her completely, having only met her five minutes before, and Margaret had forgotten all about the rest of them, so absorbed was she. It was, quite literally, love at first sight. Peter reached for Sal's hand and pulled her gently away. He was close to tears.

'One little boy with a future, and with any luck his twin brother too, if we can find him,' said Peter.

'We'll find him,' Sal swore. 'If we have to tear Bucharest apart, we'll find him.'

Back in the wards they had passed through earlier, they found Diana Wainwright cradling a tiny baby, tears pouring down her face.

'Who have you here?' Sal asked.

'Her name's Lilianna. I shall call her Lily.'

The child was tiny and pale, her skin almost trans-lucent. She was awake and big brown eyes stared up at Diana. 'They were feeding the babies just now,' she said to Sal, almost inaudibly. 'They stick a bottle in the babies' mouths, and then after a few minutes, whether they have finished or not, they take out the bottles and literally throw the babies in a heap on that bed over there. Swaddled like this, it must be so uncomfortable and dangerous – they could suffocate if they fell awk-wardly. When it came to Lilianna's turn, she would not take the bottle. She spat it out, so they just threw her on the heap anyway. She's had nothing to eat.'

'She is very underweight,' Sal said. 'There is AIDS in this orphanage. I think you should have her tested before you commit yourself emotionally.'

'I've already committed myself emotionally,' Diana said defiantly. 'It's too late.'

'But if she has AIDS?' Sal asked gently.

'We'll just have to see, won't we? I can't abandon her, Sal. I can't explain it, you'll probably think I'm mad, but the moment I saw her I just felt totally committed.' The carefully applied make-up had long since disappeared. 'You do understand, don't you?' Diana asked desperately.

'Of course I do,' Sal told her. 'The way you and Margaret are reacting, it's a sort of relief.'

'How do you mean?' Diana asked.

Sal sat down beside her and put out a finger; Lilianna gripped it strongly. 'I'm the only woman, English woman, who's seen these orphanages, as far as I'm aware, until today. Ever since I visited the first one, orphanage Luca, my emotions have been all over the place. I don't seem to have any control of them,' she smiled at Diana. 'Ask my colleagues, I'm considered to be a fairly tough individual, but not any more. I hope you don't mind me saying this, but yesterday you seemed quite cool and distant, very efficient, very together, but certainly not the sort of person who would normally wear their heart on their sleeve. Now you're a complete emotional wreck, committed to a little baby you met five minutes ago, and it's such a relief.'

Diana smiled at her. 'I'm glad you said that, it

helps.' She gazed around her for a moment. 'This is far worse than I'd envisaged. Don't misunderstand me,' she added hastily, 'your description in the paper was very graphic, but— '

'If I can adopt Lily,' Diana said, 'it won't end there. I won't forget the rest. I'll do what I can to help them always.'

Sal looked down at Lily. If she was well, she would be a beautiful child. 'I won't insult you again by asking whether you're sure about Lily,' Sal said, 'but I will ask Cristian to organise a blood-test quickly.'

On Sal's instructions, Peter did not photograph Diana and Lilianna. Sal was very nervous about the way the child looked. She was relieved when Cristian returned to the orphanage; everything was happening so fast.

'How did Jill get on?' she asked.

'She is already at the hotel with her daughter.'

'You're joking,' Sal said.

'No,' Cristian smiled. 'In the maternity hospital, it is possible for the children to be released immediately. They are not, how do you say, "in the system". The child we found for Jill either had to go into an orphanage, or come with us. The mother was leaving today. I have the mother's consent already, so I can begin processing her papers immediately. She is a lovely little girl, and all the better for not coming to a place like this. She is only five days old. She has been breastfed, so she will have no infections.'

'And Jill, how is she?'

'Very happy,' Cristian grinned. 'She cries a lot, but she is very happy.'

'Has she enough things for the baby?'

'I think she is going to try and contact her husband so that he can send out more supplies. I have told her that she will be here for at least another week.'

'Good,' said Sal, 'then we have plenty of time to talk and photograph her. Cristian, we have some problems here. We have a lost twin and I'm worried about the baby that Diana wishes to adopt. I think she may have AIDS, she looks so frail.'

'OK,' said Cristian. 'If the women have selected their children, we will arrange blood-tests right away and try to obtain the mother's consent for adoption.'

'I wouldn't get too deeply in with Diana's baby until we have the result of the blood-test,' said Sal. 'I just have a bad feeling about her.'

'OK, OK, now tell me about this twin.' Sal explained the situation and half an hour later they found themselves careering across Bucharest towards orphanage Number Six, Sal sitting in the front seat, cradling two phials of blood. 'We will drop these off at the laboratory on the way,' Cristian had told her.

Diana had stayed on at the orphanage. She had persuaded a nurse to give her a bottle of milk and she was coaxing Lilianna to take some. As with Margaret, Sal marvelled at Diana's total commitment to a child she had only just met.

In orphanage Number Six, they met a great deal of resistance, until Cristian took the Principal away, clutching a carrier bag, which Sal could only assume contained some of the whisky and cigarettes that they had brought with them to help oil the wheels of bureaucracy. Yes, the boy was there. His name was Mikhail and they could see him, but he was not suitable for adoption.

Mikhail was in a side ward, which contained three other cots. The children in the other cots were in a terrible state. One crowed continually, another beat his head against the cot bars rhythmically – something that Peter and Sal had become used to seeing, but which still upset them dreadfully. The third child was tied down in his cot – for his own safety, they were told, as they had often been told before. He was a skeleton and his eyes burnt feverishly. Mikhail alone was sitting up, staring out at the world with his brother's scowl.

'Oh God,' said Margaret, 'they're identical.' She went ahead of the party and everyone else held back. 'Mikhail,' she said. The little boy looked up at her. His smile was less radiant than his brother's, but it was there. She stretched out her arms to him and he came to her. He seemed much smaller than his brother, but was otherwise apparently identical, except for one heavily bandaged leg. Margaret turned to them. 'I don't understand. He is identical, and yet he is so much smaller.'

'I don't think he *is* smaller,' Sal said. 'He's the same height, it's just that he's so thin. Maybe they don't feed them so well here.'

'Their faces, except for the fact that Mikhail's is so much thinner, are just the same,' said Margaret.

'I know the answer to this,' said Cristian. 'He is

damaged and therefore they have never given him any priority when it comes to feeding. That is why he looks different.'

There was silence in the little group as everyone absorbed this. 'That's terrible,' Sal said.

'Maybe it is, maybe not. If there is little food to go around, they give it to those who are strongest and most likely to survive. Maybe it is not so terrible.'

As they spoke, Margaret had found a chair and was sitting down with Mikhail on her lap. She pointed to his leg. 'Can you ask the doctor what the problem is?'

Cristian talked to the rather sullen-looking doctor who had accompanied them. 'It is a twisted leg. They are trying to straighten it with bandages.'

'Can I take the bandages off? They looks so uncomfortable,' Margaret asked. The answer was no. 'It doesn't matter,' she said. 'Can you tell the doctor I would like to adopt Mikhail as well.'

A heated exchange took place between Cristian and the doctor.

'What's going on?' Margaret asked, desperation on her face. 'They can't say no, can they?'

Sal shook her head. 'I don't know.'

The shouting became louder. 'Stay here,' said Cristian, 'I'll be back soon. I'm going to see the Principal.'

They waited, Margaret and Mikhail clinging to one another. The boy could not know what was going on, but somehow he seemed to sense that his future was hanging in the balance. His eyes were wide with apprehension but all the time he snuggled closer and closer in Margaret's arms. 'They have to let me have him,' she sobbed. 'How could they have separated identical twins, how could they?'

They waited, the crowing from the boy in the other cot the only noise breaking the silence. Sal tried to soothe him, but he shrank from her. At last they heard footsteps in the corridor. The moment they saw Cristian's face, they knew all was well. 'It was not easy, it cost us most of our whisky and cigarettes, but it is OK – you can have the boy.'

'Can we move him to orphanage Number One, to be with his brother?' Sal asked.

Cristian hesitated. 'I think it would be dangerous to ask any more favours. It will not be long before they can be together for ever, but if we try and upset the system, it will cause problems and they may change their minds. I will arrange for a doctor to do a blood-test on Mikhail too, and tomorrow I will seek the mother's consent.'

Margaret was crying – they all were. 'Peter,' she said through her tears. 'Do you have a Polaroid camera?'

'Yes, I do,' said Peter.

'Could you take a picture of Mikhail for us to give to Ion, and then we can bring a picture of Ion to Mikhail.'

'That's a lovely idea,' said Sal.

'I have spoken to the doctor,' Cristian said, 'and arranged for Mikhail to be moved out of this ward. It is sad the state of these other children, but it is not right that he should be in here. They have agreed to this.'

'Thank God,' said Margaret.

'Come, let us go outside and we will take your photographs and you can give him something to eat.'

By the time they returned to the hotel, they were all emotionally spent. It was after five o'clock. They were dirty, exhausted and hungry, and both Diana and Margaret were clearly shell-shocked. Both disappeared quickly to their bedrooms to try and ring their husbands.

'Come on, Peter,' Sal said. 'We'd better go and find Jill. I hope she's all right.'

When they reached her bedroom, the door was ajar. Sal pushed it open, tentatively calling, 'Jill?'

'Shush,' came from inside the room. Sal and Peter crept in, followed by Cristian. Jill was lying on the bed, and in the crook of her arm was a tiny baby, fast asleep. The baby was dressed in a pink babygrow. She was clean and warm, wrapped in a cocoon of love. The contrast to what they had witnessed during the day was total.

'Oh, Jill,' Sal whispered. 'This is just what I needed to see – she's beautiful.' Jill nodded, smiling up at them.

'I have to have a photograph of this,' Peter said. 'I hope the flash won't wake her.'

'What's her name?' Sal asked.

'She didn't have one. Her mother hadn't given her one, so I'm calling her Emma – it's my mother's name.'

'Emma,' Sal repeated.

Peter took his photographs and left. He and Cristian said they would be in the bar. Sal lingered, watching the mother and her new daughter. Jill had changed. She was suddenly confident. It was extraordinary. She had never had a child before and yet, instinctively, she seemed to know what to do. When Emma stirred in sleep, she stroked her gently, whispering to her until the child relaxed.

'Have you enough food and clothes?' Sal asked.

'I have enough for four days.'

'I'd better arrange for some more to be sent out for you then,' Sal said.

'It's all right,' said Jill, 'I've already organised it. I hope you don't mind, but I rang the paper. There's another batch of women coming out tomorrow and they're going to bring more food, clothes and nappies for everyone. I spoke to your editor — David Thorson, is that his name? He was lovely and he asked for you to ring him when you can.'

Sal smiled. This immature girl, who would not say boo to a goose, had organised her baby supplies without a qualm.

'Did you meet Emma's natural mother?' Sal asked.

'Yes, I did. I liked her very much. She was only nineteen and Emma was her fourth child. She said that she didn't love her or want her, but she did want her to have a good home and was very pleased that she didn't have to put her in an orphanage. She has kept her first child, but her other two children are in homes. It's so sad, Sal. She wasn't a wicked person, she just couldn't cope.'

'Still, at least Emma's going to be all right,' Sal said. She left Jill and went out into the corridor, walking slowly towards the lift. What an extraordinary day it had been. Three women who up until yesterday had led ordinary, ordered lives, had their world turned upside down, and now there were four, not three, children with a chance of a new life.

*   *   *

In the bar she found only Cristian. 'Peter has gone to sort out his pictures,' he said. 'This means we are alone.'

'So it does,' said Sal, with a smile.

'I have work to do for these babies, but I thought maybe I could come back to see you later?'

'I ought to say no,' said Sal.

'But what are you going to say?' Cristian asked, grinning wickedly.

'I rather think I'm going to say yes.'

CHAPTER SIXTEEN

F our days later, Sal was waiting with Andre outside the Principal's office in Orphanage Number One. Nothing in Romania was straightforward, she was learning. Cristian had said that the paperwork for adoption would be no problem – in reality it had been one problem after another. Officials promised one thing one day and something else the next. The women involved seesawed from elation to despair: one moment it seemed that the children they had given their hearts to would be theirs any day, and the next, the whole thing seemed impossible.

Of the three of them, only Jill remained untouched by what was going on around them. She and Emma were totally absorbed with one another and, of course, they were together. Margaret and Diana had to content themselves with visits to their children, seeing them suffering daily. Although they augmented their diet as best they could and gave them as many cuddles as possible, the circumstances of their daily life were still terrible. For Margaret, particularly, the strain of travelling between the two orphanages was starting to tell; she looked exhausted. However, the results of the blood-test on Ion and Mikhail had been clear. The battle now was to stop them being given any further injections at the orphanages. At Number One, where there were now nearly a thousand children, Sal had discovered that they were using just two needles to administer drugs. It was a nightmare. No wonder AIDS was spreading like wildfire.

Little Lilianna, it turned out, was mercifully not HIV positive, but she was carrying Hepatitis B. The orphanage had been adamant that Diana should consider another child – Diana equally adamant that she should not. Her husband, being a doctor, was already scouring London for the best possible treatment for the little girl he had yet to meet, but whom he already called his daughter. Sal continued to marvel at the total commitment from everyone. Diana was only too aware that Hepatitis B, particularly in one so young, could lead to liver cancer, but she was taking this child warts and all. Sal had to admit that Lily was already looking a great deal better. Diana had coaxed her into feeding properly and the love and attention were also starting to have an effect.

'How much longer are we going to have to wait here, Andre?' asked Sal. They were supposed to be collecting some papers for Ion.

'I will go and check,' he offered. 'Do you have any

cigarettes with you? It will help.' Sal smiled and handed over a packet. 'OK, you wait here.'

Behind her Sal heard the sound of trolley wheels in the corridor and a child screaming. She resisted the temptation to turn around. Every time she came to the orphanage there was a new horror. She had reached the point where she couldn't cope with any more emotion. Her desperate sadness for the children by day, her nights with Cristian, each one more passionate than the last, were wearing her out physically and emotionally.

The sound of a cot being pushed over the floor came nearer. She sneaked a look – the screaming child was much closer now. An angry-looking nurse abandoned the cot a few feet from Sal, muttering under her breath, and disappeared. The child continued to scream. Sal tried to look away, but could not. Taking a deep breath, she walked up to the cot. A tiny child lay on its back crying hysterically. One arm was bandaged and suspended from the side of the cot. Sal caught her breath. Clearly it was broken and the arm was twisted into the broken position. Every time the child shifted, the bones must grate. The movement of the cot over the cracked linoleum floor must have been agony.

For a moment she thought she was going to be sick – that, or faint. Then she pulled herself together and looked up and down the corridor. There was no one in sight. Quickly she leaned over the cot and examined the filthy bandages. The child, sensing that help was near, stopped screaming. The bandages had been knotted. Sal was desperate and then she remembered the little pocket knife she always kept in her handbag.

Scrabbling through her bag, dropping the contents all over the passageway, she found the knife and sawed through the bandages. The child lay perfectly still. Sal talked encouragingly as she worked. At last, she managed to saw through the last thread and gently, supporting the arm, lowered it into the cot beside the child. Then she looked at the little one's face. Their eyes met and the child smiled. Sal smiled back and somewhere deep inside her something stirred.

'I'll see your arm's mended,' she said. 'Don't worry, I won't let them hurt you any more.'

At that moment Andre appeared. 'I have the papers – we can go.'

'No, we can't, Andre. This child's arm is broken: it was tied to the cot in a most agonising position. I'm going to take it to hospital and have the arm fixed. I'll need to tell the Principal.'

'There is nobody in charge here today,' said Andre. 'That is why it took so long to get the papers.'

'All the better,' said Sal. 'Let's just find a doctor – a nurse, even – someone who will let us take the child to hospital.'

It was surprisingly easy. Sal signed a paper saying that she would return the child the same day. No one seemed to know who the child was or why it had been tied up. Using a remnant of the cot sheet, Sal carefully strapped the child's arm to its body and lifted it gently from the cot. Soon she and Andre were driving across the city to the paediatric hospital. The child smelled terrible, but in the car it leaned against Sal, relaxed and apparently no longer in pain.

'I don't even know whether it's a boy or a girl,' Sal said. The child's head was shaven, only tiny tufts of an indescribable colour sprang from the scalp.

At the hospital, Andre worked miracles and soon they were led away by a woman doctor. Whether Andre had bribed her or not, Sal did not know, but the woman asked no questions, simply X-rayed and plastered the arm and an hour later they were out of the hospital, complete with a bottle of painkillers. Sal had been able to find a nappy and the hospital had lent her an old gown for the child on condition that it was returned. In the process of a very rough and ready clean up, Sal had discovered that her little friend was a girl.

'Where now?' Andre asked. 'Back to the orphanage?'

Sal hesitated, her mind in a whirl. 'No,' she decided. 'To the hotel.'

'But you said that you would return the child!'

'I know,' said Sal, 'but first I'm going to make sure that she has a good meal and a rest in a comfortable bed. She has been in so much pain. I'm sure the orphanage will never give her the medicine, and at least if she can have a good night's rest and I can get plenty of the medicine down her, she'll feel better by tomorrow.'

'I do not think this is sensible, Sal,' Andre said.

'They won't miss her.'

'I do not mean that,' Andre said. 'I just wonder if by the morning you will be able to take her back to the orphanage.'

'Of course I will,' Sal said dismissively.

Peter was out for the day. He had gone to the Home for Irrecuperables to meet the aid lorry he had organised. Cristian was chasing parents' consents, blood samples and paperwork all over town. There were now eleven would-be British parents in Bucharest, and he was working flat out to process the adoptions.

Sal told Andre that he would not be needed again until the morning, and then she took the little girl straight up to her hotel bedroom where she ordered bread, spaghetti and fruit. She laid the child on the bed and sat down beside her, holding her hand. She wondered how old she was. She was tiny, with a beautiful little heart-shaped face and, unusually for a Romanian, cornflower-blue eyes. Her size suggested she could be as young as seven or eight months, but clearly from her expression, she was a lot older than that – two, perhaps. She seemed very relaxed and placid. They sat together holding hands, Sal talking a little, until the meal arrived. She chopped the spagetti up fine and crumbled the bread, then sat the child on her lap and began to spoon it into her mouth. The child ate ravenously and drank a whole mug of water, followed by another at the end of the meal. Sal peeled and sliced an apple, and most of this disappeared too.

By the end of the meal the child was becoming drowsy. Sal washed her hands and face, spooned some medicine into her and snuggled her into bed. Within seconds she was fast asleep. It was still only seven o'clock but Sal realised that she was terribly tired, too. She had a quick shower, put on a nightshirt and lowered the lights. She assumed that at some stage

Cristian would come to her, but tonight this no longer seemed relevant. She kept glancing towards the bed where the child lay in blissful slumber. There were two beds in the room. Sal made to climb into the other one, then hesitated. What if the child fell out of bed in the night on her broken arm? Carefully she climbed in beside the sleeping little body and put an arm around her. The child snuggled into her shoulder as if it was the most natural thing in the world.

Cristian found them thus some hours later when, exhausted from a day of bureaucracy, he let himself into Sal's room. For a moment he thought he was seeing things. He crept close to her bed. The scene of the woman and child sleeping was enchanting. He noted the arm in plaster – clearly it was an orphanage child. It did not smell good and he wondered how Sal could possibly take it into her bed. He felt a stab of irritation. After the day he'd had, a night with Sal was what he needed. No woman had ever made him feel as she did. He shook her none too gently. She opened her eyes and looked up at him and then at the child. 'Shush, Cristian. Careful, don't wake her!'

'Who is this?' he asked.

'I don't know,' Sal replied with a little smile. 'I found her in Number One. Her arm was broken and they had tied it to a cot. She was in terrible pain.'

'And you took her?'

'I got permission first.'

'From whom?'

'A nurse. I signed a piece of paper to say that I would take her back.'

'Was the Principal there?'

'No.'

'You should not have done this thing – it is bad news. You are not allowed to take the children from the orphanages. We will be in big trouble.'

Sal was irritated. 'The child was in pain. I couldn't leave her there in that state.'

'There are many children in pain in those places. You were able to leave all the others, why not this one?'

'I don't know,' answered Sal truthfully.

'We must take her back first thing tomorrow. The Principal trusts us; this will not be good for relationships.'

'Drat the Principal,' said Sal, 'this child needed help.'

'OK, OK, don't let's argue. Leave her now and come to bed.'

Sal stared at him. 'I'm not going to sleep with you in the bed next to this little girl – I couldn't, it wouldn't be right.'

'Why not? She's fast asleep.'

'Because I can't and I won't,' said Sal. 'I'm sorry, Cristian, please leave us. I'll see you in the morning.'

'Oh, so you do not need me now you have this child.'

'Don't be silly,' Sal said wearily. The little girl stirred. 'Look, you'll wake her up. I'll try and explain it all to you in the morning.'

Cristian turned on his heel and left, shutting the door none too quietly. Sal stared after him. He was a good man, a wonderful lover, but they were so far apart in so many ways. What was she doing, becoming involved with him? Beside her the little girl suddenly opened her eyes, staring around her. When she caught sight of Sal leaning over her, she smiled – enigmatic, captivating. Sal bent and kissed her. 'Don't worry, little thing, you're safe. Back to sleep now.' The child shut her eyes and drifted off. Sal lay there. Her right arm had gone completely numb, but she did not care. She tried to blank off her mind and sleep too, but thoughts kept running around in her head. What was to become of this child? Would anyone take her back to the hospital to have the plaster removed? Why had she been tied up in the first place?

At last she drifted off to sleep and when she awoke, it was after six. Except for the interruption by Cristian, she had been asleep for eleven hours. The child had still not woken. Sal carefully eased herself out of bed and quietly ordered breakfast by room service, and then went for a shower. When she returned the child was awake, lying placidly, staring around her. She smiled as soon as Sal appeared. 'Hello, little one. You had a lovely sleep. Breakfast will be here soon, shall I give you a wash?'

The child was absolutely filthy. Sal took her into the bathroom and sat her under the shower. She began shampooing the fine stubble. The little girl did not think much of this, but her screams soon turned to chuckles when Sal dried her and put talcum powder on her sores and chafed skin, tickling her as she did so. She had no clean nappy so Sal sat her on a towel and dressed her in one of her own T-shirts while they ate breakfast together. The child ate a Weetabix and more bread and a cup of milk, and seemed to have settled into her new environment without question. At the thought of taking her back to the orphanage, Sal felt a terrible stab of pain. How could she, and yet, how could she not? Andre had been right. What she had done was to create a very dangerous emotional commitment.

On the spur of the moment, Sal picked up the little girl and went along the corridor to Jill Cookson's room. She knocked on the door. 'Come in,' Jill called. She was sitting in an armchair by the window, feeding Emma. Despite the turmoil in her mind, Sal could not help but smile at the scene. 'Good heavens,' said Jill, 'who have we here?'

'I don't know,' said Sal, and told her the story. 'I just wondered whether you have any spare clothes, anything that might fit her, and a nappy, of course?'

'I have a jumble of stuff with me of all shapes and sizes,' said Jill. 'Have a look in the suitcase and help yourself to whatever you want.'

'Oh, thank you.' Sal put the little girl down on the bed. 'Let's see what we can find you,' she said, pulling open the suitcase.

'So what's going to happen next?' Jill said.

'How do you mean?' Sal asked.

'Are you taking her back to the orphanage?'

'I'll have to.'

'You're not going to adopt her, then?'

'No – well, I can't, can I? I mean, I hadn't really

thought.' Yet as she spoke the words, Sal realised she had been thinking about nothing else all night. 'How can I? I'm a single parent as it is.'

'Oh, I don't think there's any problem about that. Fred, my husband and I, have been looking into adoption for ages, and I know that Social Services are quite happy with single parents in certain circumstances, provided they can give enough financial support. You say you already have a child?'

'Yes, a son, he's eleven.'

'Well, there you are then. You're already providing a home for one child. You have a track record. I can't see a problem.'

'And I am going to give up my job,' Sal blurted out, her excitement mounting.

'Are you?' Jill said, surprised. 'But that's terrible, you're a national institution. What will the paper do without you?'

'I shouldn't have told you that,' Sal said. 'I haven't told anybody yet – only my son knows. I haven't been a very good mother in the last few years and I'm going to give it all up and he and I are going to live in the country, and I'll freelance.'

'Well, there you are then,' said Jill. 'It's perfect. Do it – you can't abandon her after this. Look at her, she loves you already.'

Sal looked at the little girl. She was sitting on the bed smiling, listening to the conversation. Her hair, Sal saw with a shock, now that it had been washed, was the same colour as Toby's.

*   *   *

'The Principal says it is not possible to adopt this child. You took her without permission.' Cristian seemed almost to be enjoying the Principal's rejection.

'I had permission,' said Sal, 'and look, I have returned her. Why can't I adopt her?'

'Because she is mad.'

'She's not mad. There's nothing wrong with her, and even if there was, that's up to me, surely.'

'Her mother died of mental illness, and her father is unknown.'

'Well, at least that means no parental consent is required,' Sal said.

'But it does mean that you need the Principal's consent,' Cristian replied. 'Just try and keep calm.'

'What is the child's name?' Sal asked.

'Florina.'

'Florina,' Sal said reverently in a whisper.

The battle raged to and fro. Before, in such circumstances, Sal had been able to be at least partially detached. Not now. This time yesterday it had never entered her head to adopt a child. Now, she was desperate to save Florina. How could they think the child was mad!

At one point Cristian turned to her. 'Are you sure you know what you are doing? They say the child has all sorts of problems.'

'Only the problems that have been created here in this evil place,' Sal said hotly.

'OK, OK!' There were more agitated discussions in Romanian, more cigarettes. Sal's heart was pounding, her mouth dry. She was terrified. She wanted to scream

– 'I'll do anything, give you anything, only please, please let me have her.'

'Do you have any whisky?' Cristian asked after a while.

'Yes, there's some in my handbag,' Sal said.

'Well, get it out then.'

The Principal produced some plastic mugs. Cristian tipped whisky into all of them, and handed them out summarily to the Principal, the doctor – who had joined in the conversation – Andre, Sal and himself.

'What is going on?' Sal pleaded.

'I give you a toast,' Cristian said. 'To Florina and her future in England.' Sal managed a sip before dissolving into hopeless tears.

'But why can't I take her back to the hotel?'

'I've explained it to you over and over again,' said Cristian. 'Orphanage children have to *stay* in the orphanage. It's different in a maternity hospital, but Florina must stay here until the adoption is through.'

'But I'll have to go back to England to get the Social Services report.'

'I know. We'll arrange for my sister Mariana to look after her like we did with Martin and Sadie's little girl. It'll be OK.' Florina's cot was now on a ward with other children. The baby next to her was head banging.

'Leave her to the doctor,' Cristian said. 'Come on, you know it's best.'

'No. I must take her to her cot myself and try to explain.'

'She's only two years old and she's Romanian. She doesn't know what you're talking about.'

'She trusts me,' Sal insisted. 'I have to try and make her go on trusting me.'

Florina had been silent and preoccupied ever since they returned to the orphanage. Sal carried her to her cot, hugging her tightly. 'I'll be back, darling. I promise I'll be back.' She lowered her into the cot. The blue eyes stared up at her, for a moment years older in understanding than her tiny body suggested. 'I'll be back. Please, please trust me,' Sal whispered, and blew her a kiss. The child smiled slightly. Sal turned, feeling as if her heart was being pulled from her body, and walked to the door. When she looked back, she could see Florina's little face pressed against the bars of the cot. There were tears on her pale cheeks, but the child made no sound.

In the hotel bar that evening, Sal was strangely quiet. Peter watched her surreptitiously. The news that she was going to adopt a baby had astounded him initially, but now he saw that strangely it had had a calming effect on her. He had been so worried about her in the last few days, seeing how close she was to breaking point. Now, suddenly, she seemed far more in control. It was hard to define why. Perhaps all her grief and sorrow for the children now had a focus. At last, through Florina, in her own eyes, she could really make a difference.

He went to the bar and ordered a round of drinks and then he returned and sat himself next to her. 'Lucky you,' he said, 'home tomorrow.' It had been agreed that Sal would return to England for a few days. There was some paperwork that needed sorting out for several of the prospective adoptive parents, and in Sal's case she needed to organise her own Social Services report, as nothing further could be progressed on Florina's adoption until this was done. Peter had decided to stay on until her return.

'I don't want to go, Peter – not now.'

He grinned. 'Because of Cristian?'

'No, because of Florina. I am very fond of Cristian, but . . .' Sal hesitated.

'Don't you think I deserve a gold star for not saying "I told you so"?' Peter said.

'I think you probably do,' Sal admitted. 'Do you think I'm doing the right thing about Florina?'

'Yes, I think you are,' said Peter. 'I know if my circumstances were different, if I was in a committed relationship with someone, then I wouldn't hesitate to adopt a child.'

'Florina seemed to choose me, rather than the other way round,' Sal said. 'It was extraordinary. I watched the other women make these instant emotional commitments, and I thought it was admirable, but not something I could ever do. And yet there it was, happening to me – and it was wonderful. Of course, one cannot help but be aware of all the other children who won't have Florina's chance, but it does seem to ease the pain a little. Do you think that's wrong?'

'No, I don't.'

'Peter, there is something else.' Sal put her hand on

his arm. 'I know I can rely on your discretion for a day or two. The other reason I'm going back to London is to tell David that I'm giving up the job after Romania.'

'Giving up?' Peter's face paled.

'Shush,' said Sal, looking around her anxiously.

'But Sal, you can't!'

'Even before Florina, I'd taken the decision. Toby and I need some time together. I've been a lousy mother in recent years, Peter, and now I've taken on a second child, it becomes even more important. I hope to be able to get some freelance work.'

'I'm going to hate it,' Peter said. 'We work so well together, Sal — we always have. Isn't there some honourable compromise?'

'I don't think so,' said Sal.

'Well, I know what I'm going to do,' said Peter, standing up.

'What?' Sal looked up at him anxiously.

'I'm going to get horribly, comprehensively pissed. This is about the worst news I've heard in ages.' Without another word, he stamped off towards the bar. Sal watched him go. His reaction had been inevitable, typical of Peter. She would have liked to have talked some more, to have explained, but clearly he was not in the mood.

'You've done a superb job in Romania, Sal, but I don't really want you to go back there.' David lounged back in his chair. Sal said nothing. This was not going to be an easy interview in any circumstances.

As it was, her emotions were already at sixes and sevens.

'Look, I know how involved you are with the children, but I think we're getting the whole of the Eastern European thing out of balance because of your reportage. You are our Eastern European expert and you've been concentrating all your efforts on Romania. Look what's happening in Poland, Czechoslovakia and Bulgaria. Their revolutions have been less dramatic than Romania's, but nonetheless, they have all rejected Communism and are struggling to form their own democracies.

'I've got Jack and Edward covering those countries,' he went on, 'but they don't have your knack of getting to the people, judging the real stories. Compared with your reporting on Romania, I just can't give them houseroom. I want you to visit the rest of Eastern Europe, go into the streets and talk to people – find out how the average Bulgarian is feeling. I need your magic, Sal.'

Sal took a deep breath. 'You're not making this any easier, David.'

'Not making what any easier?'

'I'm resigning.'

'You're *what*?'

'I'm giving up my job on the paper. Romania is my last overseas assignment. If you're not too angry with me and if you can see your way to giving me the odd piece of freelance work, that would be great, but I'm going to be based in the UK from now on.'

David stood up and came around to Sal's side of

the desk. 'What in God's name has prompted you to do this?'

'My children,' Sal said.

'Your children? What do you mean, your children?'

'Toby, and also Florina. I'm adopting a little girl from Romania.'

'You have to be joking.'

'I'm not. She's two, and is currently in Orphanage Number One.'

'I don't want to hear about this, Sal. This is crazy. You can't even be a proper mother to Toby, so how the hell do you expect to look after this child as well.'

'Do you know, David, you make me sick! You have such double standards. On the one hand, you criticise me for being a lousy mother, and on the other, you insist that I keep going abroad to furnish your bloody paper with stories. You can't have it both ways. If I'm a lousy mother, it's because you keep sending me away from my son.' They glared at one another.

'So how on earth is Toby going to feel about this? You've never been prepared to give up your job for him, and suddenly you're happy to give it up for some Romanian orphan.'

'It isn't like that,' said Sal hotly. 'Toby and I had a long discussion last time I was home. I hadn't even met Florina then; I hadn't even remotely considered adopting a child. Toby and I agreed that after Romania I would give up my job. He knows I did it for him, not for her. He's over the moon at the idea of having a little sister. You yourself said what makes him insecure is that he only has

me in his life. Well, that's in the past — there's me
and Florina now.'

'I think you're mad, Sal. You'll never stick it, it'll
drive you crazy, and that house of yours isn't big
enough for another child.'

'I'm selling it. We are going to move down to my
mother's old cottage. Toby and I went there when I
was last home. We've got it all organised — it's going
to be great.'

'I'm prepared to give you a month's leave. You
have been working very hard recently, and then perhaps when you've had a rest, you'll come to your
senses . . .'

'David, I've come to my senses: that's why I'm giving
up my job. I'll do one more trip to Romania for you
and that's it.'

'Like hell you will. If that's the way you want it,
you're off the paper and the payroll right now.'

'But I have to go out to Romania once more, to take
my file and collect Florina. I thought I could cover
everyone bringing home their babies.'

'I'll put someone else on that story. If you go back
to Romania, you're going at your own expense. I can't
believe you're doing this — just get out of my sight,
will you.'

'David, can you just stop and think, as my friend,
rather than my boss. Can't you see this is the right
thing?'

'Out,' David said. 'Just get out.'

In a daze Sal left his office and went back to the
newsroom, and as surreptitiously as possible cleared

her desk. One or two people queried what she was doing. 'Just having a spring-clean,' she said pleasantly. Within half an hour she was out of the building. She expected to feel a sense of remorse, but strangely there was none — just an odd feeling of relief. She was sorry about David, but knew he would come around. They had been friends for too long. Once his professional pride had recovered, he would be back in her life. In the meantime she could not wait to get home to Toby.

At home there was an air of celebration. The previous evening, when Sal had told Toby all about Florina, they decided between them that it would be sensible to ask Jenny if she would come to live in the country with them for a while, to help with the baby. After all, Sal would have to work at something in order to support them. Jenny had been thrilled at the prospect, only too happy to get out of London. Peter had taken some photographs of Florina, which had become well-thumbed in just the few hours Sal had been home. Toby had one pinned up on his bedroom wall beside his bed. It was Jenny who pointed out how alike they were. 'They could be brother and sister,' she said.

'They *will* be brother and sister,' Sal said with more confidence than she really felt.

This time she was in England for ten days, days which were totally taken up with preparing her file, obtaining a home study, getting the documents translated and certified, and making plans for the future. She put her house on the market and she, Toby and Jenny travelled down to Horton-cum-Studley for several days to reorganise the cottage. They decided which would be the baby's room, and Toby and Jenny said that they would redecorate it in Sal's absence.

A week after her stormy meeting with David, he turned up at the house unannounced. He greeted Toby warmly and then asked if Jenny was about.

'Yes,' said Sal. 'Why?'

'Would you mind, old chap, if I took your mother out to dinner, while you babysit Jenny?' Toby, who adored David's company, was disappointed. 'We're going to talk about work,' David said. 'You'd be bored to tears.'

'Are you still as angry with me as ever?' Sal asked, once they were in the car.

'I'm angry because I'm losing my best journalist, I'm angry that you've chosen this moment to throw up your career, just when Eastern Europe is providing so many opportunities, but I understand what you're doing, and I think you are right to do it.'

'Really?' said Sal. 'That's a bit of an about-face.'

'Oh, don't rub my nose in it.'

'I'm sorry,' said Sal. 'I appreciate what you're saying very much.'

'It's not just my heightened sensibilities which have made me understand, it's your chum Peter who really showed me the error of my ways.'

'Peter?'

'Yes, he flew in yesterday and refused point blank to go back to Romania to do the final photographs of the children coming home, unless you were there with him. He said nobody else has your understanding.'

'Oh, so this is all about work, really,' said Sal flatly. 'You have to climb down because you need me to do one last job.'

'Naturally,' said David, smiling, 'but genuinely I've done a great deal of thinking, and what you're doing has to be best for you and Toby and, of course, Florina.'

They arrived at the restaurant and talked inconsequentially while they ordered their meal.

'Do you have a photograph of her?' David asked casually.

'Of whom?'

'Of Florina, of course.'

'Yes, I have,' said Sal. 'Do you really want to see it?'

'I'm not quite such a miserable old bugger as I would have you believe.'

'Oh, really?' said Sal, teasing him. She produced a set of photographs from her handbag.

'She's lovely. What's happened to her arm?'

Sal told him the full story and David listened gravely. As she finished, she realised there were tears in his eyes. 'No one tells a story like you, Sal, no one ever can.'

'It's not a story, David, it's real life.'

He wiped his eyes. 'I wish you well with your little girl. Is everything working out OK this end?'

'Yes, I think so. The paperwork should be ready by the middle of next week.'

'Good. The latest report from your lawyer friend, Cristian, suggests that the first three women will be ready to leave Bucharest next Thursday, or at the worst on Friday.'

'So much for adoptions taking a week,' Sal said.

'Still, three weeks is not a long time to wait, given all the circumstances.'

'It seems an age out there,' said Sal.

'Yes, I can imagine.'

'David, it's my turn to grovel now. I have been thinking a lot about what you've said concerning Eastern Europe and I'm sorry I won't be helping you,' Sal said. 'You're right, of course – the other Eastern European countries *do* need more exposure. It's such an extraordinary thing that's happened, and painful too.'

'Painful? In what way?' David asked.

'Before the collapse of Communism, of the Iron Curtain, we had an excuse for ignoring what was happening inside those countries as many of them were virtually impossible to visit. They were also under the thumb of Moscow which meant there was nothing one could have done to help the people anyway.'

'Go on,' said David.

'Now we know how the other half of Europe are living – the Eastern half. How women have to queue for hours for a single chicken wing to make a broth for their children. How heat and light are usually only available for a few hours a day. We know about hospitals without proper equipment and drugs and of mothers who have to give away their children because they can't support them. We know all these things now, and we need to do something about them. We have everything – they have nothing.'

'I don't think they'd agree with you in Cardboard City. A trip down the Embankment here in London is probably very reminiscent of Eastern Europe.'

'Every society has its problems,' Sal said, 'but we have too much and Eastern Europe has too little and it's all wrong. We are part of the same continent.'

'You've just got your first freelance assignment,' David said with a smile.

'What's that?'

'When you're settled in,' he told her, 'write me a piece on what you've just said. You can have a page. I want my heartstrings twanged and I want to feel guilty at the end of it. Can you do that?'

'Well, there's a challenge, if ever there was one,' Sal said drily. 'Twanging the heartstrings of Hard Man, David Thorson. Thank you David, I appreciate the chance.' They smiled at one another, all differences forgotten.

'David, there was one thing I wanted to ask you,' Sal said thoughtfully. 'I've been thinking about it while we've been talking.'

'What's that?'

'I don't expect the paper to cover his expenses, of course, but I thought I might take Toby with me when I go back to Romania.'

'Is it safe?' David said.

'It's safe, as long as he has a few jabs before he goes, and is careful what he eats. I just feel he should be a part of rescuing Florina – that he should see where she came from, so that in a few years, when she's being an irritating little monster, he will remember that. It will also make it *our* adventure, not *mine*.

'I think it's a splendid idea. Of course you may take him, if you think he can cope.'

'He'll cope,' said Sal.

CHAPTER SEVENTEEN

Sal spent a rather lonely flight on her return to Bucharest. Although Peter and Toby knew a great deal about one another, they had never actually met before. They instantly liked one another, and Peter appointed Toby his assistant cameraman. As a result, they spent most of the flight talking about how all the equipment worked. Toby was enthralled. Every time Sal ventured to make a comment, the two of them looked at her vaguely and then resumed their discussion. She was definitely a wallflower.

At the airport Cristian and Andre were there to meet them. Cristian swept Sal into a huge embrace, which embarrassed her in front of Toby, but he seemed hardly to notice in the confusion of the airport.

'Everyone's papers are signed,' Cristian said. 'Tonight there will be much celebration. I already have Emma's passport and I will collect the twins' and Lily's in the morning. Lily is already out of the orphanage. The boys we collect tomorrow, I think you would like to be there, when the twins meet – yes?'

'Oh yes,' said Sal. 'How is Florina?'

'She is well. My sister looks after her, and little Daniella flew to America yesterday.'

'Oh, I'm sorry I missed them.'

'They left me a letter for you. I have it, and I will give it to you later.' His words were full of meaning.

'I'll be sharing a room with Toby,' Sal said under her breath.

'Why?' Cristian said, too loudly. 'Why do you do this to me?'

'We'll talk later, I promise,' Sal said.

There certainly was an air of celebration at the Intercontinental. Fred, Jill's husband, had joined them. He was over the moon with his little daughter, Emma, who had grown hugely in the ten days Sal had been away. Diana's GP husband could not escape from his practice to come out, nor did they think it was sensible to leave their son, but she didn't mind – she had her little Lily with her, at last. Lily was quite unrecognisable – plump and pink-cheeked, clean and alert.

'There certainly doesn't look much wrong with her now,' said Sal.

'As soon as she's settled in, we'll take her up to London for tests,' Diana said. 'I know it's a ridiculous thing to say, but I feel it in my bones that she's going to be all right.'

'Me too,' said Sal, meaning it.

Margaret was full of nervous apprehension as to how

the boys would react to each other. 'They haven't seen one another for about fourteen months,' she said, 'a third of their lives – or nearly. Up until then they shared a cot together, but will they even remember each other now?'

No one knew the answer.

Toby settled in extraordinarily well with everyone. He seemed to take the whole thing in his stride and was particularly struck with little Lily, sitting for a long time with her on his knee.

'You're certainly not going to have any problems with him and Florina,' Peter said quietly, nodding in Toby's direction.

'Yes,' said Sal. 'I hadn't realised that he was so fond of small children. I suppose he's never really had any exposure to them before now.'

'I'm very pleased for you, Sal,' Peter said.

'You know I've told David of my decision?'

'Of course I know.'

'It's just that you didn't mention it on the flight.'

'It's just that I was too busy with my new assistant,' Peter grinned. 'I am sure you're doing the right thing for you personally and I'm sorry I didn't react better when you told me. I was upset, you see. God knows who David will try and team me up with – whoever he choses, I shall hate on principle.'

'I gather I have you to thank for this last trip.'

'David was behaving like a spoilt brat, and I told him so. You're going to be a great loss, but at least if you freelance from time to time, you'll perk up the old rag a bit.'

'Who knows, maybe when the children are older we can work together again,' Sal said.

'Yes,' said Peter. 'I keep thinking about the fact that this is our last trip together — extraordinary, after all these years.'

This was something that, with all the other things on her mind, had not occurred to Sal. She felt a stab of sadness. Was she doing the right thing? She looked around her at the smiling happy faces — yes, she was. For the first time in a long time, if ever, she was putting people before her work and she had got it right at last. She put out a hand and squeezed Peter's. 'You will keep in touch, won't you?'

'You bet your life,' said Peter.

Cristian was sitting alone at the bar, sulking.

'I think you ought to go and sort him out,' said Peter. 'We can't afford for him to blow a gasket at the moment. There are too many little lives at stake.'

'All right,' said Sal reluctantly.

'What's wrong, Cristian?' she asked, joining him at the bar.

'You know what's wrong,' he snapped. 'These children, everywhere. I need to be with you, alone with you.'

'I'm sorry, Cristian, but you're being unreasonable,' said Sal. 'Toby is my son. I'm expecting him to take on the responsibility of a little sister — a sister with whom he'll have a relationship long after I'm dead and buried. If I'm expecting him to share me with her, I have to involve him from the very beginning.'

'You could have booked into separate bedrooms.'

'No, we couldn't. Bucharest is quite a frightening

place, and I couldn't put a child of eleven in a room on his own.'

'I don't understand you English – the children always come first. In our country, children have their place. Adults are in charge, life is run by them and the children must fit in.'

'And look what's happened to your country's children,' Sal said quietly.

There was a heavy silence between them, Sal suddenly aware that she had gone too far. After a moment Cristian slammed his drink down on the bar. 'You are right, I suppose.'

'We do have a very different attitude to children,' Sal said. 'Jill told me that one morning at breakfast-time, she decided to take Emma down to the restaurant. The baby was very good and lay in the crook of her arm while she ate her breakfast and had her coffee, but people kept giving her hostile looks, as though she was doing the wrong thing, having the baby there. In England people would have come up and said, "How sweet. How old is she? What is her name?"'

Cristian nodded. 'It is all part of Ceauşescu and what happened to us. We have no idea how to care for others.'

Sal laid a hand on his arm. 'Cristian, I'm sorry, but in any case, where can our relationship go from here? I owe you such a lot. You've helped all these people and all these children, and you've found out so much about my family for me. We caught each other at a vulnerable moment. We are very good together, but you wouldn't be prepared to live in England, would you?'

'No,' said Cristian. 'I must help the new Romania.'

'Exactly,' said Sal. 'And I couldn't live in Romania. Toby and Florina are my future.'

'Will you do something for me, Sal?' Cristian said.

Sal nodded.

'If I can manage to quickly process Florina's adoption, will you come away for the weekend with me — you, Toby and the baby? There is an hotel I know in the Carpathian Mountains. Maybe you would let the boy and the baby share a room and maybe we could have a little time together.'

'I'm not sure,' Sal said. 'I don't know how Toby would feel about it.'

'Toby need not know; we would be very discreet. Please think about it.'

'OK,' said Sal. 'Now please tell me all about Florina.'

The following morning, Margaret was due to pick up the boys at ten o'clock. She had the two precious pieces of paper signed by Iliescu.

'Can't we go and see Florina first?' Toby asked at breakfast.

'Duty calls,' Sal said, 'but when we pick up Ion, then we can see Florina. They're in the same orphanage.'

Margaret had decided that it was best to bring Mikhail to Ion, without being quite sure why. They arrived at Orphanage Number Six. The Director looked at the paper, said she would need Mikhail's clothes and disappeared back into her office. Sal was stunned by the lack of interest. Margaret stripped off Mikhail's filthy rags for the last time and unwrapped the bandages from his twisted leg. She then dressed him in a cheery shirt, dungarees and a thick coat to ward off the cold outside. It had been snowing all night and the roads were slippery and dangerous.

Margaret and Mikhail knew each other well now. There was no problem about him being carried outside to sit on her lap in the car. He did not even glance backwards at the place that had been his home for the first four years of his life.

When they entered the courtyard of Orphanage Number One, Sal did not know how to control herself. She longed to leave the party and rush to Florina. Sensing her feelings, Margaret said, 'Do you want to see your baby first?'

'Absolutely not,' said Sal through gritted teeth.

'Then would you hold Mikhail, while I fetch Ion?'

Sal nodded. 'Of course.'

Sal took the little boy in her arms and they mounted the steps. Margaret went ahead. Peter loaded his camera, and told Toby to stand beside him, with a spare roll of film. Everyone was tense. Mikhail looked very serious, as if recognising something momentous was about to happen.

Moments later Margaret appeared with Ion in her arms. Sal stepped forward with Mikhail and walked towards them. Just feet away from one another, Ion caught sight of Mikhail. He gave a cry and struggled from Margaret's arms. She set him down on the floor, where, with awkward gait, he shuffled towards his brother. Sal crouched down. Mikhail could not stand but she supported him in an upright position.

Ion reached them, and without hesitation, threw his arms around his brother. The two little boys clung together, while Peter kept shooting, shouting to Toby for more film. He did not know it then, but from this sequence would come the most commercially successful photograph of Peter's life, making the front page of *Time* magazine. It was to be reproduced again and again in the years ahead. Everyone, except Toby, was in tears – even Cristian. The doctor who had been responsible for Ion, and who had been so against Margaret adopting Mikhail, began talking urgently and rapidly to Cristian. Sal, still supporting the two children, was alarmed. 'What's she saying, Cristian?'

'She says that she was wrong and you were right.' He turned to Margaret. 'She says you did a good thing, Mrs Margaret. She did not guess at the bond between these boys. She wishes you God's blessing for what you have done.'

Margaret came and scooped up the two little boys, cradling them to her. She looked up at Sal, smiling through her tears. 'I dreamt it would be like this. I prayed it would be like this, but I was too frightened to believe it was possible.' The boys were each cuddled into her shoulder, but were still holding one another's hands, smiling at each other.

'They're going to be very hard work, Margaret,' Sal joked.

'They certainly are,' Margaret said, with deep satisfaction. 'Mikhail will have to have a number of operations on his leg, but even the doctors here in Romania reckon he should be able to walk eventually.

With them both tearing around, I'll be old before my time.'

'Never,' said Sal. 'A new lease of life, more like it, and if anyone deserves it, it's you.'

'No,' said Margaret, 'it's these two who deserve that, and all the other children here. Sal, I'm being selfish. I have got my boys. Go off and see your baby, and do bring her out to show us – I haven't met her yet properly.'

Sal turned to Cristian. 'Can I see Florina now?'

'Yes, of course. This way.'

'Come on, Toby.' Sal took his arm and they set off down the now-familiar corridor and into the ward. Sal rushed forward. Florina's cot was empty. 'What's happened to her? Where's she gone? Oh my God, what's happened?' Sal was seized with panic.

'I'll go and find one of the nurses,' said Cristian. 'Be calm, I am sure all is well.'

Sal and Toby stood hand in hand by the empty cot. 'What's happened, Mum?' he asked anxiously. 'Where is she?'

'I don't know, Toby. It's probably all right.'

When Cristian returned, his face was grave and Sal felt her heart flip. 'What is it? What's wrong?'

'My sister was not happy with the baby's condition this morning. Florina has a bad chest infection, so she took her to the hospital. They are there now. We will go, yes?'

'How badly ill is she?'

'I do not know the details. Come on.'

Sal and Toby spent three days at the hospital while

Florina hovered between life and death. Sal managed to file her story and David arranged for a journalist to meet the families at Heathrow. That organised, Sal gave herself up to Florina.

The hospital found a mattress, which Toby and Sal took it in turns to lie on, beside the cot. Sal was all for flying Florina back to England, but the doctors were adamant that she would not survive the journey. They had the drugs to treat her, they insisted, and certainly the treatment she received seemed to be doing her good.

On day three, there was definitely a small improvement. On day four, her eyes were focusing.

'She knows you,' Toby said, as they leaned together over the cot. 'Look.'

'I should never have left her,' Sal said, full of remorse. In her mind she was sure that Florina's illness was her fault.

The doctor joined them. 'The worst is over, she will be OK. She is a strong girl.'

There was no question of Florina going back to the orphanage. Iliescu had signed the adoption papers and all they were waiting for now was a passport and visa. After five days, nervously Sal and Toby took Florina back to the hotel. Her chest was still a little wheezy, and she was very tired all the time.

'The mountains,' Cristian pronounced. 'That is what she needs now – that weekend in the mountains you promised me.'

It was Thursday. Sal knew that the passport and visa would not be through until the following Monday. 'I

don't like to take her so far away from the hospital,'
she fretted.

'I will arrange for a doctor to examine her when we
reach the mountains if you like. Trust me,' Cristian
said.

'But the journey in a cold car. Suppose it breaks
down?'

'The car will not break down; we will take care.
Toby can ski, it will be good fun.'

Sal was too exhausted to argue. Cristian arranged it
all and Toby was certainly excited. She was sorry to
have missed Diana, Jill and Margaret going home, and
that her last assignment with Peter had come to such
an abrupt end. But in a strange way she felt she could
not cope with any more emotion — it was all used up.

On Friday morning, with Florina bundled up in a
snowsuit and blanket, they set off for the mountains.
Their hotel was surprisingly civilised: a little chalet-
type structure, set into the side of the mountain with
log fires blazing in every room.

'Is this OK?' Cristian asked anxiously.

'Yes, it's wonderful,' said Sal, and meant it.

After lunch Cristian suggested that he should take
Toby skiing. 'And leave you girls to rest,' he said. Sal
was immensely grateful. Florina was still fretful. She
took her up to the hotel room and laid her in the
cot provided, but she would not settle. Eventually she
lifted her out and snuggled her into bed beside her. In
seconds the little girl was asleep. 'I shouldn't have left
you,' she whispered. 'We nearly lost you and it was
all my fault for going home. And yet, how else would

I have been able to adopt you? I had to go back.' The pale gold stubble was starting to grow. Sal nuzzled her face against it – her daughter. Within seconds Sal, too, had drifted off to sleep.

The weekend was an enormous success. The mountain air did suit Florina. Each day Sal took her outside for a little sunshine and then sat in front of one of the log fires, cuddling her. All the time it seemed to her that the child was relaxing, starting to believe that the comfort of Sal's arms was there to stay. Toby and Cristian had a wonderful time, skiing and tobogganing. Any resentment which Cristian had expressed earlier seemed to have gone. He genuinely enjoyed Toby's company, and the feeling was certainly mutual. At night, while the children slept, Sal and Cristian made love, and yet there was a reluctance in Sal as she knew it was something that could not last.

On their last night together she tried to explain to Cristian how she felt, but he did not want to hear. 'We will meet again somewhere,' he said to her. 'I will come to you, or you to me. I want to see those children of yours again, but above all I want to be with you. This is not the end for us.'

It was a cold, starry night. Sal peered out of the window at the mountains all around them. It was such a beautiful place. She had her two children safe next door, a man who loved and wanted her. If only . . . Sal leaned her head against the cold window pane. Cristian was standing behind her, kissing her neck, caressing her breasts and pushing his very obvious erection against her buttocks.

'Come to bed,' he breathed in her ear as he bit on her earlobe.

When Sal lifted her face to look at him he fiercely took possession of her lips, forcing them apart and thrusting his tongue deep into her mouth. He grapsed her buttocks and pulled her into him, rubbing his erection against her. Sal felt suddenly weary and although her mind wanted him to stop, her body was already surrendering to his demands. He picked her up and almost threw her on to the bed. She lay motionless where he had thrown her and as Cristian stood up and quickly undressed, she felt a thrill run through her at the sight of his nakedness. He knelt on the bed and started to take off her clothes. Sal put up no resistance. At first he was unhurried, but by the time he had reached her underwear he was almost ripping at the flimsy material. His breath was coming in gasps, as though he found her passiveness an incredible turn on.

When she was totally naked, he bent over and kissed her again. He knelt astride her and laid his throbbing penis in her cleavage; squeezing her breasts together, he started to move backwards and forwards, and each time he thrust forward his penis would push against her chin. 'Lick me, Sal,' he ordered, and she put out her tongue to lick the moist head every time it came within reach. Cristian groaned with pleasure. Sal felt curiously detached from the whole action, as though she were floating above the bed watching what was happening. Her body, however, was beginning to respond in that familiar way to his almost brutal lovemaking. She found herself reaching up and grasping his buttocks, pulling and pushing with the movement of his body and digging her nails into his flesh. She then released her grip to take hold of her breasts and squeeze them even tighter round his penis. Each time he thrust up into her face, her tongue licked the juices that were beginning to trickle out. Cristian took a deep breath and gradually slowed his movements, so as to stop his climax. He took away Sal's hands and rolled over, taking her with him, so she suddenly found herself on top.

Sal leaned over him and slowly started to move. She lifted herself so high that he almost came out of her, then waited, keeping the head of his penis just touching her inner lips, then thrust her body down and took him deep inside her. With every downward thrust, Cristian let out a cry. Sal increased the waiting time so that Cristian was almost whimpering, waiting for her to take him back inside. Sal was feeling good; being in control made her feel powerful. She sat up, stopping all movement, and he gave a cry of protest. Sal looked down at him and smiled a slow, sensual smile. 'You put me in the driving seat,' she said, 'so you'll have to accept the way I change gear.'

He glared at her for a moment, then laughed. 'I will buy you a chauffeur's cap, my darling, to add authenticity to your fantasy.' Sal grinned and, letting him slide out of her, she reversed her body; as she pushed herself into his face, she bent and took his penis in her mouth. Cristian obediently started to lick, taking the rhythm from her; as she went quicker, so did he. Sal climaxed very quickly, letting him slip out of her mouth and burying her face in his pubic hair as the intense waves swept over her.

He was on top of her again and slid himself inside her. He was teasing her now, moving slowly, so slowly, but the sensation was wonderful. Sal felt the tension start to build again. Cristian reached down and gently sucked on her nipples, first one then the other, until Sal was on the brink of her orgasm. When she started to come, Cristian kissed her, pushing his tongue deep into her mouth at the same moment as he pushed his penis deep into her body. It was the most intense orgasm Sal had ever had with him; the sensation went on and on, hardly diminishing as wave after wave swept over her. Cristian had not come, but he did not stop moving his body or kissing her. As he started to come, Sal could feel herself building to another climax with him. She could not believe it, but as he came, pumping inside her, her body echoed his climax and he broke from their kiss at last, to shout her name over and over.

The next morning they left the hotel and drove straight to Bucharest airport where Andre met them with Florina's documents. Saying goodbye to Andre was hard, for Sal knew it was unlikely they would ever meet again. At Passport Control, Cristian, too, said farewell. He embraced Toby, kissed Florina and gently kissed Sal on the lips. 'I will call you to make sure that you are home safely,' he said.

'No, I'll call you,' said Sal, conscious of how much a phone call cost in Bucharest.

'And maybe I will see you soon?' he said.

'We'll think of something,' Sal promised.

He turned then without a word and walked with his hurried stride across the airport foyer. Suddenly the big man did not look so big any more – just another Romanian struggling to survive in a difficult world. And in that moment, all the doubts Sal had felt about their relationship disappeared. She had brought him love and comfort at a time when he had needed them. That in itself was enough. If they never met again, it would be all right.

'I like him,' Toby said. 'Will we see him again?'

'I think we should, don't you?' said Sal. Toby nodded. 'Come on,' she said. 'Let's go home.'

CHAPTER EIGHTEEN

It was, in fact, seventeen months before Sal and Cristian met again – months which proved to be the most fulfilling of Sal's life to date.

On their return to London, they learned that an offer had been made on the London house and within a fortnight Sal, Toby, Florina and Jenny were settled into Horton-cum-Studley. Toby seemed completely unworried about switching schools to a local one in Oxford into which he settled very quickly. Florina blossomed before their eyes. The plaster was removed from her arm at the John Radcliffe Hospital in Oxford, and an X-ray showed that, miraculously, it had knitted perfectly.

When the children were asleep that night, Sal and Jenny sat over a bottle of wine. 'I never would have arm believed, you know, when that plaster was put on her in Bucharest, that when it came off she would be in Oxford and be my daughter, more or less.'

'You still have to go through a UK adoption process over here, don't you?'

'Yes,' said Sal, 'but it's not for at least a year.'

The year in question had shot by. David, as good as his word, had passed several freelance jobs Sal's way. She had also written a number of articles for women's magazines on the subject of adoption and Romania in particular. Life became very tranquil. She developed a passionate interest in gardening and began growing her own vegtables. Toby was amused. 'I never really saw you as a gardener, Mum.'

'And why not, pray?' she asked.

He shrugged his shoulders. 'I like it, though,' he added, 'it's homely.'

She missed her friends, but not enormously so. Plenty of them came down for the weekend. Florina began attending the playschool in the village and, spurred on by David, Sal began writing a book about Eastern Europe.

It was not until March the following year that, out of the blue, she received a telephone call from Cristian. 'It is a year today that Florina left Romania,' he said.

'I know,' said Sal.

'How is she?'

'She's very well, thank you, and how are you?'

'OK. Listen, I have an idea.'

'What is it?' said Sal.

'When I was in Yugoslavia, I fell in love with Slovenia. It is so beautiful. There is a lake — Lake Bled. In the middle is a church, a Roman Catholic church, on an island. There are mountains all around.

Oh, I love mountains, Sal. There is also a wonderful hotel called the Grand Hotel at Toplice. I have a little money saved, so why don't we have a holiday there – in July?'

'Cristian, I'm not sure it would be a good idea. We said our goodbyes.'

'Look, I know we have no future together, we have been through all this, but I would like to see you and the children. I have very little in my life except work these days. The adoptions, they still go on, as you know.'

'Don't tell me I'm the only woman in your life, because I shan't believe it,' Sal said.

'Then you would be wrong,' said Cristian. 'There has been no woman since you. I want you, Sal, I want you badly. Come, please, if only for a week.'

Toby thought it was a wonderful idea. He had several times asked about Cristian. The thought of a holiday pleased Sal too, for by then she knew that Florina's UK adoption would be through and the little girl would be entitled to a British passport. Encouraged by everybody's enthusiasm, she booked a fortnight's holiday for them at the Grand Hotel. Cristian was unable to join them for the full time, but promised to be with them halfway through the first week.

He had been right about Slovenia. Sal adored it the moment she arrived and felt strangely at home. It made her wonder whether perhaps her father's family had originally been Slovenian, but of course now she would never know. She had made all sorts of enquiries through her journalist friends about Georges, but no one had been able to find out anything. Helped by her involvement with her children, she was more or less reconciled to the fact that she would never find Georges, but in the elegance of the hotel, surrounded by the glorious Julien Mountains, she could not help but wonder if somewhere, within a few hundred miles perhaps, her brother lived.

Toby had a wonderful time, swimming in the lake and boating. Florina was now an exceptionally pretty little girl, with blonde curls. She was a tremendous chatterbox, and always the centre of attention. Sal tried not to mention her origins, but one afternoon she confided to an elderly couple, who had taken a particular interest in her, where she had come from, and it was soon all around the hotel. From then on the children were spoiled relentlessly, which suited them both very well indeed.

By the time Cristian arrived, they were well settled and relaxed. At the sight of him, Sal felt as if they had never been apart. There had been no man, not even a hint of a man, in her life since she had left Romania; it had been a period for concentrating on her children and adjusting to life in the country. So when Cristian embraced her, she wondered how she could have been away from him for so long.

The week together was magic. They walked and swam and played with the children, and their nights together were wonderful. But both of them knew that nothing had changed. Their relationship still had no future, and in a strange sort of way, it heightened its intensity with a bittersweet quality, which made every day more precious and every night more precious still.

On their last night together, without discussion, they made no attempt to get dressed to go down for dinner. They were both restless, wondering how they would cope with their goodbyes.

'I'm not sure we did the right thing,' Sal said, 'meeting again, opening old wounds.'

'Of course we did,' Cristian said.

'But I shall miss you.'

'And I shall miss you,' he said.

They had talked during the week many times of Romania and her problems and it was clear that, if anything, the situation was worse now than immediately after the revolution. Sal ached for the people. She had felt such a part of them, so excited when they had finally rid themselves of the Ceaşescus. And for what? The same queues, the same lack of everything which the civilised world considered basic.

'And the orphanages?' she asked, with dread in her voice.

'As full as ever. Birth control is allowed, but is not available, so it amounts to the same thing.'

'Why don't you come and live in England?' Sal said suddenly.

'Are you asking me to marry you?' Cristian was deadly serious. He was lying on the bed watching her carefully.

'No . . . I don't know,' said Sal, all at once on the defensive. 'I hadn't thought that far. I just thought that Romania's problems seemed so acute, maybe you would be better in England for a few years, and we could be together.'

'You would not like me if I came to England,' Cristian said wisely, 'and nor would I like myself. How can I leave my country now? And besides, what would I do? I am not trained to practise law in your country, and I am certainly too old to retrain. So do I become a shopkeeper, a bus driver?'

'I don't know.' Sal fell silent. 'You're right, of course,' she said in a small voice.

'I would grow angry and disillusioned, and despite all the problems of my country, I would miss it. You and I would irritate one another, make one another sad.' Sal nodded. 'Look, let us not spoil our last night together. Come to bed, Sal.'

She looked up and smiled at him, her smile matching his, wicked and inviting. 'I might consider it if you took your clothes off,' she said. He threw back his head and laughed and Sal felt a twisting pain in her chest when she realised that this would probably be the last time she would see him laugh like that. He leaped up and started throwing off his clothes.

'No, no,' giggled Sal. 'Let me, please, Cristian.' She slowly undressed him. As she undid the buttons of his shirt she kissed each inch of tanned skin and curly black hair as it was slowly and sensually exposed. She gave him gentle bites and took some of the hair in her teeth and pulled it quite hard. When he protested, she licked him like a she-cat washing her kittens. Sal licked round his nipples and sucked them until they hardened and Cristian's breath quickened, then she drew his shirt off and threw it on the floor. She then undid his trousers and found he had no underpants on. 'Wicked man,' she said, laughing.

'I thought you would appreciate it, darling,' he replied. She drew down his trousers inch by inch, gently kissing as she went. When she reached the thick mat of black pubic hair, she stopped and started to go up again, to tease him. He was groaning softly now and stroking her hair. She finally pulled his trousers right down and taking his penis in her hand she slowly slid him into her mouth. Cristian let out a long moan as her warm mouth sucked him in. She ran her tongue round the tip as she kept him deep in her mouth, and reaching down she began to run her fingers up and down the inside of his thighs. He was rock hard now and Sal could taste the lubricating drops of his juice in her mouth. She slid his rigid penis out of her mouth with one last suck and smiled up at him. 'You do look silly with your trousers round your ankles. Let me make you more comfortable.'

She deftly removed his trousers and tossed them over her shoulder. He lay back on the bed and opened his arms. Sal slid up his body and he wrapped his arms around her and held her very close. 'You make me feel so good, Sal,' he whispered into her hair.

Sal, trying to make light of the fact this would be their last night together, joked back, 'You're always so good to feel, Cristian.'

'It is not just sex, you know that,' he went on. She looked into his eyes and found that she had a lump in her throat that stopped her from speaking.

'You will always be very special to me, Sal,' he

said, and he gently rolled her over and bent his mouth to hers. He kissed her gently and tenderly, but suddenly their kiss ignited and the fire and passion started to build between them. Cristian's hand moved down Sal's body, first stroking and circling her breast, then gently raking his nails over her stomach until he finally reached the hot, wet centre of sensation, and she moaned with pleasure as he started to rub her clitoris. He plunged two fingers into her. Sal was writhing and moaning under him and he suddenly took away his hand and thrust himself deep inside her. Sal let out a cry as he entered her and they lay there in each other's arms, not moving at all, just enjoying the moment of ultimate togetherness.

Sal opened her eyes and found him looking at her with such warm tenderness that tears came to her eyes and slid down her cheeks. Cristian did not say a word, just brushed them away with his fingertips. He rolled her over, managing to keep inside her, and smiled his wicked smile. 'There you are, your favourite position, the driving seat.' Sal giggled tearfully and started to move up and down on him. Cristian closed his eyes and whispered over and over, 'So good, so good.' Sal quickened the pace and brought him to the edge of orgasm and then slowed down again. Cristian murmured her name, but did not open his eyes. Sal repeated the process and this time he looked up at her and said, 'Right. I, too, can play that game.' He reversed their positions so quickly that Sal did not even realise what he was going to do. He reached down and started rubbing her clitoris in a gentle circular motion as he moved slowly in and out of her. Sal floated in a sea of sensation. As she started to tense for her orgasm, he thrust into her and stopped all movement. She groaned in frustration and he whispered in her ear, 'You see, I can do it, too!'

'Can we call a truce, Cristian?' she asked, and he laughed, starting to move inside her again. He picked up the rhythm and Sal was moving too, thrusting her body up to meet his, feeling him fill her totally. Cristian was kissing her face, her eyes, her throat and her mouth as he plunged into her. They came together, Sal moaning and crying and Cristian shouting her name. He collapsed on top of her and Sal felt her tears start again. They clung to each other, almost desperately, and when Sal tasted the salty tears in her mouth, she was not sure if they were his or hers.

CHAPTER NINETEEN

On their return from holiday, for the first time
Sal felt oddly restless with her new life. Almost
immediately Toby went off to a summer camp with a
schoolfriend, and Jenny was taking her annual leave in
Scotland. On impulse, Sal decided to spend a couple of
days in London and look up old friends. She booked
herself into the Portobello Hotel with Florina, who
adored hotels.

On the first day she visited the offices of the *Daily
Record* and had lunch with David. The paper virtually
ground to a halt with the arrival of Florina, who dashed
from one department to another, causing havoc in her
wake. David and Sal had lunch at an Italian restaurant
which was just as well, since they tested the Italians'
traditional love of children to the hilt. Florina went
crazy, running around, talking to people. The waiters
bore her away to meet the chef.

'You certainly have your hands full there,' David said.

'She's gorgeous, though, isn't she? I'm quite besotted with her,' said Sal.

'Well, that I can quite understand. She's going to be quite a handful when she's older, though. Not unlike her mother, I imagine.'

Sal smiled. 'I shall ignore that.'

'Sal, there's talk of trouble in Yugoslavia. Have you heard anything about it?'

'No, nothing, and I've only just come back from there myself, well – from Slovenia. The children and I were on holiday.' She purposely didn't mention Cristian, fearing a lecture from David.

'This is around Dubrovnik. I don't understand the politics quite, but Yugoslavia is cutting herself up into bits, declaring independence – Slovenia, Croatia and Bosnia–Herzegovina – and it seems to be causing trouble. Slovenia has taken herself away from the Yugloslavian Federation, just in the last few weeks. Didn't you hear anything about it?'

'Nothing,' said Sal, 'but then it was a holiday.'

'There has been some trouble in Eastern Slovenia, in a place called Bregana – it's between the Yugoslavs and Slovenians; and then also in Croatia, between the Serbs and the Croatians. It's a very confusing situation and the reports we're getting are very patchy. You wouldn't like to go out and take a look?'

'No, I would not,' said Sal firmly. 'We've been through all this. I have doubled my responsibilities, if you remember.' She indicated Florina, who was being carried around the room by a waiter.

'I understand all that, it's just that, bearing in mind it's your country in a way because of your father, I thought perhaps you might like to become involved.'

'A bit below the belt, David, even for you,' Sal said.

'I'm not trying to persuade you – I'm simply asking,' David said firmly. 'I have a feeling about this, Sal. I can't put my finger on it, but I don't like what I hear and I believe things are going to get pretty bad out there.'

'Oh, I'm sure you're wrong,' Sal said casually. 'There's been so much blood shed to obtain the peace they have, they must value it beyond rubies. I can't imagine they'd want to start a civil war.'

'I'll remind you of what I said, and of what you said, in six months' time.' David's voice was grim.

'Then you must know something I don't.'

'Not really, but I tell you what – why don't you write me a piece about the various countries that go to make up Yugoslavia? The Serbians, I gather, don't like Croatia being split out from the Federation. Why would that be?'

'I imagine because a great many Serbs live in Croatia,' said Sal.

'It's that sort of thing I need to know.'

'Is anybody interested?'

'I'm interested,' said David. 'I'm not promising that I'm going to publish it, but I'll pay you for it anyway. Write me a piece which explains exactly how Yugoslavia works, who's who, what religion everybody practises. Use a map, do it simply as if for a small child – you know I like my facts simple.'

'All right,' said Sal. 'Now, when are you coming down to see us?'

'Soon, very soon, I promise,' he said.

The following day, Sal had promised herself, she would devote to shopping. The children both needed new clothes. She had been warned that there was little point in buying Florina much, as children newly out of an orphanage grew like weeds. Certainly this was true of Florina. Sal had felt at times she could almost see her growing. Within recent months, however, her growth had slowed down and it was time for a big splurge on clothes.

They were just leaving Peter Jones in Sloane Square, Sal laiden with parcels and Florina mercifully strapped in her buggy, when she heard her name being called. She turned and came face to face with Evelyn Noble. She felt herself blushing and stammering like a teenager. 'Evelyn, how nice to see you. How are you?' she managed.

'I'm fine,' said Evelyn. 'It's nice to see you too, Sal, and who is this?' Evelyn had always loved children. She knelt down and looked at Florina. 'Hello,' she said. 'I've read all about you in the papers. You're a very beautiful little girl, aren't you?'

'Yes,' Florina agreed readily.

Evelyn looked up at Sal from where she knelt. 'I really admire you, Sal, for what you did out there. Not just for Florina, but for all the other children you helped. It was a great job.'

'Evelyn . . .' Sal stammered, 'I am sorry about everything.'

Evelyn stood up and smiled. She was much slimmer than she had been and prettier too, with better clothes and make-up. 'Sal, I'm sorry, too, about that phone call. It was just too soon, but honestly, everything is OK now.'

'It can't be OK, you must hate me,' Sal said.

A cloud seemed to cross Evelyn's face. 'Yes,' she admitted, 'I did, but not any more. Look, I tell you what, why don't we go somewhere and have a drink?'

Sal looked down at Florina. 'It's really time for her midday sleep. If she doesn't have it, she gets really bad-tempered. What we could do is go back to my hotel and I could put her down for a nap while we talk.'

'That would be great,' said Evelyn.

'Are you short of time?' Sal asked.

'No, not at all. Louis . . .' she hesitated over his name, 'Louis is up here at a conference and I just came along for the ride. I'm a free agent until six o'clock.'

'What does he do now? Don't you live in London any more?' Sal asked.

'He works for Oxfam, and absolutely loves it. He's away quite a bit of the time, but he really adores the job. It's been a great thing for him. We're based at Hawkhead permanently these days.'

'Sounds good,' said Sal.

'Come on,' said Evelyn, 'let's get a taxi.'

In the taxi, they talked of Florina, and once they reached the hotel, Evelyn went down to the bar while Sal took Florina and the parcels upstairs and settled the little girl for her sleep.

When she came down to the bar, Evelyn had already organised some wine. She poured them both a glass. 'What shall the toast be, Sal?'

Sal shook her head. 'I'm not in a position to make any toasts in front of you.'

'How about "To friendship – no matter what".'

'I can drink to that,' said Sal. 'To friendship – no matter what.'

'How long have we known each other?' Evelyn asked.

'Well,' said Sal, 'since we were nine, but let's not add it up.'

'I agree.'

They drank and there was a silence between them for a moment. 'So how are things?' Sal asked. 'Are you all right?'

'Yes,' said Evelyn, 'and in a strange way, thanks to you, much better.'

'I can't believe that,' said Sal.

'Well, it's true. As I said, Louis' job has been a great thing for him. He really hated Lambeth Palace and all the politics. He'd set out to be a career clergyman and that's what he became. Because it was his chosen path he wouldn't have changed his job, but for having been forced to resign. He always used to complainn that he never actually *did* anything. In fact, the nearest he ever came to doing anything at all was that ill-fated trip to Moscow.' Sal blanched. 'Now, in Oxfam,' Evelyn continued, 'he feels he's making a real contribution – getting stuck in. He's a much happier man.'

'And you?' Sal asked.

'Well, I can't pretend it wasn't tough to start with. He wouldn't talk about it, you see. I mean, he's an Englishman for a start, that doesn't help, but somehow it was all so painful and embarrassing, I suppose. I wanted to talk it all through; I wanted to understand. You know me, I'm like you, we're better if we have things out in the open. So there was I, desperately needing to talk, and him being unable to. I don't know what would have happened quite, but he landed this job at Oxfam very quickly and was sent out to Palestine almost immediately. He was away for three months, and much to my fury I found I missed him dreadfully. I thought I was being a silly old fool, but when he came back, I found he felt the same. I can't pretend it was a second honeymoon, or anything as dramatic as that, but things were certainly a lot better and have continued to improve. I'd let myself go after the children were born. I was too fat and I had totally given up so far as my appearance was concerned. All I could think about, actually, was the children. What happened between you and Louis brought me up short. I was faced with two alternatives – either to accept the marriage was over or to fight for it. I fought for it, and it was the right decision.'

'I'm so glad,' Sal said again.

'We married so young, I suppose an affair was almost inevitable, but because of him being in the Church it never occurred to me. Perhaps if I'd been less sure of him, I'd have made more of an effort before and it would never have happened. As it is, and I suppose you would be a better judge of this than me, I don't think it would have happened if it hadn't been you he was out there with in Moscow.'

'What makes you say that?' Sal asked.

'I think it was because after nearly losing his life, he was in the company of someone he knew really well. I doubt it would have happened otherwise, would it?' For the first time, Evelyn seemed unsure of herself.

'No,' Sal agreed. 'If it's any consolation,' she added in a low voice, 'the whole thing never made him happy.'

'It isn't a consolation,' said Evelyn.

'No, I suppose not.' There was silence between them.

'Is there anyone in your life now, Sal?'

'No, not really. I had a brief thing with a lawyer out in Romania. We are very fond of each other, but we have no future together, we can't have. He's committed to Romania and I'm committed here. In any case, I'm not sure it's the stuff of long-term relationships.'

'You never pick the right man,' Evelyn said, smiling warmly.

'I know,' said Sal. 'I never do, do I?'

'Still, if you don't have much luck with your men, at least you do with your children. Tell me about Toby.'

They talked about each other's children for a while and then Sal glanced at her watch. 'I haven't a baby alarm and Florina will be waking up soon. I don't want her to get in a fuss and wonder where she is. It might put her off her midday sleep and I really need that, even if she doesn't. It's the only chance I get for a breather.'

'I can imagine,' said Evelyn, laughing.

'So, where do we go from here?' Sal asked.

'Well,' said Evelyn, 'I'm quite sure that Louis couldn't cope with meeting you again, and I'm not sure I could cope with that either, to be honest.'

'No, no, I can see that,' said Sal.

'And the children are still pretty resentful about what happened. We couldn't keep it from them, any more than I imagine you could keep it from Toby.'

'No,' Sal said. 'So that just leaves you and me, Evelyn.'

'Yes. As I said, Louis is away for at least four months of the year, and sometimes five, and the children are old enough to stay with friends for a few days. Why don't I come down and spend some time with you and the children at the cottage, the next time Louis goes away?'

'We'd love that,' said Sal. 'It would be great for Toby to see you again. I don't want you to feel . . .' She hesitated. 'You're not doing it because you feel you ought to, are you? Out of some sort of misguided loyalty for old times' sake, or anything? I behaved like a rat, Evelyn, and you owe me nothing. I owe you everything.'

Evelyn reached across and took Sal's hand. 'You're still my friend. You behaved like a shit, no one is denying that, but you're still my friend and I couldn't bear to think that we would never meet again, could you?'

Sal shook her head, tears in her eyes. 'No, I really couldn't.'

'Good,' said Evelyn, 'then that's settled.'

*   *   *

It was just after five o'clock the following afternoon, as Sal turned off the motorway. It had been a blazing hot day in London and Florina had been fretful. More than once she wished she had cut short her stay in the capital. It was strange, having been a city girl for so long, but she missed the country. Florina had fallen into an exhausted sleep as soon as the car cooled down on the motorway. She was not going to be easy to get to bed that night, Sal thought ruefully. Still, it would be good to be home.

As she drove through the village her thoughts were full of the next hour or two. She would wake Florina and play with her in the garden to wear her out, then give her a nice bath and with a bit of luck she would go off. Toby would be home tomorrow. He had only been away for ten days, but Sal had missed him dreadfully and wondered how on earth she had ever been able to leave him for weeks on end. It seemed inconceivable now.

She turned into her drive, but was prevented from parking outside the front door because a battered old Morris Traveller blocked the way. 'What on earth?' Sal said, aloud. The car meant nothing to her. She drew up behind it, slammed on the brakes and turned off the engine. Florina woke with a start and began to cry. Ignoring her for a moment, Sal jumped out and walked up to the car.

Slouched in the driver's seat, his head awkwardly resting on the doorframe, was Peter. He was asleep, but even in sleep he looked terrible — he had several days' growth of beard, and dark circles under his eyes.

Florina's screams were becoming more persistent. Sal glanced in her direction and then shook Peter gently. He woke with a start, staring at her for a moment with unseeing eyes. 'What the . . .? Oh Sal, it's you. I didn't know what to do. I didn't know whether you'd be back.'

'What's happened, Peter? What's wrong with you? You look awful!'

'I've just come back from Yugoslavia. It was terrible there. I was with my girlfriend, she's been shot – killed and it was all my fault. I just didn't know where else to come. You seemed to be the right person.'

'Oh, Peter,' said Sal. 'Listen, I'll just rescue Florina. Come into the house.'

Once inside, Sal broke the rules and gave Florina a packet of crisps and a drink to keep her quiet, and without being asked she poured Peter a whisky. It was a lovely evening. She ushered him through to the garden, settled him in a chair and took the cover off the sandpit for Florina, who mercifully settled down with her crisps. Then she joined Peter, taking his hand. 'What happened? Tell me all about it.'

'I've had this girlfriend, Gilly Holloway, for some years. It's always been tricky – a sort of on/off relationship. David had given me a couple of weeks' holiday. I'm no good at holidays, so I decided to go and photograph some mountains for no particular reason. I suppose it made a change from photographing the world's horrors.'

Peter sounded uncharacteristically bitter. They had only met once since returning from Romania for a slightly stilted lunch in London. He had aged, Sal thought.

'We started off in Austria. We looked at the Italian Alps, and then somebody said that Slovenia was beautiful, so we meandered into Slovenia.'

'You did it all in your Morris Traveller?' Sal asked, trying to lighten his mood.

'No, no, Gilly's car. She's in advertising, she earns proper money – *earned* proper money,' he corrected. 'From Slovenia we wandered into Croatia. We followed the Hungarian border along towards Serbia. We stayed in little hostelries each night. They are so cheap, the food's so good and the people so nice. Gilly was really taken with it. She had a week's more holiday than me and she was all for pressing on, she fancied going down towards Dubrovnik. One evening it was getting dark as we approached the outskirts of a village called Borovo Selo. Suddenly we came across a roadblock. We were still in Croatia, but only just – on the Serbian–Croatian border, I suppose you'd say.' He hesitated and took a hefty slug of his whisky. 'We didn't speak Serbo-Croat and they didn't speak English. They were all young men. I discovered afterwards that they were probably Serbian vigilantes, but we didn't know that at the time. They were very drunk and, it has to be said, so was I.'

'Oh, Peter!' Sal said.

'We'd stopped for a late lunch at this wonderful little restaurant. We'd drunk a couple of bottles of wine, or at least I'd drunk most of them. Gilly had volunteered to drive after lunch. The young men were quite abusive and unpleasant. They seemed to be making insinuations about Gilly – their gestures were all too obvious. I didn't like it – I just wanted out of it, so I told Gilly to drive through the roadblock. At first she refused, but then they started trying to get us out of the car. She panicked and put her foot down . . . They shot her in the back of the neck.' He stared out again across Sal's pretty garden.

'Oh my God, Peter. How terrible!'

'The only merciful thing is that she can't have felt any pain. She was dead instantly. The car careered off the road into a tree and I was thrown forward and hit my head.' He ran a hand through his floppy hair and revealed an enormous cut with stitches across the top of his forehead. 'When I came around, I was in a Croatian hospital, and everyone was denying everything. Gilly's body was in the hospital, too, and there was the bullet wound, I saw it. I got in touch with the British Embassy and, of course, her parents, and she was flown home two days ago. The Croatians say it was the Serbians, which seems the most likely story. The Serbians, of course, say it was the Croatians. Either way, Gilly's dead and the British Embassy don't seem able to do a damn thing about it.'

'I had lunch with David yesterday,' Sal said. 'He was talking about trouble brewing out there. I'm afraid I didn't take him seriously.'

'Something's going on all right,' Peter said quietly, and he broke down.

'I'm sorry,' he said shakily, 'I just feel so damned awful about it. If I hadn't had that stupid alcoholic lunch, I'd have had my wits about me. I'd have got out of the car and shouted and screamed and waved my British passport and they'd have probably let us through. I was asleep, you see, when we reached the roadblock, and I didn't know what the flipping heck was going on. I came around with all these men shouting at us and I just didn't react properly. Then to tell her to drive through it — it was so bloody irresponsible!'

'Look,' said Sal, 'one doesn't expect to get shot on a holiday in Croatia!'

'But they had guns and even though I was pretty pie-eyed myself I could tell they were drunk. I could smell the drink on their breath.' He wiped his eyes. 'Sal, do you know what the most awful thing about it is?'

'No,' Sal said gently.

'To crown it all, I didn't even love her.'

'Oh Peter, I just don't know what to say.'

'I'm sorry to land on you like this. I just had to talk to someone who would understand what I was saying. I just can't believe it happened. When you think of all the tight spots we've been in over the years, Sal, why have I survived and Gilly died? Why did they shoot her and not me?'

'Because she was in the driving seat, of course.'

'And why was she in the driving seat? Because I was too bloody pissed to drive!' His voice rose as he spoke. Florina looked up from the sandpit. Peter saw her. 'I'm sorry, little one, I didn't mean to startle you. She's beautiful, Sal, unrecognisable. You've done very well.'

'She's done it herself,' said Sal. 'Look, I'll give her a bath and put her to bed. You nurse the whisky bottle and then I'll make you something to eat. You'll stay the night?'

'Yes, please,' said Peter, 'if you wouldn't mind. I can't face going back to our flat. I've just been with her parents. You put Florina to bed and we'll talk later.'

By the time Sal returned, the whisky bottle was half-empty. 'Come and talk to me while I cook. I'd better produce some food a bit smartish, I think,' she said.

'What a pathetic creature I am, aren't I?' Peter said, shambling into the kitchen.

Sal set about making an omelette and salad. 'Tell me about Gilly's parents.'

'They're a lovely couple,' Peter said. 'They live in Cambridge. He's a don, and the wife teaches. 'They're very academic – heads in the clouds – that sort of thing. The terrible part is that Gilly was their only child. Neither of them cried, they were all stiff upper lip. They said she was such an adventurous girl and I wasn't to blame myself. I thought they'd want to go out there and cause a stink, find out who did it and string them up, but they're not that sort of people at all. They said they were happy to leave it in the hands of the British Embassy, which means that nothing will ever happen. They certainly won't catch the bastard who shot her.

'They asked me if I'd like to stay the night,' he went on. 'I gave them the key to our flat and said that I'd pack up Gilly's things, but they said no, that would be too harrowing for me, so Gilly's mother is going down to London tomorrow to do it. I can't understand why they were so kind.'

'Because although you're blaming yourself, Peter, they clearly aren't blaming you.'

'They should be. Jesus Christ, I should have married their daughter years ago.'

'Tell me about your relationship with Gilly, if you want to, that is,' said Sal, putting the omelette in front of him and cutting some bread. She poured herself a glass of wine. 'You'd better not . . . Oh, what the hell, have a glass of wine too.'

They sat either side of the kitchen table. 'We lived together for six, maybe seven years. She wanted us to get married and have kids, but I didn't. I wasn't ready for settling down. Besides, my job is hardly conducive to a permanent relationship, is it?'

'No,' said Sal.

'So, I sort of used her. Now and again we'd have an awful row and one of us would walk out, but we'd always get back together again. Me, because it was convenient, she, poor girl, because I think she loved me.'

'You *must* have loved her too,' Sal said.

'Well, after a fashion, yes, but it was never goosebump stuff, none of the grand passion. We were just comfortable together, more like brother and sister really – at least, that's how it was for me. Still, if I'd married her and had a couple of kids, we wouldn't have been in Croatia.'

'Oh, for heaven's sake Peter, you can't think like

that. It's like saying, "If I hadn't chosen to cross the road then, I wouldn't have been run over by a bus"!'

'Or, "If my parents hadn't made love on a particular night, I wouldn't have been conceived",' Peter said. 'Probably it would have been a damn good thing too.'

'Oh, come on. Now you're being maudlin and feeling sorry for yourself. That's the drink talking – it's not the Peter I know.'

'I just feel so bloody awful, Sal. I've buggered this girl around for years and then I get her killed. She was a decent person, she deserved a good husband, instead of which I messed her about and didn't take care of her when I should have done.'

'I bet she was proud of what you did in Romania,' Sal said sensibly.

'Yes, she was,' Peter admitted. 'She loved children. She wanted us to adopt a child. When she heard that you had brought home Florina, she suggested that we did too, but I wouldn't have it.'

'Why not?' said Sal.

'It would have meant making a commitment to her, wouldn't it? If we'd adopted a child, I'd have had to stay with her for ever. That's my problem, you see, I'm too bloody selfish. Do you know what I feel like doing right now, Sal? I feel like giving up the whole thing, opting out like you've done, although I've got no reason to do so – I haven't a couple of kids to care for. Still, all that will have to wait. I have a job to do.'

'What's that?' Sal asked.

'I'm going back to Croatia to find the bastard who shot Gilly.'

'Peter, you can't do that, it's ridiculous.'

'I can and I will. Her parents aren't going to take any kind of action and the Embassy doesn't give a toss, so somebody has got to make sure that the bastard is strung up – and it's going to be me.'

'It's the drink talking again, Peter. It makes no sense, you'd never find him. You don't know which one of those young men it was, you can't speak Serbo-Croat and as you said yourself, when you were in hospital, each side was blaming the other. Nobody is going to admit to anything. Come on, you can sleep in Toby's room. Everything will feel a bit better in the morning and then we'll make a plan.'

But everything was not better in the morning. When Sal peeped around the door of Toby's bedroom the following day, there was a note on the pillow: *Gone to Croatia, thanks for everything. Love Peter. Kiss, kiss.*

Sal stared at the note for a long time; a feeling of terror gripping at her heart. David had been right – something *was* happening. She could feel it in her bones, and for some reason it terrified her.

CHAPTER TWENTY

Peter never found Gilly's murderer. By the time he arrived back in Croatia, a war was beginning. Soon Osijek was under daily and nightly bombardment, and then Dubrovnik.

Sal, at home in Horton-cum-Studley, was obsessed. Jack Templar had been sent out to join Peter. He was a brave man, they both were, but as David had said in the past, he did not have the gift for capturing the reader's imagination. Still Sal hungrily devoured every word he wrote.

Toby, newly turned fourteen, was genuinely interested in what was happening. Sal explained it to him as best she could.

'Let's hope your brother doesn't get hurt in the war,' he said one night as she kissed him goodnight.

'I've been thinking about that too, Tobe.'

'It's a pity you never found him.'

'Yes,' Sal agreed. Thoughts of Georges were once more becoming an obsession. Her preoccupation with her children and her new life had made it possible for her to bury her feelings about her brother. From time to time, when anyone mentioned Yugoslavia, she felt the familiar stab of regret and still, at the back of her mind, she saw the need to continue her search for him as something of a life's quest. In reality, though, she knew the chances of finding him were remote. Now, though, with a war threatening to spread across Yugoslavia, Toby's thoughts were very much a mirror of her own. But what could she do? The feeling of frustration was enormous.

David joined them for Christmas. It was a good Christmas, but somewhat overshadowed by events in what the world's press now referred to as 'the former Yugoslavia'.

'I've always hated January and February, and this year it seems more cold and miserable than usual,' Sal complained to Jenny.

The countryside looked dead but the children continued to thrive. Florina was loving nursery school, but it meant Sal had more time to herself, which meant more time to brood. There was not really enough for both her and Jenny to do. 'I could get a part-time job in the village,' Jenny suggested, 'if it would help the budget.'

'There's plenty for you to do, Jenny, it's me who needs a job,' said Sal despondently.

Jenny gave her a sharp look. 'You remember what you promised Toby.'

'I remember,' Sal said.

On 16 March 1992, Jack Templar was killed by a mortar shell on the outskirts of Sarajevo. Three weeks later Peter arrived on Sal's doorstep again. He looked thin, but very different from the last time Sal had seen him. He was very much in charge of himself, refused a drink and asked for coffee instead.

Toby was home from school when he arrived and was doing homework on the kitchen table. Peter was in a hurry. 'Sal, I'm not going to beat about the bush. I want you to come out with me to Northern Bosnia.'

'I won't,' Sal said. 'You know I won't — it's not fair of you to come here and ask me.'

'Just listen to me a moment, hear me out,' Peter said. 'The Serbs are putting up a smokescreen. They're turning the world's attention on to Sarajevo. Yes, what's happening there is awful, and so that's where all the media are focusing their attention, but in Northern Bosnia, they're doing something far more terrible.'

'What?' Sal asked, instantly hooked.

'The term being used to describe it is "ethnic cleansing".'

Toby looked up from his homework. 'What does that mean?'

'The Muslims are being driven from their homes. If they won't go, they're killed. Whole villages are being destroyed, burnt to the ground. If people haven't left their houses when the Serb soldiers arrive, they are simply burnt inside them. There's an enormous refugee problem building up and the Serbs are showing no mercy. Women and children are suffering awful atrocities – I can't speak of them in front of Toby – but terrible, terrible things. We need to get out there and report on it because nobody else is doing so.'

'How do you know it's happening?' Sal asked.

'I have contacts out there because I've spent so much time in the last few months roaming about. Jack, God bless him, was very pedestrian and I needed to take off on my own from time to time. It was me who should have got killed, not him. It's me who took the risks.'

'Don't start that again,' Sal said.

'No, you're right, of course. Will you come, Sal?'

'No,' Sal said. 'For two reasons. Firstly, I made a solemn promise to Toby that I would not become a war correspondent again, nor, indeed, even go abroad again. As well as my promise to Toby, I now have Florina. Florina is someone else's child by birth and is therefore a big responsibility. I cannot put myself in danger. It's not as though either of the children has a father.'

Peter slumped down at the table, opposite Toby. 'What the hell can I do to persuade her to go, Toby?'

Toby stared at Peter for a long moment and then looked up at his mother. 'I think perhaps you should go, Mum. I think perhaps people need to know what's going on, and you know how to tell it.' There was a break in his voice. 'Only please, please be careful.'

The Intercontinental in Belgrade seemed totally unaffected by the war that was spiralling out of control, except in one respect. The self-styled President of the Serbian Republic of Bosnia-Herzegovina, Radovan

Karadzic, seemed to be living in a suite of rooms there and using it as his headquarters. Sal attempted an interview with him, but he was horrendously drunk and would only talk about the past and how much the Serbs had suffered at the hands of just about everyone else. Of the present and the future, he seemed vague.

'The only thing for it,' said Peter, 'is to head out towards Banja Luka, where most of the so-called "cleansing" seems to be taking place.'

'Will we be able to get through? I gather many of the roads are mined.' Sal said nervously.

'I think so. We may get some support from the UN.'

'Peter, I . . .' Sal hesitated. 'I'm not a coward, you know that.'

'But you think I've flipped,' said Peter. He was looking gaunt and drawn.

'Well, not exactly.'

'You could be right. Gilly and Jack have both died in the space of just a few months in this God-awful place, with me beside them. Now I'm dragging you into it and you have two children.'

'I suppose that's about the gist of it,' Sal said.

'I'm very fond of Toby,' Peter said, 'and I do have a very special feeling for Florina, having been there when it all happened. I wouldn't put their mother in danger lightly. I do believe it is terribly important that we find out what's going on, but at the same time I can't pretend that you won't be in some danger.

'I tell you what,' said Sal, 'we'll go, but if I say at any point that we're pulling out, we're pulling out – right?

And that doesn't just apply to me, it applies to you, too. In other words, I make the decision for both of us.'

'I'm not sure I can go along with that,' Peter told her.

'OK, then I don't accompany you. Those are the only terms under which I'm prepared to go.'

'You drive a hard bargain.'

'I drive a sensible one. I'll know when to quit. In your current state, I'm not sure you will.'

They were lucky. Within twenty-four hours they discovered that a UN convoy was heading up towards Banja Luka. The going was slow, the roads through the mountains were bad anyway, but every so often the convoy had to stop because mines were spotted ahead.

'I'm glad we're not in the leading vehicle,' Sal said to Peter.

Every mile or so, there were checkpoints. Always the same Serbian gunmen, very young, often drunk, menacing, and hellbent on making life as difficult as possible. They passed over the border from Serbia into Bosnia and pressed on. They had left Belgrade at five in the morning as it was imperative that they reached Banja Luka before nightfall. As one UN soldier put it: 'The snipers in the hills are mad. If they see a Red Cross, rather than respect it, it gives them a good focal point for target practice.'

As they ventured deeper into Bosnia, they began to see the signs of war. At first it was the odd house reduced to rubble, then they began to pass through village after village that was burnt out and deserted. What made it particularly heartbreaking was the beauty of the surroundings. At one point in the middle of a ruined little village, they were held up while the road was checked for mines. Enclosed in an armoured car, Sal asked if she could just step outside for a moment, to get a feel of the place.

'I wouldn't,' the soldier advised.

'Why, is it dangerous?'

'Yes.'

She ignored him, climbing down on to the village street. Immediately she was hit by the terrible stench of rotting bodies. When she looked closely, she could see them lying all around her in the grass. There was a woman who had been hanging out the washing. Her body lay beneath the washing line, and beside her was a little girl, close to her abandoned doll's pram. It was so soon after the atrocity that the gardens were still neat, and the beauty of the place stood out in stark contrast to the grim reek of death. Roses climbed up cottage doors, mountains rose above, the sun beating down. It was Alpine in a way, but softer. Peter, beside her, was busy photographing. There was a shout from behind them and the convoy was off again. They sat in silence, devastated by what they had witnessed.

'Do you think you captured the contrast?' Sal asked after a while, almost conversationally.

'I think so,' said Peter.

'The doll's pram, the little girl, the washing line . . . it was all so ordinary – or should have been. This is unbelievable, Peter.'

'Do you see now, Sal, why I had to persuade you

to come? You see things other people don't; you tell them in a way other people can't. In that village back there, I felt exactly the same as you did, and if you hadn't asked to be let out of the armoured car, then I would have done.'

Sal smiled at Peter and patted his knee. 'It's just that we've worked together for so long, we know how the other one ticks.'

'No, it's not as simple as that,' said Peter. 'The same things seem to be important to us; we react to things in the same way. I've found the last couple of years awful without you, Sal. I really can't work properly with anyone else. It's pathetic, isn't it?'

She grinned at him. 'Yes, I think it is rather,' she agreed, 'but now you come to mention it, I don't know how on earth I'd fare with another photographer. It's so long since I worked with anyone else but you, on the major stories at any rate.'

'I'm sorry I dragged you into this,' said Peter heavily. 'It wasn't right of me. I won't do it again.'

'No, you won't,' said Sal. 'This is a one-off – I want to make that quite clear. But we're here now, so let's get our story and then get ourselves out – preferably with all our bits and pieces intact!'

'I'll drink to that,' said Peter. 'which brings me on to the crucial matter of my hip flask. Would you care for a swig?'

'I most certainly would,' said Sal.

By the time they reached Banja Luka, they were too exhausted to do anything other than roll into their hotel rooms. The next morning Sal went straight around to the United Nations High Commission for Refugees headquarters. She found a sympathetic and helpful woman, who was only too happy to talk.

'New villages are being cleansed every night,' she said. 'Sometimes as many as two hundred homes are being burnt or dynamited at a time. We estimate that there may be half a million people who are now refugees, but we have no idea how many are dead. It is an enormous catastrophe and no one seems to know what is going on, or to care.'

'They'll know now,' said Sal, 'I promise.'

She went next to the newly opened Office for Population Resettlement and Property Exchange. Here the response was very different. This was a Serbian-run organisation. In theory, the office was arranging for Muslims to be sent to Zenica and Serbs to be brought into the Banja Luka area in return.

'What happens if the Serbian people do not want to be rehoused here in Banja Luka?' Sal asked.

The spokesman laughed. 'We'll be sending the Muslims, all the same.'

'How many?'

He shrugged. 'About twenty thousand a week.'

'And what will happen to them? Where will they go? How will they live?'

He shrugged again. 'That's up to them.'

During the day Sal began to piece together what exactly had happened. It had begun early in the year. First Serbian thugs had come to the doors of Muslim homes demanding money or jewelry.

They gradually became more violent, smashing up

Muslim shops. Then the police had insisted that all Muslims needed permits to move around: this was, in effect, a curfew. Then the Serbs starting driving through towns, shooting at random into Muslim homes, and so the violence escalated until the Serbs thought nothing of barricading up a house containing the elderly, women and children, setting fire to it and watching them burn to death for entertainment.

During that long and shocking day Peter and Sal made a brief sortie into two of the outlying villages which had been cleansed. There was a terrible eeriness about them. Not a cat, nor a dog, nor even a chicken appeared to have survived. They were grateful for their UN escort, because as Peter took his photographs in the second village they visited, a group of Serbian soldiers confronted them. In fact they were easily placated in true Eastern European style, with some cigarettes. It was, none the less, a terrifying moment.

Back in Banja Luka Sal visited the hospital, and then, steeling herself, the overcrowded orphanage. The doctor in charge there said they were bursting at the seams; soon they would have to open a second orphanage in the town to cope with the number of children. She was a wonderful woman, caring, obviously devoted to the children. It was all very different from Romania.

'The terrible irony,' the doctor said, 'is that here we have all denominations of children. Of course, they are mostly Muslim, but we have Serbian and Croatian children, too. Their parents have killed each other, and we pick up the debris.'

Sal toured the orphanage. There was little of anything, particularly medicines, but the children were clean and, for the time being at any rate, relatively well-fed. There was no head banging or rocking. Many looked shocked and disorientated. They had seen their homes burnt and their parents killed in front of them, so it was hardly surprising. The care given by the staff was the most heartening. It consoled her worries about Georges. Maybe Cristian had been right; the Yugoslav people did seem to have a different attitude to children. She hoped so.

Their journey back to Belgrade was more tortuous. The road had been damaged by mines in a couple of places, and at one point they came under sniper fire which was terrifying. Both Sal and Peter had been wearing bulletproof vests ever since leaving Belgrade, but they brought little comfort as bullets ricocheted off their vehicle.

Back safely at the hotel at last, they both rested for an hour and then sat up half the night trying to make sense of everything they had seen. Northern Bosnia was being destroyed; a way of life that had existed for hundreds of years was at an end. The biggest evacuation of people since the Second World War was underway. The hospitals had run out of equipment, the refugees were without food or clothes and the deaths and atrocities were continuing unabated. There was no one to stop it, and all the while, the world's focus was on Sarajevo.

The story they had to tell made headlines three days running in the *Daily Record*. They were the first

British journalists to report on what was happening in Northern Bosnia, indeed the first journalists in the world. They arrived back in London to a heroes' welcome from David, who saw it as a massive scoop.

'The trouble is,' said Sal, as they sat over a sandwich lunch in David's office, 'we've told the world what's happening. Now is anybody going to do anything about it?'

As the days rolled by, she got her answer. *No, they were not.*

Sal and the children spent a pleasant summer. Both children had now acquired a fairly hectic social life locally and Sal was forever ferrying them about to parties and outings. Florina continued to amaze her. She was such a confident, outgoing little girl. If there was a dark side that reflected her suffering, Sal never saw it, except in the early days when she had been prone to the odd nightmare. She was hyperactive, vivacious and very hard work, but her love of life, sense of humour and capacity for fun were unquenchable. Toby adored her and it was more than reciprocated. Indeed, the pride each took in the other was touching. Seeing them walking through the village street, hand in hand, or Florina sitting on Toby's lap while he read her a story regularly brought tears to Sal's eyes.

As the war continued to rage in former Yugoslavia, she felt frustrated at her inability to take part, but never for one moment did she seriously query the decision she had made. Toby was a different boy from the anxious child of the London years, and having Florina made a huge difference to him. On the night she had returned from Belgrade, Toby had confessed to Sal how frightened he had been for her. Then, almost as an afterthought, he added: 'But at least I thought that if anything had happened to you, I would have Florina. I wouldn't be on my own any more.'

Jenny confirmed this. 'He was a little boy lost in London,' she said, 'but not any more. He has responsibilities now, and he loves it.'

So when Peter arrived on her doorstep, one day in early October, with that expression on his face she had come to dread, she found it easier to discuss with Toby what her answer should be. This time, Peter wanted her to go to where the cauldron was reaching boiling point – Sarajevo. This time there were practical reasons for her going. One was credibility, the other was cash.

The summer had passed in a great flurry of activity. Sal and Jenny had raised an impressive amount of money for the refugees, and in between, Sal had written a number of articles concerning the war. However, her credibility was wearing a little thin. She had not been out there since May, and her fundraising activities had meant there had been little time for writing, so now money was starting to be a problem.

Peter's argument was equally persuasive. 'Sarajevo has been a living Hell for months now. It has reached a point where quite literally the Serbs could take the city any time they wanted to, and the people know it. No one can capture the human stories as you can. Sarajevo needs your help, Sal.'

'Like the help I gave Northern Bosnia, you mean?' said Sal, her voice heavy with sarcasm.

'At least it made the world aware of ethnic cleansing. It has resulted in an enormous amount of aid and the sanctions on Serbia.'

'And still the ethnic cleansing goes on,' said Sal.

'You're sounding even more of an old cynic than me,' Peter said. 'It wouldn't be a long trip. We'll fly to Split and go overland into Sarajevo. I imagine we'll be there about a week and then come out. You will be away from the children for inside a fortnight.'

'As long as I can avoid the snipers,' Sal said.

'We won't take any unecessary risks.'

Sal gave a hollow laugh. 'No comment,' she said, 'but I have to discuss it with Toby first.'

'He'll go for this,' said Peter. 'He knows it's important.'

'But it has to be my decision,' said Sal. 'It's not right to put responsibility on to Toby. If anything did happen to me, he must be sure in his own mind that I made the decision, not him.'

'You can do it,' said Peter. 'We'll fly out next Wednesday. God bless you, Sal.'

CHAPTER TWENTY-ONE

The journey from Split to Sarajevo made the journey to Banja Luka seem like a picnic. They passed mile after mile of devastated countryside. 'How on earth will this country ever recover?' Sal asked Peter.

'I suppose an awful lot of Europe looked like this after the Second World War. Look at France, and think what it's like now.'

'Yes, but all that needed to happen in France was for the Germans to get out. Once they'd gone, the country as a whole could pull together and set about putting things right. It's not that simple here, is it?'

'No, I suppose not.'

In places the summer's crop was dying in the field. Occasionally a group of houses still seemed to be standing, but as they drove closer they saw that the windows were shattered and the places deserted.

'When I was a little girl,' Sal said, 'my biggest

nightmare was the atom bomb. I think this is how I imagined the world would look if the Russians had chucked a bomb at us. Where have all these people gone, Peter?'

'The lucky ones are in refugee camps, I suppose. On my last trip over here, the one I've made since I saw you last, I visited Mostar. I met an old lady there, in a cellar beside the bodies of her son and her husband. She said to me, "Only the dead are lucky." Sometimes I wonder if she isn't right.'

It was getting dark as they drove into Sarajevo. The driver of their armoured car was very tense, as they approached what was clearly the airport perimeter road. 'If they want to blow us up this is the moment they'll do it,' he said conversationally. 'Sorry to frighten you, but I thought I'd mention that if you want to make peace with your Maker, this is a good time.'

'Thanks,' said Sal nervously.

The convoy proceeded in tense silence, and ten minutes later, to everyone's enormous relief, they turned into the UN Headquarters. In that ten minutes all Sal could think about was her children and about the decision she had made.

'Peter,' she said, 'this is the last time I'm coming anywhere with you. It's not fair to ask me again.'

Peter put his hands on her shoulders and looked deep into her eyes. 'I really appreciate it, Sal, you know that.'

'You appreciating me isn't enough,' said Sal. 'I love you dearly – you're my old friend and colleague, but my children have to come first. I'll do this story, and then we get the hell out, and that is it.'

'OK,' said Peter. 'I promise I won't ask you again.'

'I'm really going to hold you to that, Peter, if you want us to stay friends. You know the only reason I keep coming with you is something to do with my background, the fact that I'm half-Yugoslavian, the fact that somewhere in this poor benighted country I may have a brother, if he hasn't already been killed. If you'd asked me to join you in a war in Afghanistan or Korea I wouldn't have hesitated to say no.'

'I realise that,' said Peter quietly.

'So you've deliberately played on my background to get me to come with you?' Sal said.

'Yes, I suppose I have, but I think I've justified it in my own mind by assuming that you'd want to know what was going on.'

'I do, of course I do,' said Sal, 'but I have to put the children first. Georges may not have survived his orphanage years, he might have been killed in a car crash in his twenties, or he might have died in the last few months, in Osijek, in Mostar, here in Sarajevo even Toby and Florina are alive and well and need a mother. Please, Peter, I beg you, don't ask me to come again.'

On the wall of one of the burnt-out buildings someone had inscribed the words *Welcome To Hell*. For Sal that just about summed up what she found.

With the help of the UN she moved from house to house, talking to ordinary people. She was amazed by their bravery and their humour – albeit somewhat black – and their generosity. In one block of flats, which was two-thirds bombed out, an old lady insisted on making them coffee. Aware that coffee was like gold dust, Sal tried hard to refuse, but the old lady would not have it. As she and Peter sat drinking the coffee, Peter asked, 'Where did you get this?'

'Oh, from the lady in the flat below me. She was given it when her son was killed last week. She shared it with all the other flats in this block.' The interpreter translated. Sal and Peter looked at each other aghast. A tin of coffee had been a woman's consolation for losing her son. She had distributed it amongst her neighbours, and here was one of those neighbours giving it to them.

'I feel very humble that you should share it with us,' Peter said, through the interpreter.

The old lady smiled. 'In this world, we must all share.'

'I'm going to do something about that old girl,' Peter said when they left. 'Have you any money on you, Sal?'

'A bit,' she said.

'Well, give me what you can spare.'

When they met again two hours later, Peter had raided the UN stores and delivered a big food parcel to the old lady.

'How did she react?' Sal asked.

'She cried.'

'And you?'

'I cried, too.'

'You're a big softy,' Sal said, hugging him. 'Please don't change.'

In the afternoon they visited the city hospital and spent several hours there talking to doctors and patients. All the time fresh casualties were coming in. A little girl had lost her arm and was receiving emergency treatment to stop her bleeding to death. What she did not yet know was that her mother, father and baby brother had died in the same attack. An old lady, who had lost the sight of one eye, described in graphic detail how the mortar shell flying through their window had simply cut her husband in half, while they sat at the table having breakfast. And so the stories went on, from ordinary people who, up to a year ago, had led ordinary lives.

Driving back to the UN Headquarters, a mortar shell exploded on the road in front of them, and then another behind them. The driver turned down into a side street. 'How many days are you staying here?' he asked.

'Five or six,' said Peter.

'Too long,' the driver replied. 'You won't survive – just get your stories and get the hell out.'

The following morning they were taken to the city orphanage. The woman who ran it was desperate to have the children evacuated. She asked for their story to be told. The babies lived in the basement, and had never seen the light of day, since they lost their parents.

'We do not know who they are, many of them. They were simply scooped off the streets and brought to us.'

The older children lived in dormitories. After the playground had been shattered by mortar shells, one half of the orphanage was quite unusable as it faced towards the Serbian guns. The children were cheerful, as children are the world over, despite everything. And again, in the midst of their deprivation, Sal felt a sense of caring that had been starkly absent in Romania.

The stories Sal heard were pitiful. One boy of eleven had gone out into the streets, risking his life to try and find some bread for his family. His father was already dead and he was the eldest child. His mother had stayed behind with his five little brothers and sisters, and when he got back with the bread, triumphant, he found the house flattened, and his family all killed. He told the story without tears. Watching him as he talked, Sal could see that his childhood had gone for ever, and so had his zest for life. He said that he was not afraid of the Serbs any longer as they could do nothing to him that they had not done already. He seemed indifferent to danger.

'I do not let him out of my sight,' the Principal confided. 'I'm always frightened that one day he might just walk out on the streets in the hopes of getting shot – just so he can be with his family again.'

On the journey back to the UN Headquarters, Sal felt deeply depressed. She had never visited Sarajevo before but knew that, by repute, it was one of the most beautiful cities in the world. The blackened buildings, the destroyed bridges and the pock-marked masonry were bad enough, but what had the war done to the cultural heart of such a fine city? Where was the art, the music, the theatre? And most of all, of course, what had it done to the people? She knew it had been a cosmopolitan city, with not just Serbs, Croats and

Muslims living together, but also Jews and Turks. How could these people have turned against one another to such devastating effect? These were people who had shared hundreds of years of history, had lived and loved together, had suffered much but come through it all – only for this . . .

Suddenly, ahead of them there was an enormous explosion. Their driver jammed on his brakes and turned quickly to the right. There was another explosion and the apartment block ahead of them seemed to take a direct hit. Masonry began falling on to the street, blocking it completely. 'Shit!' the driver said, putting on the brakes. 'We'll never get through this lot. I think we'd better abandon the car. We'll duck behind the buildings and I'll call for help on the radio. If we can make it a couple of streets to the south, we'll be OK. We're in the middle of Dodge City here and it's obviously party-time!'

Suddenly the war they had been observing was their war; they were in the thick of it. Sal, her legs like jelly, scrambled out of the car and ducked behind the building, as the young soldier indicated. Peter followed. The world seemed to go mad. The Muslims were responding to the shelling; there was a *rat-tat-tat* of machine guns somewhere to their right. 'Ready for a firework display?' said the young soldier.

Sal marvelled at his calm. 'What's your name?' she asked.

'Bill. So you want to know who you're getting blown to bits with, right?' His humour was genuine.

The noise all around them was deafening. Then

suddenly there was a lull. 'Follow me,' Bill shouted. He ran, bent double, down a little alleyway. At the end he stopped. Sal and Peter followed, bumping into him, panting hard. 'Now,' said Bill. 'We have to get across this street and down the alley on the other side. When we've done that, we've made it, more or less. We'll certainly be picked up from there. Are you ready?'

'Yes,' said Sal.

'Right — go for it!' Sal did not so much hear the explosion, as feel it. The ground underneath her began vibrating and she was catapulted through the air, although the sensation was more of floating. She must have lost consciousness before she hit the ground, because all she could remember afterwards of the mortar shell was the strange sensation of floating through the air.

When she came around, she was in a big room — like a hall. The walls were cracked and in one corner, they appeared to have been reduced to rubble. She was on a makeshift camp bed and there were people all around her lying prone, some groaning. There was a terrible stench of blood, vomit and fear.

A young woman was crouching beside her. It seemed to Sal that she had the face of an angel and, fleetingly, she wondered whether this woman was indeed a celestial being. Then the vision began speaking in Serbo-Croat.

Sal shook her head. 'Where am I? What's happened to me?'

The woman sat back on her heels. 'Ah, English,' she said.

'Yes,' Sal managed.

'I find English-speaker for you, OK?'

The room began to swim again. Time passed. 'Hello, can you hear me?' Sal tried to focus on a hazy image of a middle-aged man, careworn and clearly exhausted. His face swam before her, he seemed awfully familiar. She tried to focus better, but found it impossible.

'You are going to be OK. You have concussion and a nasty gash on your right arm and shoulder and I think you have broken your collarbone. You still have both legs and both arms, though. You are very lucky.'

'Peter?' Sal asked.

'Your colleague? He was more severely wounded – but alive. We are trying to arrange to have you both airlifted by helicopter out to Split. They are organising the transport now. Your colleague needs help quickly.'

'And Bill?'

The man looked confused. 'Who is Bill?'

'He was the soldier with us.'

The kindly face clouded. 'I'm afraid he died.'

'Your English is very good,' Sal said weakly.

The sound of another English voice drifted across the room as Sal fought for consciousness. 'Georges, Georges, come here quickly, I need your help.'

Georges. Suddenly the delirium left Sal. She tried to sit up, but the man put a restraining hand on her good shoulder and Sal winced with pain. 'Do not try to move,' he insisted.

'I know this sounds stupid,' she gulped, 'but is your name by any chance Georges Kovic?'

'Yes.' The man looked puzzled.

'Oh,' said Sal, and began to laugh and then to cry. 'You see, you won't believe me, but I think you could be my brother.' A wave of pain hit her and she slumped back on to the pillow. Vaguely, she heard Georges' name being called again and was aware of him leaving her side. She tried desperately to call to him, but everything turned black.

The next sensation was of being moved. She opened her eyes to find herself on a stretcher. Georges was beside her. 'You are being taken by truck to a helicopter,' he said. 'You should be in Split in an hour. What makes you think that you're my sister?'

'Hurry, Georges,' chivvied a pale-faced Englishman at the front of the stretcher. 'We haven't got all day.'

'Just hang on a moment, Dick, please. What makes you think that you're my sister?' Georges repeated.

'My name is Salvena,' Sal said. 'My father was Serge Kovic, my mother an Englishwoman, Marie. We lived in Belgrade and my father was a – ' she hesitated '– a traitor.' Georges' face remained a blank.

'Look!' Suddenly she had an inspiration. 'Does this mean anything to you?' With her good arm, she reached up to her neck and pulled out the silver chain, on which hung the *gusle*.

Georges gasped and then stared at her. 'Yes,' he said, his eyes instantly bright with tears. 'That does mean something to me.'

'Come on, Georges, we have to be quick. The man ahead is dying.'

Sal gasped. 'Is that Peter who's dying? Oh my God!'

'He'll be all right if we can get him to hospital quickly,' Georges assured her.

'I work for the *Daily Record* in London,' Sal said urgently. 'You can contact me there. Where can I find you?'

'I'm always here,' said Georges.

'But where do you live?'

'I live nowhere. Working for the Red Cross is a twenty-four hours a day job. We will find each other again, don't worry. Here, take this.' He handed Sal a small bottle.

'What is it?' she asked.

'It's plum brandy. It'll help you with the pain on the journey. Sorry, but the morphine is kept for amputations.'

The stretcher moved on. They clasped hands briefly and then were forced apart.

'Georges, oh Georges,' she shouted ineffectually.

She sobbed on the journey to the airport, oblivious of the dangers. She sobbed in the helicopter all the way to Split. When at last she was lowered into a hospital bed, she passed into an exhausted sleep.

She woke to find her head was clear. The pain in her arm and shoulder was excruciating but her head no longer hurt. Immediately she remembered those moments in the Red Cross station and Georges. Had she imagined it? Had it been part of the nightmare? Then she became aware that she was holding something beneath the covers, and pulled out the little bottle of plum brandy. So it had not been a dream; it had really happened.

Just then there was a knock on the door. She was in a tiny room on her own. A young man put his head around the door.

'Ah good, you are awake. I'm Dr Gamic. Have you drunk your brandy yet?'

Sal smiled. 'No.'

'I thought it would all be gone. We tried to take the bottle from you when you arrived here last night and you nearly killed us.'

'I'm sorry,' Sal said, 'but the most extraordinary thing happened to me. I found my brother. I'd lost him all my life and I found him at the Red Cross station in Sarajevo and he gave me this bottle.'

'Are you sure it was your brother?'

'You think I'm still suffering from concussion?' Sal said. 'It's true, really. At least I think it is.' With a jolt of horror, she remembered Peter. 'My colleague, Mr Blakeness, how is he? Please tell me he didn't die. Oh please tell me he's all right.'

'We have stabilised him. He suffered a great loss of blood and nearly lost his leg. I am reasonably sure it can be saved if we can airlift you to London today. That is the plan. Your newspaper has arranged it.'

'What about my children? Has this been reported in the news?'

'Yes, I think so.'

'Will anybody have told my children I'm all right?'

'I don't know, I'm afraid.'

'Can I see Peter?'

'Not at the moment, he's very weak.'

'But he's going to live?'

He smiled. 'You know us doctors. We're the same the world over. We hate to make firm commitments – but yes, I think so. Last night I did not, but this morning . . . well, he is a strong man and we have been able to give him a transfusion. It's just a question now of whether he loses his leg or not. I think, too, he has fractured his skull, but it is not a bad fracture. It seems you were both very lucky.'

'But not the soldier who was with us,' Sal said. 'I believe he died.'

'I believe he did,' said the doctor. 'I'm sorry.'

For what seemed a long time, Sal lay alone in the ward. She fretted about Toby, fretted about Peter, she wanted to get up and relive her meeting with Georges again and again, but every time she attempted to move, her head swam and the pain in her arm and shoulder was unbearable.

At length a nurse came in. 'I have been told to give you no food, in case you need an operation in London,' she said. 'But here is a drink of coffee. I hope it will be all right.'

'It will be wonderful.' The moment Sal had drunk it she felt better. The nurse sat on the end of the bed. 'Peter – the man I was with – how is he?' Sal asked.

'He is awake now,' the nurse said. 'I think he will be a very bad patient. He wanted to get up to come and see you; he is very cross.'

Sal smiled. 'Do you think I could go and see him?'

'You will meet on the aeroplane. I think it is better to wait until then. Neither of you should really move.'

'Can I write him a note?'

'Of course. I will fetch you paper.' She returned a few moments later.

Sal wrote on a piece of the paper – *Love you, Peter. Sal, kiss, kiss, kiss!* She folded it and gave it to the nurse. A few moments later she returned with a note – *Love you, too, Peter.*

The pen and pencil gave Sal an idea. 'Does this hospital have regular contact with Sarajevo?'

'Oh yes,' said the nurse. 'Every day we receive people from Sarajevo.'

'So if I wrote a letter to my brother, who is at the Red Cross Headquarters there, could someone deliver it?'

'I'm sure they could,' said the nurse. 'It would be best if you gave it to Dr Gamic and he could arrange it. I will fetch you more paper, yes?'

'Yes, please.'

It took Sal a long time to write the letter, with the awkwardness of trying to write lying down, and for once in her life, great difficulty in expressing herself.

Dear Georges, she wrote, *I am writing to you from the hospital in Split. I am OK and Peter will be too, I think. This is my address in England and my telephone number. Please contact me if you can. I only learned that you existed three years ago and I have been trying to find you ever since. With love from your sister, Salvena.*

She addressed it to *Georges Kovic, Red Cross Head-quarters, Sarajevo.*

By three o'clock in the afternoon a plane had been organised. Sal gave her letter to Dr Gamic, who promised to see that it was delivered, and in the ambulance, on the way to the airport, she saw Peter for the first time. He was wired up to a portable drip, and bound from head to toe, like a mummy. He looked pale, but surprisingly alert.

'Hello, old girl,' he said. 'How are you feeling?'

'Better for seeing you,' Sal said. 'Bill died, you know.'

'I know,' said Peter. 'Another couple of inches and that would have been us. If we'd tried to cross that street ten seconds earlier . . .'

'Don't,' shuddered Sal.

'I'm sorry – I should never have involved you in this. I'll never be able to look Toby in the face again.'

'Peter, we're alive. We came out of it and – you're never going to believe this – but I think I've found my brother!'

'What?' Sal told him the story. 'Are you sure you're not dreaming?' Peter said.

'I keep wondering that, except look . . . here it is.' Still clutched in her hand was the little bottle of plum brandy. 'So I can't have imagined it, can I?'

'Give us a swig then,' said Peter.

'Not on your life,' said Sal. 'Not when you're wired up like that.'

Twenty-four hours later Sal was home. She had an impressive-looking bruise across her forehead and her left arm was in a sling, heavily bandaged. She had lost her passport and her money, but luckily she had filed all her stories, except for the one about the orphanage, which presumably had been blown to bits. Peter was to keep his leg – or so it seemed. He would be in hospital for a month and then it had been agreed that he could go down to convalesce in Horton-cum-Studley.

Toby was in surprisingly high spirits. 'You're a real heroine at school,' he said. 'Everybody thinks I'm really lucky to have a mother like you.'

Jenny was less than enthusiastic. 'When David arrived on our doorstep, I thought it was to tell us that you were a goner,' she said. 'I didn't know what to do with myself. The children were both home and I didn't know how I was going to cope. Then when he said you'd only been wounded and that you were definitely going to be all right, I'm afraid I kissed him. He looked terrified, poor man.'

'I'm sure he was thrilled to bits. Thank God he got here before they put it on the news.'

'Only just,' said Jenny, 'by about half an hour.'

In the weeks following her return from Sarajevo, Sal was busy. Christmas was not far away. She visited Peter twice a week in hospital and treasured the time she spent with her children. But without telling anyone, she was making plans. After a meeting with the Home Office, given all the circumstances, they agreed to grant her brother Georges a holiday visa for a month, on condition that Sal supported him fully during that period.

On the afternoon she collected the visa, she also collected Peter from hospital and drove him down to Oxfordshire. She told him about her plans in the car. 'I'm going back to Sarajevo,' she said, 'to bring Georges home for Christmas.'

'You have to be joking, Sal. You can't go back there!'

'I have to.'

'But he may not want to come.'

'If I've made the effort to get to Sarajevo, he'll damn well have to come back with me. I've got him a visa, it's all fixed.'

'He may not have a passport.'

'We'll just have to sort something out there.'

'Couldn't you contact him through the Red Cross, to save you having to go out there yourself?'

'I've thought of that,' said Sal, 'but it will seem like a kind of summons. I think I have to go out there in person to demonstrate how much I want to see him. Judging by the look of him, I should think he is very dedicated to his job. It won't be easy to extract him.'

'Is he a doctor?' Peter asked.

'I don't think so, he didn't seem to have the authority. It was only an impression – I've no idea really, but I somehow feel not.'

'Then one Red Cross worker more or less isn't going to make much difference,' Peter said.

'It probably does in Sarajevo,' Sal replied.

Jenny had hysterics; David completely blew a gasket. Only Toby was calm. 'We should have him here for Christmas,' he agreed. 'I'd love to meet my uncle.'

'There isn't room anyway,' Jenny objected. 'I suppose we'll still have this great lump hanging around,' nodding her head towards Peter. She was devoted to him but their whole relationship was founded on insults.

'I'll go,' he said.

'Oh no you won't,' said Sal. 'Jenny is just looking for

problems. There's plenty of room for everyone. Besides which, Peter, I'm relying on you to look after everyone while I'm away.'

'He couldn't look after anyone,' Jenny snorted. 'It's us having to wait on him hand and foot.'

'As is only right and proper,' said Peter, ducking to avoid the cushion Jenny threw at him.

'Well, I'm glad to see you two are going to get along fine while I'm away,' Sal said with a grin.

CHAPTER TWENTY-TWO

He was standing by an open window, or rather a hole in the wall which served as a window, paper cup in one hand, cigarette in the other. She stood watching him in silence for a moment. From the moment she had left home, to the moment she arrived in Sarajevo, she had been consumed by fear. Now that fear was gone. Looking at the slightly stooped figure standing alone, she knew she had been right to come.

'Georges,' she said. He turned abruptly, and seeing her, dropped his cup of coffee.

'Salvena!' He stood rooted to the spot for a moment, and then he opened his arms and she ran into them. As she stood encircled in his embrace the memory of Ion and Mikhail came back to her. So this is what it was like to find a long-lost brother.

When at last she drew away, she was laughing and

crying, and he was too. 'You're mad! What are you doing back here?' he asked.

'I've come to get you,' she said.

His face clouded. 'I cannot leave here.'

'I'm bringing you home for Christmas, to my family in England. I've fixed it all with the Home Office. You have a month's visa. Do you have a passport?'

'Yes.'

'Then everything's fine – you can come.'

'I can't leave Sarajevo, not at the moment. There's so much happening.'

'Georges, it's for a holiday, not for ever. Please come.'

He gently stepped away from her, drew deeply on his cigarette and then stubbed it out on the floor. 'I do not know how to explain this to you. All my life I have been looking for something – something to do which is useful, something where I'm needed, and I've found it here. I cannot turn my back on it.'

'Georges, I'm not asking you to, but I am your sister and we need to spend some time together. We have so much to talk about.'

'After the war, perhaps.'

'And how long will that be?' said Sal. 'And will you survive it?' As if to emphasise her words, the sound of a mortar shell thudding into a building nearby silenced them both for a moment. Reaching up to her right side, Sal slipped the jacket and shirt off her shoulder. An ugly scar ran from the base of her neck to just under her arm. 'It wasn't easy coming back here, Georges.'

He stared at the wound, and then at her. 'No, I realise that.'

'Then please, let's go and talk to whoever is in charge here. I have children, they need to see you too.'

'Do you? And a husband?'

Sal shook her head, and smiled. 'No – it's a long story.'

'It must be,' said Georges, smiling in return. 'A month's visa, you say?'

'Yes.'

'OK, let's see what we can do.'

On the journey to Split they talked only of the war. Extraordinarily, at the time that Sal was in Banja Luka, Georges had been close by in Prijedor visiting friends. He, too, had witnessed the savage ethnic cleansing and had been a victim of it. His friends were Muslims, he explained. With them, he had escaped over the mountains to Zenica, and from there he had returned to Sarajevo, which had been his home for several years. He had given up his job, which he said was of no consequence anyway, and thrown himself into Red Cross work.

Only on the plane to Gatwick did they begin talking about themselves. Sal told him first about the children and about her life. Then she reached the tricky subject of their mother. 'She died in March, 1989,' Sal said. 'She was run over by a taxi cab in London. As she lay dying she told me about you and our father. Up until then, I'd always believed the man she married in England was my father. It was a terrible shock.'

'So, she remarried,' Georges said. There was pain in his eyes. He had smoked constantly since leaving Sarajevo, interrupted by persistent bouts of coughing. He had a coughing fit now, which racked his gaunt frame.

She waited until it stopped; instinctively she knew she had to be very careful what she said.

'I would so like to know what Mother was like when you knew her,' she said. 'I realise now that she spent all her life with me being frightened, but of course I didn't know that at the time. She wanted to keep herself to herself – private. She wanted us to be very proper, very ordered. I can see that the whole thing was geared towards not drawing attention to ourselves. My father, my step-father that is, was a lovely man. I don't understand why he married her – he was so full of fun and she spent her life disapproving of everything. I of course rebelled against all of that. I left school with good qualifications, but did not go to university. Instead I got pregnant, refused to have an abortion, and ended up as a journalist, supporting my illegitimate child. That wasn't at all popular, as you can imagine. Mother never showed any enthusiasm for my career as a journalist, and at the time I was terribly hurt. Now I can understand it. She didn't want me to become a well-known figure in case it drew attention to me, or her. I assume she imagined that either Father, or someone from Yugoslavia or Russia, would come after us. Although it must have become increasingly less likely, clearly the fear never left her.'

'The *gusle*,' Georges said, pointing towards the little gold emblem around Sal's neck, 'how did you come by that?' Sal told him about the cash deposit box and the discovery of the photographs and birth certificates.

'Why do you particularly remember it?' she asked Georges.

'Because she always wore it, even when she was going to some smart dinner. It used to make my father mad. He bought her diamonds and pearls, many, many jewels, but she loved this. She said it always brought her good luck. Strangely enough, he bought it for her when they were on holiday in Sarajevo.'

'In Sarajevo?'

'Yes, I'm not sure but I think it might have been on their honeymoon, or if not their honeymoon, it was very shortly after their marriage. They had a wonderful holiday. They always used to talk about Sarajevo as though it was a magic place. It's why I made my home there.'

'You loved her very much, Georges,' Sal said quietly.

Her brother turned from her and stared out of the window of the plane. 'Yes. The mother I knew was not at all like the one you describe. She was very . . .' he hesitated. 'I think it is a word you do not use now – gay.'

'Yes,' said Sal with a smile, 'but I know what you mean.'

'She loved playing with me, she loved parties, she loved everything. She always made people around her happy. My father was not an easy man, but she could handle him. She was years younger than him, but she could have him eating out of her hand. I know he had to marry a Western woman for political reasons, but I do believe he truly loved her.'

'Did he?' said Sal. 'Did he have to marry for political reasons?'

'Yes. I have much to tell you about Father, but let us wait, we are both tired. I met him two years ago, just before he died.'

'He died only two years ago?'

'Yes, he was in his nineties. I travelled out to Kiev to see him shortly before his death.'

'If I'd only known, oh Georges, I could have come too, met him with you. It would have made such a difference.'

'Yes,' he said.

'Georges, there's something I'd like to tell you.' Sal paused. 'The last words Mother spoke were about you. She said, "I never saw my beloved son again," and then she died. I think the spark in her that you describe died when she had to leave you. She was like a person lost without you.'

Georges' knuckles were white where he clutched the arm of the seat. 'Me also,' he said, barely above a whisper.

For a man whose only journey outside Yugoslavia had been to Kiev, Georges settled into English country life with the greatest of ease. Toby and Florina adored him, but they exhausted him too. Sal had never seen a man so tired. He slept fourteen hours a night, and even then needed a siesta after lunch.

He smoked continuously and his cough was painful to hear.

'He's not a well man,' Jenny said. 'You should get him to a doctor.'

But Georges staunchly refused to go. 'The cigarettes will kill me only if the Serb guns do not,' he said philosophically.

'Don't say such things,' Sal told him sternly.

With the presence of Peter in the house and the children and Jenny, it was not until the second night of Georges' stay that brother and sister were left alone in the evening, when everyone else had gone to bed.

'Will you tell me about Father now?' Sal asked. She refilled Georges' wine glass.

'He was deported, you know, soon after you and Mother left.'

'I know,' said Sal. 'I haven't dared ask you about your childhood yet.'

'In time,' said Georges. 'I did not see him from the age of eight, until last year. With the collapse of Communism, suddenly it was easy to travel. I was still in touch with a friend of my father's, who he had known during the war – my Uncle Ivan, who helped me so much. I contacted him and asked him how I could find my father. He, in turn, wrote to someone in Moscow, and the next thing, I had an address. I had expected to be told that he was dead – he was very old, after all. I had some money saved and I travelled to Kiev.'

'And how did you find him?'

'Frail, sad, lonely – but I would have been angry if

he was happy. I blamed him for everything, Salvena. I had hated him, you see. When I saw him I could not hate him any longer. He had taken everything from me – my mother, my home, my family life. My childhood. In the orphanage, everyone knew I was a traitor's son. It was not until Uncle Ivan had me moved to Croatia that I was free of that. I could never forgive him for what I had suffered.'

'So what made him become a traitor? I did some research, too, and the man who helped me said that Father had been approached while he was at Cambridge.'

'Yes,' said Georges, 'that is right. He told me all about it, he was very frank. Cambridge, in the thirties, was where all the famous spies were recruited – Philby, I believe – and Blunt.'

'That's right.'

'He fell in love while he was at Cambridge, with a girl named Brigitte; she was half-French, half-English. A very strong-minded young woman, he described her as. She was a post-graduate and therefore older than him. She introduced him to the Communist way of thinking, which was in direct contrast to his former way of life. He came from a very upper-class Serbian family, very close to the Royal Family, very important people in Belgrade – absolutely as far away from Communism as you can imagine. So this girl must have been very persuasive, and eventually he was approached by the KGB. He said, and I believe him, that he rejected the idea. He returned to Belgrade and in doing so, found the life there so shallow and bogus

that he began to wonder if he had done the right thing.'
Georges paused to sip his wine and then inhale deeply
on his cigarette.

'Brigitte, meanwhile, had returned to Paris. In 1935
she wrote to him and asked if he would like to come and
stay with her. He went, and while he was in Paris he met
Tito at a party. At that time, Tito was trying to recruit
people for the Spanish Civil War. Initially he tried to
persuade Father to fight for him, but when he learned
of his background and also of his political confusion,
being a shrewd man, Tito could see that Father could
be a great deal more useful than simply as another
fighting machine. He therefore suggested that Father
should return to Belgrade and join the Yugoslav Army
– all the time acting as a spy for Tito and his Partisan
group. The idea appealed to our father enormously –
remember, Tito was a most charismatic man. So, he
joined the Yugoslav Army, which pleased his parents,
and became a spy – which pleased Tito.'

'What happened then?' Sal asked, fascinated.

'The war broke out and he found himself in Cairo,
working as a liaison officer because he had an excellent
command of Arabic, French, and, of course, English.
It was while he was in Cairo that he met Mother. She
was out there with her parents because her father was a
journalist and Cairo was an excellent place from which
to cover what was happening in the war.'

'I never realised my grandfather was a journalist,' Sal
said excitedly. 'Mother always just said that he was a
writer. That's where I get it from, I suppose.'

'Probably,' Georges agreed. 'Certainly he was a

war correspondent and in the thick of it most of the time.'

'It seems an unlikely match – a Yugoslav Army officer and an English girl.'

'Perhaps, but he was a very good-looking man and I expect Mother was bored. There would not have been much to do in Cairo in the middle of the war. In any event, as I have told you, politically for Father it was a good match. It confirmed his right-wing tendencies in the eyes of the world. Anyway, they married and came to live in Belgrade. Once the war was over, Tito took control of the country and naturally enough Father resigned his post in the Army and took a job in Tito's Government.'

'And he was concerned with economics, I understand,' said Sal.

'That's right, he took his degree in mathematics. Without doubt he was a bright man and it was just the area in which Tito needed the most help. It was about this time, shortly after his appointment in the Government, that the KGB approached him again – this time he accepted.'

'But why?' said Sal. 'He had spied for Tito all those years and then at last he was legitimate. Why on earth did he take up the job of spying on Tito for the Russians? It just doesn't make sense!'

'I asked him that,' Georges told her. 'He said it was not purely for ideological reasons, although that must have come into it; it had something to do with having become used to the thrill of a double life. He needed the excitement – it was apparently as simple as that.

Being a spy, I suppose, is something of a drug, if that is the sort of thing that turns you on. Anyway, the rest you know, I suspect. They had a son in 1945 – me. And then in 1953 a daughter – you. I do not know the background to it, but somehow Mother found out that Father was a spy.'

'Really?' said Sal. 'I hadn't realised that.'

'I hadn't either, until Father told me. She somehow discovered it and threatened to expose him. She was appalled, she couldn't believe that he had been leading a double life all these years and betraying their friends. Initially it seems that her life was in danger. Father said he would have to inform the KGB of her knowledge, and that would probably mean she would be assassinated. He was clearly a fanatic, despite his denial. Then at the last minute he relented and allowed her and you out of the country, fabricating your deaths. He kept me as an insurance policy. He knew that while I was still with him, Mother would never betray him.'

'Oh Georges, that's awful.' Sal was deeply shaken. 'I've always known somehow that we owed our freedom to you. Did you believe that we were dead, or did you know the truth?'

'I found it strange that you were dead. One moment you were well and the next I was told that you had been sent to a sanatorium. It all happened while I was at school one day. I know though, that however ill my mother was she would somehow have found a way to write to me and send me a message – but there was nothing. When I queried it, my father said he did not understand it either, and then a couple of days later he said you were both dead. I accepted it because I had to.'

'And yet you weren't surprised when I said I was your sister?'

'Ah, that's because Father had told me by then that you were alive. When I saw him in Kiev he told me.'

'So you've only known of our existence relatively recently — how extraordinary! I'd assumed that you'd always known about us and it was only me who didn't know about you.'

Georges shook his head. 'Until Kiev I thought you and Mother were dead, although somewhere, deep down, there was an element of doubt. When Father told me that you were alive, it felt as if he was telling me something I already knew.'

'That is very strange,' breathed Sal.

'Why do you say that?' Georges leaned towards her, the firelight illuminating his handsome but gaunt face.

'When my mother told me, as she lay dying, that I was not my father's child, but half-Yugoslavian and that I had a brother — you — although initially I rejected the idea, what kept returning was this sense of foreknowledge, that she was telling me something I already knew.'

Georges took Sal's hand in his. 'I wonder how much they damaged us,' he said quietly. 'On the surface, you seem fine. You have created this family, and this Peter — you will marry him, yes?'

'Oh no,' said Sal. 'It's not that sort of relationship at all. He's just a friend.'

'But you care for this friend very much.'

'Yes I do, but it's not like that.'

'Still, you have your children and your home. I hope you're not too hurt by what our parents did.'

'And you?' Sal asked. 'What of you?'

'I don't know. It's true that I haven't been able to form permanent relationships with anyone. I don't just mean marriage, I mean friendships of any kind.'

'Why is that?' Sal was curious.

'I suppose because I was afraid of being betrayed again. When I discovered that my mother was alive, it didn't make me happy as it should have done. It had broken my heart when she "died" – and yet, to know that she was still alive and that she had abandoned me – however impossible things had been for her at the time, made me feel worse, somehow. I was rejected twice, by my father and by my mother.'

'Not rejected, Georges. Circumstances forced you apart – those circumstances being Father's ill-chosen second career.'

'But neither of them made room for me in their new lives! Mother remarried, brought up my little sister and made her home in England. Father never remarried, but lived a relatively contented life in Kiev. *Yet neither tried to find me.*' His face creased with misery.

'You don't know that,' said Sal, desperate to comfort him. 'I tried to find you, and I couldn't.'

'That was because my name was changed by the orphanage,' said Georges. 'I only reverted to using my old name when I grew up.'

'This feeling of betrayal and rejection,' Sal pursued.

'Is that why you didn't try to contact us once you knew
that we were alive?'

'Yes,' said Georges. 'When Father told me, a part of
me wanted to go straight to England, to try and find
you both and confront my mother with what she'd
done, to ask her why she'd done it. Then I decided that
was stupid. I needed time to think over my reaction, and
in any event I had no idea of how to set about trying
to find her. Then, of course, the war came and there
was no time to think of anything but survival . . . and
then you arrived.' He smiled at her. 'I remember you
as a baby – beautiful, beautiful – as you still are, my
Salvena. I am a very lucky man to have such a sister.'

Sal went to sit on the floor beside him, resting her
head on his knee. 'I just wish I could have been a proper
sister to you. Was the orphanage awful, Georges?'

'I do not want to talk any more tonight,' he said.

The month sped by. Peter grew stronger and began
physiotherapy on his leg. He could still only walk with
crutches, but at least he was vertical. When it came to
Georges' last week, Peter announced one evening that
he was going back to London.

'Will you be able to cope?' Sal asked in concern.

'Yes I will, thanks to you and Jenny.'

'I've aged ten years looking after you,' Jenny said
wearily, and winked.

After supper Sal took Peter aside. 'You don't have
to go. You can stay as long as you like.'

'I know, but I think you should spend Georges' last
week as a family, without me butting in.'

'You are family, almost, Peter.'

'I know, but it's not the same. You can have your evenings alone now — it will be better all round.'

'I'm not going to feel very good when he goes back.'

'I'll come and see you then.'

'Thanks,' said Sal.

One bright, cold afternoon in his last week, Georges and Sal set out to walk alone across Otmoor. She had been trying to get as much fresh air into him as possible. Although his cough seemed to have improved not at all, at least his colour was better.

'I would rather be with the children round the fire,' he grumbled.

'A walk will do you good,' said Sal.

'So this is what having a sister is like. I think I had a lucky escape,' Georges said, putting an arm around her and squeezing her. 'Tell me how you found Florina. I know she is from a Romanian orphanage but I have never asked you for the details.'

Sal told him about her time in Romania and about how she found Florina. 'And do you know one of the most ghastly parts about it all?' she said.

Georges stopped and shook his head.

'It was while I was in Romania that this friend of mine discovered that you had been sent to an orphanage. There I was in Bucharest, surrounded by all that horror, and then to discover that my own brother had suffered the same fate . . . It was just awful.' Her voice broke, tears flooded into her eyes.

'The orphanage was not too bad,' said Georges,

linking an arm through hers, 'although it felt tough at first. It was awful being dragged away, seeing my father dragged away also, and then the contrast to everything I had known. I had been used to luxury, you see, and then suddenly I had nothing. I had this teddy bear our mother had given me, and foolishly, I took it to the children's home with me. I had only been there about ten minutes, when a boy discovered it. He kicked it about like a football and then threw it over the high wall outside in the grounds. Do you know, I think I was more upset about that teddy bear than I was about losing my father.'

'It was because it was all you had left,' Sal said, fighting tears.

'Yes, yes, I suppose it was. When they discovered who I was, I had a bad time; there was a lot of bullying. Then, after Uncle Ivan came to see me, he had me moved. It was he who lived in Prijedor, just close to the Croatian border. He sent me to a home in Croatia and used to visit me regularly.'

'He sounds wonderful,' Sal said.

'I would not have survived without him.'

'What happened to him,' said Sal. 'Is he still alive?'

There was a pause. 'He was killed by a Serbian sniper as we tried to escape over the mountains.' Georges' voice was hoarse with emotion.

'God, I'm sorry, Georges.'

'It was bad,' her brother said. 'By then I knew my father had died, then Uncle Ivan – there really was no one left, except perhaps you and Mother.'

'Not Mother any more,' said Sal, 'but at least you have me, Toby and Florina.

'Yes, yes, that is true.'

They were silent for a moment. 'So what happened next?' Sal prompted.

'I left the home at sixteen and then had many different jobs. I was a farm labourer, I worked in a library, I drove a bus. I moved from one job to the next, from one place to the next, and that really, Salvena, has been the story of my life. As I have told you, I have never stayed anywhere long enough to put down roots, or to form relationships.'

'A bit like me,' Sal said.

'Really? I would not have thought so.'

'Why aren't I married?' Sal said. 'As soon as I find myself getting close to someone, I shy away. My very good friend Evelyn thinks I pick unsuitable men on purpose, so that I do not have to make a commitment to them.'

'And Toby's father? What of him?'

'I couldn't have lived with him.' Sal's expression, so open a moment before, was suddenly closed.

'Why not? Is he a bad man?'

'No, not a bad man,' said Sal, 'a very good man.'

'You know him then, still?' Georges sounded surprised.

'Yes, I do. Why?' said Sal.

'Because that is not what you have told Toby. You told Toby that you do not know who he is.'

'You have spoken to Toby about this?' Sal was suddenly angry. 'Why did you do that, Georges?'

'Because you invited me here to get to know your

family, so naturally I asked Toby about his father, and he tells me that you do not know who he is. Why did you lie to the boy, Salvena?'

'Because it would not have been good for Toby and me to live with his father – it would not have worked out.'

'Does this father know that he has Toby?'

'No,' said Sal.

'Do you not think, Salvena, that you are running the risk of allowing history to repeat itself?'

'No, I'm not,' said Sal, hurt. 'How can you say that?'

'Well, you didn't know who your real father was, and I believed my mother was dead. Our parents deceived us until we were nearly middle-aged people, and they damaged us – me, irrevocably – I hope not so in your case. So you would do the same thing to Toby, is that right? If you know who Toby's father is, then you should tell him.'

'I don't think you should interfere over this, Georges. You don't know the circumstances.

'No, I don't know the circumstances, and I'm not asking you to tell me, but I am interfering because I am your brother and I care for you. As I said, you invited me here, Salvena. What do you expect me to do? To accept your hospitality, your love, your family – and not make any contribution in return? You are a wonderful mother to your children, no one can deny that, but I think perhaps over this one particular issue – the true identity of your son's father – you are allowing the damage done to you to feed on itself. You should tell him; you should tell them both.'

'I don't want to have an argument with you, Georges,' her voice was shaking. 'I couldn't bear it, not when we have so little time together.'

'As you wish,' said Georges.

Sal stared at him helplessly. Suddenly, in the grey sky ahead of them, she saw a familiar shape moving towards them. 'Look — a heron,' she said. They watched as it flapped overhead and away towards the river.

'Come on,' said Georges. 'It is cold, let us go back.'

'Talking of going back,' said Sal, immensely relieved at the change in conversation, 'do you really have to go back to Sarajevo?'

'You know that I do,' said Georges.

'You say that, but is it really true? Your country has not served you particularly well. Don't you deserve to put yourself first? After all, you are half-British. You could have a good life here.'

'Salvena, I cannot turn my back on what I have seen and witnessed in the last year. After all these years of isolation, of wandering from place to place, at last I feel I have found my home: it sounds strange to you, I am sure — a Red Cross centre in the heart of war-torn Sarajevo — but I feel I belong there and I know I am making a contribution.'

'Have you many friends in Sarajevo?' Sal asked.

'A few, yes — although, of course, they get shot. I lost a good friend just a few weeks before you arrived — I shall miss him. He and his wife caught a mortar shell on their way back from visiting me. I didn't find that easy.'

'No, I'm sure you didn't,' said Sal.

He smiled at her. He was really a very attractive man, she realised. The grey skin, the cough, the gaunt face and body were what struck one first, but he was tall and basically broad-shouldered. His eyes were fine, his features – a stronger version of their mother's – surprisingly attractive on a man. 'I just wish you had a family and a wife to go home to,' Sal fretted, 'and I wish you weren't going back to a war. I want you safe, Georges. I just couldn't bear to lose you now I've found you.'

'Then I will do my best to see that you do not,' said Georges.

Sal left Gatwick airport with a heavy heart. Saying goodbye to Georges had been one of the most difficult moments of her life. He had looked so much better, but he was still not well and seemed far older than his forty-seven years. 'I need you,' she had whispered to him at the last moment.

'No one has ever said that to me before,' he replied.

'It's true,' she said with difficulty.

'I'll remember,' he said gently.

She cried intermittently all the way home. So much of his life she could see, in a strange way, she had echoed. The extraordinary lives of their parents had affected them deeply. They were both, in different ways, lost souls. Although her life had been easy compared with his, she had never really belonged anywhere or to anyone, and until now she had not known it. If only her mother had told her from the beginning the truth of her origins, she could have coped with it. But then it was no good blaming Barbara, she had only been trying to protect her. It was her father's political convictions and love of his double life which was really the root cause of all their problems, if blame was to be apportioned.

'I'll make it up to you, Georges,' she said to herself aloud as she drove, 'if it takes me the rest of my life. I'll make it up to you, for all you've suffered.'

CHAPTER TWENTY-THREE

When, one week later, on a damp Friday evening, David arrived on her doorstep, Sal had no sense of foreboding.

'Oh David, how lovely. Have you come to stay the weekend? I haven't asked you and forgotten, have I?'

'No,' David said awkwardly.

'Come along in. You're all right, are you?'

'Yes, I'm all right.'

For the first time, Sal looked properly at his face. 'David, what on earth's the matter? What's wrong?'

'Where are the children, Sal?'

'They're watching television with Jenny in the kitchen.'

'Come into the sitting room then. Sal, I've got something to tell you.'

Sal's heart began to pound. 'Something's happened to Peter, hasn't it?' She followed David into the room.

'No, not Peter – Georges.'

Sal's hand flew to her mouth. 'What's happened to him? Has he been wounded?'

'I'm afraid he's dead, Sal.'

Sal stared at him. 'But how could you possibly know, David? How can you be sure?'

'A Red Cross vehicle took a direct hit in Sarajevo yesterday. We've got a chap out there at the moment and when they released a list of the people who had been killed, he sent it through with his report because there was an English doctor involved. Georges Kovic was one of the names on that list. I put a fax through to our man out there and got him to double-check. There is no doubt about it – it was the Georges Kovic working for the Red Cross. There can't be two, Sal.'

Sal began to sob. She collapsed into a chair, head in her hands. David came and knelt beside her and put his arms around her. 'I'm so desperately sorry, Sal, but I felt it ought to be me who told you, and as quickly as possible.'

'I can't bear it. I'd only just found him, and now to lose him.'

At the sound of her crying, Toby came into the room. 'What is it?' he said anxiously. David told him and Toby rushed crying into his mother's arms. When Florina and Jenny joined them, they too began to cry, caught up in the emotion of the moment. They all clung together, trying to bring each other comfort.

'I tell you one good thing that's come out of all this,' said David after a while.

Sal looked up at him. 'What possible good could there be?'

'Two months ago, Georges Kovic had nobody to cry for him. Now he's got four of you at it.'

'Five,' Toby corrected, seeing the tears sliding down David's cheeks.

Sal's initial intention was to go out to Sarajevo to make sure that Georges was properly buried. The family vetoed it, even Toby this time. 'You're not helping Georges by getting yourself killed,' was the general feeling, and in her heart she knew they were right. She sent money out to the Red Cross, as much as she could afford, asking them to use it in Georges' name as they saw fit. Otherwise she tried to get on with her life, to keep going for the sake of the children.

David visited her every weekend and commented on how much weight she had lost and how ill she was looking. 'I've got a little cottage in Cornwall,' he said. 'I bought it a few years ago, thinking that the kids would use it, but they never do, and I certainly never have time to go there. It's on the Helford River, a tiny hamlet called Durgan, right on the water. Why don't you take the children and go down for a week or two? The weather is bound to be lousy, but at least it would be a change of scene.'

'I'd like that,' said Sal. 'It's half term next week.'

'There you go then,' said David. 'Do it.'

The weather was indeed awful. The cottage was perched against a cliff; below them was a schoolhouse and a stretch of beach. Although they were tucked away up the estuary, the wind whipped the water into a cauldron and it crashed on to the beach and on to the surrounding rocks with unbelievable venom. Strangely, though, it suited Sal's mood. She and the children walked over the cliffs to the Ferry Boat Inn most days for lunch. They did a little shopping in Falmouth, played Scrabble in front of a log fire and all slept a great deal. The lady who came in each day to clean the cottage assured them that they were becoming 'Cornished'. 'Once you've been here a day or two, you can't stop sleeping,' she said, and certainly it seemed to be true for all three of them.

Jenny had taken the opportunity to have a quick trip up to Scotland and Sal found it was good to have the children to herself. Yet when they had gone to bed and she was alone, she was inconsolable. For the first time in her life she felt she had lost her sense of direction. Georges' death seemed to have affected her in so many ways. She kept thinking back over their conversations, the advice he had given her, and felt that somehow now she should be living for both of them. He had never been given the chance to lead a normal life, and why? Because he had been her insurance policy – the pawn who made it possible for her and her mother to be free. In life, she had never been able to make it up to him. In death, somehow she felt she had to do so.

In June she was going to be forty. She had lost her parents and her brother, and although she had two wonderful children, she had no adult with whom to share her life. It seemed to her that everything she touched of an emotional nature, she messed up. She thought of the grief she had brought to Evelyn and to Louis, of course, and the lack of commitment that had hurt Cristian. He still telephoned her from time to time, but she could not find it in her heart to renew the relationship. And then, looming largest in her thoughts, was Toby's father. Was Georges right? Was she allowing history to repeat itself? She felt so unsure, so lacking in confidence.

It was while she was still in this mood that one day, as she and the children wandered back across the cliff-tops from The Ferry Boat, they saw the familiar, battered Morris Traveller parked outside their cottage. Sal felt her spirits lift.

'I wouldn't have thought that car would have made it down to Cornwall,' she said to Peter.

'There you go then, o ye of little faith.'

'How did you find us?'

'David told me, of course. Have you any objections?'

'None,' said Toby. 'We're very pleased to see you, aren't we, Mum?'

'Yes,' said Sal. 'I think you could say we're pleased. How's your leg?'

'I'm walking on it now, and it's extremely sore, but I'm being impossibly brave,' said Peter.

'Which means,' Toby said, 'if Jenny is to be believed, that he's going to moan about it the whole time he's here.'

'We'll cope with that,' said Sal cheerfully.

After the children were in bed, Sal cooked supper, and Peter settled comfortably in front of the fire.

'So, when do you go back to work?' Sal enquired.

'Next week.'

'But nowhere too exotic, I hope.'

'There is talk of me going back to Bosnia,' Peter said. 'I don't know how I feel about it yet.'

'I know how I feel about it. You're not to do it, Peter.'

'You went,' Peter reminded her.

'But that was different.'

'I'm sorry about Georges,' Peter said. 'I should have written to you — I should have telephoned, but I couldn't find the words.'

'Don't worry, I couldn't have coped with your sympathy — not right after it had happened.'

'It must be very lonely without him,' Peter ventured.

'Yes,' said Sal. 'Yes, you're right.' She was surprised at his understanding. 'It's ridiculous, isn't it? I only had him properly in my life for a month; I only knew he existed for three, and yet now he's gone, there's a great big gap.'

'That's why David sent me,' Peter said softly.

'David sent you?' Sal echoed.

'More or less.'

'Why? To keep me company?'

'No.'

There was something odd about Peter's tone. Sal came and sat down in the chair opposite him. He was staring fixedly at the fire, his hair flopping into his eyes as usual so that she could not read his expression. 'Why then, Peter?' she asked.

'Because he knows I'm in love with you, and he thought it was about time I declared my hand.'

'What?' said Sal. 'Is this a joke?'

For the first time Peter looked up and met her eyes; his own were full of pain. 'I knew you'd be like this, I knew it was silly for me to come, but David insisted. He said you had the right to know.'

'Are you serious?' Sal said.

'Yes, deadly serious.'

'Since when?'

'Oh, I don't know. In Romania, I think. Yes, that's when it happened.'

'And so you told David rather than me. Isn't that rather odd?'

'Sal, you are a very beautiful, clever, talented and elegant woman. I'm a bumbling photographer, dressed in Oxfam cast-offs, and as you rightly say, driving a clapped-out car. You deserve someone a lot better than me, but for some reason David convinced me that it was a good thing for you to know how I felt, even if there was nothing you wanted to do about it.'

'I don't know what to say,' Sal said. 'I can't quite grasp it. I do love you, Peter, but I never thought of it like that.'

'Is friendship such a bad basis for marriage?'

'Are you asking me to marry you?'

'Well, I suppose I'm trying to, and making a bit of a hash of it, aren't I?'

'Yes,' Sal said, 'I'm afraid you are.'

Peter got up abruptly and walked to the back door. He opened the top part of the stable door and leaned out as a rush of cold air funnelled in. 'I'm a stupid bastard,' he murmured into the night.

Sal went to join him. 'Peter, you could try kissing me, or something.'

He turned and stared at her. 'Do you want me to?'

'Oh, for God's sake, man. Come here.'

Peter bent his head and his lips met hers. It was a slow kiss, a gentle exploration, a soft play of tongues and lips that made Sal think that this was the sweetest kiss she had ever experienced. When Peter finally broke away, he looked down and stroked her face, tracing the line of her nose and mouth with one finger.

'I love you Sal,' he said. 'It's not very original, but I don't know what else to say.' She opened her mouth to speak, but he laid his finger over her lips. 'Just kiss me, please,' he said.

This time their kiss had a new dimension and Sal was conscious of a great warmth spreading through her. Peter held her very tight as the kiss grew in passion and Sal was very much aware of his lean, hard body. His hands started to move over her, stroking, caressing, setting her alight.

It took them an hour to reach her bedroom. For the first time in her life, Sal was not in a hurry. The flustered marriage proposal, the declaration of love, lay between them, soothing her soul, making her feel that if it was what she wanted, this was something which could last a lifetime.

When at last their need for one another became impossible to ignore, Peter looked at her half-apologetically. 'I have to take you to bed, Sal, do you mind?'

'Am I behaving as if I mind?' Sal asked. Her shirt was unbuttoned to the waist; she had responded to his kisses and his touch with a passion that startled them both.

'I just so want it to be right for you. I don't want to rush you, and yet . . .' His voice became husky. 'Oh Sal, I'm so frightened of messing this up.'

'Peter,' Sal whispered, taking his face between her hands. 'You're my best friend, there's nothing to fear.'

'I thought you'd laugh in my face, tell me to piss off. I can't believe this is happening.'

'Peter.'

'Yes?'

'Please take me to bed.'

During their long night together, Sal felt as if she was learning about lovemaking for the first time. When their bodies moved, they moved together. Their passion was intense, but there was a gentleness and consideration in everything Peter did which Sal had never experienced before. She felt like a young girl again – untried, untested, moving in a new and unfamiliar country, and at some point during the night, she realised what it was: she was in love for the first time in her life. She felt safe, whole and no longer alone.

In the early hours of the morning, Florina woke up, confused by her unfamiliar surroundings. While Sal soothed her, Peter went downstairs and made them mugs of tea. It was just a little gesture, but it was the right one.

'Why didn't we know before? Why didn't *I* know before?' Sal asked.

'I don't know,' said Peter. 'Maybe there were things we had to work through.'

They slept then, like children, in each other's arms – warm, secure, confident of their love.

When Sal awoke it was still quite dark, but her clock showed her that it was already six o'clock. She slipped from the bed into the bathroom for a shower. When she returned the bedside light was on and Peter was lying there, watching her. 'How are you?' he asked.

'How do you think?' Sal grinned, coming to sit beside him.

'Sal, what's happened between us, does it mean that you'll marry me?'

'I've run away from any such kind of commitment all my life, and Georges showed me why,' Sal said. 'Somehow though, after all these years, just when I thought I'd lost my way, I feel ready. I love you Peter, and I'm yours if you really want me.'

'I've been no good at commitment either. I'm thirty-seven, and yet I still behave like an overgrown schoolboy most of the time.'

'You should be marrying somebody younger, somebody who will give you children.'

'You can still give me children, it's not too late. Besides, even if we can't make babies, we'll have Toby and Florina, and that will be fine with me.'

'I've been a selfish bitch for most of my life,' Sal said ruefully, 'and I've always been in such a hurry. Only in the last few years have I started to ease up a bit. I suppose my mother dying was the watershed. Peter, I would be very honoured to be your wife, but there is something I have to do first. I decided finally in the shower just now.'

'What's that?' Peter asked.

'Georges taught me many things, one of them being that blood really is thicker than water. I want to tell Toby who his father is, and I want to tell his father, too. I thought it was better they didn't know, that it would complicate things, but I realise now I was very, very wrong.'

'Who is Toby's father?'

'I can't tell you that until I've told Toby,' Sal said. 'I have to lay a ghost, sort my life out and put it in order before linking it to yours. Can you understand?'

'I'm trying to,' said Peter. 'Does that mean you might want to get together again with Toby's father?'

'Of course not, you old silly. I'm yours, if you're really sure you'll have me. I just want everything out in the open.'

He kissed her and rolled her on to the bed beside him.

'No,' she said, wriggling away reluctantly, 'the children are going to be waking in a moment.'

'There is tonight,' Peter said comfortably.

'And many nights to come,' added Sal.

David Thorson had particularly asked for no interruptions. He was trying to write a difficult leader article and his mind was straying. He kept wondering how Peter and Sal were getting on. On the one hand he wanted terribly for her to find happiness, on the other there was still that edge of jealousy which he tried to control, but which was never far below the surface. She had so nearly been his.

He had known her father, Timothy Saunders, off and on since childhood. Timothy had been best friends with David's eldest brother, Martin. When Martin was killed in the war, Timothy and David had remained in touch. Timothy was a man's man, who missed his best friend keenly; becoming friends with Martin's little brother was a blessing. In due course, David had met Timothy's wife and daughter. Having married young, David's own daughters were approaching the teenage years and were becoming morose and difficult. He was enchanted by Salvena, a cheerful, outgoing little girl. He had found her mother far from easy, though, and therefore rarely visited the family. Instead he and Timothy tended to meet at the pub near David's office, interspersed with trips to Lords, Henley and Cheltenham – a particular favourite.

Timothy had contacted David out of the blue one day, to say that Salvena was proving something of a problem. She had obtained three good A levels, but was refusing to go to university. David, by this time, was Deputy Editor of the *Daily Record* and Timothy was wondering whether he could find Salvena a job, as she had expressed some interest in journalism. David was intrigued to meet the teenager whom he had not seen at all during her boarding-school years.

He had interviewed her, he recalled, in this very office, the Editor being away. She was a startlingly good-looking girl – beautiful, yes, but almost eclipsing her beauty was her personality. She called him Uncle David, which he did not like over much.

'You see, Uncle David, I have to get away from

home. My mother's driving me mad. She won't let me do anything or go anywhere. I will be kept so short of money if I go to university, I'll never be able to do a thing in the vacs either. You see, if I got a job and a flat in London, I could be my own person. You do understand?'

He had understood, he had helped her and three months later they had become lovers. It was crazy – she was a girl in her teens and he was over forty. They had made love in the back of his car, in her flat, hurriedly before her flatmates came home. She had been a virgin and he, a married man, felt guilty and at the same time proud to have taken her virginity.

He stood up and walked over to the window. He remembered the last time they had been together. They had managed to organise a weekend away from his family. He had pretended he was going golfing with some colleagues and instead had borrowed a cottage in Sussex from a friend. It had been a weekend full of magic. He had not dreamed that love could be like this – so tender, so passionate and yet such fun.

But it had been during that weekend that she had issued him with her ultimatum – either they married, or their affair was over. She could not live with the half-life which was all he could offer her, and he had not the courage to leave his wife. Five years later his marriage was over anyway – his wife had left him for someone else – but in those five years he had lost Sal for ever. He had never tried to win her back, he had just been her friend, helping her where he could, initially with the problems of being a single parent by providing her with as much freelance work as he could, and then by helping her build her career. Not that he had been doing her any favours – she had always been good, very good, but her love-life had never been satisfactory and he had always felt guilty, sure that he was responsible for her disastrous relationships with men. Now that the truth of her identity was resolved, now that she had set aside the main thrust of her career in favour of parenthood, she needed a man. He was free, but he was too old, far too old . . . but still hopelessly in love.

'Toby.' Sal put her head round the door of the sitting room. 'Do you fancy a walk on the beach?'

'I'm locked in this Scrabble match with Peter,' said Toby, 'and he's winning. I didn't know he could spell as well as take pictures, Mum.'

'Cheeky young sod,' said Peter. 'Do as your mother says and go for a walk.'

'I bet it's raining,' whined Toby.

'Can I come, can I come?' piped up Florina.

'No,' said Peter. 'You're going to stay with me and we'll get tea while they're out. You can show me what to do.'

'OK, Peter.'

Toby and Sal stared at Peter, full of admiration. 'How did you do that?' Toby asked incredulously.

'What?' Peter asked.

'Get her to do something she didn't want to do.'

'Charm,' said Peter.

Sal grinned at Toby, putting an arm around his shoulders. 'A shy, retiring sort of chap, isn't he?'

'No confidence,' Toby agreed.

'Be off then, you two. Florina and I have a lot to do.'

As they left the room, Peter's eye caught Sal's. He smiled at her, a smile full of love and understanding.

It had stopped raining but it was still very windy. Grey clouds scudded across the sky and the waves pounded against the beach.

'Stiring stuff,' Sal shivered.

'Where do you want to walk to?'

'I don't mind,' said Sal. 'I just wanted to talk to you.'

Toby looked at her curiously. 'What about, Mum?'

'Can we wait until we just get clear of the cottage?'

'All right.'

They climbed up the steep path which led to the clifftop and Helford Passage. When they reached the cliff, they paused. '"The wrinkled sea beneath him crawls; He watches from his mountain walls, And like a thunderbolt he falls",' said Sal sagely.

'What on earth are you talking about?' Toby scoffed. 'You're not cracking up are you, Mother?'

'Tennyson – "The Eagle". Don't tell me you never learned that at school.'

'Not knowingly,' said Toby. 'So come clean, what's this all about, Mum? You're nervous.'

'Does it show?'

'I'm afraid so. You're not going away again, are you?' He suddenly looked very vulnerable.

'No, I'm not, Toby. I'm never going away again, at least not until you two are both grown up.'

'So what is it then?' he persisted.

'I've always told you I didn't know who your father was, haven't I?'

The cheerful expression left Toby's face. He was suddenly very solemn. 'Yes,' he said cautiously.

'Well, it wasn't true. I've always known who your father was.'

'Who is he?' Toby asked, his voice very small and young, trembling slightly.

'David,' Sal managed. 'David Thorson.'

Toby stared at his mother. 'David, our David? My father?'

'Yes,' said Sal.

'Does he know?'

'No,' said Sal. 'Not yet.'

'Mum, I don't understand. Why couldn't you have told me from the start that it was David?' His eyes were over-bright, his face flushed. Sal would have given anything to have spared him this.

'I so want to make you understand,' She said. 'Only it's so hard. I had an affair with David when I was very young. I was only a teenager, he was already in his forties. He was the first man in my life and I loved him to distraction. It's strange, you know, Toby, bearing in mind that my real father, your grandfather, spent his whole life being a spy. I'm no good at leading a double life. When I was involved with Louis I hated it, and the same with David. He was married with two grown-up children. He seemed to be able to cope all right with having – well, I suppose a mistress on the side – but I couldn't bear it. I just couldn't bear the deceit. So I issued him with an ultimatum.'

'What does that mean?' Toby asked.

'I told him that either he had to leave his wife and we had to get together, marry and all that, or else we had to end our relationship.'

'And he decided to stay with his wife?'

'Yes.' Sal's face creased with pain at the memory. 'The thing is, darling, I didn't know at the time that I was pregnant. I was so angry, you see, and so hurt. I loved him so much. You were conceived in such love, Toby, never doubt that. I couldn't have killed my child and David's, but equally I couldn't throw myself on his mercy. How could I go crawling back and say, "Oops, it's OK, I'll be your mistress again because I need help now I know I'm pregnant." So I soldiered on, on my own.

'After you were born, when things got really tough and I hadn't enough money to support you, I approached him very formally and asked for some freelance work. Your existence in the world made it easier. I hinted, and he obviously assumed, that I'd had another relationship after him and that you were the result. I think it helped him come to terms with his decision and to cope with me on a platonic basis. The trouble was that once I'd started the lie, I couldn't stop it. It became compounded because as I couldn't tell David, I couldn't tell you either. Do you understand?'

'I think so,' said Toby. 'I just wish I'd known. It would have made so many things so much easier.'

'I realise that,' said Sal. She put out her hand tentatively. Toby took it and smiled at her.

'It's OK, Mum,' he said gently.

'Toby, it's not OK, I got it so wrong. You see, the thing I'd never considered, never bargained for, was how well you and David would get along in your own right. I never imagined that you'd become firm friends. David really loves you, but without knowing why.' They stood hand in hand in silence for a moment, looking down at the sea below.

'So what made you tell me now?' Toby asked.

'Let's walk,' said Sal. 'Have you got a handkerchief?'

Toby passed one over. 'I must be growing up,' he said, grinning.

'Why?' Sal asked tearfully.

'Mothers usually provide their children with handkerchieves, not the other way around.'

'Oh Toby, I do love you so much,' said Sal, 'and I'm so very, very sorry.' They stopped on the path and embraced. 'Come on,' she said, at last. They linked arms and continued on their way.

'The first person who really made me realise I'd been so wrong was Georges. I suppose because I'd really had no close family but you, I hadn't understood the importance of the blood relationship. He confronted me about it one day. He told me that he'd spoken to you about your father and that you didn't know who he was, and he asked me point blank if I did. He assumed I must and, of course, he was right. I didn't tell him who it was. David would have meant nothing to him anyway, but he urged me to tell you the truth.'

'Good old Uncle Georges,' said Toby quietly.

'And the second thing is . . . oh Toby, I think I'm rather overdoing the shocks for one day.'

'Go on,' said Toby.

'Peter's asked me to marry him, and I've sort of said yes.'

'I thought so,' said Toby. 'I thought Peter looked really pleased with himself this morning. I'm really glad, Mum, I like Peter.'

'I know you do, but will you be happy having him as a step-father?'

Toby nodded. 'You bet, he'll be great fun – but what's that got to do with me and David?'

'Just that I couldn't embark on a marriage with Peter, with us all starting out together as a family, without everything being truthful between us. I can't believe how nice you're being about this, Toby. It's more than I deserve. You should be so angry, like I was with my mother.'

Toby grinned. 'If you'd taken as long to tell me the truth as your mother took to tell you, I might not have forgiven you.'

'As it is?' Sal said.

'As it is,' said Toby, 'I think you've told me just in the nick of time.'

There was a knock on the door, and before he could shout in protest, it flew open and Sal was standing there. For a moment he stared at her like a madman.

'What's wrong, David?' she asked anxiously.

'I'm sorry.' He came forward and embraced her. 'I was just thinking about you, and then here you are – strange.'

'Nice thoughts, I hope.'

He blushed slightly. 'Yes. How are you? I thought you were supposed to be in Cornwall.'

'I came back a day early. I had something important to do.'

'Oh,' he said, trying to sound casual. 'Did Peter come down to see you?'

'Yes he did, and you put him up to it, I gather.'

'Yes, I suppose I did.'

'I can't quite see you in the role of Cupid!' She was teasing him.

'OK, I'm sorry. I shouldn't have interfered but I just want you to be happy.'

'I know that, David, and I am. Peter is a good man and I do love him very much – I just hadn't realised – but I don't want to talk about him right now.' She hesitated. 'David, there's something I want to tell you – something I have to sort out first before I can look to my own future.'

'You're nervous,' said David, astonished. 'That's not like you, Sal. What's wrong?'

'David, our affair – it caused us a great deal of heartache at the time. It wasn't an easy period, was it?'

'How strange, I've just been thinking about it. I wish to God I'd kicked my marriage into touch when there was a chance of us being together. All those wasted years.'

Sal sat down heavily. 'They weren't wasted, David. I was too young, I'd have made a poor companion for life and I wasn't in a position to commit myself to anyone. I knew you wouldn't leave your wife but I just couldn't bear the deceit. So I issued the ultimatum knowing it could only result in one decision. It broke my heart at the time, but it was the right thing to do.'

'I see. Why are you raising this now, Sal?'

'Do you remember our last weekend together, in Sussex?'

'Of course I do,' said David. 'I'll take it with me to my grave, you know that.'

'I've spent the last fifteen years trying to find a way to tell you this, and I still don't know how to. I'm afraid it's just all going to come out in a rush. I got pregnant that weekend, David, and the result was Toby. Toby is your son.'

The colour drained from David's face. 'What? What are you saying? It can't be right, the dates weren't right, you said so.'

'They were,' said Sal. 'There was never a one-night stand, I made it up initially to protect you and your marriage. Toby was late in coming; I pretended he was premature. If you remember, you didn't see him until he was five months old and men have no idea about these things. You didn't notice what a big bonny baby he was for one who was supposed to be premature.' She smiled slightly. 'You see, at the time I didn't expect you to be an ongoing part of our lives. I knew you were helping me in those early years out of a sense of guilt, but I thought it would stop. I didn't know we'd go on and have this friendship and that you'd become so involved with Toby's life.'

'Toby's my son. You say Toby's my son?'

'Yes.'

David sat down and put his head in his hands. 'Oh Sal, why didn't you tell me?'

'Because I didn't realise how important families were until I met Georges. Because now I want to start a new honest life with all the skeletons in the cupboard out in the open, and because if Toby is going to have a step-father, he needs to know who his real father is. I don't want him to be in the same position that I was – not knowing, until it was too late. Georges showed me that I was in danger of allowing history to repeat itself. I would never have believed I was like my mother in any respect, but I appear to have inherited her ability to keep a secret.'

'But we've wasted fifteen years!' David groaned.

'But you have years and years ahead of you both,' said Sal. She went over and slipped an arm around him. 'I can't understand why you didn't realise it. You are so alike – you look alike, and you *are* alike, it's why you get on so well. I suppose, too, it's why you've always had that sense of protection towards him.'

'Then why didn't you let me help? All those years when you had to go off and leave him with Jenny. I could have been there, as a father.'

'But you were there,' Sal said.

'Yes, but I could have given him that feeling of security he's always lacked until recently.'

'I made a mistake. You see, I didn't think we needed

anybody, Toby and me, and I was still so hurt and angered by your rejection. The longer I left it, the more impossible it became to tell you. You'll never know how many times it has been on the tip of my tongue . . . but David, you can be so aggressive. You were always criticising me for not being a good mother. I kept thinking that if you knew that Toby was your son, you'd be even worse. I know I did wrong, but I just got deeper and deeper into the deception.'

David looked at her keenly for a moment. 'Give me a hug,' he said. They stood entwined, her head resting on his shoulder. 'I'm very proud to have him as my son, you know that,' David murmured into her hair.

'I think you'll find that it's reciprocated,' Sal said.

'Does he know, then?'

'Yes,' said Sal. 'I told him yesterday.'

'Was he pretty shattered?'

'He was surprised,' said Sal, 'but very pleased.'

'After all this time, to find that we share a child, not just any child, but Toby, it's incredible, wonderful. Is he really like me?'

'Spitting image, I'm afraid,' Sal said. She was smiling, but tears were still rolling down her face.

'May I kiss you?' David asked.

'You don't normally ask,' Sal whispered.

'I mean properly.'

Their lips met in a lingering kiss that brought back long-ago memories of the passion that had once been between them.

'It *was* good, wasn't it?' David said. 'It's not just my geriatric mind playing tricks?'

'It was good,' Sal assured him. 'I told Toby he was conceived in great love and I spoke nothing less than the truth, did I?'

'Oh yes,' said David, 'you spoke the truth. Are you sure he doesn't mind?'

'You'd better ask him yourself, he's waiting outside.' She gently eased herself from David's arms. 'I don't know if it's a good idea or not, but I booked a table at the Wig and Pen Club. I'll leave you two alone and hope to see you both there, unless you both decide I'm so awful you can't bear to have lunch with me.'

Trembling with nerves, she walked to the door and opened it, not daring to look back at David, afraid of what she might see. Toby was sitting outside. He raised his eyebrows in query at his mother. She smiled encouragingly. 'It's OK,' she whispered, 'go on in.'

'He's not cross?' Toby said.

'Certainly not with you, Tobe. Can you cope, darling? Are you sure?'

'No sweat, Mum.'

By ten past one Sal was sick with nerves. Being a Friday, the Club was busy and so she decided to wait for them in the comparative seclusion of the table she had booked in advance overlooking the street. She saw them crossing the Strand. They were talking animatedly. As they crossed the second stream of traffic, David put an arm around Toby's shoulders. They smiled at one another. It was unbelievably touching. They, at least, were all right together, thank God, but what did they truly think of her? Her heart was pounding. She heard their voices and footsteps on the stairs.

'Hi, Mum,' Toby said casually.

Sal stood up. 'Is everything all right?' she said, and much to her horror found her voice wobbling.

'Everything's fine,' said David.

The three of them stood in an embrace, Sal weak with tears. 'Are you sure, Toby? Are you ever going to forgive me?'

'Everything's fine, Mum, I promise. As I told you, if you'd asked me to choose a dad, I'd have chosen David.'

'I don't deserve this kindness and understanding,' Sal said, her voice hoarse.

'We've all talked enough. I think the occasion requires us to drink a little champagne, don't you think so, old boy?' David addressed Toby.

'Definitely, Dad,' he replied.

CHAPTER TWENTY-FOUR

'Logs crackling, soup bubbling, snow falling outside. There's not a lot more one could ask for really, is there?' Peter said contentedly. 'Are you happy?'

'Of course,' said Sal with a smile, snuggling up to him.

'I mean about life as a whole, not just about us.'

Sal leaned forward and poked at a log on the fire. 'Ah, life as a whole is another matter, isn't it? Three years ago, I set out on a sort of quest, I suppose, to find out who I was. I know the answer to that now, but tragically I found and lost Georges in the process. And then there's my life's other quest, my life's work, my involvement in Eastern Europe, almost an obsession, you could say – all very understandable, now I know my own background, but sadly, quite unresolved. Throughout my working life I have tried, through the paper, to make Western

Europe understand the problems of Eastern Europe, and essentially I've failed.'

'It's not that you've failed, it's just that people don't want to listen. Anyway, who says you've failed? Everyone's still talking about the war in Bosnia. That's not failure, that's media success, surely?'

'But they're ignoring all the other countries – Bulgaria, Poland, Czechoslovakia, Romania, the Russian States. They've no medicines, no proper hospital care, not enough food, not enough heating, abortions instead of birth control, overflowing orphanages . . . what we throw away in a rubbish bin at a single sitting would feed an Eastern European for a week. The Romanian orphanages are fuller than they ever were, the conditions worse than when we discovered them, but no one cares any more. Those children are yesterday's news.'

'Maybe one day,' said Peter.

'No,' said Sal passionately. 'If the children of Romania didn't make people care enough, if the horrors of Bosnia didn't do it either, what else possibly could?' She smiled suddenly. '"Second to the right, and straight on till morning".'

'What on earth are you talking about?' Peter asked.

'The way to Neverland, Peter Pan's travel instructions to Wendy; and Neverland's about the right description for what I had hoped to achieve. I just see no end to the war in Bosnia. People read about the atrocities, they shake their heads in horror, but nothing happens. Peace talks follow peace talks, new promises are made and broken and the world continues to watch . . . and yet does nothing.'

'We can try again, if you like?'

'What, and get ourselves shot again?'

'If that's what you want.'

'I want us to be married, Peter, and if it's not too late I want us to have a couple of children. I want to raise them to be happy and healthy, like Toby and Florina. I want to shut out all the horrors of the world and go and live somewhere remote, with no telephone or television.'

'It wouldn't suit you,' said Peter. 'You're always going to be in the thick of it, one way or another.'

'Not any more.'

'I don't mean necessarily by risking your life, I mean by helping in the way you know best – with your pen. Don't give up just because no one seems to be listening. Keep at it – if not for your sake, or my sake or the children's . . . for Georges.'

'I'll try, if you think I should.'

'I do,' said Peter. 'After all, you have the directions.'

'What do you mean?' said Sal.

'Second to the right, and straight on till morning.'